Also by Linda Broday

Bachelors of Battle Creek
Texas Mail Order Bride
Twice a Texas Bride
Forever His Texas Bride

Men of Legend
To Love a Texas Ranger
The Heart of a Texas Cowboy
To Marry a Texas Outlaw

Texas Heroes
Knight on the Texas Plains
The Cowboy Who Came Calling
To Catch a Texas Star

Outlaw Mail Order Brides
The Outlaw's Mail Order Bride
Saving the Mail Order Bride

Texas Redemption
Christmas in a Cowboy's Arms anthology

Saving the
MAIL ORDER
Bride

LINDA
BRODAY

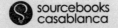
sourcebooks
casablanca

Published by Sourcebooks Casablanca, an imprint of Sourcebooks, Inc.
P.O. Box 4410, Naperville, Illinois 60567-4410
(630) 961-3900
sourcebooks.com

Printed and bound in the United States of America.
OPM 10 9 8 7 6 5 4 3 2 1

Dear Reader,

Often life throws us for a loop and we have to scramble for footing. This is certainly the case with Jack Bowdre, arrested and on his way to jail one day shy of his marriage to a mail order bride who finally said yes. But fate intervenes. I love these surprises.

In steps pretty Nora Kane, and his world isn't quite as bleak. She's running from something too, and together they make quite a team as they race toward safety with nothing but the clothes on their backs.

I hope this entertains and leaves you wanting to know more about the outlaw town of Hope's Crossing and its people.

Happy reading,

Linda

One

North Texas

Early Spring, 1880

It was a plain, ordinary March day with nothing ahead but dusty miles and a wide expanse of sky overhead. Ordinary...

If you didn't count the manacle around Jack Bowdre's wrist.

If you didn't count the marshal sitting next to him.

And if you didn't count the fact that he'd soon be in a hoosegow in Saint's Roost.

The stagecoach slammed into a large hole in the narrow road, almost jolting half of his teeth out. He ran his tongue over the pearly whites, checking to make sure he still had them, and shivered from the cold air coming around the leather flap on the window.

Just ordinary. Same rough road. Same regrets. Same barren scenery he'd ridden across too many times to count. Maybe it'd been one time too many. He glanced down at the iron bracelet handcuffing him to the marshal.

The weak afternoon sun would be going down in a matter of hours. Jack flexed his jaw. There was sure to be a dark bruise there soon enough, to go along with his split lip. He tried to brush the dirt from his black trousers and shirt. The blood from the fight would have to stay.

Damn!

To his satisfaction, the marshal appeared in worse shape, still bleeding from his nose. After subduing Jack—with help—the lawman had flagged down the stagecoach about ten miles back.

Jack silently cursed himself for getting caught. All the times he'd outrun the posse, why'd it have to be now, when he was set to marry?

Movement on the seat across from him drew his attention to the young woman, the only other passenger, whose knee practically touched his. She kept her gaze averted, probably pondering his crimes and the wages of sin. He thought about listing them all for her just to smooth the wrinkle in her brow, but that would take quite a while, and he didn't want to shock the delicate beauty.

The stagecoach lurched across what must have been a series of large holes. The lady's dark lashes lifted and his nerve endings stood at attention, something he'd not felt in a very long time. He touched two fingers to his hat with his free hand, and smiled.

She was most definitely *not* ordinary.

Unlike so many reed-thin women running around, this one had curves. He preferred a little meat on a woman's bones. Her fair hair reminded him of freshly churned butter and the dusky eyes meeting his were the hue of his favorite chestnut roan. High, sculpted cheekbones and a determined jawline spoke of strength and grit.

Jack quirked one eyebrow. Her face heated and she gave him a frown, hurriedly turning her gaze back to the window. Not that she could likely see a blessed thing through the crack of the leather flap that was supposed to keep out the cloud of dust from the churning wheels.

Anything must be better than looking at his sorry face.

A glance sideways at Marshal Dollard found him sleeping. Now if only Jack could find a way to get that door open. But the racing stage and the manacle put a halt to escape plans—for the moment.

While he marked time, he resorted to a guessing game, studying the moss-green traveling dress that peeked from the opening of the lady's dark wool coat. Was that fox fur around the collar and cuffs? The outfit was a little too fancy for the wilds of Texas. At least the dress was slimmer than most. He hated those large bustles and petticoats that made some dresses balloon out until a man couldn't walk past without crushing the fabric. Her plumed hat was a bit fancy as well. Feathers and a bird's nest? Really? He gave a soft snort.

Definitely an easterner. He'd bet the price on his wanted poster that this was her first time this side of the Mississippi.

He leaned forward slightly and craned his neck. There on the floor of the stage, peeking beneath her hem, was the rest of the tale. The little he could see of her high-top shoes was worn and scuffed beyond a polish's magic, which led him to believe either she'd borrowed the finery—or her funds had dried up before she could get to shoes.

The lady's clothing was probably nothing more than window dressing meant to fool some poor soul. Thank goodness not him.

Her age? Hard to say, but he'd put it somewhere between twenty and twenty-eight. She'd done some living.

Why was she here in Texas? Now that was the real question.

A job? No. Although gloves hid her hands, he knew in his gut they'd be soft. She didn't appear to be the kind of woman to do hard work. No, she seemed a bit pampered.

Family? Maybe.

Married? He lowered his gaze and studied her through the fringe of his lashes. Hmmm. That one puzzled him. Something about her seemed to say she wasn't the marrying kind, that she craved her independence a bit too much. After all, what man would let his wife travel alone through wild country? No, he couldn't see her married. At least not yet. But definitely looking.

Though not at him. Him, she was bound and determined to ignore.

Forgetting his right arm was still attached to the marshal's left, he lifted his hand to rub his sore jaw, stubble sharp against his palm, the six-inch chain rattling.

The old lawman startled awake and glared. "Quit your fidgeting and be still." He jerked Jack's arm down with a resounding thump.

"Watch it, Marshal! You don't have me as restrained as you think." Jack had woken in a cold sweat from nightmares just like this too many times over the years—manacled to a lawman, heading for his doom. He always knew they'd catch him one day, seeing that the odds had been stacked against him from the start. Fact was, he'd grown careless. Jack bit back a curse, wishing for his ivory-gripped Colt that the marshal had taken off him and put God knows where outside the coach. *Damn!*

"If that's a threat…you're lucky I don't strap you to the top." The marshal smiled at their lady traveler. "Sorry that you have to endure this a bit longer, ma'am. He's little more than a savage animal."

Marshal Dollard said it like Jack had a case of rabies or something.

Dollard continued in a tone full of righteous contempt. "Why, he's so mean the rattlesnakes won't even come near him. I heard his own kin disowned him."

Like Dollard knew a damn thing about his family. The puffed-up lawman would say anything to impress the lady. Jack eyed the Colt on Dollard's right hip. If only he could reach it…

❧

Lenora's gaze traced along the outlaw's long legs and lean form. Power radiated from him—enormous power barely held in check. She could almost feel his deep irritation, and his anger. She'd read about men like this one in dime novels that were all the rage back East, men who lived outside the law. But reading about them and coming face-to-face with one in the flesh were two totally different things.

Awareness sizzled between them, and his tiniest movement captured her attention. When he turned his gaze to her, a rush of heat flooded her cheeks. She found herself pinned like a butterfly under glass.

His chiseled features appeared hewn from the hardest stone that the good Lord probably reserved for those like him. Outlaws. The marshal appeared barely able to contain him. In fact, she got the impression the prisoner merely bided his time until an opportunity for escape came.

He glanced toward the window, allowing her to study him better. The outlaw had uncommon good looks, his hard, angled jaw sporting light-brown stubble. The bump on the bridge of his nose indicated it had been broken few times. *Ha!* She wasn't surprised by that.

Most striking were his gray eyes—gunmetal gray. When he'd first climbed into the coach, they were stormy, and other times, like when the marshal shot warnings and threats, they became icy and hard. Yet amusement always colored his gaze when he turned his attention to her.

Was it her appearance or her nervousness that brought out the twinkling glint?

Lenora thought about leaning across the space and slapping his brazen face. Except that she'd never struck anyone in her life, even though she'd been sorely tempted quite a few times over the last year.

The way his body tensed, swinging measured glances at the door, then back to the marshal—could he really be planning an escape?

He suddenly gave her a smile that could've charmed the devil's own mother. Lenora stilled and held her breath, her pulse racing.

Would he use her in his escape plan somehow? Maybe take her hostage? Oh dear. She glanced at the marshal, wondering if he'd pull his gun and shoot the outlaw if he tried anything.

The handsome outlaw lifted a finely arched brow. "Here in Texas, they make you pay to gawk, ma'am. But I reckon this is the first time a gentlewoman like yourself has laid eyes on a born and bred killer. Who knows? Maybe you can come to my hanging. That'll be a real treat."

"I don't think I could bear such a sight."

"You don't know what you'll miss. It'll be the social occasion of the year. Big, bad Jack met his end. He was as sorry as his father." He raised his free hand to his eyes and released a long sigh.

Beneath his mocking tone, she saw the layer of sorrow, felt his heavy heart, tasted his bitterness. Whatever had happened to land him here had two sides to the story.

❧

"When shall we reach Saint's Roost?" Refinement echoed in her crisp Eastern accent, swept along by her melodious voice.

Definitely not Jack's type. He preferred them a little rough around the edges. The fun lay in smoothing those over a little. Not too much though, so they wouldn't get the notion they were better than him.

This lady probably already thought herself better than the uncouth outlaw.

With his free hand, Dollard reached for his watch, hanging on its gold chain, and flipped it open. "Another hour or so, ma'am. Frankly, I can't wait to get this stinkin' outlaw behind bars. Every marshal, sheriff, and bounty hunter in the state has been hunting him for years. By last count he's killed over fifteen men. He's one dangerous *hombre*."

Their fellow traveler didn't appear one bit afraid of him.

Jack rolled his eyes and bit back a curse. As far as dangerous, that all depended on which person you asked. The men he'd killed would agree most heartily, them having done what they did. But Jack never shot without a reason—and once he pulled his gun on someone, it was because he meant to send them to hell.

He'd never been sorry, except for once. His breath grew ragged with the recollection. He pushed the pain aside and inhaled.

To his best friend, Clay Colby, and the people of Hope's Crossing, Jack was a hero who stood tall against evil, seeking justice however, whenever he could. He didn't go out of his way to end someone's life—he tried to be sure that it only ever happened because of a wrong choice the other made.

The coach jolted and shifted, jarring Jack again. The driver shouldn't be going at such an unsafe speed. Stagecoaches were notoriously top heavy, and it took next to nothing to turn one over. But that was beyond Jack's control. Quite a lot was at the moment.

A sigh full of regret escaped him. Tomorrow was supposed to be his wedding day. His mail order bride would arrive in Hope's Crossing about sundown today, and he wouldn't be there to greet her. Just his luck that she had decided to go through with it. *Hell!* A lot of good that did him. Unless he got to the marshal's Colt, he'd be sitting in a cell instead, sleeping on a thin mattress stretched on a cement slab.

Dammit!

How had the marshal known where he was? Dollard must've tracked him.

Another thought struck and froze his blood. Hope's Crossing could have a traitor in their midst. But who? He couldn't imagine any of his friends turning on him.

His thoughts spun like a roulette wheel and ice slid down his spine. Three new men had come to the town a few weeks ago. Maybe one of them was working with the law.

Or it could be a longtime friend. The thought of betrayal made his stomach clench.

Or maybe he just had rotten luck.

The lady on the opposite seat fiddled with her light-blond hair. The curve of her jaw and elegant neck drew him. Near perfect, very kissable. His lazy gaze slid over her body—what little he could see, that is. No harm in looking. It appeared he'd be getting his neck stretched instead of marrying now anyway, and what he saw definitely intrigued him. He nudged his knee over ever so slightly until it touched hers. The light connection sent unexpected pleasure coursing through him.

She swung her eyes to him, anger flashing from the brown depths. She shifted in her seat, breaking the contact.

In an effort to stifle the boredom and to ruffle the lady's cool gaze, Jack caught her looking again and winked.

She gasped and tilted her chin several degrees. If her stare were a sharp knife, it would've impaled him.

The stagecoach careened around a corner and slid sideways. Jack waited for the slide to stop and the coach to straighten up, only it kept going. The tilt threw him against the marshal.

He grabbed for something to hold on to, which ended up being the lady. She screamed. The team of horses screeched in terror, and the driver yelled curses, the noise outside turning to holy hell as the driver tried to right the stage.

The wooden coach cracked and groaned as it fell, tumbling, cartwheeling down an embankment.

The sides caved in, the whole wall breaking apart.

All Jack could do was hold on and pray to reach the bottom in one piece.

Pain pierced his leg, the one that still carried a posse's bullet from a few years back. He let out a yell. His head cracked against something solid, and for a minute, stars twinkled in his vision.

When what was left of the stagecoach finally settled, he slowly moved his legs, then his arms. Nothing felt broken, but the lady passenger lay on one side of him, and he was trapped on the other by the marshal's weight. He yanked on the manacles, which didn't give. Pain shot up his arm.

Dollard's sightless eyes were open and his mouth hung slack, his thick body half-on and half-off the seat. A piece of wood protruding from his chest said there was no need trying to save him.

Jack lowered the man's eyelids with his free hand and turned his attention to the woman's low moans. "You all right, ma'am?"

"What happened?" She pulled herself to a sitting position, holding her forehead. Blood trickled from under her hand. Her hat sat askew, the pretty green ribbon under her chin still holding it on, the bird's nest hanging over one eye. She shoved it back in order to see.

"An accident. We rolled down an embankment, would be my guess. The marshal is dead." He tugged at Dollard's large girth again but couldn't free himself. The chain was twisted around the man's arm and pinned beneath his body. "I need your help. Do you think you can?"

"Can what?" She appeared dazed. Maybe the blow to her head had been harder than he'd thought.

"Get the key to these manacles from the marshal's vest so I can free myself." When she didn't budge, he tried again. "Please get the key from his vest pocket. I'd do it, but I can't reach it with my arm trapped."

Finally she appeared to slowly comprehend the situation and crawled to the marshal. Though she seemed calmer than he'd expected a fancy lady to be, her hands trembled as she searched. The first pocket had nothing. She tried the other side and pulled out a small brass key.

"Good. Now give it to me." He would be loose in a moment. By the time help arrived—which shouldn't be long, since this was a well-traveled road—he'd be gone.

But she shook her head. "No, I'll unlock it. I can do that much."

She stuck the key into the lock of the marshal's manacle and it swung open.

"Good. Now hand me the key."

She stared at him a second through wide eyes. In a swift move, she yanked the chain free from Dollard's body and, before Jack could utter a word, snapped the cuff on her own wrist.

Hell and be damned!

"What are you doing?" He tried to grab the key from her.

"You're crazy if you think I'm going to let you get away. I'm safer with you next to me than those rattlesnakes the marshal mentioned." Then she did the unthinkable. She drew back her arm and pitched the key out the smashed side of the coach before he could blink.

So much for this being a plain, ordinary day.

Two

THE BRASS KEY FLEW OUT AND LANDED SOMEWHERE IN THE rugged landscape, vanishing among the cactus and patches of sharp-spiked yucca.

"Hell," Jack growled and tried to scramble for it, but his handcuff was now attached to her. He fell back against her softness, disappointment and anger choking him. Freedom had been so close! He could have wrung her pretty neck.

Fury rose faster than floodwater. "Do you know what I could do to you right now, with no one here to stop me?"

Eyes wide, she swallowed and scooted back as far as the chain allowed, which was only the length of one of her shoes.

"I can do most anything I take a notion to." He wrapped his steely words in velvet to soften the impact a tad. "All you did was ensure you can't run from me. I've got you, lady. You heard the marshal say I'm an animal. I can prove it if you'd like."

She inhaled sharply. "You wouldn't."

"Try me. What you did was very, very foolish." Jack hovered over her. She cringed, and realizing his size intimidated her more than he intended, he moved back. Not that she was that scared of him. She appeared ready to clobber the daylights out of him. Lord help him if she got hold of a length of metal.

She glared, raising that god-awful mulish chin. "I'm not sorry. I just did what was right. A judge will decide your fate." Then she muttered barely loud enough to hear, "I won't mess up again."

Not about to let her win this round, Jack glowered back and slowly lifted an eyebrow. "I don't think you fully understand your predicament. Wherever I go, you go. And I'm a whole lot stronger than you."

"Is that a threat, mister?"

"Simply stating fact." He finally managed to rise from the floor of the coach and yanked on the six-inch chain. "You're coming with me."

The stubborn lady wrapped her free arm around Dollard's thick leg and leaned back, wedging her feet against the doorframe. "I'm not going anywhere, and neither are you."

Hell and be damned!

Jack jerked his black hat from the space between him and the floor and reached for Dollard's gun, sticking it in his waistband. Then he pulled off the marshal's boots and threw them out. They could come in handy later. He saw nothing else that might be of use.

"You're going to find that key if it's the last thing you ever do." He bodily lifted her up and over the dead lawman. At the last second, he removed the U.S. marshal's badge off Dollard's chest and pinned it on his shirt. Jack ripped aside the splintered wood and mangled metal of the broken coach. When one piece wouldn't budge, he picked her up a second time and lifted her over it.

The north wind had a bite to it, and he was glad for his heavy duster. Winter still hung on, even though the calendar said early spring had arrived. The stiff breeze caught her hat and sent it sailing away across the jagged terrain.

"My hat! It cost me five dollars." She forgot about the chain that held her rooted as she tried to race after the piece of millinery only to be brought up short. She gave a loud huff and kicked a clump of dead grass, muttering to herself.

"See what I mean? I think you're getting it now," Jack said grimly.

"You don't have to gloat."

No, but it was nice to finally have her see the gravity of what she'd done.

"It's only a hat. That's the least of your problems, lady. By the way, do you have a name?"

"Lenora—and that's all."

"Fine, Lenora That's-All. Now get busy scouring the ground."

She chewed her bottom lip. "The key has to be close. I'm such a poor thrower. I really am. I have a weak arm, you see."

All the evidence pointed to the contrary. So far, he saw no brass glimmer. "Keep looking." Jack listened intently for sounds of life above the high embankment. The driver had to be dead or he'd be making noise. It would be hard for a man riding up high like that to survive with nothing around him for protection. Jack thought he heard a horse snuffling, but it had to be the wind. The horses were probably dead along with the driver…or else had run off.

After looking for what seemed like an eternity and finding nothing, he gave up and turned to her. "Enough. We're going to climb to the top and see if any of the horses are alive so we can get out of here."

Lenora glanced up. "That's very steep, and we have nothing to hold on to."

The young lady had a point, but that wouldn't stop him. He grabbed her hand and tackled the incline only to slide back down. He tried again. Still no luck.

"Let's go back and try to find the key," Lenora suggested. "With you free of me, you could probably make it."

He grunted and turned back to the brush, praying to spy the small piece of brass. Then…hoofbeats pounded above. A lot of them and shouts. More lawmen? Probably. He wasn't going to lose this chance at freedom no matter how difficult his escape had become. He yanked the chain between them. "We've got to go."

"Where?"

"Away from here."

"I can't. Not without my bags. Everything I own is in them."

"Sorry, ma'am." The hoofbeats and snorts got louder, and men were yelling curses.

Lenora opened wide to let out a bloodcurdling scream. Jack quickly clapped his hand over her mouth, silencing the alarm before she could do more than squeak. He held her in a tight grip and pulled her along, cursing Lenora's high principles.

Jack let out a disgusted swoosh of air and glanced around to get his bearings. He figured they were a good distance from Hope's Crossing. It'd take a while on foot, but hopefully they could get there inside a week. If he didn't get caught again. *And* if righteous Miss Lenora didn't do something else to mess up his plans even worse.

"I'm going to remove my hand. Don't scream. Got it?"

At her nod, he released her. She tried to pull away only to be held fast by the chain.

Jack picked up Dollard's boots and took her hand. They only made it a few hundred yards when he stopped in a draw, out of sight from anyone above.

He glanced at his companion and rolled his eyes. She was already struggling.

"Can you pick up the pace?"

Flames flashed from her eyes. "I'd like to see you walk in narrow shoes with a wobbly heel."

"Give me your foot."

Lenora eyed him suspiciously. "Why?"

"Let me see your foot. It's a simple request."

"Well, forevermore. I don't understand you. First, you're far too familiar in the coach. And now you want me to just lift my foot." She narrowed her gaze. "Why?"

"I won't hurt you." Jack glanced at the sky, the need to hurry screaming inside him.

Although she got all huffy, she lifted her left foot. Jack anchored it against his leg, unlaced her high-topped shoe, pulled it off, and threw it into some thorny brambles.

She gasped and gave a sharp cry. "You…you…shoe stealer!"

"The other one, please."

"No." One shoe might not do her much good, but she was keeping it.

"For God's sake, you can't walk on it anyway and we need to move faster."

"Well, I guess you might as well, since I can't very well hobble on one." She raised her right foot and he did the same thing.

Jack reached for Dollard's boots, which seemed small for a man's. "Now give me one of your petticoats."

"I most certainly will not."

"How else do you propose to make these boots fit?"

"You're not making me wear those." Lenora put her hands on her hips. "Look, you took my shoes and made me leave everything I owned in this world behind. Are you going to undress me as well?"

Jack took in her flushed face, wild hair, and heaving breasts and didn't think he'd ever seen anyone so enticing. Or mad. "One petticoat, and it's for your own comfort."

"You only get one."

"I believe that's all I asked for. You'll still have oodles." Or at least the dress certainly gave that appearance.

"Don't look." With a good bit of maneuvering and tugging, she got one off.

As he listened for sounds of riders, he tore the voluminous petticoat into strips, wrapped them around each foot, and slid the boots on her. "How does that feel?"

"Not too bad."

He handed back what was left of the petticoat, which was only from the waist to her thigh. "Put this back on. We may need it."

She gave him a scathing look, snatched what remained of the garment, and wiggled into it, muttering, "Here's a notion. Why don't you wear the darn thing?"

"I'm sorry for my high-handed ways, Lenora. I don't mean to be, but I've been far too long from a woman's parlor." Jack scrubbed the back of his neck, needing to voice the apology he knew she had coming. "I shouldn't have threatened you back there. My mother would've tanned my hide. She drilled into me to act like a gentleman, but in my surprise and frustration, I'm afraid I forgot those lessons. I won't do it again."

Lenora's eyes softened. "You're forgiven. I probably would've reacted the same way in your situation."

"Thanks. Are you ready to go?" Unless something else went wrong. Jack wasn't placing any bets—given how his day was going, he was sure to lose.

"I simply have to go back. My things—"

"Look, if you hadn't thrown the key away, I'd be free and far from here and you'd be back there with your cases and that precious, god-awful hat. You have only yourself to blame for the situation."

"Believe me, if I could undo things, I would." She gave the chain an angry yank.

"Best to save your strength. No talking." Jack's leg was killing him, and his limp became more pronounced the longer they walked, but he could do nothing about that except push through the misery.

He imagined it would take a little bit for whoever had ridden up on the wreck to figure out what had happened—or even that Dollard was a marshal. So they were pretty safe for a while. Unless the rider had known Dollard, and that Dollard had made an arrest that day. Always that possibility.

The afternoon sun had sunk much lower in the sky, with darkness about an hour or so away. He needed to get farther from the wreck before stopping for the night. He glanced at his partner. She looked far from the elegant woman from earlier. Tendrils of blond hair had fallen from her upswept arrangement, straggling around her face and down her back. Still, she was keeping up, even if anger fueled her spunk. He grinned, recalling how she'd stood up to him, hands on her hips, fire flashing from her eyes. He hoped Miss Kane had half of Lenora's grit.

A knot formed in his stomach. Maybe sending for a bride had been a mistake if he could be attracted to someone else so quickly. He'd never thought he had a roving eye, but she made it difficult not to stare.

The whole idea had probably been a bad one from the beginning. He'd only exchanged a few letters with his bride-to-be and still hadn't told her that he was a wanted man. Keeping secrets never boded well. He'd figured he'd come clean about everything once she arrived. He did better face-to-face. Only now, circumstances were conspiring against him.

Jack pulled the marshal's Colt from his waist, flipped open the cylinder, and let out a yell. Of all the low-down, dirty tricks! *Empty.*

"What's wrong?" Lenora stumbled over a rock, and he grabbed her arm, hauling her upright.

Hell! You'd think a marshal would keep his gun in firing order. Jack kicked himself. If he'd only known, Dollard wouldn't have gotten the manacle on him or gotten Jack anywhere near that stagecoach.

"Bad news, Lenora. There're no cartridges. We have no way of defending ourselves."

"You mean we can't shoot a wild animal if it's attacking us?"

"Animal or a man either. We won't be able to hunt for food. Period."

"Oh dear." Then she brightened. "Maybe we'll reach a town soon."

"Five days—if we're lucky." A lot longer if anything else happened. At the rate they were going, they'd do well to make it to Hope's Crossing in six months. He gave her a smile, determined to put a happy face on the situation. "We'll survive. There are lots of things to eat out here."

Worry filled her eyes, then she tried for a faint smile, mirroring his. "I really need to lose a few pounds."

"Don't look at it that way. I won't let you starve." His throat was parched and he knew hers was probably the same. "There's a little creek up ahead, if it hasn't dried up. Think you can make it?"

"I'll match you step for step."

"This isn't a competition. We can rest if you need to."

"I'm just dandy. If I'm going to die, I want to get it over with."

Okay then. They walked in silence as the sun set and twilight descended, folding like a blanket around them. Up a slight hill, down the opposite side, putting one foot in front of the other. Onward they trod.

At last the creek came into view. They rushed forward, dropped on their bellies, and drank.

Once they'd satisfied their thirst, Jack helped her up and glanced around. This was as good a place as any to camp for the night, but not right at the water, where they'd be easily found. On the left was a stand of mesquite. The darkness in there might hide them.

"Let's find a spot where we can sleep." He pushed back a mesquite limb and caught his hand on a thorn. He sucked away the blood, ignoring the sting.

Lenora dug in her heels. "I'm not going in there with rattlesnakes. Or scorpions."

"Lady, you're trying my patience. We can't stay out here in plain sight."

"You mean *you* can't. I'm not wanted." She muttered low, "In Texas."

A strange comment. Just who was Lenora?

He rattled the chain, holding it up. "We're together, in case you've forgotten." Possibly a matched set if his gut was right. Miss Lenora That's-All had secrets.

An unholy fear widened her eyes. "Those trees will rip us to shreds. They all seem to have sharp thorns on them. And who knows what wild animals—snakes—are living in there?"

Maybe he was being repaid for trying to get under her skin.

After all, he was as good as married, even if he hadn't laid eyes on his future wife yet. He was promised to Miss Kane at the very least. Yet here he was feeling interest he shouldn't for Lenora.

He needed to remember that he wasn't free to act like a single man any longer.

"I can't possibly go in there."

Jack pinched the bridge of his nose and counted to ten before he answered. "Ma'am, what else do you suggest? I see no hotels."

"There's a hill just ahead. Let's look on the other side. It couldn't hurt."

"Fine," Jack growled.

Fit to be tied, he set off, his limp much worse. He had to rest his leg soon, or he'd be crawling. In no time, they topped the rise and discovered a small clearing that was shielded from the wind. The hill would also block them from view, and they could have a small fire.

"Does this suit Your Majesty?"

Lenora's head lifted slightly higher, and she gave him a nod. "It does."

"Good." Irritation rose that she was right. This *was* much better.

More pressing—he'd tried to ignore nature's call, but no longer could. "This is going to shock your delicate sensibilities, ma'am, but I have to…uh, you know…relieve myself. Sooner or later you will too."

Her eyes darkened and grew round.

"I'm sure you see the problem."

She worked her mouth and finally loosened her tongue. "I'll just turn my head and quote Scripture. I don't want to hear anything." She tilted her head and wrinkled her nose. "No, on second thought, maybe poetry. I never was much of a Bible reader."

They moved over into some high brush, and Lenora pulled as far from him as she could get. She began to quote some such about a nightingale being a melancholy bird, then moved on to something about wandering lonely as a cloud. Jack listened to her musical voice and could no more make water than flap his arms and fly.

She pursed her lips and began another poem:

> Whene'er I wander, at the fall of night,
> Where woven boughs shut out the moon's bright ray,
> Should sad Despondency my musings fright,
> And frown, to drive fair Cheerfulness away,
> Peep with the moonbeams through the leafy roof,
> And keep that fiend Despondence far aloof!

At last a trickle. Far better than nothing. But when she suddenly launched into a fervent rendition of "Battle Hymn of the Republic," the dam broke and he sighed contentedly.

He made himself decent. "You can stop now. It's your turn while I sing."

"Oh, I just couldn't. A lady needs privacy."

He barked a laugh. "Your privacy extends six whole inches."

"I'll wait."

"Suit yourself."

She helped gather some pieces of wood and he made a fire, thankful for the matches he always carried. They made themselves comfortable against a large boulder, their shoulders touching. A shiver raced through her and she clutched her coat tighter around her.

"I'd share my duster if I could free my arm." Jack reached for her gloved hand.

"I'm fine. Really." Lenora leaned against him and laid her head against his arm. Those soft curves nearly did him in.

"I'm very sorry," she moaned. "If I had thought things through. If I had only known. Oh, I wish I could go back. I wouldn't have touched these shackles, and I sure wouldn't have thrown the key."

"Lesson learned. We all make mistakes, albeit that was a whopper. Lord knows I've made some bad ones myself, but we'll be all right." He patted her hand. She smelled nice. It felt good having her near. It would feel a whole lot better if he had these manacles off. He'd try his best with that problem come daybreak. "Where are you from? It's plain you're not from here."

"Buffalo, New York."

He whistled. "That's a far distance. What brings you to Texas?"

"I was on my way to be married. I went through a mail order bride service. A different sort—a private one." She rubbed a weary hand over her eyes. "You know, I never asked for your name."

"Jack. Jack Bowdre."

"From Hope's Crossing?"

"Yep."

She jerked and glanced up with a confused stare. "I... we're...you're the one I was coming to marry." She flailed at him with her free hand, landing a soft blow. "You're nothing but a low-down criminal! You...you deceived me. You're despicable!"

Three

JACK SHIELDED HIS FACE WITH AN ARM TO FEND OFF THE attack, his stomach bunching tight. "Lenora—Nora. You're my Nora Kane?"

"I'm not your anything. Yet." The glare she gave him could've stripped the hide off a buffalo. "Why didn't you tell me you're a wanted man? Just explain that." She hauled off and slugged him with her free hand.

"Watch it, lady." Jack had wanted rough edges on a wife, but Nora's needed to come with a warning label. "I wanted to tell you face-to-face. Something like that's hard to put into a letter."

She slapped his arm. "Don't tell me you can't *spell* either. 'Outlaw' is easy." She squinted at him sharply, probably thinking he'd gotten someone else to write them, a common enough practice but not one he needed.

Jack got hot. "For your information, I can spell *and* write *and* cipher. I'm not dumb." At the moment, mind you, he wasn't too sure about that last part. He had shit for brains for omitting his lawless ways from his letters. And he sure hadn't shown any sense when he let down his guard that morning and Marshal Dollard had arrested him.

"Well, that's a relief. I wouldn't want an illiterate outlaw husband."

He'd better not tell her about the rest of his day, because it would only confirm her opinion of him. He wasn't supposed to be anywhere near the small community of McDougal Springs, and he wouldn't have been if Dr. Mary hadn't gotten an urgent message about a woman having a difficult childbirth. Like always, she'd asked Jack to drive her.

Hell! It was obvious he'd stepped into a trap. Only, who had tipped the lawmen off? Certainly not Dr. Mary. That woman was a saint and had been as stunned as he. But a traitor again came to mind and was something he meant to explore at his leisure.

"Exactly what kind of husband do you want, Nora Kane?" Better to know now.

She was silent so long he was about to repeat the question when she said, "A kind one."

Kind? The answer stopped him. Would that apply to him? He'd never beaten any woman or child, but he didn't think that made a man kind. Kind seemed to be putting other people's welfare before his own. But had he? Jack scowled, searching his memory.

Nora picked at the chain binding them together. "You said in your letters you were once a lawman. Or was that a lie too?"

He rubbed his sore jaw and removed Marshal Dollard's badge from his shirt, staring at it. Memories swirled like dry leaves piling one on top of another, and he couldn't stop them.

Another time, another place, another life when he'd loved and been loved. Then lost it all, in the blink of an eye.

"I spent five years as a U.S. marshal, wearing a badge like this one."

"What happened?"

Her tone had softened considerably. Or maybe he simply wanted to imagine that she cared. "Too much water ran under that bridge and washed it out." Jack leaned for a piece of wood, snapped it in half, and tossed it on the fire. If he were free of her, he'd stalk off into the darkness where she couldn't see his pain.

Maybe there with the night around him, he'd find the strength to tell her that his try for marriage had been his last hope.

To find some good still left inside him.

To claim the life and the family he dreamed of.

And to find the respectable man he used to be.

"No, please. I'm curious. What turned you into an outlaw?"

"Revenge." He regretted the harsh snap in his voice. Regretted the dark places his thoughts took him. Regretted more things than he could count. "Enough questions. I'm not some bug you can poke and cut open to examine. I guarantee you won't like what you see."

The fire crackled and popped in the welcome silence. Thankfully, Nora appeared to have run out of questions. Finally. She was quiet so long he thought she must've gone to sleep. Some night creature scratched at the ground and a nearby bush, dry and bare of its leaves, stirred.

Nora jerked. "What's that?"

"Just some animal, maybe a rodent. It won't hurt you." It baffled him how she could stand her ground and fight him tooth and toenail yet seemed terrified of everything natural around her.

"It could be a rattlesnake slithering across the ground." She drew her feet up under her dress. "I've been told they can sink their fangs into someone, and their venom is deadly."

"Their bite doesn't spell instant death. Folks can survive with proper treatment."

She shook her finger at him. "I know what you're doing. You're just trying to humor me."

Jack gave a soft snort. "Where did you get all your information about Texas anyway? Dime novels?"

"Books and esteemed newspaper accounts." She sniffed. "Many folks back home assured me it was accurate."

"Don't believe half that stuff. Besides, that's not a snake. Those are silent. It's more likely a skunk or armadillo."

"Do they bite?"

"No. Try to relax."

She fidgeted and squirmed. "I can't. Jack, I have to go. Oh dear, I have to go. I must hurry."

The strong urge had Nora afraid to move, much less stand. Why had she waited so long when there were creatures prowling about?

Jack helped her to her feet and they moved off into the bushes, where there was no light. At least he couldn't see her embarrassment in the pitch black.

"I'll turn my head. Do you want me to sing?" He appeared a little too eager to assist. "It's not easy doing something so personal with a stranger chained to you."

It touched her that he recognized how she must feel. "Please sing. Just don't listen. If I ever make it back to civilization, I'm never crossing the Mississippi again."

Jack chuckled. "It's not as scary as you wish to believe."

Maybe not, but she'd take no chances. Maybe the singing would keep varmints far away. Everything was so different here, even the air. The slight breeze smelled fresh and clean—really nice. He sang an unfamiliar tune, something about whiskey and rye. For an outlaw, he had a very good baritone. And she liked hearing him talk in that low voice of his. Something about it sent quivers dancing along her spine.

With the singing to muffle the sound, she fought with her skirts. Try as she might, she couldn't raise her dress and petticoats with one hand *and* fight to keep the stupid steel-hooped bustle out of the way.

Finally, she swallowed her pride. "Jack, do you think you can...help?"

Thankfully, he didn't say a word, just held the yards of fabric so she could get her pantaloons open. Another thing not exactly easy to do one-handed, but she sure wasn't going to ask for any help with that. The thought made her cringe and heat flooded her face.

As Jack switched to a jaunty tune about tumbleweeds and Texas, she let loose. What were tumbleweeds? Could tumbleweeds kill a person? Probably. Everything here was so new and frightening. Here, even the simplest things seemed capable of bringing death—even the sun. The sun never shone this hot in New York. And what was this weather about? Frigid one day and burning up the next? It sent a person's body into shock.

When she finished, she untied her bustle and yanked it off, throwing it as far as she could—which probably wasn't as far as the key to the manacles. However, without the bustle, the dress dragged on the ground. She solved that for now by tucking her skirts up higher.

On the return to their little campsite, Jack broke off some branches of scrub oak and a few wide, lacy ones from a juniper. "For our bed," he explained.

It would be a lot better than the bare ground. Jack seemed to think of everything.

Back at the fire, Nora felt considerably better. She helped Jack spread the branches out and dropped down on them. "I wish we had a nice cup of hot chowder."

"Never heard of that, and to my knowledge, I've sure never eaten any."

"It's a thick soup. Very hearty and most tasty."

"When it gets daylight, I'll find you something to eat." He leaned to toss another piece of wood on the fire. "Come morning, one way or another, I'm going to break this chain."

She couldn't be surprised by how badly he wanted to be separated from her. Nora chewed her bottom lip. Maybe he'd go off and leave her. After all, she hadn't really endeared herself to him. She'd been nothing but a thorn in his backside from the start.

What would she do if he insisted they part ways? Worry twisted her insides into knots.

Nothing had prepared her for the possibility that her letter-writing Mr. Bowdre might not want her. If he didn't, what then? She'd burned all the bridges behind her. There was no going back. Ever. Her lip trembled.

She studied his long, whipcord form, broad chest, and muscled arms. He could probably break her like a twig. But something told her that Jack Bowdre wouldn't hurt her. No matter that she made him mad enough to stomp and cuss, all he'd done so far was bluster. If he really had a mean streak, he'd have shown it by now. He hadn't hit or thrown things, only looked exasperated and counted beneath his breath. And that odd rumbling in his chest when he was annoyed, as though he had to gain a head of steam like a train trudging uphill. Then when it erupted, his temper hadn't been half as bad as she'd anxiously feared.

This man she'd come to marry sight unseen had honor.

Despite circumstances and the fact that she hadn't made it easy for him, he was taking care of her as best he could. He had grit too. Instead of stopping to rest when his leg obviously pained him until he turned white around the mouth, he gathered strength and limped on, fighting for each step.

She wondered what had happened to him.

Sure, Jack was an outlaw and undoubtedly wanted for many crimes, but she'd hear his story before passing judgment. After all, she was no lily-white saint. She fumbled with the folds of her dress for the little ledger she'd tucked into the hidden pocket of her skirt, relaxing when she found it still there.

If not for that book, she'd be dead right now. The pages and pages of names and numbers were the only thing keeping her alive. Once she was safe and Flynn O'Brien couldn't touch her, she'd turn the book over to someone she could trust to stop the rich, powerful crook.

By the flickering light of the fire, Nora admired Jack's strong profile—from his rugged jaw sporting that dark bruise, his tantalizing mouth and high cheekbones, to his thick, dark lashes.

He would be a good kisser—she just knew it. Not that she *wanted* to kiss him.

Still, the thought sent tingles up her spine and her stomach quickened. No, to be separated from him forever was not anything to look forward to.

"Tell me something. Why do you dress all in black, down to your hat and boots?"

Jack shrugged. "Simple. I wear black clothes for every person who's been wronged, beaten down, deprived of a living, and for the poor and hungry. Why did you discard your bustle?"

"It was in my way, and I'm tired of wearing what men decide women must."

His lips twitched. "Rebellion is good for the soul. Do you make a habit of revolt?"

"Only in certain instances when things are unfair." Her answer was soft. A strange urge came over her to touch his bruised jaw, trace the lines of his mouth—smooth the crow's feet at the corners of his eyes. But she didn't dare touch him so familiarly.

She blurted out without thinking, "Do you have a price on your head?"

His eyes darkened. "Yep. Last wanted poster said nine hundred dollars, dead or alive. Could've gone up since, I don't know. It's not something I can control, so best not to worry about it."

The price staggered her. Such a reward would bring lawmen and bounty hunters down on him in droves. "No, I don't suppose it helps to dwell on it."

Death didn't seem to be what a man liked to think much about, even under normal circumstances.

He rubbed the back of his neck and stretched out his long legs. "Nora, I'm sorry I wasn't truthful when I wrote you. I should've told you everything right out. Only I was afraid if you knew, you wouldn't come. And I couldn't take…" He gazed into the flames. "I was set to marry a woman last fall, only she decided the barren days of a nunnery were preferable to making a life with me."

"That's wrong. That's just plain wrong." The woman must've been an imbecile to pass up a man like Jack, even if he was an outlaw.

Marshal Dollard claimed he'd killed fourteen people. Or was it fifteen? All she knew was he didn't seem the sort to kill in cold blood, so they probably deserved it. Jack had seen lots of chances to kill her and been plenty mad enough to do it—only he hadn't.

Until recently, she'd worked with men who made Jack look like a choirboy, men who wouldn't hesitate to cut out a person's tongue or drive nails into their fingers. A shudder ran the length of her body. If they found her…

They'd torture her first and then throw her in a hole in the desert—one filled with deadly snakes.

The threats alone had terrified her. Nora swallowed hard. She was more afraid of the cold-blooded, slithery reptiles than anything else on earth. Maybe more than the lizards and alligators that lived in the swamps that she'd read about.

Maybe an outlaw like Jack was all that could stand between her and trouble.

"You have to understand about Darcy," Jack said, bringing her attention back to the subject of his original intended, the one who'd joined a nunnery. "She'd been locked in an asylum for a while and tortured. She wasn't crazy though. Her uncle put her in there to keep her from telling anyone about his crimes. I don't fault her—it just stung is all. For a man to feel like a second choice stomps on something inside him."

They lapsed into silence and Nora thought about what he'd revealed. More telling was what he couldn't bring himself to say—the real reason he'd turned to crime. It had to have been something terrible if he couldn't forget.

Whatever it was had left him wearing black, his soul scarred. Maybe one day he'd open up. If they managed to live long enough.

"Do you mind if I ask why you limp?"

"An old injury, about five years gone. A posse was chasing me, and one got off a shot. The bullet's still lodged near my hip. When I'm on my feet for any length of time, it feels like a damn badger's gnawing my leg off."

She wanted to ask if he got chased often but didn't want to appear too nosy. An outlaw's business was his own. Guilt littered the chaotic landscape inside her. She hadn't been truthful with him either.

The fact was, she had men on her trail. She'd glimpsed one at the train station in Fort Worth but had managed to lose him. Right now, they were scattering in a frenzy like a bunch of cockroaches when the lamp was lit. Her luck wouldn't hold.

They would find her no matter how careful she was.

Tomorrow she'd tell Jack. It was the only fair thing to do, even though he might hate her for keeping silent.

She thought a moment and gave her head a shake. On the other hand, what difference would it make to mention even more trouble? She'd probably do him a favor by keeping quiet.

They were on foot, handcuffed together. Even worse, they had a gun with no bullets and the town they were headed for was five days away. He couldn't very well fight. Or run. Except she couldn't see him doing that. Jack Bowdre was a stand-your-ground sort of man.

And that didn't count the men scouring the countryside for him.

No, she didn't have the heart to tell him things were far worse than he knew.

She stared up at the stars, wishing for a miracle. Yet all she saw up there was the same thing she saw when she closed her eyes. Murky black water that smelled like rotted flesh—water that hid untold danger and death.

And when trouble closed around her, cutting off her air supply, she wouldn't even see it coming.

Four

THE MORNING SKY WAS AN ODD SWIRL OF LIGHTER AND DARKER
pink when Nora woke with a start. The realization that she lay
curled in Jack's arms, her skirt and petticoats bunched halfway
up her legs, shocked her into action. She bolted upright, tugging at her skirts to make herself decent.

A chuckle jerked her around. His gunmetal gray eyes didn't
have one bit of sleep in them.

"How long have you been awake?"

"About an hour I guess. Nice legs." The chain of the
manacles rattled as he sat up.

"You could've woken me." What else had he ogled
while she was dead to the world? She groaned and quickly
straightened the gap between the buttons of her bodice.
She'd provided him with a free tease, like the women at the
burlesque shows.

"What for? You needed sleep." He stood and pulled her
up. "We'll go back to the creek to wash and then get moving.
I expect riders will come this way after me very soon. I'd like
to keep ahead of them."

The stubble on Jack's jaw, a shade darker than his light-
brown hair, sent Nora's heart into a spin. That and the muscles
working along his arms did funny things to her stomach. She
told herself it was this Texas air.

Yet she knew it wasn't. Outlaw or not, behind his gruff
complaining, this man was gentle and kind. Not once had he
done anything to make her really afraid for her life. In fact, she
felt far safer with him than she had for a long while. He even
shortened his long stride to the length of her legs and reached
for her hand. She hummed all the way to the water, noticing
he barely limped.

"Jack, about this posse. Who exactly are they?"

"A group of ordinary men who've been deputized, with one or two lawmen in charge. Why?"

"No reason. Just trying to figure the odds, that's all."

"Slim and none. If we get out of this, it'll be a pure miracle." He led her around a bed of cactus. "Watch out for those thorns."

"I appreciate the warning."

Before they set off across the rugged landscape, Nora helped Jack stuff the bustle she'd discarded in the night behind some rocks. Hopefully, if a rider passed by, he wouldn't see it. She prayed not, anyway. Too late, she realized she should've burned it in the fire. That would've been best. Finally, with the bustle out of sight, she helped him get rid of the branches they'd slept on and wipe away their footprints until the camp-site showed no evidence they'd been there.

An hour later, Nora's growling stomach reminded her they had yet to eat.

He stopped in front of a bed of cactus. "This is about it in the way of food right now. Sorry."

"We're eating…that?" She leaned down for a closer look at the round pods covered with thorns. That was going to hurt. "I don't think I'm quite that hungry."

"Don't let the appearance fool you. Cactus is good food in a pinch. You might even develop a liking for it."

"Don't count on it." She'd already formed an opinion on the subject.

"I just have to wrap my hands so I won't get stuck." The shackles clanked as he removed his right arm from his duster and encased his hand in the heavy fabric. Carefully, he yanked on a large pod from the nearest vicious-looking plant, tore it off, and laid it on the ground. Then he removed another, laying it on top of the first and picking them both up together.

Nora moved with him behind the shelter of a group of rocks, where he built a fire. Thank goodness they weren't going to eat the cactus raw.

"Hand me that stick behind you, please." He reached for another near his foot.

Whatever he had in mind, this would bear watching. She'd never lived in the wild before, and she might have to do this on her own at some point. She handed him the stick and perched on a rock beside him. Jack stuck the sticks through the pods and set them in the flames, turning them until they began to roast. When he removed the pods from the fire, the thorns were gone.

Where had he learned to do that anyway? Or did he live like this all the time?

Oh good Lord, did he even have a house or a bed? He'd lied to her in his letters already, which meant she knew nothing about him. He might expect her to do without even the basic necessities. She couldn't live like this. She needed *stuff*. Not a lot, mind you, but more than she had now.

Jack laid the roasted cactus on a rock, a smile teasing his mouth. "We'll let them cool a minute. It's too early in the year for the fruit, but they're tasty and sweet."

"I need to know—what do these roasted pods taste like?"

"Have you ever had okra?"

"No. Are you sure those are edible?"

"I've eaten them many times. You'll like the taste, and they're very moist."

After a few minutes, he handed her one. Much to her surprise, she did find the taste and texture halfway agreeable. Her hunger was too great, and before she knew it, she'd finished.

"Well?" he asked.

"I've certainly had worse. They're pretty good. Thank you."

When she sat back, her stomach full, she knew there were lots of worse things than being shackled to Jack Bowdre. Why she trusted him was hard to explain. Abused as she'd been for so long, she should be wary, but something in his eyes, on his face, assured her he wouldn't hurt her. Growing up with Flynn, she'd become very adept at sizing men up. In fact, to make a mistake would've meant death. This outlaw wasn't a threat—not to her.

But others should definitely take heed.

She gave Jack's rugged profile a sideways glance. He seemed deep in thought the way he stared into the distance.

Maybe how to get rid of her?

Out here on the plains, there appeared to be certain freedom in the primitive conditions that she hadn't considered. Still…she didn't want this for the rest of her life.

Panic swept through her. What if Jack didn't want her? What if he got loose from her and left? How would she survive in this strange place alone, without anything?

He rose. "We'll have some more later. Right now, I need to find a good rock and see if I can break this chain. I had planned to shoot out one of the links, but without bullets, the gun is useless."

"You can break these iron links apart with a rock?"

"Exactly what I plan."

"What size rock are you looking for?" There were hundreds in the immediate vicinity. This part of Texas sure didn't have much to commend it. In each direction, she looked she saw the same barren landscape. How did people live out here?

"I'll know when I see it."

A lot of good that did *her*. "Can't you use the butt of the Colt?"

"That'll damage it and it won't fire." He said that like it was something everyone should know.

"But we have no cartridges. Why keep something that doesn't work?" Lord help this poor outlaw. He didn't seem quite right in the head sometimes.

Jack stopped and stared as though she'd suggested he gnaw through the iron links with his teeth. He inhaled a slow breath and seemed to be…counting? Oh dear. "Even if a gun has no ammunition, it still has plenty of worth. If someone corners us, I can still point it at someone. They'll think what I want them to. I'm very good at making men believe they're about to die. Besides, I have friends who roam this land. I can borrow some cartridges from them."

"Oh. I guess that's why you're the outlaw and I'm…a bride you kept secrets from."

The way color flooded his face and the kick he gave a clumpy weed of some kind said he didn't appear to appreciate her remark. As long as he didn't start counting again.

"Over there." He pointed to a group of rocks that appeared to have been stacked on purpose.

She allowed him to pull her to them, and he chose a hefty one, about nine by six inches. Although he had very large palms, she still had no idea how he'd lift the makeshift sledge-hammer and slam it onto the chain with one hand.

With his inability to accept criticism, she thought it prudent to hold her tongue.

With the few inches of chain stretched across a boulder, Jack lifted the rock. The mighty blow jarred her, sending vibrating waves along the chain and stinging her wrist. Plus, the impact didn't even put the slightest dent in the iron. He slipped his arm out of the only duster sleeve he could get off and tried again. Nothing. He unbuttoned his shirt, tugging at the collar, and Nora sucked in a breath at the sight of that broad chest with rippling muscles.

My oh my!

To run her hands over that. She'd always assumed men who lived by the gun would be too thin, too pale, their bodies too…standard. After all, what work did an outlaw do other than ride his horse and shoot?

Apparently, Jack did far more. He had to do physical work of some kind to have a chest that brawny. She tried not to stare, but her eyes refused to obey.

Over and over, he pounded the chain. With each strike, she flinched and dodged the flying chips of stone. Over and over, the metal failed to yield. Sweat poured off him despite the cool day. Frustrated curses slipped from his mouth, although he restrained himself far better than she expected.

"I have a hairpin if you want to try picking the locks." That idea made more sense to her, rather than thrashing the daylights out of a chain that wouldn't budge.

"I'll get this in a minute. It's just stubborn, that's all. I have to hit it just right."

The sun rose higher, he kept working, and the *rock* finally broke right in half…but the chain held fast.

He met her gaze. "Failure is just the opportunity to begin again. We're not licked."

Nora cocked her head, catching a faint sound. "Someone's coming."

"Hurry." Jack took her hand and led her down into a ravine, where they flattened against the side. "Don't make a sound."

Her heart hammered in her ears. Or was that *his* heartbeat? He put his free arm around her and pulled her against all that brawn. The scent of the wild Texas land melded with leather and manly sweat, and Nora could do nothing but sag against him as limp as jelly left sitting in the sun.

His mouth was mere inches from hers.

Perspiration trickled between her breasts, and she could barely draw a shaky breath into her lungs. No one had a right to be so rugged, so enticing, so…so sensual.

What would it be like to feel his lips on hers? Her pulse raced.

He shifted a little, knitting his brows, frowning down at her. Shoot! Had she spoken aloud?

The empty Colt tucked in his waist pressed into the area above her belly, reminding her they were in grave danger. In truth, she was having trouble forming a complete thought.

A few minutes passed, and the hoofbeats became louder until the rider was right above them. The horse snorted with impatience. Other than the horse, all was silent.

Good. That meant only one person, not a whole posse of bloodthirsty men.

Jack removed his hat, gripped the empty gun, and took a look. The suspense proved too much for Nora. She raised on tiptoe to peek, and fear raced through her. She clamped a hand over her mouth to hush the startled cry.

The horseman was the man she'd caught following her in Fort Worth. The white of her discarded bustle bulged from his saddlebag.

The gray gelding he rode ambled by, almost stopping, the rider scanning every rock, cactus, and blade of straw grass.

Looking for her.

She ducked, pressing the trembling length of her body tightly against Jack. How could the tracker have found her? Had he watched her board the stage in Fort Worth and followed? If so, he'd seen the stagecoach wreck and knew she had to be in the area. Then he had found the bustle they'd stuffed between the rocks. She mentally kicked herself. Who was he? The man definitely wasn't from New York. He knew far too much about this land, moved in it too easily.

Jack's hard gaze followed the tracker until he rode on. He kept his voice low so it wouldn't carry. "Who was that? You recognized him."

Oh God, she had to tell him. But then—that meant mentioning everything else—and the ledger she'd stolen.

Careful. The lies would pile up on top of each other until she couldn't keep them straight.

"I thought I saw him in Fort Worth when I got off the train." Nora twisted a button on her coat, keeping her eyes lowered. "I'm sure I was probably mistaken. I didn't get a very good look at him just now. The sun was in my eyes, you know, and I could barely make out anything."

He narrowed his stern gaze and pinched his eyebrows together. "Why would anyone follow you?"

"A case of mistaken identity?" She finally glanced up and widened her eyes. "Although I'm sure I imagined that whole thing. No one here in Texas would have absolutely any interest in me. I came to marry you, Jack, and I have to say it's been a rather arduous trip. Some of the hardship was my own making, I admit. If I could just go back to the moment when I unlocked the marshal's handcuff."

She smiled brightly, refusing to let the outlaw's dark scowl worry her.

"Repeating that won't unhook these. We'll have to talk about the marrying part." He took her hand and they moved north, staying in the ravine. The chain stayed on their wrists, breaking it forgotten for the moment.

Talk about it? What did that mean? She chewed her bottom lip.

Thick brush grew in the long slice in the earth, providing many places for snakes to lurk. She stumbled several times, too busy looking for the slithery reptiles with their beady little eyes and long fangs. Jack didn't seem one bit concerned. Maybe the marshal had it right back in the stage. Jack was so mean the rattlesnakes wouldn't come near him. Whatever it was, she was glad they stayed away.

The marshal's other comment—about Jack's family disowning him—raised other questions, and she wondered if that was true. Sometimes he stared off into the distance with such sorrow.

Only someone all alone in the world wore a look like that. She should know. Her current situation was due in part to that. Flynn O'Brien had come sniffing around, taking advantage of her vulnerability and the fact that she had no family of her own. At first, he'd seemed like a caring benefactor. Then he'd trapped her in a web of lies, murder, and fear.

For years, she'd struggled to free herself from the labyrinth of horror only to find every turn led deeper and deeper, away from the blessed light and freedom.

Jack's letters and offer of marriage had been her first real hope in a very dark time. *Come to Hope's Crossing and marry me. Start a new life. Help settle a raw town and find more contentment than you've ever known.*

Nora wiggled her fingers inside his warm palm. Now he wanted to "discuss" the marrying part. Had he changed his mind and was sending her back to that nightmare?

Fear slid up her spine. She'd barely escaped by the skin of her teeth. She wouldn't be so lucky again.

What about her? Although he set her pulse racing, did she want to marry an outlaw? Someone always on the run? Hunted like a wild animal? A husband who could be shot or hanged at any time, and maybe leave her with children to raise alone?

Wasn't this what she sought to escape from?

A tiny voice whispered in her ear: *Honey, you're no better than he is.* For sure, she and Jack were two of a kind...and he didn't even know it yet.

She jumped when he placed his mouth to her ear. "There's a cave nearby. We'll hole up there until I decide our next move." His gray gaze sought hers. "I have to know something right now before we go further."

"Sure."

"Given the opportunity, will you cry out and turn me in? Let the posse take me?"

Nora studied his face, saw the pain dulling his eyes, saw a hint of his tortured past and knew the answer. "No. I think you suffer enough. If they arrest you, it won't be by my doing."

Relief eased his stony features. "Good to know. Then be as quiet as possible in case that rider or others are close."

With a nod, Nora gripped his hand and let him lead her from the ravine. But was he saving her or, like Flynn, leading her into greater danger?

Or possibly death?

Five

THE CLIMB TO THE CAVE WAS DIFFICULT, AND FINALLY JACK
had to pull Nora up the side of the steep hill. To her credit,
she didn't cry out or complain. Determination lined her face
instead, and that grit made her someone he'd be proud to ride
the river with. He'd never seen another with her strength—
except maybe Tally Shannon, wife to his friend Clay.

Still, Nora Kane made him mad enough to rope a rabid
coyote. It had taken all his self-control at times not to strangle
her. If only he could smash the chain between them so he
could go off by himself for just a few minutes.

There was close, and then there was so close it smothered.
A man craved space to breathe.

Yet chained to her for a day and night, he'd come to know
a little of what went on in her head. She had a gentle touch
and endeavored to look on the bright side of a situation. He
liked that. Even as bloody as he'd been in the stagecoach and
afterward, when she should've been afraid of him, she'd stood
toe to toe. But like everyone, she had her faults. Hers was
being impulsive. Handcuffing herself to him and tossing the
key. He gave a soft snort. And, Lord, that woman would argue
with an iron jenny.

Galloping hooves and riders fast approaching caught
his notice and set his heart pounding. "Hurry. Someone's
coming."

"Oh no." That built a fire under her, and she clawed the
rest of the way to the large cave.

His lungs burned as panic raced through him. He couldn't
get captured again. Not with Nora there. They'd get the
wrong idea, and that would sure lead to the gallows, even with
her denying he'd touched her. Didn't matter.

Jack scrambled the last few yards to the flat ground in front of the shelter and pulled her up into the cool dimness, praying they wouldn't encounter angry varmints.

The entrance was high enough to stand, the ceiling gradually sloping down the farther they went. "Hurry to the back and don't talk. Pray they don't look up here."

Although the whites of her round eyes revealed her fear, she did as he asked.

Jack's boot brushed against a length of shed snakeskin. He should probably tell her that they might've invaded a den of hibernating vipers. In the fall, the snakes sought dry, dark places such as this. But here in March, they'd be waking up and moving about, looking for food. Still, she was already terrified enough. No need to worry the excitable woman more.

He sank down beside her against the cold earthen wall and took her trembling hand. His mouth was as dry as month-old bread, and hers had to be the same. The next available water he knew was a day's walk. Nora wouldn't last that long.

And now trouble was hot on their heels, which would keep them hunkered down for a while. If they weren't detected. If the members of the posse didn't decide to make camp here and trap them.

And if…a thousand ifs and maybes ran through his head.

By now, his friends at Hope's Crossing would have heard about his predicament. Clay and the others would come looking for him when they learned the stagecoach hadn't made it to Saint's Roost. If they could stay alive until then.

The pulse in Nora's wrist throbbed fast against his hand. But why? They weren't after her. All she had to do was holler and they'd rescue her. She held his life in her hands.

Yet he got the impression she might not want to be found.

Shouts and the sounds of horses reached him. The men would scour every bit of ground. They wanted him that bad. He pulled the empty Colt from his waist and stared at it, cursing Dollard for removing the cartridges. *Hell and be damned!*

He felt naked, vulnerable.

Even one bullet could mean the difference between life and death. He'd been in far worse spots, but never without a pistol and some ammunition. Had no knife either. No kind of weapon.

Nora leaned in to whisper, "What if they come inside?"

"I have a plan." What it was, he didn't exactly know. Bash them over the head with the Colt? With Nora there? He couldn't fight or do much with her shackled to his side. She could get hurt.

One minute dragged by. Then two.

Bootheels struck pebbles. Jack tensed and squeezed Nora's icy hand, praying she didn't rattle the chain or utter a word. Something nearby rustled, feet scurried. A rodent or maybe a badger. Please not a skunk. He'd been sprayed once, and it had taken forever to get that scent off. No one would come within a mile of him.

Next to him, Nora shivered and pressed against his shoulder.

Footsteps stopped on the rocky ledge just outside the entrance. Though the day was chilly, sweat popped out on his forehead.

Two men entered the cave. Where had the second one come from? Jack's stomach twisted at being caught by surprise. No excuse for overlooking the second rider. He had to get his head back on straight before he got caught. Nora Kane had messed with his good sense, cuddling up to him in her sleep the way she had.

Without a light, the two members of the posse couldn't see very far. Just as Jack thought that, the tall one struck a match and held it up. Jack and Nora shrank deeper into the shadows.

"I don't see anything. Do you, Red?"

Jack barely breathed. He'd messed up in not brushing away their footprints. If the men glanced down…

"Not a thing, Gilbert. There's no telling what's back up in there. You can go look if you want, but I've got the shivers." The man pushed back his hat and scratched his forehead. "I lost a real good friend once who poked around in a cave this same time of year. A damn wildcat leaped out and mauled him to death before we could save him."

"A bad deal." Red paused a moment, then added, "I keep

thinking about that young woman Bowdre took. She must be real cold and scared. Bowdre's a killer. Who knows what he'll do to her? We'll probably find her broken body lying on the trail."

Jack seethed. He'd heard whispers of the same talk before, but none spoken as plain as this. He'd never ended anyone's life because he enjoyed it. And though the men he'd killed deserved what they got, each death had bothered him. And he'd never—nor would he ever—touch a woman in anger. He restrained the urge to jump up and set them straight.

The tall, hefty one named Gilbert held up a new match and stepped farther into the cave. The hair on Jack's neck twitched as he lowered his head and blocked Nora's eyes, leaving nothing to glitter.

She stiffened, her chest heaving. *A sneeze.* Hell! If she couldn't contain it... Holding the chain so it didn't clink together, he pinched her nose until she relaxed.

"You know what bothers me, Red?" Gilbert peered closer into the shadows. "What happened to the manacles that Marshal Dollard had on Bowdre? Why did he take them?"

"Well, I'm betting he put them on that pretty young woman so she couldn't run."

"Yep, that's probably what he did, the bastard." After several long heartbeats, Gilbert swung around. "I don't think Bowdre's here."

"We should get down the trail. We've gotta be gaining ground, him being afoot and all. He shouldn't even have gotten this far."

"I just hope we ain't too late to save that lady."

Mumbling to each other, the searchers left, and quiet descended. Jack became extremely aware of Nora—how close his mouth was to hers, her breath brushing his cheek, and the special scent of her drifting near. Stifling the chain's rattle, he quickly put six inches between them. "Don't talk. Those lawmen could be just outside."

"That was close. I wanted to tell them that I'm in good hands," she whispered.

It touched something inside him that she would see her situation as positive. But why? They were cold, hungry, thirsty. She had no reason to feel that he was taking care of her, because he wasn't. Irritated, he stuck the empty Colt back in his waistband.

They waited there awhile longer, until he was certain the posse had ridden on. "I think they're gone. It's safe to talk."

"I'm really thirsty."

"Me too. Try not to think about it."

"Hard not to." Nora reached down beside her and held up something long. "What's this, Jack?"

"A snakeskin. They shed once or twice during a year's time."

She sucked in a quick breath, jerked back, and threw it. She slapped his arm. "Why didn't you warn me?"

"What's to warn? A skin can't bite."

"You know how I feel about snakes." She glanced around. "Do you think any live ones are in here?"

"Most are still in hibernation for another three weeks."

"What was that rustling and scurrying I heard earlier?"

"Probably a rodent of some sort. Won't hurt you."

"Why are you always saying that?" She fumbled underneath her dress and pulled out something about five inches long that gleamed in the dim light. She held it out in front of her with a tight grip.

Jack stilled, his eyes narrowing. "Is that a knife?"

"Yes, and quite a good one."

"You had it all this time?" He couldn't help the rising anger. Here he'd needed something to feed and defend them with, and she'd had it right there the whole blessed time.

Hell and be damned! Besides all that, she could've killed him in his sleep. The only thing that probably kept her from it was having to drag his dead body around. He turned away, took calming breaths, and started with number one again, reaching the forties before he began to cool off.

"Oh, for heaven's sake, you're counting."

It took the nineties before he allowed himself to speak

calmly, although his voice remained tight. "I could've used that knife."

"You managed quite well." Nora shot him a glance. "You really can't blame me. A woman traveling alone has to have protection of some kind."

Everything inside Jack froze. "To defend yourself—against me?"

Did she honestly think he'd hurt her? Had he been that threatening and mean? The answer was yes, he *had* threatened her. Quite a bit, in fact.

"Against you, against everyone." She rested a hand on his arm. "Please try to see it from my side."

Which was what? Then he suddenly found himself admiring her for having the gumption to arm herself. A woman alone did face all kinds of unsavory people. And why should she have trusted an escaped outlaw, a killer? His clothes were covered with dried blood, he could feel his bruises, and he'd messed with her on the stagecoach, touching her leg with his knee.

Still, the truth that she felt safer with a weapon pricked him.

His thoughts were in a turmoil, but admiration won out. Here he'd let the marshal strip him of his gun and knife, leaving him with only his hands, but Nora had kept *her* knife.

Maybe she needed to be the outlaw, because she was smarter by far.

Another calming breath. "Do you have anything else you forgot to tell me about, Nora?"

"No, I think that's all." The way she chewed her bottom lip failed to convince him.

If he stripped her down, what would he find? A small derringer and cartridges? Other things they needed?

"Nora, tell me the truth. I have to know."

"Well, there's one teensy little thing." The smile she gave him was shaky at best.

"Whatever it is, give it to me. I might have some use for it."

"You really won't need this."

"Let me decide."

Nora swallowed and dragged her gaze from his. She reached into a hidden pocket of her dress and pulled out...What? A book? "Here. This is everything."

"What is this?" He opened the small ledger and glanced at the lines of names and numbers.

"My insurance. That book contains evidence that will put a bad man behind bars for a long time. Please help me make sure nothing happens to it."

"What man?"

"The vile one I used to work for. He kept me a prisoner for years."

Jack stuck the ledger inside his duster and pulled her up. "Let's find some wood to make a fire, and then you're going to tell me everything. About this insurance of yours, and about the rider we saw this morning. Deny it all you want, but I know you recognized him. I saw it in your eyes."

"All right, I'll tell you what you want. Just don't judge me. Never judge until you've walked in a dead man's shoes."

He glanced down at Dollard's boots on her feet and laughed. "Nora, you are something."

At the mouth of the cave, he held her back. "Let me make sure it's safe." Cold wind slapped his face when he leaned out, but he didn't see any riders. He turned back to button up her coat, avoiding her large brown eyes. He'd be lost if he let them pull him in. "All clear."

They quickly gathered wood and soon had a fire going. He prayed they reached town before they ran out of matches, or that would spell disaster in the worst way.

Seated by the flickering fire, Jack glanced at Nora's stoic features and removed the ledger from inside his duster. "Everyone has a story. Tell me yours and how this book fits into it."

"You may as well know, since we're in this together now." She sighed. "I was thirteen when my parents died of cholera. I lived with an old aunt for a year, until she too passed. With no other relatives, I found myself on the street, sleeping under porches, chicken coops, or whatever I could find. I was dirty, freezing, and hungry. A man by the name of Flynn O'Brien took me in. He was the richest man in town and had the best of everything. He had a nice way of talking. I had the softest bed a girl ever slept on and plenty of food. He never raised a hand to me. At first, I thought of him as a surrogate father."

Jack could picture her as a bright-eyed young girl, lost and alone. Men preyed on the vulnerable. At least this Flynn O'Brien hadn't stolen her innocence—not in that way at least. He suspected O'Brien had taken other things that were as valuable.

Nora put a weary hand to her forehead. "One day about six months later, I was exploring the huge house and stumbled into a meeting between Flynn and a group of rough-looking men. They were discussing city officials and businessmen who hadn't paid protection money—and they caught me listening. After that…it sent me in a downward spiral.

"Flynn often played dice and card games with me and knew I was good with numbers. Since I'd accidentally learned of his racketeering, he put me in charge of recording the protection payments. Not long after, I learned they hurt or killed those who didn't pay. But by then I was in far too deep to get out."

"I'm sure you saw too much." Jack reached for her hand and found it icy. He knew what men did to those who saw more than they should.

She shivered. "I watched him—and others—torture men in the basement with my own eyes. They did things you wouldn't believe. I still hear their horrible screams inside my head. Everything is written in that book. Money. Deaths. Bribes. And I was caught in the middle, threatened daily, fearing for my life."

She lapsed into silence for a moment, the quiet broken by a rumble of thunder.

Jagged lightning flashed outside the cave. Jack glanced through the opening at the brewing storm. "It's raining."

"Wonderful! I'm so thirsty." Excitement colored her voice as she slipped the knife back into its hiding place and hurried with Jack to the opening.

Jack removed his hat and held it out. The wind drove the pouring rain sideways, which made it difficult to capture. They stood at the entrance for quite a while. When the hat was full, they held out their hands and drank from the sky. He watched Nora, head tipped up and laughing like a young girl. He didn't think she'd had reason to laugh in a long while. Come to think about it, he hadn't either. Happiness bubbled up inside him at her smile.

Back on the stagecoach, he'd thought she was a pretty girl. She was much more than that. Nora had brains and strength all her own.

They finally went back to the fire that had almost gone out. Jack added wood. "Did you try to escape O'Brien?"

Nora nodded. "Many times. Once I even made it to the train station and got into a seat, but before the locomotive could pull out, two of Flynn's men caught me. After that, they watched me day and night. Then I met Millie Kent. She's a young woman from here, and she told me about Luke Legend's private mail order bride service. I contacted him through her, and she secretly delivered your letters."

"Such as they were," he growled.

Her voice was soft. "No, you offered hope of a new life. I loved how proud you sounded of Texas and your friends in that town you're building. I heard your loneliness between the lines, and your longing for family touched me."

"Be honest. Would you have come if you'd known I was a wanted man?" He stared into her brown eyes, dreading the answer.

She was quiet for what seemed a long time, brushing water droplets from her wool coat. "Yes. Yes, I would've. Texas is a lot better than Buffalo any day. Truthfully, I think I'd be dead if I hadn't escaped. I had seen too much, knew too many things, and I'd become a liability Flynn couldn't afford. The night I ran, I overheard him tell his closest confidant they had to silence me soon."

"Flynn let you keep this ledger in your possession?"

"No. He locked it in a safe every night. While I waited for

you to send the money to come, I searched for the combination and finally found it." She lifted her gaze. "I wasn't leaving without this evidence. He has to be stopped."

"So, your plan is what now, exactly?"

"I'm not really sure. I guess take it to a trusted U.S. marshal who won't be bought."

"The rider we saw this morning. Who is he? The truth this time."

"I believe he's one of Flynn's men. He followed me when I got off the train in Fort Worth. I had a time losing him." She gave him a wry smile. "Or so I thought. He must've followed the stage."

"How far is O'Brien's reach into Texas?"

"I don't know. Flynn seems to have eyes and ears everywhere. Money buys anything you want."

"Not always." No one bought Jack or his friends. If Flynn O'Brien wanted a war, he'd sure get one. But he should bring an army with him, because the men of Hope's Crossing wouldn't die easy. He returned the book to Nora. "Slip this back into your secret pocket for now."

Seated near the fire, Jack took her hand, remembering the softness of her voluptuous curves against him as they'd slept the previous night. Her creamy legs were forever branded into his vision whenever he closed his eyes. His attention was drawn to her moist mouth, something he was sorely tempted to explore.

What would she do if he kissed her? Or ran a finger down the column of her throat?

"Jack?"

"Yeah."

"I'm glad you were the one who wrote those letters and not someone else."

"Yeah." A strange protectiveness filled him. No one was harming Nora Kane with him around.

Six

"JACK, ARE YOU HAVING SECOND THOUGHTS ABOUT MARRYING me?" Nora worried with the links of the chain. He'd appeared so distant in the hours after she'd bared her sordid past.

They'd bided their time in the cave, waiting for the rain to slacken, and Jack's mood reflected the gloomy afternoon. He hid his feelings behind grim features. His gunmetal eyes had grown icy, reminding her of a winter storm. She could take anything but cold silence.

The question of what she'd do if he didn't want her rose up in her mind again.

The pain of the possibility brought a sob that lodged in her throat. Anything was better than being unwanted.

"I know I'm not much, but I'll work hard at being a good wife," she added quietly.

The silence extended several more heartbeats. Finally, he swung his piercing gaze to her. Dark turmoil swirled in his eyes. "I understand your reasons, but I might find it hard to marry any woman who keeps a knife close to protect herself from me."

"I had to make sure I could trust you first. It's not like you've been a soft, cuddly lamb, you know." She hated the panic in her voice. Despite not having an alternate plan in place for her future, she wouldn't beg. "Having said that, you do have your moments."

"What about you? You'd still marry me—an outlaw?"

"You make me feel safe. Yes, I will marry you." She sucked in a quick breath. "Unless you've changed your mind."

Nora watched the dark storm in his eyes fade.

"You have to be sure, because this will be for keeps. I won't let you go if you later decide that you can't abide life with me—or want to join a nunnery." His forbidding scowl returned.

"Don't worry. Black makes me look like an old crone." She laughed. "All I need is a black cat and a broom."

At least the corners of his stern mouth twitched. Definite improvement.

"We need to give this lots of thought. The time it'll take to reach Hope's Crossing will allow us to see if we're a match. Marriage is nothing to rush into lightly. Or for the wrong reasons."

"If we're not compatible?" She might as well know what to expect.

"I'll pay your way to any place you want to go." He took her hand. "I won't leave you high and dry. Or at the mercy of men like Flynn O'Brien."

Although even that offer worried her, she forced a smile and adopted a cheery outlook. "Then Hope's Crossing will give us two things to look forward to. We should kiss, don't you think? To see how we fit together?"

Jack frowned. "I usually don't put a lot of thought into kissing. If I like a lady, I just do it. And if it feels right, I do it again."

Good heavens. Did he like her enough to try or not?

"So you just go around kissing random women? How is it some husband or father hasn't shot you by now?"

"You're twisting my words." The troubled sigh he released did nothing to help her confusion.

"I've never kissed a man before." Her confession slipped out before she could stop it. But there it was. If Jack kissed her, he'd be her first.

His startled expression had at least gotten rid of the frown. "Not one?"

"No. There was a boy a long time ago, when I was a child, but not since."

Jack quickly lowered his gaze to her hand. Evidently, he found the subject of kissing nothing to discuss. "Let me see your wrist. That cuff is digging into you." He gently took her bloody wrist and inspected the painful welt.

"I hated to complain, but the metal rubbing against my skin really hurts."

"Do you think you can part with another petticoat?"

She sucked in a shocked breath. "I beg your pardon!"

"I only need a piece. How about the ruined one?"

"So you can do what exactly?"

The request hung in the air for a long moment.

"Fine. I wanted to bandage your wrist, but it's entirely up to you."

Nora stood and managed to shimmy out of the one he'd already ruined. She opened her mouth to tell him how dear every piece of clothing was and remind him that everything else she owned was back at the wrecked stagecoach. But before she could speak, he grabbed it. A cry hung in her throat when he ripped off a long section.

"Sit down."

Mr. Bossy dipped the piece of cotton in a small amount of water that had yet to leak from his hat, took her handcuffed wrist, and washed the injury. Then he covered it with a dry strip of soft fabric. "This will protect you while I try to unlock these. Does that feel better?"

For a moment, his tender touch made her lose her train of thought. He truly was a man of contrasts. Hard and gentle. Gruff and caring. Threatening one minute, and full of concern the next. But she remembered how he'd protected her when the tracker rode above them. He'd been ready to give his life for her. And he'd fed her and kept her warm.

"Yes." She smiled up at him, watching how the firelight flickered across the hard planes of his face. "Now let me wrap yours."

"I'm fine. Don't worry about me."

"It wasn't a question." Her firm statement whipped his head around. "Your wrist is bleeding. I don't want you to attract that wild creature that's scratching and scurrying around behind us. Yes, I know. It's probably not dangerous. That's why I haven't dragged you from this cave."

"You're a high-handed woman. Know that?"

"Seems to make us well-matched, don't you think?" She tore another strip from her petticoat with precise movements. "Now, your wrist, mister."

Irritation darkened his eyes, but he offered his hand to her.

"My father often told me that I was my mother's daughter. Neither of us were very biddable then, and I'm still not. That's one reason I tossed away the key to these. You ordered me to give it to you. Taking orders has never been my strong suit." She wet a piece of the petticoat and gently washed his angry, raw welt. Although it had to hurt, that man would cut out his tongue before he admitted it. They appeared to share that trait too. "What are we going to do, Jack? Don't you think we should get going? It'll be dark in a few hours."

"It's lots better to be behind a posse than in front of one. We'll let them put some distance between us and leave in the morning."

That made a lot of sense. She finished doctoring his wrist and tied the end of the wrapping. "That should do it. Now, if you'll stand, I'll put the few remaining inches of my petticoat back on. I'm sure you'll need the rest soon at the rate we've been going."

"Obliged, Nora." He held her upright while she slipped back into the ruined clothing. "Now I'll see about getting these cuffs off if you'll lend me your knife." They sat down, and he took the sharp blade Nora handed him.

She smiled, watching how the flickering fire played across the light brown of his hair and touched his tanned skin that told of hours spent outdoors. Doing what? What did outlaws do when they weren't...well, outlawing?

The stories in her dime novels hadn't mentioned the subject.

Maybe he worked with horses. Or maybe outlaws did like regular people—built houses, raised chickens and cows, cooked, washed clothes. She stifled a giggle at the thought of Jack in his hideout, washing his clothes and hanging them on the line to dry, sweeping the floor.

Warmth seeped into her as the wood crackled and popped. Even in the cave full of noises, she felt safer than she had in years. There was no need to worry about someone springing from a dark corner and killing her. Flynn O'Brien was far away—probably planning his next murder.

For sure hers—when and if he could get to Texas.

Jack's feather-soft breathing brushed her skin as he bent over, working on the lock. A jolt of awareness swept along her body. His fingers were long, his hands strong. And, she reminded herself sternly, they belonged to someone who lived by the gun.

Those dime novels of hers had portrayed outlaws as ruthless men, for the most part. That wasn't Jack. She admitted his hard exterior had given her the wrong impression at first, but inside, he was gentle when he'd helped her cross difficult terrain, at night when she slept beside him, and he'd washed and bandaged her bloody wrist.

Now each of his touches sent sizzling sparks through her, like when she'd once stood too close to lightning.

She inhaled a ragged breath, trying to steady her heartbeat. What was this thing between them?

"You all right?" Jack glanced up, his eyes meeting hers.

Nora smiled. "Never better. How's it coming?"

"About to get it." He bent his head to closely examine the workings of the lock.

A strand of his hair brushed her hand, the feeling more pronounced than his breath. The soft texture reminded her of a bird's wing, and a memory of when she was eight or nine flashed across her mind. After a storm like this one. She'd found a mama tree swallow with a broken wing. Unable to fly, she managed to hop to her babies, their nest lying on the ground. Her fierce struggle to get to them stuck in Nora's mind, especially how the mama had tried to pull them underneath her injured wing even though they were dead.

Tears blurred her vision. That was what mamas did. That need to protect their children overrode everything.

Her mother had loved her with the same fierceness. Her father too.

If they hadn't died, she'd never have met Flynn O'Brien. Yet if not for Flynn, she'd never have come west to marry Jack

Bowdre. Everything seemed to have happened in order for something else to take place. Maybe life was just like dominos in a row, each one toppling over the next.

Jack's hair tickled her again. Without thinking, she lightly touched it with her free hand and found it like soft velvet. The thought struck her that her parents would've liked this man. He shared some similarities with that wounded tree swallow. Jack had protected her and left himself exposed.

She'd taken that mama bird home and patched it up, but the minute Nora released her, she'd flown right back to the same spot where her babies had crashed to the ground.

Maybe birds never forgot. People either. Nora knew that if she was lucky enough to have children one day, she'd give her all for them.

The fire crackled in the silence. Jack let out a frustrated breath and mumbled a curse, then sat back. "The damn thing won't open."

Nora took a hairpin—the only one she had left—from her hair. "Just try it with this. Please. It can't hurt."

He stared at her like she'd called him every vile name she could think of. "Do you know how often outlaws have tried to unlock handcuffs with those flimsy things?"

How could he scoff at her suggestion? She was only trying to help. He hadn't been able to make headway, so why not at least give her idea a shot?

"I would have no reason to know anything that outlaws do." She sniffed and moved as far as the chain allowed, which was only a matter of inches. "The next time you need a petticoat, use your own."

"Look, I'm sorry. It's just that hairpins almost never work. In fact, in all my years on the run, I've never seen one of those unlock handcuffs. I just haven't. They bend and twist and lack the strength." He shoved his hand through his hair and blew out a loud breath. "But I'll try. As you rightly pointed out, it can't hurt."

The earth must've shifted on its axis. Hardheaded man! She handed him the hairpin and stuck out her wrist.

With a long-suffering sigh, Jack bent over the lock again. Minutes passed, and the fire became glowing embers.

"Dammit to hell." Jack sat back and handed her the small piece of metal. "No luck."

Her heart plummeted into her stomach, the very last bit of hope gone. She stared at the pin in disbelief. He had twisted and mangled it into a shape she'd never seen before. They couldn't even try it a second time. "Jack! What did you do? Try to bend it into a pretzel?"

"What's a pretzel?"

"It's a kind of German biscuit that's twisted into the shape of a knot and baked. Very tasty. The immigrants brought the recipe from the old country."

"Never had one." He poked around in the embers and added sticks of wood to the fire. "I'm sorry I couldn't unlock the cuffs."

"How am I going to keep my hair back now? I've lost all my pins but that one."

"Maybe you can tie it into one of those pretzel things." He wiggled his fingers in the air.

The urge to hit him was powerful. But before she could punch his arm, something scratched very close by. Alarm rang in her head. "What is that, Jack?"

"Just a small animal. It's harmless."

She wasn't an imbecile. Some things could eat you alive, and she had no intention of leaving anything to chance. She slid her right foot from Dollard's boot. Having a hefty weapon gave her a sense of security. If it came closer, she'd bludgeon it to death. Unless it was big. Then she'd stick Jack in front and see if the varmint had a taste for stubborn outlaws. Maybe it would gnaw the chain in half and she could run.

Although she was as mad as a box of drenched cats at Jack, she pressed tightly against him. He seemed lost in thought and didn't glance her way. Maybe he was thinking about those pretzels.

Two heartbeats later, something ran across her leg. Nora let out a bloodcurdling scream and jumped to her feet, slamming her boot down on a black form about six inches long. She kept pounding whatever it was until Jack pried her boot from her hand.

"I think it's dead, Nora," he said in a quiet tone.

"How can you be sure?"

"It's as flat as a pancake." He laughed and held the thing up by its long tail. "Hard to tell what it used to be, but it resembles a wood rat."

Nora blew her hair out of her eyes and tried to calm herself. She must look like a harridan, with her heaving chest, wild eyes, torn dress, hair stringing down.

After a moment to gather herself, she jutted her chin in defiance. "I'm glad he's dead."

It occurred to her that she'd said *he* and realized she meant Flynn O'Brien.

If only he were. But it would take more than a bootheel to kill a man like him.

❧

Jack held the rat up. "Unless we want to eat this, we need to find some food while we still have a little light left. It's a good time of day to catch a rabbit."

Nora swayed unsteadily on the one boot until Jack balanced her. "You can catch a rabbit by hand? Aren't they too fast?"

"Sometimes. But often I've walked right up to them without them hearing me." He lifted her foot, slipped her boot back on, and grinned. "Maybe you can use Dollard's boot to kill it. I have to say you have a pretty good aim when you're mad. I don't want to get on your bad side."

She arched an eyebrow. "How do you know you haven't already been?"

"Right." He knew she'd been angry enough to sling a buffalo when he couldn't unlock her handcuff with the hairpin. He had tried his best, but the slim piece of metal kept slipping out of his fingers. "I'm really sorry I couldn't free us. I want it even more than you do."

"I doubt that." She smoothed the make-do bandage underneath the handcuff.

"You know, at the rate we're going, you're likely to be naked by the time we reach Hope's Crossing. I can't imagine what folks will think when I walk in with you in tow."

At least she gave him a half smile. "They'll probably arrest you for taking advantage of me."

"Can't. I'm the only law in town."

Nora rolled her eyes. "Heaven help us. I'm hungry. Let's go hunting."

He helped her down the embankment as the sun broke from behind the heavy clouds.

Nora sucked in a breath. "Look, Jack."

The rainbow was exceptional, the bands wide, the colors vibrant. He always felt happier when he saw one—except for today. A burden sat on his shoulders. He had to find some food for Nora. She needed to eat. Although he was hungry enough to cook the wood rat, she needed better. Come to think of it, he had no appetite for rats either. He selected the right shape and size of rock and hoped for something to use it on.

The rain-fresh air soothed his ragged spirit. He'd been sure the knifepoint would open the cuffs, and the disappointment had been a bitter pill to swallow.

It was just that he needed to be free so he could fight. When that posse didn't find him ahead, they'd double back. So would the man looking for Nora. Worry crawled along his spine like thousands of millipede legs, warning him to stay vigilant.

"Don't speak, Nora." His gaze scanned the low brush, his senses sharp.

They moved quietly along the wet ground, and he noticed a cottontail about twenty feet ahead, sitting underneath a mesquite tree. Barely breathing, he drew back and launched the missile. But by the time the rock reached the spot, the rabbit had scampered into some dry brush. Jack muttered a curse.

Nora rested a hand on his arm. "You'll get the next one. You're quite good at throwing."

"Almost as good as you, huh?"

"Almost."

Jack picked up another rock and motioned her forward. They walked until he could see her getting tired. The sun was setting. It would be night soon, and he'd rather not climb the embankment in the dark. "Let's head back."

They'd taken about a dozen steps when another rabbit hopped from cover and sat with its nose twitching. Jack quickly threw as hard as he could.

The rock struck the rabbit squarely. He rushed toward the small mound, in case he'd only addled it. Loud huffing behind him made him realize he was dragging Nora, and he slowed. "Sorry."

"Don't worry about me. Get our food."

He picked the rabbit up to examine it. "It's dead."

"You did it, Jack." Nora's smile was wide this time. "I didn't want to eat that wood rat."

"Me either." He wished he had the manacles off so he could put an arm around her. But no need wishing for that. She probably wouldn't want him to anyway.

"How did you learn to hunt game with a rock?"

"I pretty much taught myself to make do in a pinch. Out here, we don't always have everything we need, and the nearest town is often days away. The prospect of starving is an excellent motivator. So is making noise and getting caught. Sometimes I can't afford to fire a gun."

"Yes, I suppose it is. Your aim is very good."

He caught her look of admiration and winked. "Apparently, so is yours."

By the time they reached the safety of the cave, Nora was winded. Jack stirred the sleeping embers and added more wood. "Get warm while I cook supper."

With the aid of her knife, he prepared the rabbit and slid chunks onto a skewer fashioned from a small stick. After putting the meat into the flames to char, he cleaned his hands with the last of the rainwater from his hat and sat next to her.

"It won't be long. I'm sorry I don't have more."

"Don't fret over it, Jack. It's lots better than our other choice."

Jack chuckled. "I wish you could've seen yourself. You were whacking that poor rat with everything you had. Even gave my leg a lick or two." He rubbed his knee.

She laughed. "I probably resembled a wild-eyed woman for sure, but I wasn't about to let it get away."

The lady was quite a picture even now, with her flushed cheeks, twinkling eyes, and messy cloud of honey-hued hair. She was doing things to him no other woman had ever done. His heart thudded against his ribs.

He couldn't stop staring. "You're quite beautiful, Nora Kane."

Her eyes lowered as he pressed his mouth to hers.

Although he meant to merely brush her lips, the kiss held hunger and desire. Shaken, he leaned closer, the chain rattling. How he yearned to put both arms around her and hold her against him.

Nora touched his stubbled face with her free hand and parted her lips ever so slightly, her soft breath mingling with his, and Jack found the only peace an outlaw knew.

Seven

THE LOW FIRE GAVE OFF AN EERIE GLOW THAT PAINTED THE dark walls of the cave red. Their bellies full, they'd called it a night. Unlike Nora, whose soft breath indicated deep sleep, Jack had yet to close his eyes. His jumbled thoughts had him in an uproar.

Before, he'd always known where he was going—at least for the short term. The long term was to the grave, and that was a given. How he got from one to the other seemed mostly unimportant...as long as the grave didn't shift to a short-term destination.

The pressure of Nora's plump bottom against his groin was a big reason for the upheaval twisting and turning inside him until *he* was one of them pretzels she talked about.

Then there was the kiss.

It shouldn't have affected him that way. He'd kissed a lot of women. True, most were of the paid variety, and the amount of money exchanged determined the depth of the passion. Yet Nora had kissed him because she seemed to like it.

To be honest, the moment their lips had met, his stomach twisted upside down and sideways, the same way it did when he was riding a bucking bronc.

The kiss meant something more than the mere touching of lips. What was it he'd really expected of her when he wrote those letters anyway? Fantasy was one thing. Reality another. Maybe he hadn't really thought she'd come.

He draped a protective arm across her stomach and tried to ferret out his motives.

Only the lowest kind of weasel would send for a bride without wanting her. She wasn't a fish to throw back after deciding he could catch a bigger one. He wouldn't even think of returning her to O'Brien, and she clearly had nowhere else to go besides.

Gentle memories of his Rachel drifted across his mind. He couldn't even recall her face now, which shamed him, but her warm touch remained branded on his skin. She'd had real beauty on the inside, where it mattered, that much he remembered. Each morning and night, he would hold her close, kiss her, tell her he loved her. Rachel was an extension of him.

And his four-year-old son, Alex's, bright, inquisitive spirit had always brought a smile, even on the most frustrating days.

The answer to what he wanted from Nora suddenly emerged from the fog in his brain—to share a life with someone. To not have this loneliness burrow bone-deep inside and become permanent. To ease the noise inside his head.

Still…what could he offer her? A life of running, dodging bullets, waiting for the grim reaper. That was all he had.

You can have more. A good life. A family again. Could he believe that small voice in his head?

Nora mumbled something unintelligible and shifted. The slight friction of her bottom rubbing against him did nothing for his already ragged self-control. He clenched his teeth and inhaled sharply. This forced closeness was pure torture. If he could just remove these handcuffs, he'd throw them as far as he could send them.

There was only so much a man could take, and he'd reached the end of his limits.

Nora's unpredictable nature added to his stress and put a niggling worry inside his head as well. He couldn't quite figure her out. Something had been bothering him, and now he knew what it was. Maybe she wasn't as chancy and erratic as she appeared. That could be an act. She hadn't told him about the knife right away or the people following her. It occurred to him that she could've known he was an outlaw all this time and was using him to rid herself of her problems.

He froze. If that was true, she might be planning to leave him the minute the coast was clear. Just as Darcy Howard had changed her mind at the last minute, Nora Kane could be ready to snatch away everything.

The moments ticked by and the fire turned to embers.

As his eyes finally drifted shut, he remembered a sign he'd once seen scrawled on a board in Cimarron: *If you climb in the saddle, be ready for the ride.*

❧

Nora was gone. Jack jerked awake in the gray dawn, holding up the empty handcuff that had been around her wrist when they'd laid down together.

What the hell! Of all the low-down tricks. Maybe she'd had the key all this time and only *pretended* to throw it after the stagecoach wreck. That could be why they hadn't found it. Narrowing his eyes, he saw no sign of her in the cave. Just wait until he caught up with her!

Only she could be on horseback now if she had this planned out and someone had been following to help her.

He sat up and ran a hand through his hair. "Listen to yourself. Stop that."

The truth was, she had no motive for disappearing. He hadn't done anything for her yet, except find the cave and feed her. The men trailing her still were after her, *and* he had her knife. But he'd returned that strange ledger to her keeping.

One end of the manacles dangled off his wrist as he pushed to his feet and let out a loud curse.

Footsteps crunched outside. He spun around ready to fight, but he saw no enemy. Nora strolled in, her arms full of wood. "Good morning. I'm glad you're awake. I thought we might want to warm up before we leave. It's a chilly morning."

The sight of Nora stole his breath, her cheeks rosy from the cold, her hair curling about her shoulders, and her moist lips slightly parted. Her chipper mood and the fact she hadn't left him behind made him feel like a fool. He'd let himself get carried away with a bunch of nonsense.

Jack held up the dangling handcuff. "Mind explaining how you got out of these?"

She stacked the wood to the side and knelt to blow on the embers. "Nothing to explain."

"How did you manage to unlock your side?"

"I straightened out the hairpin this morning and it opened right up. Jack, if you'd focused on a positive outcome yesterday and used a lighter touch instead of jamming the thing into the lock like it was something you had to kill, you could've had better results." Her glance made him uncomfortable. "But you had already decided it wouldn't work, because it never did." She eased a piece of wood on the glowing embers and sat back. "You get the effort you put into something in return. You have to admit that you barely tried with my hairpin."

The message was loud and clear. Jack growled. She should've been a Baptist preacher. He tucked in his shirt, still feeling lopsided without his gun belt. "The fire feels good."

"I took the liberty of looking around while I was out and didn't see anything stirring."

"How long have you been awake?"

"A few hours." She propped her arms on her knees. "Are you always so grumpy in the mornings? If so, it's better for a wife to know now."

He felt the need to explain, and he almost never did that. "Finding you gone threw me. For one, I'm usually a light sleeper and jump up at the sound of an eye blinking."

Nora grinned and stood. "So, what you're saying is that I've upset you and you're angry at yourself that you're slipping."

"I'm *not* slipping." Except maybe she'd hit the nail on the head. He should've heard her, felt her leaving his side. Being caught unawares never boded well for an outlaw who lived or died by his quick senses.

"You know, something my father said came to mind just now. He was fond of telling my mother that she didn't have to attend every argument to which she'd been invited. That might be sage advice here. Considering."

Jack clenched his jaw so tightly he thought he'd broken it and began to count from one.

She threw up her hands. "*Oh forevermore!* I can't believe

you, Jack. How are we going to have any children with you counting at me all the time?"

Children?

Dammit, he'd lost count.

Silence spun a silken web between them, one that added to his unease. Finally, he was able to resort to begging. "If you still have that hairpin, would you please unlock me?"

"I'll be happy to free you." She took the pin from her hair. "Let's move to the other side of the fire, where the light spills in from the entrance."

He sat down next to her and pointed out. "You didn't have any light before."

"I did it by feel. However, I prefer to see this time."

"Whatever works, go ahead. I just want the damn thing off."

Nora bent over to work on the lock. Minutes ticked by and he was still held fast.

"What's wrong?"

"Quiet. I'm concentrating." She raised her head and stared up at the ceiling with intense focus while gently working the hairpin in the lock. He was about to tell her they had to get going when the handcuff sprang open.

Nora pinned her hair back and stood, buttoning her coat. "Coming, Jack?"

Hell! He kicked dirt onto the fire, put on his hat, and draped the set of manacles around his neck, thinking they might come in handy. Nora was halfway down the steep embankment by the time he left the cave. At least the sun had come out, and that improved his spirits. That and being free. He could raise both arms and flap them like a bird if he so desired.

The main thing was that he could fight now if he had to. But it felt odd not having Nora right next to him—like he was missing a part of himself. He realized he actually liked having her near.

Tightening the space between them, he kept by her side, and they must've gone a mile or more when the deep bellow of a cow nearby reached him. The softer cry of a calf rode on the breeze.

"Nora, pull off one of your good petticoats."

"Why?"

"I'm going to see if I can get close enough to rope that cow."

She narrowed her gaze and hissed. "With my clothes? It'll only leave me with the one you ruined that doesn't even come to my knees. It'll feel like I'm naked."

Jack shrugged. "It's not like I have much to make a rope from."

"Your trousers. Use them."

"I don't think they'd work. Some milk sure would sit well in my belly. Yours too, I'm guessing."

"Fine." She turned her back, lifted her skirt, and slid out of the undergarment. "Anything else you need?" she asked sweetly, blowing a lock of hair from her face. "Maybe my corset? Or how about my shift? Would the cow be needing those to perhaps warm herself against the coolness of the morning?"

"Funny woman." He turned away to hide a grin and removed the knife. He soon had the undergarment in strips, which he tied together and braided. Yanking up a trailing vine, he wound it around the length of petticoat and tested the sturdiness. It would have to do. "It might be best to wait here."

"Oh no you don't, buster. I have to see this."

"Just don't do anything to spook the animal."

She gave him one of those I-wasn't-born-yesterday sort of looks and followed him through the tangle of undergrowth. Fifty yards ahead stood a cow with a swollen bag and a frayed rope around her neck. She must belong at a house somewhere nearby.

Slow and easy, he worked his way forward, murmuring quiet words. Just as he got to the heifer, she rolled her eyes and ran a couple of yards and stopped to stare. The cow's stubborn streak reminded him a little of Nora, but he kept that thought to himself. She *had* unlocked the handcuffs, and she *had* given him the petticoats when he asked. Oh, and tended his raw wrist with the softest touch he'd felt since losing Rachel.

Actually, she could be a big help in this current endeavor.

"Nora, if you can circle around and get on the backside of mama cow, I think I'll be able to slip this around her neck."

"I'll do my best, but don't holler at me if this doesn't work." She maneuvered her way through the tangle and positioned herself.

The milk cow chewed her cud and kept a wary eye on Nora but didn't move. Jack slowly advanced, building a loop in the long strip. Doubt rose that this would work, but he had nothing else to use.

Nora kept talking in a soothing voice and moving calmly toward the animal. So far so good.

When Jack was five feet away, he threw the loop over the cow's head and pulled, digging in his heels. The animal's eyes rolled back in her head, then she bolted, dragging him through a mud puddle and some thorny mesquite, heading directly for Nora.

The spit dried in Jack's mouth. "Get out of the way! She'll run right over the top of you."

Nora held out her arms. "Whoa. We're not going to hurt you. We just want some milk."

The mama stopped short, her muscles shuddering, and Nora walked right up to her. Jack spat out a mouthful of grass and mud.

"How did you do that?" Jack wiped the mud from his face with his bandana and stared in amazement.

"Us girls stick together. I'm sure she'll be happy with the pressure off her full bag." Nora patted the animal's hide. "Go ahead and milk, and I'll keep her calm."

Still admiring Nora's skill, Jack removed his hat and, after more than a few misses and comments from Nora, filled it with fresh milk. He released the cow and they sat down to enjoy the bounty before it leaked out through the weave of the felt.

"Tell me the truth. What just happened?" he asked.

"I lived on a farm until my parents died and I milked the cow each morning, so I learned a thing or two about them. No mystery. This milk is going to be good. I missed having fresh."

"Why is it that you didn't milk Miss Bessie? You could've done a better job."

Nora grinned. "And deprive me of watching you? Nope."

Jack got lost in her eyes and reached for her hand. "You're something, lady. You know that? And you have a soothing touch."

She pulled her hand from his. "I wouldn't know."

"I do. Let me poke a hole in the crown of the hat so you can drink."

After he did, she got underneath and let the milk run into her mouth. The liquid dribbled down her chin and onto her clothes. She wiped the mess off her face, then ever so slowly, ran her pink-tipped tongue around her lips. Her brown eyes widened as she met his gaze.

Jack swallowed hard and covered the hole he'd poked into his hat with a finger. The way the sunlight brushed her hair, turning it to spun gold, took his breath. When he could move and breathe, he gently wiped away a teasing bit of white above her top lip with his thumb. "Missed a spot."

Something sizzled between them, and suddenly the cold day grew very warm.

"Want some?" Nora asked.

For a minute, he stared, trying to figure out how to answer.

Finally, she held up the milk. "Your turn. Better hurry before it leaks out."

"Yeah." He removed his finger from the hole and drank his fill. The minute the fresh, creamy taste hit his mouth, he was in heaven.

He drank his fill, then glanced at Nora, considering their teamwork. This, and the last few, were the best days he'd had in a long time. He felt foolish to have doubted her. What had he been thinking? She didn't have an ulterior motive. She was still the woman he'd met on the stagecoach.

With their combined sharpness and skill, they might just possibly come out of this in one piece.

"I hate to leave the cow behind." Nora moved to the animal, now calmly eating in a patch of wild rye and patted the cow's side. "Can we take her?"

"No. When that posse and the man hunting you turn around, and it's only a matter of time before they backtrack, the bellowing will give us away. Besides, her owner will be looking for her."

Nora let out a long sigh. "You're right of course. Though it would be nice to have the milk."

Jack laid a hand on her shoulder. "I can get us a little more." As he started toward the mama, a mud-covered calf walked from the thicket, crying, and took its place at the cow's swollen udders. "Looks like we'd be robbing that little fellow."

"Where do you think he's been?"

"Must've bogged down in mud. When the rain comes, every hole fills up. He probably fell into one and had trouble getting out. We'd best go."

Nora gave the mama and calf a longing glance and fell into step with Jack, her long coat swishing against his leg.

"The next bit of water I find I'm washing some of this mud off my clothes and cleaning my hat. I feel naked without something on my head and my gun at my side."

"What about me? I'm wearing practically nothing underneath my dress now."

Heat flooded his senses at the thought of all that silky skin bare. He only had to lift her skirt to touch that softness.

He shook his head to clear it. "I'll buy you a dozen petticoats when we reach town."

"I'll hold you to that."

Staying well off the trail to avoid the men looking for them, they walked for about an hour. The day was pleasant with occasional clouds. Nora didn't say much, which suited Jack. He didn't talk unless he had something to say, and at the moment, he didn't know what to say to the woman at his side. At times she scowled, and he wondered what she was thinking. Probably how much she'd like to leave his sorry rear behind.

He'd done it again—he'd ordered instead of asking her to donate another petticoat to make the rope, and then did the same when he'd needed to position her on the backside of the cow.

Hell! He wouldn't blame her for giving him an earful.

The silence grew, and when he wasn't watching her, he was

constantly scanning the landscape for trouble. And water. His hat had begun to stink to high heaven. They stopped to rest in the shade of a shrubby juniper.

Nora plopped down and wiped her forehead. "I'd give anything for a drink of water."

"Wait here and rest while I scout around. The rain might've collected in a few ravines. I won't be gone long." He handed her the knife. "Keep this close. Don't be afraid to use it."

"I won't." Their hands brushed as she took it. "But what if you need it?"

"I'll be okay. It's you I'm worried about." He brushed the softness of her cheek with a finger, and her ashen expression pierced his heart. "It's all right. I'll be near. If you hear riders, move back into the protection of this juniper and don't make a sound."

At her nod, he set out and found water in a little gully not far from where he'd left her. He drank from the small pool and washed the mud from his face and milk from his hat. He rose, planning to go back and bring Nora.

The sudden sound of hooves striking the ground froze his blood. He peeked over the rim of the ravine and saw a single horseman.

Hide, Nora, and keep quiet.

But the rider had heard something. He turned toward the scraggly juniper shrub.

Eight

HOOFBEATS STRUCK THE GROUND, COMING CLOSER AND CLOSER. Nora's heart pounded, and she wished for Jack's strong arms. Gripping the knife tightly, she shrank back into the juniper like he'd told her. The tall bush poked into her like thousands of needles, but she never uttered a sound. Through the odd, lacy leaves, she recognized the tracker who'd been following her before.

He rode slowly into view, scanning every inch of the landscape. Alarm raced up Nora's spine. Why had he left the road and come so far into the brush?

His horse snorted and skittered sideways. The tracker pulled up to calm the spotted gray gelding. He removed his hat to wipe his forehead and glanced around. It was the first time Nora had gotten a good look at him, and she sucked in a breath, careful not to make a sound.

The long-haired man struck terror in her heart. Cocky self-confidence filled every movement. That and knowledge of the landscape made him a foe that would be hard to beat. It took such a man as this to make a living tracking those who didn't want to be found. His sunken cheeks, the small eyes of a predator in constant motion, and hard mouth told her that he must have the stone heart of a killer—exactly the kind of person Flynn O'Brien would hire. And this much she knew—neither Flynn nor this man would give up until they found her.

She strangled an anguished cry before it left her mouth and remained frozen in place, afraid even to blink.

A minute passed, and she kept so still that a rabbit hopped right into the tall bush with her. Once the little animal saw her and realized its mistake, he leaped out, and the flurried movement had alerted the rider.

He dismounted and strode toward her hiding place. Nora's heart hammered against her ribs.

Ever closer he came. If he peered hard enough, he'd see her through the lacy foliage.

Where was Jack? She needed his strength. But she had the knife and her wits—she wasn't helpless. As quietly as she could, she eased from the backside of the juniper.

Run!

The order sprang into her head, and she realized that it was the only choice left.

When he leaned farther into the shield of green, she lifted her skirts and bolted toward a gully. Halfway into the jump, a hand caught her dress and pulled her back.

"I've got you now," the tracker spat. "You've given me a lot of trouble, and you'll pay for that. O'Brien didn't specify what shape you'd need to be in. So I figure as long as you're breathing, that's good enough."

Nora tried to shrink away from the bold gaze that raked over her, but his grip was like a steel band. He jerked her coat open and squeezed her breast. His mouth went slack, and lust glittered in his round crow eyes.

"You an' me are gonna have a good time. O'Brien didn't tell me how pretty you were." He crushed his mouth to hers, a demonstration of how cruel he intended to be.

Gripping the knife, she sliced his arm, drawing blood.

"Hell! You'll pay for that, whore!" The tracker yanked the knife from her and tossed it aside. "I see you like to fight. It'll just make taming you more fun." His lips parted in a cruel grin.

"You'll need an army to get me back to O'Brien." She bent her elbow and rammed it into his stomach, then stomped down on his foot. Nora twisted and wrenched herself free from his grip. Her breath coming in harsh gasps, she raced toward the cover of a stand of mesquite. Maybe she could get lost in there. It didn't matter to her that they had thorns. Anything was better than what was behind her.

She'd taken about three strides when she saw movement from the corner of her eye and heard Jack's familiar bark.

"Take another step and I'll blow a hole clear through you."

She turned to see Jack planted in front of the tracker, blocking his path. Her focus was on the empty gun he jammed to the man's neck.

One second she sagged with relief; the next she clenched her hands, worrying that the tracker would notice the gun was empty. Then something Jack once said came back to her—that he was very good at making men think they were about to die. Looking at him now, even though she knew he couldn't fire the Colt in his hand, she could easily believe he was about to kill the tracker. Jack wore his hat low so she couldn't see his eyes, but she watched a muscle work in his jaw. He showed no nervousness in his grip or wide stance.

"Ahhh, you're the outlaw." The tracker gave Jack a thin smile, but his sunken cheek twitched. "This matter doesn't concern you. It's between me and the lady."

"Everything concerns me—especially her. She's mine and I'm keeping her." Jack kept the Colt pressed to the man's neck and reached for the gun hanging at the tracker's side. He pitched it toward Nora.

She thought he must've lost every bit of sense he had to keep the empty weapon and give her the loaded one, but she hurried to pick it up. Her hand shook so much she nearly dropped it as she pointed it at the tracker. For insurance. Both the unexpected weight of the heavy steel and her jangling nerves made it necessary to use two hands. This was the first time she'd ever touched a firearm. How could Jack make holding one and facing off against an enemy look so easy? His calm demeanor made it appear as though he were taking a Sunday stroll down Main Street.

His last sentence rolled around in her head and warmth washed over her. She concerned him. That had to mean he cared for her. Didn't it?

Why couldn't he say the words to her instead of a stranger?

"Lay that gun down and we'll see what you have, outlaw." The tracker released a wad of spit on Jack's boot. "You won't stand a chance in hell."

"You know, you've got a big lesson to learn. I'm awfully tempted to cut you down a notch, but I don't need to prove a damn thing to a snot-nosed kid. Got a name?"

"Darius. Guthrie."

"Darius Guthrie, remove your gun belt, drop your trousers, and get on your knees." Jack never looked at Nora, but she was sure he knew exactly where she was, down to the inch. "Twitch and you'll never bother anyone again."

"I don't think so, old man."

"Then you and me have a big problem."

Darius glared, his mouth set in a tight line. "Better kill me, or I'll hunt you down. I *will* take Nora Kane back to New York. Boss wants her and the book she stole, and I'm going to take both back to him." The cocky man gave Jack a chilling smile that sent tremors through Nora. Jack was right. Guthrie was young—too young to be in the killing business. She guessed early twenties, but just barely. Maybe even nineteen.

"I've run up against men like you all my life." Jack's voice was silky smooth as he rattled the set of manacles he'd slung around his neck. "Do you know the one mistake they all made?"

"Why don't you tell me, old man?"

"They never take experience into account. Drop the gun belt." Jack pressed the gun so hard into Darius his neck moved sideways. "I will not tell you again."

What was Jack going to do with him?

Tense moments stretched as neither man moved. Hands shaking, Nora cocked the gun, the single click sounding loud in the silence.

Her nerves frayed as time ticked by. She was ready to act in case she needed to, but Jack appeared unfazed. He'd likely faced many such moments during his life.

A bead of sweat rolled down Darius's cheek.

Neither man blinked.

"Turn your head, Nora, you shouldn't see this," Jack said softly.

A second drop of sweat made a painstaking march to Darius's chin. The young tracker shifted, finally unbuckling the belt and letting it fall. Staring an angry, defiant hole into Jack, he let his trousers drop to his ankles.

Uncomfortable, Nora glanced away. She didn't want to see. Didn't want to feel sorry for the piece of cow dung. Guthrie deserved everything he was going to get.

The man had intended to inflict great pain on her, and something in his eyes said he'd have enjoyed every second.

Steeling herself, she turned back, out of defiance more than anything, and saw the man wore ankle-length drawers. She would watch Darius get what was coming to him. That seemed fair to her, but she just wished Jack would end this quick instead of dragging it out.

The set of manacles clinked together as Jack removed them from around his neck. "Lie on your belly, Guthrie, hands behind your back."

Darius shot a nervous glance to Nora, as though pleading for her to intervene. For the first time, he appeared to face the seriousness of his situation.

Instead of lying down, he lunged, knocking the cuffs from Jack's hand. Trousers bunched around his ankles, Darius could only ram into Jack with his head and grab him. They rolled under the gray gelding. The animal reared up, then took off in a gallop, hooves narrowly missing the fighting men.

Nora made a diving leap for the horse's bridle but missed.

Jack yanked Darius up and slammed a fist into his nose. Blood spurted over the rocks where they stood as well as their clothes. Nora gripped the gun, unsure where to shoot. They hit the ground and rolled. First Jack was on top, then on bottom. Darius Guthrie was bleeding heavily. Why didn't he give up? He couldn't hope to win with his legs all tangled. Yet he kept desperately pounding on Jack whenever he could get a lick in.

If Darius Guthrie won this fight, she'd shoot him. He would never get her back to Buffalo alive, not in a million years.

"Go, Nora. Get out of here," Jack yelled.

She took five long strides when a loud grunt stopped her. She had to see, and she turned. Jack had managed to get behind Darius. He placed one arm in front of the man's throat and the other behind his head to anchor…and held him.

It didn't take long for Darius to go limp in Jack's arms, his eyes closing. Jack laid him on the ground.

Nora stood. "That was amazing. How did you put him out like that?"

"It's called a choke hold. When you can get behind an opponent, it's the best and safest way of ending the fight." Jack removed Darius's boots and yanked his trousers off.

"It certainly worked." She relaxed her grip on the gun, unsure what to do with it. "I know he deserves his fate, but please don't kill him. I can't live with myself if he dies because of me."

"You're sure?"

"Yes."

Breathing hard, Jack flipped Darius onto his stomach and handcuffed his right arm to his left leg. "I think that will hold him for a while. Some of the posse will ride by and release him eventually, but for now we can make tracks without worrying about him." He straightened and glanced around. "Did you see where the gray went?"

"It galloped off in the direction we came from. I tried to catch him, but he ran by me too fast."

"He seemed to spook easy." Jack plucked his black hat from the ground and put it on, then buckled Darius's gun belt around his hips. "He would've saved us some time though."

"Can we look for him?"

"We can't risk getting stuck here."

"Here's Guthrie's gun." Nora handed it to him, glad to be rid of the weapon. When he reached for it and stuck it in the holster, she noticed his bloody knuckles. "If you found water, you should wash first. I could use a drink something awful."

"There's water in a little gully nearby." He picked up the empty gun that had belonged to the marshal, loaded it, and stuck it in his waist. She guessed he'd hang onto it no matter what.

"Hold up your foot," Jack asked.

When she did, he placed Guthrie's boot against Dollard's. "I think Guthrie's is smaller and would fit better."

"I think so too." She sat down and slid her foot into the young tracker's boots.

Jack pulled Darius underneath a small tree out of the sun and stuffed his trousers and Dollard's boots in a crevice between the rocks. Then he put an arm around Nora, and the gentleness after the explosive violence almost did her in.

"Are you all right?"

"I'm fine. I was terrified that Darius would hurt you." Shaking, she glanced up at his bruised and bloody profile. "Even though I begged for his life, if he'd harmed you, I would've shot him then and there."

Jack froze, his face darkening. "I hope you never have to take a life. It kills something inside here." He placed his hand over her heart. "It scars you until you can't recognize yourself. Then hardness sits in, pushing out everything good and kind. Never become like me."

"Hold me, Jack. Hold me and don't ever let me go."

He pulled her against him, his heartbeat strong and steady beneath her ear. He held her beneath the pale-blue sky until she stopped trembling. It had to be nearing the noon hour and she was hungry, but she didn't want to move out of Jack's strong arms.

"We should get far away from here before trouble finds us." His deep voice rumbled and filled her with longing.

"I know." She pushed out of his embrace. "Maybe manna will drop from the sky and we can eat."

He chuckled. "I'll catch a fish for supper. Barring complications, we'll reach a small river in three or four hours."

"I don't know how you plan to fish without a pole and a hook."

"You'll see."

Yes, she would. She didn't know what he had in mind, but she wouldn't bet against him. This tall outlaw could do almost anything he set his mind to—even rope a cow with her petticoat.

After drinking her fill, Nora tenderly washed the cuts on Jack's face with a strip she tore from the bottom of her dress. "With the added bruises and scrapes, folks will think you fought a grizzly."

"I'll heal. You worry too much about me."

"Someone has to. Since we're as good as married, I guess it falls to my lot." She let out a chuckle. "I don't know which of us looks the worst. I'm wearing a half a petticoat, and your shirt needs to be in a rag box."

Jack put an arm around her. "Doesn't matter. We're still standing and that's what counts."

"You saved me." She shuddered, remembering the look in Guthrie's eyes at anticipation of forcing himself on her. Then the crude, bruising kiss.

"No matter what I had to do, I wasn't going to let him take you. Ready to go?"

She met his gray eyes, their color resembling a dove's wing in the light. "Always, as long as it's with you." Then she touched her lips to his ever so softly.

Jack Bowdre was her saving grace, her light in the darkest hours.

Nine

RIDERS DESCENDED ON THEM ALMOST BEFORE JACK HEARD THE horses' pounding hooves. He shoved Nora into a shallow ravine and jumped in after her. They'd barely hidden themselves when a dozen riders rounded a rock formation and galloped straight for them. The sunlight glistened on their badges, and he had no need to wonder who they were.

He yanked his gun from the holster, thankful he had it to use if forced.

Barely breathing, Jack put an arm around Nora. She huddled against him, trembling, quiet. He could smell her fear, feel her heart pounding, taste her salty skin beneath his lips pressed to her temple.

The lawmen scanned the area as they slowly rode through. Jack shrank against the dirt wall around them, willing the men to move on.

But one yelled that he'd seen movement, and they stopped no more than ten yards away.

A big spider crawled across Jack's arm and dropped onto Nora. She gasped but, by some miracle, didn't whimper or shriek before he quickly flicked it off.

One of the lawmen reached for his rifle. "I know Bowdre's around here. I can smell him."

"He's a slippery one, but we'll soon have him boxed in," said another.

"After the grief he's caused us over the years, when I find him, I'm going to put a bullet in his damn head. He'll never make it to a judge, and there'll be no need for a trial." The speaker was a thin man not much older than Jack, his face set in hard lines.

Deputy U.S. Marshal Seamus Belew.

Jack had crossed paths with the crooked lawman a handful

of times and come out the winner. A vein throbbed in Jack's neck. One day, he'd end their association. Had to be that way.

"Execution is not what we do, Belew," the leader admonished quietly.

"He killed my brother," Belew snapped. "I'll not rest until he's dead."

The air crackled with jagged currents. Jack's breathing became shallow, every nerve taut. Time crept by at a snail's pace. He made no sound. Belew dropped from the saddle to scour the brush above them. Jack held Nora tightly against him and pressed to the side of the ravine.

After what seemed like hours, Belew mounted up and the hunters rode on.

"They're gone." Jack released Nora. "That was close."

"I've never been so scared. I just knew they'd find us. Belew really wants you dead."

"Yeah, let's move out. We'll have to be even more careful from now on." Belew wasn't going to give up until he caught him. The man would dog Jack's trail until he ran him to ground.

Jack noticed two buttons missing from Nora's dress and wondered when that had happened, but he didn't ask. Probably the rigors of walking up and down hills, ravines, and gullies, and roping cows. He tucked a tendril of hair behind her ear and brushed her cheek with a knuckle. "You look a sight, Nora. This has taken a toll on you."

"No worse than it has you." She trapped his hand on her cheek with her fingers. "We both look like we've been dragged behind a horse ten ways to Sunday."

"I am sorry. Maybe you should try to find the posse and let them take you to town."

"No." Her eyes sought his. "I'm staying. I'm your almost-wife, and my place is with you."

Jack smiled, and suddenly the day wasn't as gloomy as it had appeared.

They walked for what seemed like forty miles, although it couldn't have been more than fifteen. Each step Jack took felt as if the bone in his leg was poking clear through the skin. It was all he could do to hold back a cry of agony. Despite his pain, he kept a close eye on Nora. Guthrie had really shaken her. She'd trembled like a newborn calf when he'd held her, and rattlesnakes and rats aside, it took a lot to scare this woman.

"How are you holding up?" He put his hands around her waist and lifted her over a patch of thorns, grimacing at the cost to his leg.

"Except for being hungry, I'm fine, Jack. It's you I'm worried about. We should stop."

Her concern touched him. No woman since Rachel had ever given two hoots for his welfare. He'd missed having someone to care about and fuss over him.

He took her hand. "Soon. I promise. I'd like to make it to the river first."

"Why the river?"

"Food. Water. And the crumbling ruins of a place there that will hide the smoke of a fire."

Nora nodded. "Then the river it is. I just pray we last."

That made two of them. Jack picked up a sturdy stick about the right length, and they began the last leg of the day's trek, keeping a wary eye out for the posse.

The landscape, comprised of mostly rock formations, gullies, and ravines, became treacherous at times, each mile a struggle. Hungry and weak, they needed too many stops to rest. They'd only found a few roots and had eaten the tender white end of yucca leaves. It'd taken quite a bit of coaxing for Nora to try them, but hunger had won out. Bottom line—this was the wrong time of the year for a mad dash across the wide-open prairie.

He thought of the gray gelding and wished they could've found the animal. The horse would've made a huge difference. Jack glanced up at the buzzards circling overhead. They were just biding their time until Jack and Nora fell, then they'd swoop in and pick their bones clean.

Nora shaded her eyes and followed his gaze. "What are those birds doing?"

"Waiting. For us."

"To die?" Her eyes widened as she licked her dry lips.

"Yep."

When the sparkling blue river finally came into view, he breathed a damn sight easier. Nora took off running the last ten yards with Jack hobbling behind. They lay on their bellies and scooped water into their mouths. Jack dunked his head in the refreshing current.

They'd made it this far at least. He raised up and glanced around. The ruins he remembered had to be over in the high tangle of brush, assuming they were still there. He'd holed up in them once after getting shot. Clay Colby had found him then and saved his life. Over the years of riding the trail together, they'd become as close as brothers. What he wouldn't give for Clay and Ridge Steele to come riding up about now with saddlebags full of food.

Jack stood and scanned the area, listening, then moved toward the brush, his duster slapping against his legs.

"Where are you going?" Nora jerked upright. "We just got here, Jack."

"I have to find us a place to hide."

"I'm coming too." She lifted her skirt and waded into the thorny foliage as though it were high tide on Galveston Bay. Her gaze was in constant motion, apparently looking for four-legged predators, ready to bolt if something leaped out.

But she was getting better at adapting; he'd give her that.

He waited and helped her navigate the waist-high thicket. "Best I can recall, it's right over here a bit."

They pushed through the jungle of bare boughs, yucca, and thistle, and there it was. The little that remained of the crumbling sod walls with a small portion of sagging roof would shelter them for the night.

Jack gave her a wry smile. "It's not the fancy hotel I know you wish for, but it'll protect us. You can stay here and rest."

She gave him a startled glance. "And where will you be?"

"Fishing. With any luck, we'll eat well tonight. If you can find a flat rock to cook on, that would be very helpful. Just be careful. The snakes are waking from hibernation."

"Great. What if I come with you? I've never seen anyone fish using nothing."

The yearning in her face bruised something deep inside him. Jack figured she hadn't had much quality companionship, except what little she got from Flynn O'Brien and their dice and card games. Hell of a thing, living in fear.

It might be best to stay together in case of trouble.

"Come on, then, but you have to be quiet." He draped an arm around her neck and couldn't miss her big smile.

Everything had gone to pot in his life lately, but Nora Kane felt right being next to him. He'd gotten used to having her near so quickly that he had trouble remembering when she hadn't been. This was the kind of feeling he could see lasting forever.

Only one thing was wrong. Jack no longer believed in forever.

A cold breeze blew from the north, and Nora pulled her coat closer around her as she sat down on the riverbank. Jack removed his duster, rolled up one sleeve, and squatted to dip a hand in the rippling current.

"Remember. Don't talk or move around." His soft voice was markedly different from the way he'd spoken to Darius Guthrie.

Irritation crawled up her spine and stiffened her words. "I'm not a child."

"Nope. I doubt I'll forget that. I didn't mean to belittle you."

"I know." She watched his every movement. "I'm just hungry and tired."

He peered intently into the blue water for several minutes, then stretched out on his belly. He eased his arm down past his elbow and held perfectly still. The minutes passed silently by as Nora waited for something to happen. She wondered if Jack had pulled a trick on the dumb New Yorker. But from everything she'd seen, he didn't appear that kind, and he was as hungry as she.

Jack seemed to do everything by the order in his head— safety, water, food, shelter.

While he was occupied and couldn't turn his piercing gray

eyes on her, she took the liberty of admiring his long, muscular legs, trim waist, and tight backside. Her stomach quickened. He must have his pick of women. So why wasn't he already taken? Maybe being on the run had kept him too busy.

Suddenly, Jack swung his arm and flung water on the bank. "Dammit. Missed him."

Nora smiled encouragement. "It appeared close from what I could tell."

No answering smile came. He stood. "I'll move down the river a bit. Coming?"

"Lead the way."

A few yards from where they had been, Jack stretched out again and slid his arm into the water with barely a ripple. Now she had the gist of it but still wondered at the quick reflexes this kind of fishing required. Her stomach rumbled. She'd have to eat something soon or gnaw on a piece of cactus.

The waiting began again, and her stomach refused to be quiet. Jack raised his head and glared, to which she shrugged her shoulders.

The sun disappeared behind a cloud, and Nora found the March day suddenly very cold.

In the silence that crowded out her thoughts, time seemed to have stopped. The day had turned even gloomier while they waited, the sky gray, the wind picking up.

An abrupt thrashing about snapped her attention back to Jack. Water splashed out onto the bank, and a large fish landed in Nora's lap. She let out a yell and jumped up. The fish stared at her through angry, sullen eyes, flopping in the dead grass like line-drying clothes on a blustery day.

"Get it!" Jack hollered. "Don't let it get back in the water."

Nora tackled the wet, slimy thing, trapping it against the ground with her body. Now what? A sudden icy chill raced through her as the fish wiggled against her bare skin.

She let out a sharp cry and leaped up, flinging her arms. "Oh, Jack, it's inside my dress! Help me, Jack. Get it out!"

Jack knelt, sliding his hands through the open folds of her coat and into her dress. His fingers probed against her flesh.

She gasped. "Jack Bowdre! That is *not* the fish."

"Sorry." He jerked back. "I didn't mean to touch you." He shoved his fingers through his hair. "Tell me what you want me to do."

Nora blew a curl from one eye. "I don't know. I just want it out." The fish appeared as desperate to escape her dress as she was to have it gone, but in trying to escape, it settled deeper and deeper into the wool folds.

Wiggling. Twisting. Flapping its tail.

She danced in a circle, clawing at her dress. "Help me, Jack! Oh God, help me!"

"You'll have to stand still."

"I can't. It feels worse than a snake. Oh God, oh God, oh God!"

Jack took her arm. "Be still a moment."

"Oh, this is slimy! I can't." She grabbed it with both hands, her dress between her and the catfish. "I've got it trapped. Slide your hand inside and get it. Please, Jack."

"Just remember, this was *your* idea." Very carefully, he slid his hand down into her dress until he could touch the fish. "Now release your hold. I have it."

"Are you sure?"

"Positive."

Only then did she remove her grip on the fish and Jack carefully pulled it out. The thing glared at her, its mouth gaping open. She could barely feel her hunger now and was ready to just forget eating. It wouldn't hurt her to lose a few pounds anyway.

"Thank you, Jack."

"I think you might've killed it."

"Then I saved you the chore. I'll look for that flat rock you need." She hurried back to their hideout, anxious to evade Jack's gaze. He'd touched her in places no one had.

While Jack cleaned the fish with the knife he'd taken from Guthrie, she found the right size rock and got a fire going. Then she slipped off to a secluded spot on the river and rinsed the fish smell out of her dress and off her skin. She put her coat on over her undergarments and buttoned it. Then when she was back at the campsite, she flung her dress over the bushes to dry and warmed herself by the fire. She missed the added warmth of her dress, but at least it wouldn't stink. Even if she froze, she just couldn't take that fish smell.

By the time they'd filled their empty bellies, night had fallen. Jack disappeared for a while and returned with his arms full of branches from a scrub oak.

"Our bed." He arranged the branches on one side of the fire.

"Lovely. Thank you."

"Better than the hard ground." He sat down on a cedar stump.

Nora glanced across the low flames at Jack. He hadn't said a word about the fish incident, and she thought that maybe he'd felt something too.

The flickering light deepened the haunting shadows in his eyes.

What did such a man think about? Did memories haunt him? Did he see the faces of each man he'd killed? She couldn't imagine the torment. From her observations, Jack wasn't like most. He seemed to feel remorse deep in his soul.

Her dime novels had never spoken of this subject. Killing had been glorified and impersonal. She could see how wrong those authors had been. Very wrong.

Out here in the wilds of Texas, every life seemed to matter—even the rotten men's.

To some degree anyway—at least with Jack.

"Did you get full?" His voice was low, his face dark.

"Couldn't hold another bite. Maybe I was just hungry, but it tasted good." Nora leaned back, trying to judge his mood. "You know, I haven't had one day in the last ten years when I wasn't afraid. Until now. You're a good man, Jack, and I don't care what the law says. Inside your heart, you're a decent man and I feel safe when I'm with you."

He gave a soft snort. "And that's why you're sitting so far away? Because you trust me?"

"You don't seem to want me over there. You've taken turns glaring at me and the sky."

"It's not you." He let out a low curse. "Sometimes I'm not fit company, but I miss having you next to me. I got used to the sound of your breathing and now it's not there."

"Same here." Nora, too, felt as though something was missing after the closeness of the last two days. She rose, skirted the fire, and dropped down next to him. "We're a sad-looking pair, you know that?"

"Yep." Jack slid an arm around her and she snuggled against his warmth. "This is much better. You shouldn't have washed your dress this close to darkness. It won't dry unless we find a way to bring it closer to the fire."

"I couldn't help it. I wouldn't be able to sleep a wink smelling that fish."

Without a word, Jack rose and fashioned a rack by the fire out of four sturdy cedar limbs stuck into the ground and spread the dress out. Her heart warmed that he saw to her comfort. Not what she'd expected of an outlaw.

"That should do it." He sat back down and drew her close. The fire popped and crackled in the long silence and some animal howled in the distance. Finally, he spoke. "Tell me more about your life."

Nora rested her head on his shoulder. "I've already told you. What more do you want to know?"

"I want to hear about when you were happy. The things you dreamed of in the still of the night when life was good."

"My parents didn't have much. My papa was a poor fisherman, but he loved my mama. He would kiss her each time he left the house, then again when he came back. They kissed all the time. I slept in a loft above the parlor and I'd lie there and listen to them whispering to each other. I never heard what they said, but those private whispers made me feel cherished." She glanced up at the firelight flickering across Jack's face. "I know that sounds silly, but I felt so safe and loved."

"Not silly at all." Jack rested his chin atop her head.

Nora laid her hand on his chest and took comfort from the vibration of his voice when he spoke. "Papa would take me with him fishing sometimes, but I never liked to touch the fish.

I hated that slimy skin. I always told him I should've been a boy, and I still remember what he said."

"What was that?"

"He'd throw back his head and laugh and say that if I'd been a boy, he never would've gotten his little princess." For a second, hot tears lurked behind Nora's eyes. "I was his girl and I still miss him and Mama every single day." She patted Jack's vest. "Your turn. Tell me about a time when you were happy."

Jack shook his head. "I'd rather listen to you."

"No, I insist you play the game right. We each take turns."

"Never had much reason to smile that I can remember until I married Rachel. I've blocked out everything up to then. Meeting and taking Rachel as my wife was the first time I was truly happy."

The sorrow in his voice made her want to cry. "I can tell you loved her very much. What happened?"

He tensed. "She was murdered. My son too."

Shock swept through Nora, and she remembered asking what had turned him. This was what had made him an outlaw. Like he'd said—revenge.

Thick anger shook her. "I hope you made someone pay."

One corner of Jack's mouth tilted in a half smile before it vanished. "I did."

"Good." Something told her he'd shown no mercy, and that was as it should've been. "How old was your boy?"

"Alex was four." A smile drifted across Jack's face. "He used to follow me everywhere, putting his little feet in my footprints. He said when he grew up, he wanted to be just like me." His voice broke and the smile vanished. His gray eyes hardened. "I wouldn't want anyone to be like me."

The fire crackled in the stillness and cold seeped into Nora's bones. The lives Jack had taken had scarred his soul. He didn't feel he deserved any other kind of life. Clearly, he had little hope for the future. No wonder he was an outlaw. He'd opened up for that Darcy woman and she'd chosen a life of solitude over him. Nora ached to hold this stone-faced man and promise that it wouldn't stay dark forever, that the dawn would eventually come.

"As I stated before, you're a fine man, Jack. And don't you dare think you're not."

"Difference of opinion." He got to his feet and propped his arms on the top of a crumbling wall. "We'll have snow before morning. I feel it in the air."

"Snow? Are you sure?" Her gaze went to her wet dress and she bit her lip. Maybe washing it hadn't been wise.

"Doubt it'll do more than cover the ground, but it'll be cold. We'll have to sleep close to stay warm. Unless you object. If so, you can have my duster."

"Keep it. I don't mind sleeping beside you." After several minutes, she rose and stood behind him. He didn't move when she put her arms around his waist and rested her cheek on his back. "You're not alone, Jack. You have me. I'll stand by your side through sunny days and storms."

He turned to study her, and sadness drifted across his high cheekbones, his rugged profile. "I don't deserve you. I'm a bastard, and that's on good days, but I'll try to make you proud."

"I already am," she said softly. "Don't you know that?"

Something shifted in his eyes and the hardness lifted. He framed her face with his hands and lowered his head. Blood pounded in her brain and her knees trembled with need. She sagged against him and let out a little mewling sound. This outlaw made her forget all the bad in her past, filling her with thrilling new memories.

He teased her mouth with his tongue, outlining the shape before crushing her to him.

The scent of the wild land, smoke from the fire, and unmistakable desire filled her senses. Nora clung to his vest and returned the kiss, one that deepened into hunger that seared through her. She slid her arms around his neck, the locks of his hair brushing her skin like soft feathers.

A smoldering fire burned inside and spread along each taut nerve ending, tingling just below the surface as though waiting for the dry tinder to catch and erupt into a blaze. Nora saw herself standing at a deep chasm that separated her old life from the new.

She yearned to take the step that would make her a woman in every sense of the word.

His hands moved down the sides of her body, his touch so heartrendingly tender that it brought tears to her eyes. Her stomach quickened, and she swayed on her feet.

She wanted this man, this outlaw, who made her feel a hundred things she'd never experienced before. Her heart pounded like the hooves of a thousand wild horses on the plains.

Jack broke the kiss and mumbled against her mouth. "Lady, you're not too smart taking up with the likes of me."

"I've never felt this way about anyone. I wish we could stay like this forever and no one would ever find us."

"That's not possible."

"I know." And that's what scared her. The posse would never give up, and when they arrested him, what then? They might hang him. Her blood froze. In the books she'd read, posses often strung up outlaws from the nearest tree without benefit of a trial.

He already carried a bullet in his hip. What more would they do? A lot more. They could take his life. A shudder ran through her.

"What's wrong?" He tightened his hold around her. "Cold?"

"Hold me, Jack. There are monsters in the dark."

"I'll get rid of them for you."

As if he could. But for now, she'd curl into the safety of his arms and try not to think about the coming morrow.

He found her upturned lips again and branded her with a kiss while his palms slid along the curves of her hungry body. He rested his hands firmly on her bottom and anchored her to him.

Jack Bowdre was hers, and she would fight tooth and nail to keep him.

Tonight, she was going to sleep beside him, not because she had to, but because it was the only place she wanted to be.

Ten

THE LOW FIRE POPPED. NORA LAY WITH HER BACK TUCKED against Jack, his arm laying across her hip. She was cold but wouldn't complain. He must be too. "Are you asleep?"

"What's wrong?"

"My thoughts keeping me awake, I guess."

"Monsters in the dark?"

"Afraid so." She sighed. "Maybe if I talk a little more. Do you object?"

"Nope. Is Flynn O'Brien on your mind?"

"Good guess. I keep hearing his voice, hollering such hateful, horrible, degrading things to me."

"What kind of things?"

"That I was fat and ugly and made him sick. He said no one would ever want me."

Jack shifted. "I want you."

Warmth spread through her and she wasn't cold anymore. "I wasn't fishing for that."

"I meant what I said. I want you for my wife."

"And I want you for a husband." She smiled in the dim light of the flickering fire.

"What else did the rat bastard say?" Jack's low growl scared her a little.

"That I disgusted him. Said I was too stupid to live, and he wished a thousand times over I'd just get run down and trampled by horses. That started about six months after he brought me to his house. I was only fourteen. According to him, I couldn't do anything right. He'd scream it out in a fit of rage, and the sound would bounce off the stone walls of the mansion and crash inside my head. Those words hurt as much as a fist. Or more. He would tell me over and over that no one would miss me if I suddenly disappeared."

"Why did he teach you to keep the books then?"

"Because he had no one else with the skills that he could depend on, and he couldn't do it himself. He never had any schooling. His enemies would love to know that—it was a secret he guarded very carefully. He controlled every aspect of my life. Bought whatever he thought I needed and never let me shop for myself. He kept me in line with threats and insults."

She paused, fighting down crushing horror. "He used to keep a bag of snakes, and he'd threaten to let them out on me if I didn't do as he said. He liked to take a snake out and bring it close until I would beg and agree to whatever he wanted."

"Now I know where your fear of reptiles comes from."

"Once Flynn dumped the whole sack on a man who'd disobeyed him." Her voice broke. "I watched him die, writhing in pain from their bites. That's why I'm so terrified of the slimy things."

Jack released a low oath. When he spoke, his words were stone cold and as hard as granite. "If I'd been there, I would've slit his throat."

His glittering eyes were chilling. What she saw even in the dim light sent a shiver up her spine. Those who sought him had best be afraid. "I will never, ever ask you to kill for me."

"As my wife, you'll never have to."

Nora considered his soft words and the hardness underneath. She would have to be careful or she'd put him in even greater danger of arrest for murder.

With a troubled sigh, she laid her hand on his stubbled jaw. "I wish we lived far away from Texas, someplace where no one would find us. Maybe California."

"Darlin', men like these are everywhere, not just in Texas. You can't escape them. There are thousands of O'Briens and bad marshals in the world." He gently kissed her and smoothed back her curls. "I wish I could give you the life you deserve. The only thing I can promise is that I'll do my best to make you happy."

"Jack, why did you tell me that you wanted me as your wife now, instead of waiting to reach Hope's Crossing like you'd said?"

"You might as well know. We may not live to reach there."

A quiet filled Nora. He must really believe that to say it aloud, and that frightened her. "Do these lawmen know that's where we're headed?"

"I'm sure they have a pretty good guess."

"And after we reach there, you still may not be safe?"

"We'll have a far better chance there than out here in the open. Hope's Crossing was an outlaw hideout once, until we decided to make it into a town. The beauty is that there's only one way in and one way out. It's surrounded on all sides by steep walls, and it's built like a fortress. Block the entrance, and no one can get in unless they scale down the sides by rope. That's why they're desperate to stop me from reaching there."

No one had to tell her the lengths to which desperate men would go.

She snuggled against him. "Let's talk about something else. When did you kiss your first girl?"

"Don't recall. My memory doesn't go back that far."

"Come on, Jack. Everyone remembers their first kiss. Or maybe you just went around kissing all the girls." She smiled. "Of course, that's got to be it."

Jack didn't smile, not even a little. After several heartbeats, he let out a long breath that ruffled the hair at her temple. "She was Lucy Shane. She was twelve and I was fourteen, I believe. Her father caught us in the barn and laid into me with his fists. Said I was a no-account, and if he caught me with his daughter again, he'd kill me. He yelled that I was rotten, just like my father."

Nora's stomach twisted. "Why your father?"

"Orin Bowdre was an outlaw, a robber, and a bastard. He was as mean a man as you've ever seen. I always swore I'd never end up like him." Jack barked a laugh. "Now look at me."

"I never met your father, but I know you're nothing like him."

He snorted. "Maybe you're wearing blinders."

"Well, I'm not. Is your father still alive?"

"Don't know. Don't care. I saw wanted posters on him

when I was a lawman, but the last time I laid eyes on him, we fought. Over my mother and two sisters. Orin came home drunk and started beating my sisters, calling them despicable names. Mother tried to stop him, and she got the worst." Jack fell silent and she wasn't sure he'd go on.

After several minutes, he let out a troubled sigh. "Orin kept pounding her with his fists even after she fainted. Her face was a bloody mess. I fought with him and knocked him out cold, then packed Mother's and the girls' bags and drove them to the stage line. They went to live with my widowed aunt on a farm in Hardeman County. I go by to see them now and again. My sisters married good men, and Mother is happier than I've ever seen her."

"I'm glad. Everyone deserves some happiness. How often do you get to see them?"

"I try to swing by every two or three months. I'm due for a visit."

"Did you have any brothers?"

"One brother. He died when I was probably twelve or so. You?"

"No. My mother was never able to have any more. They died in the womb."

He wound a lock of her hair around his finger. "What about you? Tell me about your first kiss."

"You're going to laugh. Tommy Smith and I were out behind the house, in a cluster of blackberry bushes. We were about eight or nine years old and supposed to have been picking berries for a pie. He put his arm around me and gave me a big sloppy kiss. About that time my mother called from the back door and I jerked my head around—and as I did, my hair wrapped around a button on his shirt. The more I tried to get loose, the tighter it held me." Nora chuckled with the memory.

Jack caressed her arm. "What did you do?"

"Nothing I could do except to crawl out and let my mother get me loose. She had to snip my hair, and I had a gap there for the longest time. Tommy's face was bloodred. Once he was free, he ran home, and the only time he came back was with his mother when she visited mine. We never went near those blackberry bushes together again."

The fire crackled in the silence and something scurried nearby, only this time she wasn't afraid because Jack held her in his arms.

She glanced up at the moon overhead, praying that Jack was wrong and they'd reach Hope's Crossing safely and marry.

This man, who'd already gone through such tremendous loss and torment, held her so tenderly, as though she was a priceless treasure. She lifted his hand to kiss his palm and sent up a silent plea that they would get to live out their days together.

❧

Morning neared when Jack awoke with Nora in his arms, a hand resting on the curve of her hip. As predicted, a light dusting of snow covered both them and the ground. A surprise snow wasn't unusual in the early spring. He'd gotten up several times during the night to add wood to the fire, and it still burned, but the flames had gotten low. He carefully eased away from Nora.

She stirred. "Jack?"

"Just going to throw more wood on the fire. I'm cold and you probably are too."

"Don't be too long. I need your warmth."

He chuckled softly. "Just my body heat, not me? Isn't that just like a woman. I reckon I need yours too. It's chilly."

They should probably get up and start the day, but it was still dark, and he was cold—and, well, Nora called to him. He warmed his hands by the tall flames of the fire and lay back down beside her. He drew her lush curves against him, opened his duster, and put it around her, sharing his heat.

"Mmmmm, I could stay like this all day." Nora nuzzled into the folds of his shirt.

"We'd get awfully hungry, and I haven't been feeding you enough as it is." He closed his eyes to soak up the feel of her— contentment he'd not had in a very long while. Now if he could keep them safe long enough to claim her for his own...

But Seamus Belew was searching high and low. How long before he found them?

Jack buried his face in her hair, loving the softness. She wiggled her bottom against him and proof of his desire rose. If only they had a blanket to shield them from the snow. But even if they did, he didn't want their first time to be on the hard ground, hungry and cold, him smelling like some rank mountain man who'd missed his yearly bath.

He swept her hair aside and kissed the back of her neck. "When we get out of danger and this cold, I'm going to lay you down and make you mine," he growled.

Silently, she reached for his hand, tucked it through the opening of her coat where she'd undone the buttons. Her skin was like warm velvet. His breath stilled.

"Touch me, Jack. Run your fingers across my skin. I'm yours just as much now as when we're married."

Without a word, he slid his hand over the soft mounds of her breasts and down her ribs, memorizing, savoring—wanting.

His heart thudded with the unexpected joy shooting through him.

Nora rolled to face him and unbuttoned his shirt. Slowly, she explored his chest, kissing each inch. Then she laid her face against his flesh.

"I didn't know I was getting such a well-muscled husband. I thought at best you'd be like Lazlo Parker."

"Who the hell is Lazlo Parker?"

"He ran the mercantile in Buffalo. His sleeves bulged with his muscles. Lazlo could lift a fifty-pound sack of flour in one arm and pick up a second in the other."

"Do tell." Jack grinned. Nora seemed pretty easy to impress.

"I once saw him lift a wagon that was loaded to the gills with household goods and move it over to make room for another wagon to pass by. He was very tall too. Good-looking, if you didn't count the hair growing in his ears and nose."

"I take it that didn't earn him points."

"Good heavens, no. I couldn't stand to look at that man."

"I imagine not." A grin teased his lips.

"I inspected you while you weren't watching."

"And?"

"No hair in your ears and nose." She paused and lowered her voice. "I liked what I saw. You're a handsome man, Jack Bowdre."

"I'm glad you think so." Jack buried his face in her hair. "I still think you got a raw deal when you answered my letters."

"Do you know what I noticed right off about you?"

"Hard telling."

"It was the pain you tried to hide behind your eyes. I knew then that you'd be a man that never gave up. You'd ride hell-bent through flames with a fury no man could equal. I was looking for someone like that, and I'm glad I found him."

Something stirred in Jack that she thought him honorable and worthy. There was a day when he had been. But now?

He was different now. Older, wiser. Soul-weary and cynical.

The sharp teeth of a memory lashed out. A time when he'd shown mercy and it had cost lives.

He'd cornered the murdering outlaw Gus Franklin, and as Jack raised his weapon, Gus had begged and pleaded for his life. Jack had spared him, convinced that Gus would change his ways. Only Gus had ridden on and wiped out an entire family, stolen their large herd of cattle and everything else he could find.

Jack clenched his eyes shut against the sight of pools of blood everywhere, the daughters Gus had violated, the swarms of flies. The family had paid for his mistake with their lives.

Months later, he'd found Gus Franklin and put a bullet in his head. Only it hadn't brought back the family who'd died at Gus's hands.

Jack slowed his breathing and swallowed the bitter secret that was his cross to bear. Ever since then, he'd been determined not to show anyone a speck of mercy. Until Nora had come to be by his side.

Sleep evaded him. He held Nora until the sky began to lighten, then stood and pulled her to her feet. "Put your dress back on. It might still be a little damp."

"If so, it'll dry on me."

He held her coat and tried not to glance at all that soft, white skin as she slipped into the garment. She said it was dry except for part of the skirt.

When she was dressed and back in her buttoned coat, he put out the fire and took her hand. "Time to go."

They walked for several miles before they ran across an old abandoned wagon, the wood all busted and decayed. He poked around in the bed, tossing out pieces of cloth and clods of dirt, hoping to find something useful.

Nora peeked over the side. "What do you supposed happened that would cause someone to leave this behind?"

"Probably got ambushed."

"By who?"

"Not sure. It's been here a long time." Jack gave a cry and held up a bow and one broken arrow. The bow string was missing, but he could fix that with some rawhide or animal sinew. The arrow was a lost cause, but he could make more with the right materials. He pocketed the arrowhead.

After finding nothing else of interest, Jack jumped out of the wagon. "This bow and arrow will be silent, so we'll be able to hunt for food."

Her eyes lit up. "Hallelujah!"

"See if you can find a sturdy piece of wood for a new arrow while I try to fix the bow." He pointed to a scrub oak. "Try over there. The oak wood will be harder than mesquite."

Nora hurried to the small tree. Jack pulled off his duster and turned it inside out, looking for something he could make do with until he got a strip of rawhide. The heavy thread might work if he could stretch it tight enough—at least one time. He unraveled the edge and pulled two long pieces of thread, winding them together for strength.

"Will this do?" Nora held out a long piece of oak.

"Perfect." Jack quickly tied the string to one end of the bow then bent it and tied the other end of the string to the opposite side. He tested it. "I think this will work temporarily."

He took the oak branch, stripped all the bark away, and

sliced off a small section running the length of the wood. Whittling and notching made it a decent arrow. Taking more thread from his duster, he inserted the arrowhead into the slot and bound it tight.

"I think this might do. I'll see what I can kill."

"I'll make a fire while you're gone."

"If you hear riders, hide."

"I will. Please don't go too far, Jack."

"I won't." He kissed her cheek and left. A short time later, he killed a small rabbit.

The sun had climbed in the morning sky by the time they finished eating. They put out the fire and set out again. By the close of day, they'd covered a fair amount of ground. They'd hidden from riders twice, but by luck managed to evade them. Each step was taking them slowly toward Hope's Crossing and friends. He felt better about their chances—and evading Seamus Belew.

Nora stopped to rest, clutching her side. "Jack, how long now until we reach safety?"

"I figure we're two or three days out, barring unforeseen circumstances."

"Wonderful."

"I'm sorry I pushed you so hard today."

"You didn't." She met his gaze. "We're going to make it, Jack. We're going to be at Hope's Crossing soon and we'll be married. I forgot to ask. Does the town have a preacher?"

"Ridge Steele. We've ridden the outlaw trail together for years, and I can safely say there's none better to have near in a fight."

"He sounds like a good friend. I'm glad you have him."

That was the truth. Jack knew he'd be dead and in the ground right now without Ridge, Clay, and some of the others.

"We'd better find somewhere to bed down for tonight." Jack took her hand. "Just a little farther, where the land isn't so flat."

"Lead the way." Nora smiled at him and his stomach fluttered.

He glanced up at the sky and counted to twenty until the butterfly wings inside him settled. They only had about an hour of sunlight left. He didn't want the darkness to catch him and Nora in open country. If they could just make it to a mesa near an old burial mound, they'd find plenty of cover there. But despite Nora's brave front, he couldn't miss the tired lines on her face. And his leg felt like it was on fire, the searing pain raw.

Plus, he was hungry enough to eat a bear, and he suspected Nora was too. Still, she didn't complain. She just kept going in the boots of the man she hated.

His mouth became bone dry, and it was difficult to dredge up enough spit to swallow. He saw no water source.

On they went, putting one foot in front of the other. He didn't know how much time had passed, but relief shot through him to see the shadows of the mesa rising from the floor of the prairie.

Light flickered through the mesquites. They drew closer, and he could make out the fire of someone's camp ahead. Three horses were staked at the edge of a thicket, and a wagon stood in the circle of the firelight.

Friend? Or foe?

He directed Nora to a hiding place where wind and rain had hollowed out a deep crevice at the base of the mesa. "Wait here. Let me check them out. It could be the posse."

She gripped his arm. "Be careful."

With a nod, he crawled on his belly through the grass until he could hear the murmur of voices. He made out three men passing a bottle around the fire.

"What are you talking about, Woodrow? We gotta lay low. This land is crawling with lawmen. If we go get the money we buried and that posse shows up, our goose is cooked." The voice belonged to a thin man known only as Undertaker. He sported a long white beard, a portion of it braided.

Jack knew him well and trusted him—as long as they faced each other. He never turned his back on the old outlaw. He inched a little closer and recognized dark-haired Woodrow, and the third man, Poteet, by his stooped bearing and suspenders. He couldn't recall their first names.

Woodrow filled a tin plate from a Dutch oven. The fragrance of cooking food wafted around Jack's head, and his stomach growled in response.

"What I mean is, we can bargain with the posse." Woodrow sat cross-legged on a bedroll. "We can tell them we saw Bowdre hightailing it toward New Mexico Territory. That would get them out of our way."

Good. The outlaws were more interested in themselves than turning Jack in.

And there was the hot food to consider. Definitely worth the risk. He could almost taste the food, feel it sliding down his throat to his empty belly.

Poteet rose with considerable effort from his place near the fire to fill his plate. "I hope Bowdre gets away. I like him. He's always treated me with respect, and I wouldn't cross him. The man sure has a lightning-fast draw. How do you suppose he learned that?"

"Practice," Undertaker answered. "Lots of practice and quick reflexes."

Woodrow stuffed his mouth and talked around his chewing. "Wish he'd join up with us. We could use someone like him."

"Fat chance," Jack whispered. "I work alone."

The trio didn't seem like they'd be a problem, and Jack felt confident enough to get Nora and take a meal with them. In fact, they'd probably fall all over themselves for a chance to sit across the fire from a pretty lady.

As long as they only looked. But lay their grimy hands on her, and Jack would delight in showing them the error of their ways.

Eleven

"HELLO, THE CAMP!" JACK CALLED, AS NORA'S HEAD REELED with the smells of cooking. "Mind sharing your food?"

Nora took Jack's arm, praying this wasn't a mistake. Yet her empty stomach would revolt if she didn't feed it. She'd let Jack have the biggest portion of that one small rabbit he'd killed that morning. Since he was protecting and feeding her, he'd earned more. But now, especially after the long walk, she was ready to gnaw off someone's arm. It was all she could do to keep from running through the thorny mesquites to the campfire, grabbing a fork, and stabbing anyone with it who tried to stop her.

Curbing the desire, she tightened her grip on the bow and arrow they'd found and waited.

"Who's there?" a man yelled.

"Jack Bowdre."

"Come on in. We got plenty."

Jack spoke low. "I don't think they'll bother you, but if they do, I'll take care of it."

"I know." She walked into the circle of the firelight, tall and proud beside him.

The three men jerked off their hats and put their pistols away.

"You could've warned us you had a woman with you, Bowdre." The speaker was an odd-looking man with a very long, white beard, the front part of which was braided.

"Yep, I could've. Undertaker, meet my"—Jack paused and glanced at her—"my wife, Nora. Touch her and you'll be wishing you hadn't."

"I'm delighted to meet you, Mr. Undertaker." A strange name for a man to say the least. Maybe that had once been his profession. She smiled when he offered her a seat on a log, and Nora laid the precious bow and arrow behind her.

"These other two are Woodrow and Poteet." Jack sat next to her. "Thank you for sharing your food. We've had very little to eat since escaping the wrecked stagecoach."

"We heard mention of that in town." Undertaker stroked his beard. "In fact, me an' the boys were just talking about that." He narrowed his gaze. "When did you get married, Bowdre?"

Nora met Jack's gaze, curious of how he'd answer.

"A while ago." He turned her palm over. "She finally came to join me."

"I lived back East," Nora explained, her stomach growling.

"Woodrow, get the lady a plate," Undertaker snapped. "I reckon we ain't never seen a lady as pretty as you, ma'am."

She sat straighter, glanced down at her dirty, torn clothes, men's boots, and gathered her pride. "Thank you, Mr. Undertaker. That's very kind of you to say." Her hand shook when she accepted the plate of beans and potatoes with a little slice of ham. The delicious aroma made her weak, and she inhaled deeply, savoring the scent before lifting the fork to her mouth. Likely one of the men had already used the fork before her, but she didn't let that stop her. She'd waited too long for this. Undertaker handed her a cup.

Jack rose, poured some coffee, filled a plate, and returned next to her. He wasted no time digging in. Between bites, he told the trio about their ordeal over the last few days. "Seamus Belew is riding with the posse."

Woodrow, the outlaw with dark hair and mustache, choked on his coffee. "Hell!"

Undertaker swore. "We'll have to watch our backs even more."

Poteet, the silent one, sat hunched over and stared into the night. "Wish I'd killed the bast"—he glanced at her and swallowed—"killed him when I had the chance."

"Yeah, well, you didn't." Jack took a drink from his cup. "What are you doing out here?"

Nora caught the furtive glances the trio gave each other. They were hiding out as well, and they didn't want to tell Jack why. Poteet mumbled something unintelligible.

"This cold snap sure makes my old bones ache," Undertaker said, changing the subject. "I guess you and the missus slept in the snow last night."

"That we did." Jack shoveled more beans, potatoes, and ham into his mouth. "I didn't mind for myself, but Nora's not used to roughing it like we are."

A noise of snapping twigs beyond the firelight made Nora jump.

"This is Bittercreek!" a man yelled. "I aim to come in. Don't shoot."

Not only Jack but the whole group stiffened and drew their guns. Whoever "Bittercreek" was, she already didn't like him.

She put her mouth next to Jack's ear. "Do you know this man?"

"Heard of him is all. He's a bad one with a crazy streak. Stay close to me."

"Hell, this place is busier than a crowd at a medicine show," Undertaker spat. "This is the last damn time I'm letting you pick the place to camp, Poteet."

"Don't blame this on me," Poteet returned. "It was hidden and quiet when we got here."

The brush rustled, and the firelight fell on a tall, muscular man as he stepped into the circle, leading a horse. He shoved a boy forward. The kid managed to stay on his feet, but it was a near thing. Nora could see the fear written on his face. He was all legs, like a young colt, and she made his age about eight or nine. She fought the urge to rise and put protective arms around him.

Undertaker straightened. "Who you got there, Bittercreek?"

"Sawyer something or another. Who the hell cares? He don't got no kin. Got him from a peddler in trade for a mule. I got big plans for the boy." Bittercreek's matted yellow hair hung down his back. He shifted his heavy-lidded gaze to Nora, and she drew her coat tighter, her scalp prickling. Though it cost every bit of courage she had, she returned his stare with disdain.

She knew his kind too well.

The gangly boy appeared frozen in place, unsure what to say or do. He glanced at the pot of food with palpable longing, and the flickering firelight deepened his blue eyes.

"Sawyer, come sit next to me. We'll get you something to eat." Nora patted the space beside her on the log. Relief came into the boy's eyes, and he slowly walked to her as though afraid that Bittercreek would yank him back or hit him.

"Thank you, ma'am," he whispered, dropping next to her.

Nora put her arm around his thin shoulders. "You're among friends."

"What you whispering 'bout over there?" Bittercreek glared and wiped his mouth with the back of his hand. "Don't go making the boy all soft. I need him toughened up."

Nora ignored him and rose to fill a plate that she took back to Sawyer. "Here you go."

Bittercreek stalked to her and stood inches away. "The boy eats when I say." He reached for the plate only to be met with Jack's loaded gun, pressed to his side.

Jack had risen so fast Nora had missed it, her attention on the man whose boots touched the toes of her shoes. She met Bittercreek's stare, refusing to back down.

"The boy eats now," Jack growled low. "If you have a problem with that, we'll face off right here."

Nora backed out of the way, her attention on the man who'd just claimed her as his wife.

Woodrow drew his gun also. "I stand with Jack."

"Me too," Undertaker barked.

Poteet nodded. "I never had any use for your kind, Bittercreek. You'd best move along."

Nora admired these men for the loyalty they showed Jack.

Finding himself outnumbered, Bittercreek grunted and straightened. "Come on, kid. We ain't welcome."

"The boy stays." Jack had yet to remove his weapon from the outlaw's side.

A minute passed as Bittercreek scanned the group, evidently trying to take in the turn of events. Nora watched his glittering yellow eyes. They reminded her of a cat.

Finally, the surly man snarled. "He belongs to me."

"Not anymore." Jack motioned to the darkness. "Go. Come back and I'll finish this."

"It ain't over, Bowdre."

Nora watched Jack jerk a little in surprise. "I see you've heard of me. An admirer?"

Red streaks crawled up Bittercreek's neck. He spat on the ground at Jack's feet. "That's what I think of you. Stay out of my way. Only a coward hides behind his friends."

"I'm not hiding." A muscle worked in Jack's jaw, and Nora could feel his icy anger. "I'll meet you anywhere and come alone. Just name the time and place." He paused. "But you're more the kind who'll sneak up behind a man in the dark."

"Best watch the shadows then." Bittercreek whirled and stalked off into the night.

Only after he'd disappeared did Nora set the plate in Sawyer's lap. His hand shook as he raised a forkful of food to his mouth. Nora was sure he hadn't been allowed to eat in a while. She sat down beside the boy, her own legs trembling. Jack put away his gun and returned to his place on the log next to her.

"Not sure that was the smartest move, Bowdre." Undertaker took a swig from the bottle and passed it. "Now, you'll have the posse *and* Bittercreek gunning for you."

"Won't be the first time the odds were stacked against me. That piece of filth needed someone to stand up to him." Jack shrugged. "Might as well have been me. I'd do the same again. Besides, I didn't like how he was looking at Nora. We'd have had problems sooner or later."

"You spoke a mouthful." Poteet dumped the grounds from the empty coffeepot in the dirt, then filled the pot with water from a barrel and added coffee. He set it on the fire to boil.

Young Sawyer swallowed his mouthful of food. "Thank you."

"You're welcome, kid." Jack rose and stood with Undertaker, his arm propped on the wagon. "How long were you traveling together, Sawyer?"

"Two weeks. He was real mean." Sawyer glanced up, his lip quivering, trying not to cry. "What's gonna happen to me now?"

"Do you have any family we can take you to?" Nora rubbed his back.

"None that I know about. My parents and two sisters died of the fever about a year ago. That's when the peddler took me. I had to work to eat, but he was nice."

Nora watched Jack's eyebrows knit, saw his frown. He probably wondered the same thing she did.

"I'm curious." Flames from the fire flickered on Jack's face. He spoke in a tight voice. "Why did an outlaw like Bittercreek want you? He had to have something in mind to haul you around, and it wasn't out of the goodness of his heart."

The boy's voice trembled. "He made me stand in the road in front of a stage to make it stop so he could rob it." Sawyer licked his lips. "Sometimes he used me to draw attention away from himself and the things he was stealing. Once, he made me sneak into a corral and take the horses so he could sell 'em. Said he'd slit my throat if I didn't. Then he gave me a gun and made me—made me shoot a man." Sawyer's blue eyes glistened with tears as he glanced up, whispering. "I'm an outlaw now. Do they hang little kids?"

"Of all the low-down, sorry-assed things to do," Woodrow growled.

Jack clenched a fist. "No, they don't hang kids, and you're not an outlaw, so forget that."

Tears stung Nora's eyes as she put her arm around Sawyer. "You'll come with us. We're heading to Hope's Crossing. It's two or three days from here, I think."

Jack knelt by the fire. "You'll be welcome there, son, if you want to come. I reckon you've had a bellyful of being told what to do, so this time, the choice is yours. I can guarantee no one will mistreat you."

"Sounds like a good offer to me, kid," Poteet said. "I was left on my own when I was about your age, so I know how tough it can be. This fellow here, Jack Bowdre, is a fine man—just has one fault. He has the uncanny, god-awful ability to get into trouble without blinking nary an eye."

The men chuckled. Nora smiled and asked Sawyer if he wanted more food, to which he said no.

She was happy to see the tension at the campfire melt away. She liked these three outlaws, even if they lived on the fringes of society. She didn't kid herself about their chosen profession. Like Jack, they'd probably all done things—killed even—but mostly to stay alive. They appeared to be content to walk the world all alone, and, in a way, they were stuck in some kind of earthly prison of their own making. Wrong choices often led down the wrong path, and there was no backtracking. Her heart ached for men like Jack, Undertaker, Woodrow, and Poteet.

But if they could save Sawyer for a better life, they had to try.

"You don't have to decide tonight. Let us know in the morning." Nora patted his cold hand.

Sawyer swallowed hard. "I don't have to wait. I'm coming with you. I ain't gonna take a chance on Bittercreek getting me again."

"He won't as long as I'm alive," Jack said quietly.

Nora nodded, suddenly unable to swallow past the lump in her throat. Sawyer's decision made her happy. He needed someone to care about him, help him grow up to have honor.

It made their lives more difficult—they had the posse and now Bittercreek to try to avoid. They'd been lucky so far, but that could end at any moment. As much as Nora wanted to help, they might be putting the boy in even greater danger.

The men spent another cold night on the ground, next to the fire, giving Nora and Sawyer the wagon. Woodrow gave them an extra blanket of his, but she, in turn, wrapped it around Sawyer. The size of her heart plainly showed in the way she cared for the little lost boy. Jack had dozed between adding wood to the fire, but he was wide awake now as he sipped a cup of coffee, his gaze on Nora's shapely figure as she and Sawyer gathered more limbs and sticks to cook breakfast.

"Don't go too far!" he yelled. Bittercreek would love to get his hands on them.

Nora's smile blinded him. "We won't."

The woman and boy already seemed like they belonged together. And he'd see to it that they stayed that way.

So much about Nora reminded him of the wife he'd loved, especially the way she cared about needy children. Probably animals too, if he could hazard a guess. Except snakes and rodents. A smile curved his mouth with the memory of her whacking the wood rat to death with Dollard's boot. He might as well lump catfish in there too. She didn't like those either.

The three outlaws cooked breakfast, and afterward, Jack, Nora, and Sawyer said goodbye.

Nora smiled and complimented each man on something, although finding even a small attribute to praise seemed to be a challenge, judging by the wrinkled lines on her forehead. Poteet appeared happy she'd complimented his suspenders, Woodrow his cooking skills, and Undertaker his soft heart.

Undertaker clasped Jack's hand. "Be safe, my friend."

"You as well." Jack's gaze went to the other two. "Never approach a bull from the front."

Woodrow grinned and picked up the second line of the saying. "A horse from the rear."

"Or a fool from any direction," Poteet ended. "Take care of that woman and boy."

"Count on it."

Their breath fogged in the cool morning air, the sun just above the horizon. Jack couldn't miss how attentive Sawyer was to Nora, helping her over rocks and across thorny patches. He was a good kid who'd had some tough breaks. If the posse gave chase, Sawyer would look after Nora. That eased Jack's mind a bit. When his leg acted up, he could do little more than hobble.

He kept his gun loaded and a wary eye out for the posse

and Bittercreek. Something told him they'd not seen the last of either—especially Deputy Marshal Seamus Belew.

Nothing would ever convince Belew that Jack had been on the right side of the law when he'd shot Belew's brother. To Seamus, Max could do no wrong, but the truth was, he'd been helping himself to strongboxes off of stagecoaches for a while before that fatal day. Jack had been a lawman back then and happened to be riding shotgun. The brash young robber on horseback had burst from behind some trees and attacked the coach he was on, aiming to grab a gold shipment. They'd shot it out, and at the end, Max lay dead.

And now big brother wouldn't let it rest until he made Jack pay.

"I wish I could shoot this bow and arrow." Sawyer held it in front of him and pulled back the string. "Do you think maybe I can?"

"Sure. Go over there and practice." Jack ruffled the gangly boy's hair.

"Jack killed a rabbit with it," Nora bragged. "He also killed one with a rock."

Sawyer's eyes grew round. "No fooling?"

"Jack is very skillful. If not, we'd surely have starved." She met Jack's gaze, and he grew warm. "He even fished without a pole."

"I do *not* walk on water, no matter what Nora says." He loved that she thought him more accomplished than most men. He didn't have the heart to tell her that out on the Texas plains, folks lived off the land and were proficient in survival skills.

"How did you fish without a pole?" Sawyer asked.

Jack related the feat in detail with Nora adding the color and commentary. "She's leaving out the fact that the fish wound up down the front of her dress." He could still remember in vivid detail the feel of her skin beneath his touch, both then and later, when they'd slept in the old ruins. His blood heated, recalling the satiny texture of her skin, the taste of her mouth, her curves pressed against him.

Damn! He shifted and drew his duster over the bulge in his trousers. Longing rose for the day when he could lay her on a soft bed and take his time exploring her lush body. He wouldn't rush that.

Sawyer squinted up at him, his blue eyes sparkling. "I wish I had been there to see you catch that fish. Do you think you can teach me to do that?"

"Sure, kid. It's not that hard. Just takes a lot of patience."

The boy went to a mesquite thicket and played with the bow and arrow while they rested.

After a bit, Jack called him back and they resumed their journey. A little while later, they approached a rocky hill that had little vegetation covering it. He didn't like the looks of it. There were no birds twittering about. The stillness seemed eerie.

"Let me take the lead and keep silent," he said low.

"What is it?" Nora whispered.

"Maybe nothing." Or maybe something. He'd learned to be careful, reminded of it even more so after Marshal Dollard had captured him. Careless men ended up dead.

He slid the gun from his holster.

A shot rang out, and Jack shoved Nora and Sawyer into the brush, then dove in after them.

Trouble had found him. Again. The only question worth asking was "who?"

Twelve

THE PROJECTILE HAD COME TOO CLOSE TO JACK'S FOOT. HIS heart hammered. He scanned the thick brush, working his tongue in a mouth that had suddenly gone dry. Whoever hid among the rocks was good. He could detect no movement. Save for the absent birds, he would've had no warning.

The shooter could be anyone—Deputy Marshal Seamus Belew, Bittercreek, another posse member, or even Darius Guthrie still hunting Nora. Take your pick.

Sawyer's thin body shook, and he sniffled quietly. Without shifting his gaze from the rocky hill, Jack put his free arm around him. "Don't be afraid, son. I won't let anyone hurt you. Or Nora."

Nora moved against him and whispered, "Who do you think it is?"

"I don't know. I'm going to have to take a look. You and Sawyer stay here and keep out of sight." Jack handed her Dollard's Colt, still loaded with Guthrie's extra bullets. "Shoot if you have to."

"Don't worry." Her hand was steady, her grip firm as she took the gun. Jack sensed a new determination, new assurance in her. Maybe it was her need to protect the boy that'd brought on some changes. "Be careful, Jack."

He nodded and crawled through the tall brush, slowly making his way toward the spot where he'd seen the muzzle flash—a stand of mesquite at the foot of the hill. He had to be fast. That rifle shot would bring everyone from miles around, and the place would soon crawl with the posse. He didn't like being separated from Nora and now Sawyer. They depended on him.

The need to hurry pounded in his brain as he reached a tall juniper. He kept a sharp gaze on the brush, searching for movement.

"I told you this wasn't over!" The yell came from Jack's right. The voice was familiar.

Bittercreek.

A chill curled along Jack's spine, and his stomach clenched into a knot. He tightened his grip on the gun. "I couldn't let you starve the boy. Come out and let's get this over with. Your shot is going to bring everyone in three counties. They won't mind finding your hide."

Jack inched his way forward until he spied his quarry a few yards to the left with his horse. Bittercreek hadn't seen him. Jack reached for a rock and threw it over to the right.

When Bittercreek swung and fired at the rock's landing spot, Jack stood. "Drop it."

The man turned, his top lip curling back from his teeth, his rifle pointed at Jack. "Told you we weren't done. I want the boy. He's mine, and I got plans for him."

"Not going to happen. I can see why you need him though. You're one dumb outlaw. It's a mystery to me why they haven't hanged you before now. The kid is a whole lot better than you. He told us what you made him do." Anger washed over Jack, recalling the words. "I ought to kill you for that."

"You would've already done it if you'd had the chance. I'm taking the kid back one way or another."

"No chance in hell." Jack listened for sounds of riders but heard nothing yet. "I'm guessing you have a job you want him to do. Is that about the size of it?"

"I ain't telling you nothing. Tell you what, though. I got an idea that would work for both of us. What say I take him for two more days—treat him real nice—then I'll give him back. I'll be glad to be shed of the boy after that."

"Nope. Drop the weapon." Jack watched Bittercreek's strange yellow eyes narrow into slits, and a thin smile formed.

"Don't think so, Bowdre." The man shouted over his shoulder, "Kid, get the hell out here now or I'll kill him!"

Ice slid down Jack's spine when he saw Nora stealing from the brush, with her gun pointed at the outlaw's back.

What was she doing? He'd told her to stay put. Where was Sawyer? She'd never shot a gun before. What if she missed and hit him? His blood froze. If that happened, both her and Sawyer would fall into Bittercreek's clutches. Jack's heart pounded.

Nora came closer until she stood ten feet away. "Throw the gun down, Bittercreek!"

The outlaw stiffened with surprise and glanced over his shoulder. "Lady, you don't have guts enough to shoot a man."

Not bothering with a reply, Nora fired. She let out a surprised yelp when the force of the .45 propelled her arm up and her rear backward, the gun flying from her hand. The bullet struck Bittercreek below his right shoulder blade. Before Jack could stop him, the man staggered to his horse and leaped into the saddle. Blood had already soaked a good portion of his shirt.

"Hurry!" Nora got to her feet. "The posse's coming. Glimpsed them through the trees."

"Not without the kid."

"He's already ahead of us. We'll catch up to him."

Maybe Nora had saved them, especially if Bittercreek got away. The posse would assume Jack was the one who got shot and follow the blood trail—which would be good if it led in the opposite direction. And if they didn't catch Bittercreek too soon.

He spied Sawyer several hundred yards in front and lengthened his stride, soon catching him. Jack breathed a sigh of relief to have them all together again. The afternoon sunlight added a bit of warmth to the day. No one spoke until they reached a small river about an hour later.

Anger that Jack had held back while they escaped boiled over as he faced Nora. "I told you to stay hidden with Sawyer back there. Why did you come after me?"

"I thought you might need me," she answered hotly. "You're welcome."

"Don't ever do that again. I had it under control." Jack caught Sawyer's worried gaze. He swallowed the rest of his irritation and began counting. He reached forty and kept going.

"Oh for God's sake, Jack." Nora rolled her eyes. "I didn't mean to make you mad. All right? Next time you're on your own. I swear, I don't understand you."

Her shoulders slumped. She started to turn away, and he grabbed her. "If I lost you, I'm not sure if I'd have the strength to rebuild my life again. You're my world. I don't know how it happened in so short a time, but there it is. Maybe being handcuffed together all that while drew us closer, let us get acquainted faster." He lifted a tendril of golden hair. "All I know is that I don't want to ever lose you, lady."

Nora released a sigh. "One day, I promise I'll listen to you. I just had to know what was happening and to do something to help. I saw him holding the gun on you and thought he was seconds from firing. He blocked me from seeing you and your Colt, and I thought I had to act fast."

"Maybe you just bought us more time. We'll see if the posse assumes I was the one shot and take out after Bittercreek."

She blinked twice. "Oh, then I helped. Can you take my gun? I don't want it."

Jack took it from her and stuck it in the waistband of his trousers. Sawyer gave them worried glances from where he stood, skipping stones.

"It's all right, Sawyer," Jack assured him. "Nora and I are just discussing things. Rest here with her while I backtrack a little and get rid of our footprints."

The coltish boy's eyes lit. "I can help, and it won't take long at all. Please?"

Nora gave Jack's hand a little squeeze, and he found himself agreeing. The kid needed to feel useful, and sometimes that helped to heal a spirit.

In short order, they wiped away all traces of them. Jack glanced up at the sky and frowned. The sun had slipped lower, and the town was at least another full day's walking distance. *Damn!* Hope's Crossing seemed to be moving farther away instead of getting closer. They'd lost too much time on Bittercreek. If they just had a horse, they could make it a whole lot faster. The grind was wearing on all of them.

One more night and day of hiding from the posse—and Bittercreek.

They'd have to spend another night under the stars unless he found something. He muttered a low oath. If he were alone, it wouldn't matter so much. But Nora and Sawyer needed a bed and blankets.

They set off again with Jack looking for shelter. The area was riddled with abandoned adobe houses that sheepherders had once lived in when sheep filled the panhandle. All but a few had given up and returned to New Mexico Territory.

Over the next three hours, he kept his eyes peeled for one of those empty dwellings. If they couldn't find an empty one, maybe the folks living there would give them water and food. His throat was parched, and he knew Nora's and Sawyer's were too. As he walked, he listened to their low voices. The boy spoke with longing of his parents and the home he'd left behind.

Jack's eyes misted. He knew from experience how a longing like that could burrow deep inside and wake you from a dead sleep. So did Nora. But it was worse for a kid. Sawyer's memories were fresher and more vivid, and he hadn't learned how to push them away. Jack was glad he'd come with them. They could help the boy make a new life, one he'd be proud to claim.

Alex would've been about Sawyer's age now if he'd lived. Jack couldn't help his son, but he could help see Sawyer grow up strong with good values.

That's all a man like Jack had a right to hope for. Leaving good behind to show his life had counted for something.

Jack's memories of childhood weren't the sort to share—his mother crying, her lip split, her eye black, after Orin Bowdre came home from his latest holdup, drunk and mean. Little food, cold and scared, Jack stayed hidden until Orin sobered up. Until that last time, when he couldn't take anymore. Spoiling for a fight, his rotten father had been like a raging bull. Jack grabbed him by the neck and slung him into an iron pole, then left him lying in his own blood and urine.

Remembrances of violence were all Jack could claim.

The sun had started its downward path toward the horizon when they rounded a large clump of mesquite trees and spied a small soddy ahead. He gave a low cry.

And then he noticed about a dozen sheep and two or three goats at the side of the house. Occupied. Hell!

Nora drew close. "Do you think they'll let us have some food? Sawyer needs to eat. And we all need water."

"Yeah." Jack scanned the thick windows of the mud-brick building. "Stay here." He eyed her sternly and placed his hands on her shoulders. "I mean it. Do not leave this spot. Do not follow me. Do not try to save me or shoot anyone. Got it?"

She gave him a wounded expression and placed her hands on her rounded hips. "I am in full command of the English language, Jack. I know when my help is not appreciated."

Those large, expressive eyes bored into him like they had the day she'd defiantly handcuffed herself to him and tossed away the key. And she'd looked so perfectly innocent then too. Ha! She knew exactly what she was doing to him and wasn't one bit sorry. But right now, as he drowned in the depths of her brown eyes, his thoughts turned to the nights beside a flickering campfire when he'd held her close in his arms, listening to the sound of her gentle breathing, feeling her heart's soft beat, knowing he'd found an uncommon woman.

The breeze ruffled her hair and lifted a strand of silk, laying it across her eyes.

God, she was beautiful. Why would she want an old outlaw like him, who'd end up dead from a bullet or in a hangman's noose?

His breath caught as he brushed the strand of hair from her face and watched the sun's rays fire it to soft gold. Nora Kane made him mad enough to cuss, but despite that, she was worth more than all the glitter in the bottom of a miner's pan.

Headstrong? That was a definite yes, but she didn't run from trouble, and that was something you couldn't buy.

Her eyes twinkled as she raised on her tiptoes to brush her lips across his. He melted and turned quickly away while he was still able.

He met Sawyer's gaze, and the boy gave him a knowing grin.

After leveling both of them with another stern glance, he moved cautiously toward the humble dwelling, surveying the area for signs of trouble.

The closer he got, the more his nerves tied in knots.

Something didn't feel right.

Nothing stirred or made a sound. Even the goats and sheep seemed to have disappeared from the side of the house. The unmistakable odor of blood reached him. Someone was hurt bad. Or dead.

An icy chill formed against his spine, and the hair on his arms prickled as he drew his Colt and slowly approached.

"Hello? Anyone home?" He was met with cold silence. "I wonder if you'd mind sharing your water. Then we'll leave."

The quiet whispered caution and brushed his face with cold, bony fingers.

His pulse raced, and he became acutely aware of each tiny sound, each blade of grass moving, each tense second that ticked by. He tightened his grip on the gun.

The familiar iron tang of blood clung like a horse nettle, refusing to let go. Some sixth sense he'd acquired over the years of riding the outlaw trail told him death had come to someone.

Taking a deep breath, he stepped to the door. "I don't want any trouble. Just water."

The wind abruptly picked up, the sudden gust almost lifting Jack's hat from his head, as though trying to shoo him from the dwelling.

Not before he checked on whoever, whatever, was inside. A faint noise came from beyond the door. A weak kitten? Had someone locked an animal up inside and ridden away?

Jack pressed his ear to the door and turned the knob. The cry came again.

The sound awakened a memory of long ago.
One heartbeat. Two. Then three.
The cry. The tiny hitch in its breath.
This time he recognized the familiar noise.
A baby.

Thirteen

THANK GOODNESS THEY HAD A LITTLE TIME BEFORE THE SUN set. A large knot settled in the center of Nora's chest and clenched until she could barely draw in air. She gripped Sawyer and watched every move Jack made. The tense set of his broad shoulders as he approached the door of the lonely house spoke of wariness, maybe even a dose of fear. What had spooked him?

If anyone was inside, why didn't they open up?

She started to rise, but Jack's stern admonition to stay put echoed in her ears. Going to him was out, but she could still help by keeping watch. Where she crouched in the brush, she could see a wider swath of land and anyone who sought to creep up on them.

"What's happening?" Sawyer fidgeted.

"I'm not sure. Try to be still in case someone is looking out the window."

The next thing she knew, Jack turned the knob and went inside. A second later, he reappeared. "Nora, come quick!"

She rose and sprinted toward the dwelling with Sawyer at her side. She arrived out of breath. "What?"

"Better see." He stepped aside and let her in.

The smell of blood hit her the second she stepped through the door. Her gaze flew to the bed, where a woman lay, her unseeing eyes open, staring up at the ceiling. Blood soaked the feather mattress. At her side lay a crying baby wrapped in only a ragged piece of blanket. The young mother's hand rested on her child as though in comfort during her final moments.

"Oh no!" Nora hurried and picked the infant up, her heart melting. Cradling the babe to her, she unbuttoned her coat and slipped the wool around the tiny, icy limbs. "This child isn't going to make it unless we get it warm and fed right away. It can barely cry."

"My thoughts exactly." Jack gently closed the woman's eyes, took the rosary beads from her other hand, and pulled the old quilt that covered her over her face. "Here, Nora." He handed her the beads.

Nora took the rosary and put it in her pocket. She glanced down at the black-haired infant and its olive skin. She cradled the babe and let her gaze sweep the one-room dwelling, lighting on a display on a shelf with three candles and a small statue of Mother Mary she'd once seen in a church. "What is that, Jack?"

"A traditional family keeps things like this in their home, and it's where they pray. Clearly, the child is of Mexican descent." He crossed to the tiny kitchen area of the one-room house and began rifling through boxes that had once held supplies.

The baby captured Nora's attention. She held it close to take advantage of her body heat and crooned softly. Sawyer remained frozen in the doorway, his eyes wide. "It's all right, Sawyer, honey. Nothing to be afraid of. Jack, have you found anything to use as a bottle?"

"Nothing yet," he called. "Sawyer, can you find a pail and milk one of the goats?"

"Yes, sir." The boy appeared grateful for something to do away from the house—and the dead woman.

Nora hurried to help Jack search. "Doesn't look like much here. I wonder how long this woman's been so far from town. And where is the father? How could he, in all decency, abandon his wife and child?" Nora blinked back tears. How sad that the young mother had to die all alone.

Jack put an arm around her, and she welcomed his strength. "Try not to worry, Nora. We're doing our best here, and don't judge the poor husband yet. He could have a good explanation. I'll try to find him after we get the babe fed and the mother buried."

"If you don't see a glove, how about a clean rag that I can dip in milk and let the child suck on?"

Items flew this way and that as Jack returned to the box and dug to the bottom. "No luck."

"Try the woman's clothes. Maybe she tucked a pair of gloves into a pocket." That sounded like a better idea to her anyway. No woman would normally leave a pair of gloves in the kitchen. But save for one patched dress hanging on a nail with a man's shirt beneath it, she saw no other clothes. In fact, there was very little of anything.

"These people lived with nothing, Jack." The baby's cries were getting weaker. All the jiggling and swaying in the world wouldn't fill an empty stomach or warm a body gone that cold.

"No surprise. Sheepherders are a thrifty lot."

Nora glanced at the woman again, the membrane, cut cord, and bloody knife. "It looks like she could've given birth a few hours ago and then began hemorrhaging. It's a miracle the baby has lasted this long without warmth."

"It's a good thing we happened by." Jack pulled a white glove from the woman's dress pocket. "Found one!"

Sawyer appeared in the door. His face was dirty, his shirt ripped. "Is this enough? Those goats won't keep still."

Jack took the pail. "It's good for now. Thank you, son." He sat the milk on a small table. "I'll see if there's anywhere I can wash this glove, Nora."

"Hurry."

"I saw a small creek behind this house. Not much water in it though," Sawyer offered.

"Thanks, son. It'll have to do." Jack raced out the door with Sawyer following.

The baby occupied Nora's attention. "There, there. We're going to get you fed, little one, and you'll feel much better. Yes, you will." But Nora was anything but sure. She'd never seen any newborn this cold or hungry. She trembled as she tried to think. Then it hit her. Up north, when people fell through a frozen lake, they immersed them in warm water. That was it.

Her hand shook with excitement and she could barely

unbutton her coat. Finally, she managed to get it off and wrapped the babe in it.

"Jack!" She flew out the door. She found him squatted by a trickle of water behind the mud brick house, Sawyer at his side. "Jack!"

He jerked to his feet, his face white. "What's wrong?"

"I need water to heat and put the infant into."

Sawyer rose from his crouch. "I know where another pail is." He raced toward the animals' enclosure.

"Here's the glove. It's as clean as I can get it without soap." Jack caressed her cheek with the back of a knuckle. "We're going to save this child. Believe that with all your heart."

His soft touch gave her strength as she fought back tears. Guilt and painful memories flooded over her. She bit her trembling lip to still it and pushed a terrifying scene into the back of her mind. Now was not the time to relive the past.

Nora nodded. "You're right. We were led here to save this poor, innocent babe, and we're going to give it a fighting chance. Jack, I don't even know if this is a boy or girl. I haven't removed the old quilt."

Sawyer raced back with a pail but went straight to the creek without being told. He was such a dear, sweet boy.

"We have time for that later. Go fill the glove with milk and see if you can get the babe to suckle," Jack said. "I'll come with you and get a fire started."

Nora hurried on to the house, not waiting for Jack, who was instructing Sawyer to release the animals and let them eat. No telling how long they'd been penned. Poor things.

The sight of the covered woman struck Nora with a new bout of immense sorrow as soon as she opened the door. Maybe Jack would carry her out into the fresh air after he got a fire started.

The wet glove was freezing, yet another problem to deal with. Nora ran her free hand over her eyes. The trials just kept coming. To put the warm milk into an icy glove would give the infant a stomachache. The warmest place she knew was inside her dress. She placed the cold, clammy fabric next to her warm skin and moved toward the box of kindling next to the stove.

Jack came in. "Darlin', let me do that. Your hands are full. Where's the glove?"

"Warming inside my coat."

"I'll help you fill the glove, then carry the body outside, but it'll be dark soon. I may have to wait until tomorrow to dig a grave. How are you holding up?" His eyes spoke volumes, and she softened beneath his gaze. She'd never experienced anyone so attuned to her emotions.

"I'm fine." For now. She might tell him later about the source of her grief and the guilt it brought. Of anyone, he'd understand. "I'm worried about the babe. It's too weak to cry now."

"I noticed." A flash of anger deepened the lines around his mouth. "We might be too late to save it. Damn this land!"

His frustration reverberated inside her. Why did life have to be so hard? It took and took.

No words would help, so she kept silent and reached inside her coat for the glove. With her holding one side and him the other, he filled it with milk, then punched a tiny hole in the end of one of the fingers with the tip of his knife. Milk dribbled out onto the babe's little bow mouth. The first drop or two ran out and off the side of its face.

Jack lit some candles, and a glow filled the sheepherder's soddy.

"Come on, sweetheart. Please take this milk." Nora rubbed the baby's soft cheeks with a finger, coaxing the little mouth open. When it did, she slid a mere fingertip of the glove inside. It wasn't the best bottle in the world but would have to do for now. She gently touched the black tendrils of hair and murmured quiet, soothing words.

Sawyer entered with the pail of water and found a large kettle to fill. Then he set it on the fire and held the door for Jack as he carried the dead woman out.

Unshed tears burned the back of Nora's eyes at the life cut short. "Jack, don't let wild animals get her."

"I won't."

After Jack went out, the boy closed the door and stood, undecided—wanting to come closer but afraid he shouldn't.

Nora smiled. "It's all right if you want to watch. The babe won't bite."

"I ain't never seen one so small."

"Your sisters were older then?"

"Yep. Lots bigger. I was the baby of the family and the runt." He unbuttoned his coat and she noticed a deep scrape on his hand that was bleeding.

"You're hurt."

"I tripped with the pail of water. Ain't nothing."

The flickering candlelight played across the boy's freckled face and reddish-brown hair. She wanted to cry. He took his pain inward. Did he feel that he didn't deserve sympathy or that he'd be punished if he complained? His blue eyes held much grief. He'd seen far too much pain in his short life, much of it due to Bittercreek's treatment.

"I'll wash and bandage your injury when I get the baby taken care of."

"I can do it. You're busy." Sawyer went back out.

Jack returned, shrugged out of his duster, and strode to Nora's side. "I put the woman in a shallow hole for now and covered her with rocks. It'll do until morning. How's it coming with the baby?"

"Eating for now. With food, getting nice and warm, and finding something to make a diaper out of, I think the poor darling will be all right. I'm glad we have shelter tonight."

"Me too. I'll carry the blood-soaked mattress outside and try to scrounge up something for us to eat. If only I could get rid of the smell."

Nora chuckled. "Everything reeks, including us. When I get to town, I'm burning these clothes. What I have left is beyond saving. I'd love to take a hot bath and soak for a week. Does this town of yours have a bathhouse?" Guilt washed over her that she'd complain about stinking when the baby's mother was dead.

"Nope, no bathhouse, but we manage just fine." He swept

her hair aside and bent to kiss the nape of her neck. "I'll make sure you have everything you need, darlin'."

The light in his gray eyes drew a shiver of longing. Just a day or two and they'd be married. She found the idea very appealing. "Anywhere with you is heaven to me, Jack. Never feel like you have to make things perfect for me. I gave up on perfect quite a while ago."

The water had finished heating by the time the babe quit taking any more milk. Nora unwrapped the baby's frail body. "She's a girl, Jack. A little girl. Think of a pretty name, Sawyer."

Sawyer glanced up. "My sister was Willow. I kinda like that name. She hugged me a lot."

"Then Willow it is." Jack's gruff voice didn't fool Nora. Sawyer's wistful words had touched him and maybe brought back a memory.

"I agree." Nora tested the temperature of the water, then eased Willow's cold body into it.

Her little eyes were open, and even though she couldn't see very far yet, she looked up into Nora's face. Something turned over in Nora's chest, a protectiveness she'd never felt before. She knew in that moment she'd give her life for this innocent baby girl.

She started to tell Sawyer to come watch the bath but noticed he'd curled up in a corner, asleep.

"Jack, what's your best guess about Willow's father? He almost had to have met with some catastrophe to leave his wife. From the way we found them, she must have been alone during the birth." Nora felt Jack's hand on her shoulder and glanced up. "Maybe there was no father—at least not here. Maybe she lived all alone."

"Anything is possible. Try not to let your mind go to dark places." Jack rolled up a sleeve and slipped his hand into the water and laid it on baby Willow. His fingers, his hand, appeared so large resting on the baby's small chest. "She's tiny, but she's a fighter. My son was too, up until the end. I think of all the things I did wrong, all the regrets. If I'd only been there instead of riding off, following the bastards' trail. I didn't realize they'd doubled back until I was too far out. I should've saved my wife and son."

"What was that you said about not letting your mind go to dark places? What is done cannot be changed." She squeezed his big hand under the water and noticed the corded muscles in his arms. She'd only seen him a few times without his duster and sleeves rolled up.

How could he be so big and yet so gentle?

"You're right. I never was too good about taking my own advice."

His nearness aroused a slew of tingles and flutters inside her. She wondered if that would change after they settled into married life. For all she knew, the magic would evaporate like mist on water. She doubted it though.

They had enough magic to last a lifetime, in her estimation. Magic and trust.

"Jack, I want to tell you something."

Fourteen

THE TROUBLED PITCH IN NORA'S LOW VOICE CAUGHT JACK'S attention. What else could she have to tell?

"What is it?" With his hand in the water resting on baby Willow, Jack let his shoulder brush Nora's—a slight pressure that let her know he was there for her.

The newborn yawned and closed her eyes, seeming warm enough now.

"Finding Willow and her mother brought back a horrible memory." Her voice dipped even lower, and her lip trembled. "I must've been at Flynn O'Brien's two years when this happened. Best as I can recall, I was sixteen. Muffled screams woke me, so I crept to the door and looked out. Not seeing anything, I stepped into the dim hallway. I dared not go any farther, because I'd been warned not to come near the basement where the screams came from. A door at the far end that led below jerked opened and Flynn stomped out, holding a wailing baby. Not a newborn. I'm guessing it was probably about a month or two old. I'll never forget the look of rage on his face. He brought the child to me and shoved it into my arms, ordering me to get rid of it."

"The bastard! What did he expect you to do? Smother it?"

"I asked him that question, and he said he didn't care— just that the baby boy had better not be there when he woke up."

Jack took her hand under the warm water and gave it a little squeeze.

"I was shaking from head to toe, so scared. I took the child into my room and rocked him to sleep, then I dressed and wrapped him up. I snuck out of the house and carried him to a church not far from where I lived, left him inside on the altar." Her anguished words were broken. "I never knew...what happened to him…or his mother. Flynn told me if I breathed a word to anyone, he'd silence me."

"At least you tried to give the child some kind of start. I'm sure the boy is grateful that someone saved him. You never heard anything about where the kid had come from?"

"No, and I was too afraid to ask questions. I knew Flynn to be a man of his word. And now the memory I had buried so long ago came storming back." She rested her head on his shoulder. "I'm tired, Jack, real tired of having his voice in my head, tired of remembering the screams, the blood, the terror. If only I could go to sleep and wake up with everything erased."

"You're safe here. I won't let any monsters have you." He took his hands from the water and kissed her temple. "The water's getting cold. I'll heat what's left, and we'll put Willow in again, then try to feed her more."

She raised her troubled gaze to his. "Jack, do you think I'm a bad person for not trying harder to get away, for not telling anyone what went on in that house, for not doing more?"

The tears bubbling in her eyes made his chest tighten. "No, you're not a bad person."

"You're not either, Jack." She wrapped the baby back in the old quilt.

He thought of Gus Franklin and the family the man had murdered. But for Jack, they'd be alive.

"A lot of folks would disagree." He put the cold water onto the stove and added more wood. "We do our best, hope it's good enough, and try not to worry about the rest." He wished he could follow his own advice. Hell! "I have memories that haunt me also."

"It helps to talk."

"Maybe one day." He moved to a trunk hidden in the shadows and opened it. "Nora, I found a small stack of baby things and two large, frayed blankets for us."

"Oh thank goodness. I was wondering what we'd use."

He stuck the tiny clothes under an arm and tucked one of the blankets around Sawyer, who mumbled in his sleep, saying he'd be good.

Damn this life! It was hard on adults but devastating for kids, especially those left alone with no one to protect them.

Laying the few diapers and clothes on the bed, he went over plans for the next day. "I'll bury the mother, then head to a trading post two or three miles from here to see if they might have a bottle. I hate to leave you behind."

"I'll be fine. We have to have a better way of feeding Willow. I'll keep one of the guns just in case. If you move the sheep and goats away from the house, any passersby will think it's abandoned."

"Of course. I'll find a place to hide them."

He loved her quick mind and the sound of her voice. She was the kind of wife any man would be proud to have. When the water grew warm enough, he took it from the stove and made another bath for Willow. When that one cooled, he held the baby while Nora dried her off.

"I feel a lot better about her chances, Jack. Her skin is pink now and she has milk in her belly. Can you hand me one of the diapers?"

He brought it to her along with a soft gown. "At least the young mother had collected a few things."

"I thought she must have. She had plenty of warning."

While Nora dressed and fussed over the baby, Jack went outside to check on things and scrounge up something to eat. The odds of finding food, short of slaughtering one of the sheep, which would be too complicated and messy, were slim and none.

Darkness had fallen, and creatures of the night were rustling through the brush near the house. His thoughts were in a turmoil. He had to warn Nora not to get attached in case the baby's father returned, but he wasn't sure how to find the words.

There was no mistaking the love on her face. It was in her voice, her touch, each tender glance. That tiny girl had found a firm place in Nora's heart. To have Willow ripped from her arms would destroy her.

Maybe, in some small way, in saving Willow, she believed she could atone for not doing enough to stop Flynn O'Brien.

The sounds of the night settled around his shoulders. He listened to the wind but heard only sighs, not screams of warning, and relaxed.

A faint cluck reached him, drawing him to the back of the house. It had to be a chicken. Few sounds were similar. He inched forward, the noise getting louder. There, bedded down in the tall grass, sat three chickens. That meant there had to be eggs. Jack lifted up the hens one by one and ended up with seven eggs. He was grinning when he went inside.

Providing for his family made a man feel real good, and seeing the smile on Nora's face put a glow in his heart.

Now that Willow was fed, warm, and dry, she slept while they fixed supper. The smell of food must've woken Sawyer, and the kid almost beat the sparse meal to the table. Jack didn't miss how his and Sawyer's portions were larger than Nora's.

"Don't do with less for me. Got that?" Jack raked some of his onto her plate to make them even.

"A man needs more food than a woman," she protested.

"We're equals. Got that? Same amount of food."

Nora nodded and lifted her fork. "What are our plans after tomorrow?"

"I figure we should stay here for a couple of days to see if Willow's father shows up and let the infant gain more of a toehold on life."

Sawyer glanced up from his tin plate. "He's probably dead."

That death would be Sawyer's first thought hit Jack like a sledgehammer. That should be the last thing on a nine-year-old's mind.

"Try to look at the bright side. He might've gone hunting. There's nothing here to eat but his flock and the laying hens. We'll see what the coming days bring." Jack shoved in the last bite and laid down his fork. "I'll kill one of the chickens tomorrow, and we'll have a good supper. I have a couple of dollars tucked away, and it'll be enough to buy us a few things. I might do a little hunting with the bow and arrow along the way. It'll be quiet."

"Can I come?" Sawyer asked.

Jack met Nora's gaze and got her nod. It was best if they started deciding these things together. "You can come." Jack carried his plate to the tub to be washed and Sawyer followed close on his heels. "Did your parents teach you to clear your plate from the table, son?"

"Nope. That was what you did, so I did too. I don't want to mess up."

Jack put his hands on the boy's shoulders. "You're not going to mess up. And if you do, we're not going to get rid of you, so get that out of your head. It's good to help Nora however you can though. She has her hands full."

"I will." The boy lay down on the rough plank floor and pulled the blanket around him.

"I'm going to go out for a bit, Nora." Jack slipped his long duster on.

Worry sprang into her brown eyes. "Is something wrong?"

"I just need to make sure no one has caught wind of us. I won't be long." He kissed her cheek and slipped out into the night.

The air held a chill. He shivered and tugged his collar up, his gaze moving left and right, searching for anything out of the ordinary. He'd been lucky for too long and could sense the posse's noose tightening.

They'd made it to within one day's walk of Hope's Crossing, but would they live to see the town?

Not that he thought the posse would shoot Nora and the children, but a stray bullet could find them in a gunfight. Danger lurked around them. Darius Guthrie, Bittercreek, and Seamus Belew wanted him so damn bad he could taste it.

They waited for him to make a mistake. Searching. Ready to pounce.

These last miles to the town were going to be the hardest of all because everyone would be gathered right here, determined to keep him from reaching home. They knew he was getting close so were likely homing in on their location even now.

If he could just reach Hope's Crossing and block the single entrance, they'd stand a chance.

Yet he could almost feel the burning path of the bullet that would end him, end everything; smell the gunpowder, taste death.

It was coming.

Jack shook his head to clear it, released a heavy sigh, and began to haunt the night. Moving silently through the brush, he made two wide circles around the house but saw no sign of encroachers. Good. Maybe he was being overly cautious.

The door opened behind him and Nora stepped from the house, pulling her coat around her. "See anything?"

"No. The children asleep?"

"For now. Willow will wake soon for more milk though. I think babies eat every few hours during the first months."

He drew her into his arms and she rested her head on his chest. "I'll take a shift. I doubt I'll sleep much anyway. Too jumpy."

"I appreciate that." She motioned to the darkness. "What's got you spooked?"

"Nothing more than a feeling that won't turn loose." He tightened his hold around her, and she slid her arms around his waist. The feel of her body next to him settled his nerves a little. "We've barely had time to talk since Sawyer came with us. Are you all right?"

"Why wouldn't I be?"

"I know how deeply finding this dead woman and Willow affected you."

"It's just so sad to think of her dying all alone and never knowing if someone would save her baby. That had to lie heavy on her mind as she passed. As a woman, I can't imagine anything more devastating." Nora tilted her face to look at him. "To leave my baby would tear my heart out. Or to have my child taken from me, as your son was. The pain, the rage, the jagged hole where once your family was." She inhaled sharply. "I don't know how you manage."

"One day at a time." He wouldn't mention the nights he'd lain awake, tormented and stuck in grief. Even if he were able, telling her that would serve no purpose.

"I have this horrible premonition that we're not going to make it, Jack. I think they're coming."

So did he, but he couldn't let her lose hope. He took her face between his hands and tenderly pressed his lips to her forehead. "We have to hold on and believe. Do that for me."

"I'll try, but that's all I can promise."

The quiet, as clear and sharp as spun glass, drifted between them. Jack held Nora and searched for the right words.

When he spoke, his voice was raspy. "You need to prepare yourself for the possibility that Willow's father could show up and take her. Don't get too attached."

"It's too late, Jack. I already love that little girl as though she's my own child." Her soft words confirmed what he already knew. "For whatever reason, her father might not come, but if he does, I doubt he'll want the responsibility of a baby. He might want someone to take her."

"Don't confuse wishful thinking with fact."

Nora raised her head and met his gaze, her fingers lightly caressing his stubbled jaw. "I'll deal with that when the time comes. Meanwhile, I'll give baby Willow the mother she doesn't have. I can't close my heart to her. I'm sorry. I just won't."

"I know." He rested his chin on top of her head and tightened the warm cocoon he made with his arms. She felt everything so deeply—hurt, pain, love—and maybe that was one of the many things he adored about her. There were no half measures with this woman he'd soon marry. She was either all or nothing.

Nora wiggled away from him, unbuttoned her coat, then his, and pressed her warm body against him. He drew his duster around her and held her as though there were no tomorrows.

And no killers lying in wait somewhere in the dark.

"Much better." She snuggled again in his arms. "I need to feel you next to me without the bulky layers of fabric between us." She pressed her lips to the hollow of his throat. "I wish we were somewhere safe. I'd just be getting out of a long, hot bath. You would've already taken yours, and the heat in your eyes would devour me. You'd scoop me up in your arms and carry me to a soft bed." She opened the top buttons of his shirt and kissed his chest. "I'd strip off your clean clothes and run my hands over every inch of you."

Jack chuckled and picked up the fantasy. "Then, I'd light a fire inside you and make you my wife."

"Someone we trust would look after the children, so we could touch and whisper and kiss to our hearts' content."

"And I'd leave no doubt in your pretty little head about who you belong to," Jack finished.

He tenderly caressed the sweep of her high cheekbone, the line of her jaw, the long column of her throat. Visions of them naked burst inside his head—warm and clean, the sheets tangled around their legs. Her silken body made for loving lying next to him.

Nora reminded him of a summer storm. Thunder and lightning crashed all around, but her center was dead calm, a place where a man could find respite from the turmoil and daily struggle to survive. If only he'd lived a better life and hadn't dragged her into trouble with him.

"Jack," she whispered, running her hands across his back, kissing his jaw.

His need for her flared. He lowered his mouth and drank of her passion, tasted the velvet warmth of her mouth, listened to the mewling cry coming from her that spoke of the same heat.

Liquid fire raced through his blood and scorched a path along his limbs, creating a pool of molten need in his belly. His heartbeat pounded in his temples, drowning out everything except the hunger that demanded fulfillment.

In this harsh land, where the next moment could put you in a grave, a man had to take whatever solace he could.

Nora wound her arms around his neck and clung as if he would save her from drowning.

Damn the clothes still between them!

If only he could slide his hands along her skin, down those luscious curves that drove him mad. Shifting his feet, he trailed his fingers down her throat where her pulse beat. There in the tiny hollow, he pressed a kiss.

"I want you, lady," Jack growled. "You drive me out of my head, the way your hips sway like a river current and that funny little tilt of your head you have. You're all I think about."

Nora's smile and teasing nibble of her lips set his heart thrumming. "This may sound crazy, and if so, I don't care. I want us to say our vows to each other. Right now. Right here, tonight. We don't know what else lies ahead and we may not ever reach Hope's Crossing. Will you say yours to me?"

The request jarred him. But why not? She had a point, and if he could offer her his name, such as it was, he'd do it. Maybe the little extra security would at least help her weather the storm that was bearing down on them.

"If that's what you want. It'll probably be as binding as any ceremony Ridge Steele would've performed."

At Nora's nod, he took her hands, staring deeply into her eyes cloaked in shadow. Nerves set in as he wiped a dark smudge off the tip of her nose. He'd never wanted anyone more than her, his woman that he'd sent for and agreed to marry. He'd gotten a prize. She had a spine of steel, arms that ached to hold children, and a heart that burst with zest for living.

Inhaling deeply, he tried to steady his jitters. He blew out some air. "Here goes. I, Jack Bowdre, vow to provide, protect, and cherish you, Nora Kane. I'll do my best to be a husband you can be proud of for all my remaining days and give you all my worldly possessions, pitiful though they may be. I want to grow old with you, sleep beside you, and dream of a happy future." He dropped her hands and lightly placed his on each side of her throat. "I will care for you however long I live. That's about all, I guess."

He hadn't mentioned love. That wasn't part of the deal. He did find pleasure in sleeping next to her and sharing the days. But love? He could never give his heart to another woman. After Rachel, there wasn't enough of it left.

"My turn." Nora laid her hand over his heart, and the small weight warmed him. "I, Lenora Kane, solemnly pledge to be faithful to you, have undying devotion, and to find a bright side even when there isn't one. I'll stand by your side and hand you the bullets. I'll have your back, and I'll never steal the covers—unless you're hogging them. My love for you is eternal, a light for all the world to see. We'll make a formidable team. If you get arrested again, I'll search for a key until I find one. I'll be steady and true, the best wife I know how. This I pledge, Jack Bowdre."

He captured her slightly parted lips, slipping his arms inside her coat, rubbing her back. As the kiss deepened, he slid his hand to her waist, then rested it on her plump behind. Stirrings of wanting and something deeper swept through him. Somehow, he felt as married as he had with Rachel. Nora and her unusual vows would always remain in his heart.

But would they be enough to hold them together when the law caught up with him and Nora got the full list of his crimes? Especially the mistake he had to live with daily—the decision that had led to the deaths of a dozen innocent lives.

Then, without a preacher or witnesses to hold them accountable, would her pretty vows fly off into the sunset?

Fifteen

NORA SLEPT IN JACK'S ARMS ON THE BOX BED THAT HAD NO mattress. Her dreams were frightening, and in one of them, she desperately clutched Willow while a man tried to pull her away. His appearance sent terror into the marrow of her bones, a skull in place of a head and a gruesome smile. Then he turned away and grabbed Sawyer.

"No, you can't have them!" Nora bolted upright, swinging her fists.

"Wake up, Nora, you're dreaming." Jack shook her. "It's only a dream, darlin'."

"It was so real." She rubbed her eyes to rid herself of the image.

"What's wrong?" Sawyer raised from his bed. "Are we in danger?"

"No, son. It's just me having a nightmare. Go back to sleep." Nora turned to face Jack, lowering her voice. "I'm sorry to wake everyone. I dreamed that Willow's father came and was trying to pull her from my arms. The feeling that I was losing that precious baby was one that will stay with me for a long time."

"You're trembling." He pulled her against him and held her. "It's going to be all right. Whatever comes, we'll face it together."

She met his lips and found strength in the kiss. Slowly, her fears eased, replaced by a deep longing to be Jack's wife in every way. She wanted to feel him inside her, run her hands over his body, taste his skin.

And if possible, she would bear him some children. He'd been alone and unloved for such a long time. But no more.

"Did we actually say our vows?" she mumbled against his mouth.

"We did."

She cupped her palm on the side of his face and stared into his gray eyes. "I love you, Jack."

Just then, Willow let out a cry. Jack held Nora back when she started to get up. "You rest. It's my turn to feed her."

"I guess it is. If you need my help, holler." She lay back on the hard bed and watched how tenderly he picked Willow up, crooning softly to her.

If someone hadn't ripped his wife and son from him, he'd never have taken up the outlaw trail. He loved family too much. He cradled the baby girl in his large hands and, though his face was bathed in shadows, she could see how the hard lines softened. Then he bent his head and kissed the tiny face. Tears sprang into Nora's eyes. He was going to make an unbelievable father, filled with compassion and love enough to raise strong men and women.

Only…would he get to?

The first line of his vows drifted into her mind. *I, Jack Bowdre, vow to provide, to protect, to cherish you, Nora Kane.*

Though he'd mentioned nothing about love, a happy glow filled her. That would come later. For the first time since her parents' death, she'd finally found someone who wanted her for herself.

She drifted off with the sight of Jack feeding and burping the baby. When she opened her eyes, a pink dawn was peeking in the corner of the window, and Jack still sat in the chair at the small table holding Willow. His Colt rested on the tabletop, within easy reach as always. He was asleep with his head on his chest. Nora sucked in a breath, the sight warming her heart.

Jack Bowdre might be a big, tough outlaw, riding the plains and dispensing his brand of justice, but put a tiny babe in his arms, and he was every bit a gentle cowboy.

She rose and noticed that Sawyer was missing. Panic raced through her. She hurried to the door and opened it.

The creak of the hinges woke Jack. He grabbed his Colt. "What's wrong?"

"Sawyer is gone. I'm going to find him." Nora stepped into

the brisk morning air and relaxed when the boy came from around the side of the house.

He grinned and held up a pail. "I milked the goats."

Jack moved behind Nora. He'd lain the baby down. "You didn't have to do that, son."

"I know, but I wanted to." Sawyer handed Nora the full pail. "I thought Willow might need it—and I'm hungry too. Do you think that maybe…maybe you can make some gravy?"

Nora's heart broke. The kid seldom asked for anything. "I'll see if I can find some flour, and you will have your gravy. A biscuit to go with it too, if we're lucky."

Jack draped an arm around Sawyer. "I saw a little flour last night in a tin when I was looking for that glove. Let's see if the chickens laid more eggs or if I overlooked other hens last night."

She hurried inside to do some hunting of her own—and to make a bit of coffee, if she could locate some of that too. The flour was easy to find, but she was about to give up the search for coffee when she spied another tin, this one smaller, way back in a corner. Nora reached for it and found dark coffee beans. A grinder sat next to the stove in a box that also held a tin of baking powder. The tiny bit left in the bottom was just enough for some biscuits.

By the time Sawyer and Jack came inside with a half dozen eggs from a nest he'd overlooked before, she had coffee boiling and biscuits in the oven.

Jack sniffed the air, his gray eyes twinkling. "I think you must be an angel." His lazy gaze moved over her body and heat swept through her.

"I'm simply a wife who guesses what her man likes."

"Indeed." He slid his arms around her and nuzzled her neck. Nora caught Sawyer rolling his eyes. The boy only wanted food, and the sooner the better.

Willow woke with a cry that quickly grew insistent.

She gave Jack a playful shove. "Whatever am I going to do with you?"

Teasing glints sparkled in his eyes. "I could suggest a few things."

Heat swept along Nora's body like some wildfire, scorching everything in its path. "I'm quite sure you could."

Flustered, she grabbed a skillet and put it on a burner, then cracked the eggs. Sawyer went outside with Jack to wait for breakfast. Only then could she examine her feelings about him. The more time they spent together, the more Jack loosened up and allowed himself to feel. She understood better about his life and the kind of marriage they'd have.

Yet there were things he still couldn't bring himself to share with her.

Maybe one day he could. Until then, she'd love him and be the wife she knew she could be.

When breakfast was ready, she called them in and they ate their fill for once.

"Thank you for making biscuits and gravy, Nora," Sawyer said. "They taste like Mama's."

"I'm glad you approve." Nora leaned to kiss his cheek.

After they finished eating, and Jack had buried the young mother, he entered the soddy with a dead chicken.

Nora glanced up and spoke over the baby's wails. "Jack, I don't know what's wrong. I've tried everything, and she won't hush."

"Tell me what you tried."

Nora rocked the baby. "She refuses to take milk and hasn't since early this morning. I changed her and she's dry, so it's not that. I don't know if she's sick or has developed an aversion to the taste of the glove or what."

He laid his hand on the child's quivering body and face. "No fever. It must be the glove then. I'll go after a bottle." He handed her the extra gun. "Don't be afraid to use this."

"I won't. Please be careful."

"It may just be colic. Rub her back and it might release a burp." He gave Nora a light kiss. "Sawyer and I will be back soon."

She grabbed his hand before he turned away. "Are we

doing the right thing? Do you think we should bundle her up good and start toward Hope's Crossing instead of staying here another night?"

"Darlin', it's too far, and this baby is too fragile for the cold night in the open." He brushed a finger across her cheek. "The trading post is only an hour or so away. I'll go there and get a proper bottle. If that doesn't work, we'll head for the town. But I'm wasting time now."

"I know. Hurry, Jack." She clutched Willow's sobbing body and prayed that they could figure out what was horribly wrong.

"Please, God, let Willow be all right." If He granted that, she wouldn't ask for anything more.

The door closed behind him. Her rocking, swaying motion carried her and Willow to the window. She watched Sawyer and her new husband stride toward the outpost with a list—or as much as Jack's two dollars would buy. The day had turned nice and sunny, and he'd removed his duster. She drank up the sight of his tall, lean figure, his heavy Colt hanging at his side, and prayed both her husband and the boy would make it back to her.

"My husband." The words felt right on her tongue.

She'd found a home, family, and purpose here in the wilds of Texas.

❧

Jack kept a wary eye out for trouble and avoided the trail. The rugged landscape made for slow going, even though they were making good time. Sawyer stayed silent and at his side. The boy seemed to know when to speak and when to hold his tongue. That was rare in one so young. His son, Alex, had rattled on all the time about something or another. Jack wondered if he'd made a wrong decision by letting Sawyer come, but he welcomed the quiet company.

A flock of buzzards circled in the sky, drawing his attention. The scavenger birds always gathered where something died.

They climbed down a steep gully to investigate, and Jack

was the first to see the body draped over a large boulder. A group of birds feasting on the remains squawked at him in protest and flapped their large wings before slowly taking flight.

From the purple face and bloated corpse, the man must've been dead for three or four days.

Sawyer fidgeted. "Who do you think that is?"

"I don't know." Jack surveyed the scene—a woven basket at the man's feet, sacks of flour and meal busted open on the ground. A blanket of lamb's wool like one for a newborn was clenched in the man's fist.

Moving his gaze to the top of the gully, Jack noticed the broken limbs of the brush. Everything there told a story. The man must've lost his balance and fallen. There was no sign of a struggle, no other footprints. It was simply a tragic accident.

"Is that Willow's father?" Sawyer asked.

"Appears so. Looks like he took a tumble from up top."

Jack placed the dead man in a depression in the ground, and he and Sawyer covered him with rocks. It was the best they could do.

They set off again, and an hour later, the outpost came into sight. He waited another thirty minutes in the brush, watching, getting a sense of the place. It had a new owner these days, one who'd arrived after Jack's old friend, Pete, had met up with a bullet one dark night.

Neither of the horses tied to the hitching rail looked familiar.

Finally, sensing that the coast was clear, he and Sawyer approached. Jack eyed the two horses with longing as they walked past. Those animals would get them safely to Hope's Crossing. He felt Sawyer's gaze on him and glanced over to see disappointment in the boy's eyes. Shame filled Jack that he'd even considered taking the horses. Hell! He'd slipped several places in Sawyer's high esteem of him.

"I was just trying to see if I recognized them is all, son." Jack put his arm around Sawyer, and they stepped inside the store.

Two rough-looking men wearing buffalo robes played cards at a small table near the back.

"Morning, gentlemen." The clerk smiled from behind the counter. "What can I get you?"

"A small sack of flour, lard, baking powder, and..." Jack lowered his voice. "Would you happen to have a baby bottle?"

The two men playing cards snickered. Jack shot them a glance and they hushed.

"Don't get much call for one of those. But I do have families traveling through and stopping, wanting all sorts of stuff. Let me see." The clerk bit back whatever else he was going to say and began rifling through some boxes. Finding nothing, he pulled out a drawer and held up a bottle. "Found one. I'll fill the rest of your list."

Sawyer wandered over to the gumdrops. "Throw in some of that candy too," Jack instructed the clerk. The boy rewarded Jack with a grin.

The seediest man at the table shifted. "Where did you say you're from, mister?"

Jack tensed and met Sawyer's worried gaze. "Didn't."

The air crackled in the store and Jack watched the two through narrowed eyes. Both were about his age, but he'd never seen them before. He knew their kind, though. They were vultures, living off what they could steal. They waited for the right moment to make their move, then jumped in to pick the bones clean.

"Nope, don't reckon you did." The man turned to his companion. "Joe, who did that posse say they're looking high and low for?"

"Some fellow named Jack Bowdre. Mister, you'd best keep an eye open. They say he's a killer and took a woman hostage when he escaped. I speculate he's slit her throat by now." Joe picked his teeth with the tip of a knife. "Better keep that gun of yours handy in case you cross his trail. They have a reward out—one thousand dollars, dead or alive. Ain't that right, Toad?"

"Yep, that's right. No missus with you, mister?"

"Just me and the boy." Jack draped an arm around Sawyer's neck and whispered, "Stay close."

The one named Toad stood. "I'd sure like to claim that reward. Yes, siree."

Jack shrugged. "Well, who knows? You'll have to play your cards right."

"Some say Bowdre is sure enough quick with his gun." Joe stuck his knife into a sheath hanging on his belt. He also wore a pistol in his holster.

"You don't say?" Jack turned toward the clerk and was relieved to see him wrapping his purchases. The sooner they left the better. Joe and Toad either recognized him or they suspected who he was. "Sawyer, wait outside."

"Okay." The kid walked to the door and went out.

Jack knew he could take both men, but he didn't want Sawyer in the middle of it. At least if shooting started, he was out of harm's way.

"Of course, no outlaw like Bowdre would be risking his hide for a…baby bottle." Joe snickered, leaning back his chair. "Nope. Not some stupid thing like a baby bottle. You got a wife and a young'un, mister?"

"How much do I owe you?" Jack asked the clerk, ignoring the two rabble-rousers. No one would bait him into drawing his gun. He drew it for one reason only—self-defense. And when he drew it, someone usually died.

The clerk tallied the bill and Jack counted out the money.

"Be careful out there, mister. Danger is all around," the clerk warned in a low voice. "Including those two over there. They're spoiling for a fight. Been drinking most of the day."

"Thanks." Jack tucked his purchases under his arm. "Say, do you know a young couple living in a sheepherder's soddy not far from here?" He described them.

"They came in off and on over the last few months, but I didn't get a name. The woman was in the family way. They'd buy flour and sugar, mostly. That's all I know."

"Okay, thanks." Jack kept a wary eye on the two men at the table.

Their cold, calculating gazes sent a warning to his clenched gut. The tense air rippled with danger, raising the hair on

Jack's neck as he backed slowly to the door. One slow step at a time, keeping his gun hand free.

A guttural growl came from the table, but the men stayed seated.

He reached the door without incident, collected Sawyer, and they hurried toward the little house where Nora waited. They ducked into a gully not far from the trading post to watch. If the two hunters in the store followed, he'd have to kill them.

He wouldn't take trouble to Nora.

To hold her in his arms again would erase all the lonely days and nights when his heartbeat had been the only sound to break the silence in his head.

The thought of holding her, sleeping beside her, caring for her, sent heat through his body.

They'd dream of their life together and plan.

If this was real, he'd be as happy as a man could ever expect.

Only life had taught him not to count on tomorrow. Or even the next hour.

Sixteen

THE BABY FINALLY CRIED HERSELF TO SLEEP. NORA WRAPPED
the moth-eaten blanket around her and laid her on the hard
box bed, then plucked the chicken and put it in a pot to cook.

She felt so grimy. Maybe Willow would sleep for a while
and she could wash a bit at the creek. Even getting the dirt off
her face and arms would help. She gazed down at her dirty,
torn clothes, wishing she had something else to wear. But one
look at the dress hanging on the nail and she could tell it was
too small. Even though she'd lost a few pounds since the stage
wreck, her curves were still far too generous.

Feeling along her hem, she found the book of numbers and
names she'd risked her life for and pulled it out. Some instinct
told her to hide it in the house—just in case. There were too
many people hunting them for the ledger to be safe. She could
always come back for it later. Spying a loose board on the floor
where the table sat, she lifted it and stuck the book into the
cavity, then placed the chair over it. There, that should keep
it from falling into the wrong hands.

Before she could head for the creek, Willow woke, again
crying. Nora changed her, but she wouldn't hush or take milk.

"There, there, little one." She glanced around for something
besides the glove and grabbed the thin flour sack she'd used as
a dish towel. It wasn't the cleanest in the world, but maybe it
would work. "If only Jack would hurry," she whispered.

She dipped the cloth in the milk and Willow sucked at the
soft cotton fabric. *Yes!*

Although it was very slow, she at last got enough into the
baby to satisfy her hunger temporarily, and she drifted back
off to sleep. Nora patted her small back, loving how Willow
cuddled against her shoulder. After Willow burped, Nora laid
her down and covered her, then hurried around to the creek.

Midafternoon, she glanced anxiously in the direction Jack and Sawyer had taken. They should be back soon—unless trouble had found them. But only the tall grass moved on the distant horizon.

Maybe Willow's mother had waited anxiously in vain for her husband just like this, never seeing him again.

"Hurry, Jack. Please come home to me." But no voice answered back.

The chicken soup had finished cooking and was cooling on the table by the time she heard Jack's call. She rushed to the door, her heart leaping with joy to see him walking toward her with long, confident strides and Sawyer with his shorter ones. From the looks of it, Jack's leg wasn't hurting a lot from the walk either. Praise be.

She hurried to meet them. "What kept you? I was getting worried."

"We found a dead man," Sawyer blurted.

Nora slipped an arm around Jack's waist. He ran the backs of his knuckles lightly across her cheek. "Who was he?"

Jack pulled a lamb's wool blanket from his shirt. "I'm almost positive he was Willow's father. It looked like he fell into a steep gully and landed on the rocks. He must have been coming back from the trading post. I guessed that by a few staples lying nearby, along with a woven basket."

Sawyer took their purchases into the house, as though sensing they needed to be alone.

"The mystery is solved." Nora inhaled a deep breath. "That poor baby girl in there is an orphan. She's ours now."

Jack tenderly brushed a tendril of hair from Nora's eyes and kissed her. His touch melted her, and her knees trembled. This lean outlaw had the uncanny ability to make her weak with a single crooked grin.

"Woman, I'd do most anything in the world for you." He studied her, his face somber. "You know that, don't you?"

"Yes."

"Lord knows I wish I could, but I can't let you believe that we can keep this baby girl. We owe it to Willow to try to find her kin first."

Tears blurred Nora's vision. "Jack, don't you realize how impossible that would be? We don't even have her mother's last name to start with. How can we find her relatives without some information? Even if you put up handbills in nearby towns, how would we know they're who they say? I won't let Willow go with just anybody."

"True. But if anyone comes looking for a couple of sheep-herders, we have to speak up."

"Of course. I wouldn't dream of keeping Willow a secret."

With a quick nod, he brushed his lips across her temple, and she clung to him, not wanting to let him go. "How is she?" he asked.

"She's sucking milk from a piece of flour sack, refusing the glove. Did you get a bottle?"

"Yep." He lowered his voice. "We may have more trouble though. Two men from the trading post tried to force a show-down. They asked if I was Bowdre and made no bones about the fact that they want the reward money."

"Oh, Jack." She clutched his hand, her stomach knotting. "Maybe we should leave tonight and try to make Hope's Crossing ahead of them."

"This night chill wouldn't be good for the baby or Sawyer. We'll leave come daylight."

"All right. I trust your instincts." Nora kissed his cheek. "I missed you, Jack. I'm finding it hard to think about anything but you."

He gave her a wisp of a smile and drew in a ragged breath. "You've ruined me, lady."

The declaration, the man, the feeling that washed over her made Nora's pulse race. It seemed like there was nothing but the two of them in the entire world. She sucked in a breath, melting into him.

A slow sizzle began at her toes and ran the length of her body like some kind of current.

His gaze settled on her mouth, and the late afternoon grew increasingly warm. His gray eyes twinkling, he kissed her upturned lips, and the familiar heat she'd come to embrace raced along her limbs. This man she'd married beneath the stars made her feel like the luckiest woman on earth, and as treasured as a piece of fine bone china.

The powerful arms securing her were strong and capable and there was no place she'd rather be. He pushed her dress aside where the buttons were missing and caressed her skin. An unexpected stirring made her stomach dip as though she'd been thrown from a horse.

The scent of his sweat mixed with sagebrush and mesquite swam up her nose. The kiss was the kind that made a woman forget her name, where she was from, and where she was going. Her breath mingled with his, and raw need settled deep in her core.

When he released her, she drew back, shivery and breathless, not only thankful for each day she had with her new husband but for all the ones yet to come.

"I've waited the entire afternoon to do that." Jack's deep, smooth rumble sent warmth washing over her.

"Is it always like this between husbands and wives?"

After a long moment, he troubled himself with a reply. "Yep."

"Then I'm going to be preoccupied for the rest of my life." She traced the fullness of his lips with a fingertip. "I love you, Jack Bowdre."

He opened his mouth to speak when Sawyer appeared in the door. "Are you going to kiss all night? I'm hungry. And Willow's awake."

Nora laughed. "I guess we'd better feed you."

A short time later, they sat down to bowls of chicken soup, and Nora thought it was the best thing she'd ever eaten.

She glanced at Jack, holding baby Willow, then at Sawyer. She wondered how she'd gotten so lucky. Tears clogged the back of her throat.

Please, let them all get safely to Hope's Crossing.

And please let her make love to Jack before she died of longing.

❦

Jack rose before daylight, eased from Nora's side, and slipped from the house. He couldn't say what spooked him—a feeling more than anything. He'd known they should've left yesterday, but the cold night air wouldn't have been good for Willow.

He'd rather risk capture than to bury that tiny baby who still didn't have a firm grip on life.

The darkness was his friend, and he moved silently through the whispering grasses, his eyes scanning right and left. The goats and sheep milled about, restless in their pen. They, too, sensed trouble.

Twice around the area revealed nothing, yet the unease persisted. Jack sat down in the shadow of a stand of mesquite to await the dawn within the hour. A sudden light shone in the window, telling him Nora was up. Minutes later, he caught a wisp of smoke curling from the stovepipe on top of the house and knew she'd put coffee on. He could almost smell it, his yearning for a cup and his wife was so strong.

But Jack didn't move.

Riders were coming, and he had to protect Nora. If they caught him inside the house, they wouldn't even give him a chance to surrender. They'd just open fire. And Jack wouldn't risk her or the children's lives. They only wanted him. But they wanted him so damn bad they'd do anything, even kill everyone in their path.

At least in the open, he had better choices. And so did Nora and the kids.

❦

Nora lit a candle, then started the fire in the little stove. She didn't like what her instincts were telling her, but to ignore them might put her and the children in danger. Not only was Jack gone, but so was the bow and arrow lying next to the door. He'd gone hunting.

But for animals or humans?

She shook the boy. "Sawyer, wake up."

The instant terror on his face and the way he threw his blanket aside pierced her heart. He immediately expected something bad.

"What is it?"

"I'm not sure. Jack went out and hasn't returned. I have this feeling that we need to get moving. Can you hurry and milk one of the goats while I get the baby ready?"

"Okay." He stood and folded his blanket. "Did the lawmen get Jack?"

"I don't think so. I never heard gunshots or anything. I do think that posse is close by though. If we hurry, we might escape." She put her arm around his shoulder. "Go milk the goat now. We have to take some with us for Willow." She kissed the top of his unruly hair, loving the smell of the little boy.

In no time, he'd milked the goat and she'd filled a mason jar, plus the baby's bottle. Buttoning her coat and clutching Willow, snugly wrapped in the lamb's wool and one of the other blankets, she stepped out with Sawyer as dawn broke.

She jumped back, her heart pounding.

Pink light revealed riders surrounding her, and she stared into at least a half dozen gun barrels.

Nora swallowed hard and drew Sawyer close.

"Raise your hands, ma'am," barked a steely-eyed older man with white hair, wearing a marshal's badge.

"I have a baby. Unless you'd rather hold her…"

The lawman frowned. "Just keep 'em where I can see 'em. The boy too."

Her gaze swept the group. Jack had explained that out here a posse was made up of only one or two lawmen and the rest were ordinary citizens. Most wouldn't meet her eyes.

Sawyer pressed close to Nora, and she could feel him shaking.

A raw-boned younger man she recognized as Deputy Marshal Seamus Belew dismounted. His mouth set in deep lines, he stalked to her, so close she could smell his rank breath. "Your name?"

"I've done nothing wrong." Nora raised her chin at a defiant angle. "I'm Lenora Kane." Another rider dismounted, his bearing and manner instantly reminding her of a cold, deadly snake. He stepped from the shadows and her breath lodged in her throat. Her stomach knotted.

Darius Guthrie.

For now, he hung back, but she knew he wouldn't stay there. She'd have to face him.

Her stomach knotted, and she forced her attention back to the older, white-haired marshal. "Will you let us go? I need to get these children somewhere safe. Please."

"Over here, Marshal Hays," someone hollered. "We found a bloody mattress and a trail. Bowdre has killed again."

"He killed no one." Panic-stricken, Nora grabbed Hays's arm. "Please listen, Marshal. We found a dead woman here, this baby's mother, and buried her. That's all, I swear to it."

"You'll say anything to save his rotten hide," Belew snarled.

"Sorry, ma'am. I have to go." Hays glared at Belew. "Deputy, touch this woman and you'll answer to me. That goes for your *friends* too." Hays shot a glance at two rough onlookers dressed in buffalo robes.

Sawyer tugged on her dress and whispered, "I saw those two men at the trading post. They're mean."

She could believe it. They looked like uncivilized mountain men.

Hays hollered out orders. "Deputy Belew, keep Guthrie and the two over there with you. The rest of you men fan out. Bowdre is nearby and we're gonna find him."

They galloped away, and Nora's heart sank. She and the children had little hope.

Belew gave his disappearing superior a mocking salute and waited until the men were out of sight, then grabbed Nora's arm and jerked her up against him. Willow let out a sharp cry. "I want Bowdre. And Darius here wants that book you stole. If you don't want these children to get hurt, you'd best start talking."

Sawyer launched himself at Belew, kicking and hitting. "Leave her alone! We ain't afraid of you!"

The mean, raw-boned deputy stuck his face into hers. "Where's Bowdre? If he's in the house, you'd best tell him to come out."

"Be careful what you wish for," Nora said softly. "If he were in there, no one would have to ask him to come out. He'd be in your face and shoving his gun down your throat before you could swallow spit. But go ahead and look." Belew headed for the house, but Nora's gaze was on Guthrie, hurrying toward her. She wasn't sure who she felt safer with—Belew or Guthrie.

Or the two rotund onlookers from the trading post.

Truth be told, she wasn't safe with any of them. All wore the kind of cold expressions Flynn O'Brien had been fond of giving her. The kind that made her blood run cold.

"I want that book you stole!" Guthrie hollered. He didn't slow as he came closer. A foot away, he drew back his arm and slapped her. The sound rent the air like a rifle shot.

The explosive violence whipped her head back and she tasted blood.

Nora staggered backward, her grip on Willow giving way. She grabbed, catching the infant in time and pulled her close, wrapping the blanket securely around the child.

"You bastard!" She wiped a trickle of blood from her mouth. "You think that makes you a big man, Guthrie, but it just shows how weak you are. I don't have your damn book." She was confident about that. Even if he raised the loose board, he wouldn't spot it directly.

Guthrie slapped her again, only this time she'd steeled herself for the blow and stayed upright. "Give me the damn ledger."

Deputy Belew ran from the house, apparently drawn by the commotion.

A shot rang out. Blood stained the deputy's sleeve. He yelled and dropped to the ground.

Guthrie dragged her toward the door of the house, but never made it inside.

Nora heard a soft whirring sound and an arrow flew from the rugged landscape into Darius's thigh. He screamed and grabbed his bloody leg. "Dammit! Pull it out!"

Satisfaction shot through Nora where she stood with Sawyer against the side of the house. Jack was protecting them the only way he could.

"Damn you!" Belew crouched, holding his arm, his gun drawn, searching for movement in the deep shadows of the early morning light. "Bowdre, come out or I'll kill her!"

Silence.

"Pull it out," Guthrie managed, his face blanched, eyes filled with agony. "Get this thing out of my damn leg."

"Quit your whining. Be a man!" Belew barked, getting to his feet but keeping low.

Nora watched, quiet and still, ready to act if she got an opportunity. If only she were carrying one of the guns Jack had tried to give her. But she did have the knife strapped to her leg.

She inched her hand into the folds of her dress, slowly lifting it, when Belew swung around. "You and the boy get inside. Now!"

Putting an arm around Sawyer and clutching Willow, she did as he ordered. A second later, Belew pulled Guthrie inside by the collar of his shirt and the two men in buffalo robes raced in as well. The small house bulged at the seams with dangerous, angry, smelly men.

The deputy marshal yelled an impatient curse, grabbed one end of the arrow that pierced Guthrie's thigh, and snapped it off amid horrible screams. Then he pulled out the bloody end and threw it aside. "Satisfied?"

Shaking, Guthrie blew out a breath and tied his bandana around the wound, glaring at Nora. He stood, and rage radiated off him. She took one step back. He snatched Willow from her arms with bloody hands and thrust the baby at Sawyer. Willow wailed, flailing her small arms. Guthrie jerked Nora's coat open and ran his bloody hands over her breasts and down her body, searching for the ledger.

One of the buffalo men moved closer. "She's sure a looker, ain't she, Joe?"

"Yep. She can fill a man's mind with all sorts of pleasurable thoughts, Toad." Joe's mouth slack, he reached for a lock of Nora's hair with a dirty fingernail.

"Get away from me." She slapped at him and jerked back.

The rough men jumped when Belew bellowed, "Where is Bowdre? I want him now!"

"What you want and what you get are two different things. He's far away from the likes of you." Nora pulled her coat back over her and took Willow from Sawyer.

The boy glared at the men. "We don't know where he is."

"That true?" The deputy marshal yanked him away from Nora and put his face into the boy's. "You know what we do to little boys who lie, don't you?"

Sawyer bravely shook his head, but he was shaking. Nora could do nothing but watch. And wait. Oh, if only she had a gun. She'd put a bullet in both Belew and Darius.

"We throw 'em in jail and let the rats gnaw on them. And this ma of yours we'll put in leg shackles and make her work from sunup to sundown."

"That's enough!" Nora yelled. "Leave the boy alone."

"What are we going to do?" Guthrie asked. "He has us pinned down."

Belew put a hand to his head. "I'm thinking!"

Time crept by. The baby began to cry. Nora rocked her, crooning soothing words.

Finally, the marshal appeared to reach a conclusion. Yanking Nora, Willow, and Sawyer in front of him, he went to the door and flung it open. "We're coming out, Bowdre! Give yourself up or the woman and brats are gonna die!"

Darius Guthrie limped behind, and once they were a yard from the house, stuck his gun under Nora's chin. The tracker's cold, dead eyes glared into hers. "How much do you value your woman, Bowdre? I'll give you 'til the count of three."

The early morning shadows slid around them. Nora said a silent prayer, begging Jack to stay hidden.

Guthrie shouted. "One!"

Willow's cries became insistent and Nora could do nothing. Both men's cruel grips on her brought tears to her eyes. She glanced around, praying to see the kind marshal returning. If only someone would come to their aid.

A second later, she jumped when Guthrie yelled out, "Two!"

"I don't think he's going to save you," Belew growled next to her ear.

Oh God! She was going to die. If he killed her, what would they do to the children? Had they saved Willow only to watch her die?

A chilling grin formed on Guthrie's mouth. "Three! Time's up."

"Wait." Sweat trickled down Nora's spine. "I'll give you the ledger."

"That's more like it." Darius's rank breath, his face so close to hers, the gun pressing into the soft flesh under her chin—it all made her ill. She would give up the book to save Sawyer and Willow.

Willow's loud cries shredded her attempt to remain calm.

"But you have to let the children go. It's the only way."

"You stupid fool!" Belew shouted at Guthrie. "I want Bowdre, not some damn book."

Before anyone could move, a gun cocked, and the dark barrel of a .45 poked into Guthrie's neck. A woman grated out, "I wouldn't do that, mister. Lower your weapon and be quick about it—if you care about living."

Seventeen

Nora stared at her ally, whose face was hidden by the brim of her hat. She wore a long, dark duster, and tendrils of red hair hung to her waist. She didn't know who the woman was or where she'd come from, but Nora could've hugged her. She jiggled Willow and the baby's cries hushed.

Darius didn't move. Belew's Adam's apple bobbed when he swallowed.

The two rough men in buffalo robes inched toward their horses. "Go on. Get out of here." The woman issued the order without taking her eyes from Guthrie.

They stumbled to their mounts, leaped into the saddles, and raced away.

"You gentlemen enjoy pain, I suppose. Entirely your choice. I dearly love showing a rotten, no-good bottom-feeder the error of his ways." The woman's voice was as soft as satin, but underneath lay pure granite and a whole lot of anger.

Frustration went through Nora at being unable to see her savior's face, but she imagined a sly smile accompanied the threat.

"Sweetheart, I do think they need to be convinced," drawled a tall, lean man. He walked toward them, leading two horses. He held a long-barreled gun in his other hand, pointed at Guthrie and Belew. "I tell you, gentlemen, you don't want to mess with my wife. Tally's got deadly aim, and I've never known her to miss a target." He jammed his gun into Belew's stomach, and the angry marshal let out a whoosh of air. "And if that's not enough to convince you to toss your guns, I would feel terrible if I didn't warn you—you won't be the first she put in a grave."

"I am Deputy U.S. Marshal Seamus Belew." The man was still defiant. "You're interrupting a lawman in the performance of his duty."

The tall, dark-haired cowboy pointed to Sawyer. "Is that boy under arrest? How about the woman?"

"Not exactly. Though Guthrie here claims she stole a book from his boss."

The rugged man grinned and winked at his wife. Nora liked this couple. "He's all yours, sweetheart. I'll take care of the slimy one."

"Go ahead and fire. The rest of the posse will come running," Belew snarled and dropped his pistol. "You won't get far."

Tally's husband leaned close. "Sorry to ruin your plans, but I've taken care of them already. They're too far away to hear gunshots. They think they're hot on Bowdre's heels."

His wife gave the men a cold smile. "Now which is it?" She seemed to enjoy striking terror into Guthrie. Nora had no doubt if he moved a muscle, she'd kill him. "Take your grimy hands off the lady or I'll blow you into hell faster than you can spit."

With a growl, Guthrie released Nora and threw his gun at Tally's feet. She kicked it well out of reach. Nora pulled Sawyer close and backed up. Darius Guthrie stared a hole in her, his message clear. No matter what happened here, she hadn't seen the last of him.

A shudder raced through her. Would she survive their next meeting?

Fresh blood had soaked the bandana Guthrie had tied around his wound. Nora motioned to his thigh. "You'll need to get that wound seen to or you might lose your leg."

"Save your concern." The sullen man jerked away.

Nora's smile lacked warmth. "I believe I will."

"You will live to regret this," snarled Belew, gripping his bloody arm where Jack's bullet had found the mark.

While Tally held a gun on them, her husband removed the men's gun belts, none too gently, and shoved the pair toward a mount. "You're lucky I'm feeling generous. I'll give you one horse to share. Start riding and don't stop until you reach Saint's Roost. I see you again, you're dead." He winked at

Tally. "Or on second thought, I'll let my wife do it. She loves killing jackasses and reprobates."

"Nothing brings greater pleasure," Tally replied with a pout. "Are you sure I can't shoot them?"

"Not this time, darlin'. I'm sure it won't be long though."

Belew swung into the saddle, then pulled Guthrie up behind him. Giving them all a look that could kill, the surly deputy marshal set the horse in motion.

Tally put a comforting arm around Nora's shoulders. "I'm Tally Shannon, and over there is my husband Clay Colby. I'm glad you're safe. I take it you're Nora Kane?"

"Yes, but how did you know?"

"Clay and I are Jack's friends from Hope's Crossing. We knew you were on the stage when it wrecked. We'd been expecting you. Then Dr. Mary told us that a marshal had arrested Jack." As the woman put her gun away, the hat slid back a little over her flaming curls and Nora finally saw her face. Although age was difficult to judge, Nora guessed her to be near her own twenty-eight. Regardless, Tally was a stunning, fascinating lady.

"I've never been so glad to see anyone. You showed up in the nick of time." Nora shifted the baby. "But how did you know to intervene just now?"

"We were watching the house, sure you and Jack were here, but we stayed hidden until we saw that no-good marshal and his friend hurting you."

Sawyer raised his head, his eyes hard. "They were gonna kill us."

"Then I'm glad we stopped them." Tally draped an arm across the boy's thin shoulders. "You're a handsome young man, and I'll bet you help your mother out a lot."

The gangly kid pulled his coat tighter. "My ma's dead. Nora's my friend and I love her. Jack and Nora saved me from Bittercreek. He was real mean. Then we found baby Willow."

Tally turned to Nora. "Neither of the children are yours?"

"No, but they can be if they want. Jack and I would welcome them in our lives."

Clay took his attention from the horse carrying Belew and Guthrie and chuckled softly. "You know, that sounds exactly like Jack. Get himself in a desperate situation and take time to rescue two children."

"And me," Nora added.

Satisfied that Belew and Guthrie weren't doubling back, Clay holstered his gun. "Ma'am, we should be going. The posse might return. Do you have any idea where Jack is?"

If only she did. Nora wiped a weary hand over her eyes. "He left while I was asleep. I haven't seen him since we went to bed, but he was expecting trouble. We both were." Jack couldn't have gone far, and he was certainly close enough to shoot Belew in the arm and the arrow into Guthrie.

Clay narrowed his gaze in the direction the rest of the lawmen had gone and spoke to Tally. "Sweetheart, do you think you can get Miss Nora and the children to Hope's Crossing? I'm going to find Jack. He might need help."

"We'll be fine." Tally lifted her face for a kiss, then Clay reached for his gelding's reins.

"Please keep Jack safe." Nora could hardly speak past the painful lump.

Clay nodded. "I'll try."

"I can't—" Nora's helpless gaze stared into the sunrise. "Jack—"

Clay patted her back. "I'll find him. Try not to worry." Then he disappeared around the soddy.

Tally motioned to a horse calmly munching on winter grass. Nora thought it probably belonged to Marshal Belew. "Let's get you and the babe up. The boy and I will ride double."

Panic filled Nora. "I've never ridden a horse."

"The reins will tell the animal which way you want him to go. Pull back and he'll stop. I'll help you. Just don't be afraid."

She held the baby while Nora settled in the saddle. She felt wobbly and that she might tumble off any moment. And it was a long way to the ground.

"Find your balance." Tally was patient and waited until she became more confident before she handed Willow to her.

Nora pulled the baby bottle from a burlap sack. Unlike her, Sawyer appeared right at home in the saddle. A minute later, she cradled Willow and the little caravan moved slowly toward the safety of the town they'd been trying to reach for days.

With each clop of the hooves, her heart ripped apart. How could she leave Jack behind? She might never see him again.

Her husband. Her love. Her future.

Tears rolled down her cheeks. She swung around in the saddle to stare at the little house where she'd married Jack under a cold, starlit sky.

They were joined at the heart and nothing could sever that. But would she be a widow before she ever got the chance to be a wife?

"I'm Mrs. Jack Bowdre," she whispered brokenly into the wind. "My feelings for you will never die, not even when I take my final breath. Please stay safe."

Jack limped away from the woman he'd sworn to protect and care for. Pain pierced his heart. He drew in deep, ragged breaths and gripped his Colt with trembling fingers.

Dear God, what kind of man was he?

The posse had ridden up too fast. He'd felt them close in but thought he had time enough to get Nora and the kids away. He should've left yesterday—should've listened to Nora and his damn gut. His weakness for her had dulled his senses.

But then, he'd had the newborn to consider. One more day to let the baby gather strength hadn't seemed that risky.

Stupid.

When the posse had surrounded Nora and the kids, it had taken all his strength not to charge down the hill right into the middle of them. It had been easy to recognize the two men in buffalo robes. They must've followed Sawyer and him from the trading post, then gone after the posse. He'd seen—and heard—Guthrie slap Nora and hadn't wasted a moment in putting an arrow through the tracker's leg. At least he'd done that much, little though it was. He rubbed his stubbled jaw. A better-placed arrow would've gone through the man's heart.

Shot Belew as well, before the chicken-livered bastard had run into the house, although the sound was sure to draw the other lawmen back.

Rage still burned. No one hit his wife and lived. One day they'd both pay. Jack closed his eyes. His beautiful Nora. He'd brought her so much pain.

His hand curled around his Colt, the need for revenge burning like the fire of a smithy's forge.

If he could've gotten to Belew and Guthrie without getting his family killed…

If… He turned all the possible scenarios over in his mind and found nothing he could've done different.

He'd started back down the hill to give himself up, when Tally and Clay arrived. Thank God. His old friends would make sure Nora and the kids got to Hope's Crossing—to a warm bed and food. Nora could have her hot bath.

And him?

He'd get there somehow, even if he had to shoot every last person in his way. Hidden in the tall grass, he watched Nora's proud figure fade in the distance. A sudden mist blurred his vision. A bullet slamming into him would hurt less than this kind of pain that clawed at his insides.

I, Jack Bowdre, vow to provide, to protect, to cherish you, Nora Kane.

Like hell he had.

For a moment, he fought to swallow. The first line of his vow echoed in his head and agony doubled him over. He hadn't protected or provided for her any more than he had his Rachel. Fine husband he'd turned out to be. Again.

The lump hung in his throat as he wiped his eyes. Gathering himself, he cautiously slithered through the tall, dead grass like a snake looking to sink its fangs into an enemy.

He had a special venom reserved for Seamus Belew and Darius Guthrie.

When he reached Hope's Crossing, he prayed Nora would

forgive him. He hadn't meant to leave her to face the posse alone. It was no way to repay her for taking a chance on a sorry-assed outlaw.

He removed his hat and pinned the U.S. marshal badge to the lining. It'd be safer there.

He fought with everything he had not to go down and join her and his friends. But that would only draw the posse to them, put them in danger. He had no idea how close they were, but he knew they wouldn't leave the area without him. No, Nora and the kids were safer if he stayed away.

Pain swept through him like a raging prairie fire as he moved toward the one place where he'd be safe for a little while. There, he'd try to think of a way to make things right with Nora.

Until he did, he couldn't live with himself.

Nora rode silently, each clop of the horse's hooves taking her farther from the man she loved. The ache in her heart consumed her and breathing took effort. The sun was about two hours old when they stopped to rest. Every bone ached as she climbed from the horse.

Tally pulled some jerky from her saddlebag. "You must be hungry. I'm sorry we can't stop to hunt for game."

"This will do. Thank you." Nora took the food and handed a piece to Sawyer. They sat on a fallen log, except for Tally, who stood watch. Nora held Willow. There were trees here, and she welcomed the relief from the barren, desolate plains.

A gust of wind blew Tally's long duster open, and her bulging stomach came as a surprise.

"When is your baby due?" Nora asked.

"A few more weeks, Dr. Mary says." A smile curved Tally's mouth and she laid her hand on her stomach. "I can't wait to see it, hold it, love it. Clay and I are very happy."

Nora could certainly see that. She'd always heard a baby brought indescribable joy. Would she and Jack get a chance to fulfil this longing inside so strong that it sometimes woke her from a sound sleep? Pain shot to her heart, taking her breath. To not know if he was safe, cold, hungry—even alive—was horrible agony. If the posse did capture him, she prayed Marshal Hays would be the one to take him in. He was kind and he'd see that Jack made it to jail.

The thought of him locked up, called a wild animal, shredded her composure.

She swallowed hard and shook herself. "Congratulations. Forgive me, but what are you doing out here? Isn't that dangerous?"

Tally laughed. "I'm as healthy as a horse, and Dr. Mary said riding is good for me."

Maybe, but still it seemed very risky. "Do you want a girl or a boy?"

"We don't care. Either will be loved." Tally pulled off a bite of jerky with her teeth. "We have a daughter already who is blind. Violet came to us as yours did." She put her jerky in a pocket and straightened. "Do you mind if I hold Willow? I've been itching to cuddle her."

"Be my guest." Nora handed her over.

"How old is that little girl of yours?" Sawyer asked.

Tally cradled Willow in her arms, a smile gracing her face. "Violet just turned nine."

"She's the same old as me," Sawyer said. "Maybe we can be friends."

"You can count on it. Violet loves meeting new people. I swear, that girl is afraid of very little." The baby whimpered. Tally moved Willow to her shoulder and patted her small back. "There aren't many kids in town so far. You and Willow'll make five, Sawyer."

The boy's face darkened. "What happened to the rest?"

"Honey, we just started the town and there aren't that many people yet. And some are old." She swayed back and forth, rocking Willow, and turned to Nora. "We're glad for the help in settling Hope's Crossing. Right now, the population is around thirty, so we're growing."

"Tell me more about Hope's Crossing. Who started it?"

Nora wanted to learn everything about this place where she hoped to put down roots with Jack.

"The town was Clay's dream, and he laid down the first board. So far, we have a hotel, mercantile, bakery, telegraph, and livery. And the Mobeetie/Tascosa Stage Lines recently added us as a stop." Tally nuzzled Willow's cheek. "There's something about holding babies that makes me all squishy inside. I love the sweet smell of milk on their breath."

"I know what you mean." Nora agreed. "Willow makes my chest tighten. Her life is very fragile, and yet she fights so hard to live."

"It was a miracle you found her when you did."

"I say a prayer every day and try not to think about what might've happened." Nora's gaze followed Sawyer as he rose and walked out away from them, staring toward the direction they'd come. She went and put an arm around his shoulders. "Jack knows how to stay safe. He's going to be all right. And Mr. Colby is with him. Clay Colby's his best friend and won't let anything happen."

Tears bubbled in Sawyer's eyes. "But bullets can find him. I don't want Jack to die. He's my friend too."

"No, honey, he's not going to die. Don't even think that." Yet even as she said it, she knew there was a very real possibility that she might never see Jack again.

And that fear shook her to the core.

Careful and quiet, Jack moved toward a place nearby where he'd often hidden. If he could just make it there, he might have a chance. The posse was so close he could sometimes hear the soft snort of their horses.

What had happened to Seamus Belew and Darius Guthrie?

As soon as he'd known Nora and the kids were safe, he'd taken off.

They were one less worry, but he missed them like he would miss breathing. He closed his eyes and felt Nora's soft curves pressing against him.

Ahhh, those curves that could make a man lose his mind.

The best thing he'd ever done had been writing and sending for her. He'd saved her from a horrible fate, as well as saved himself from a lonely existence.

Yes, Nora was a keeper, and he'd do whatever it took to get back to her.

Between hiding and walking, Jack kept a steady pace and, two hours later, peeked through the branches of a scrub cedar at a tiny, rundown cabin surrounded by bluffs on each side. The bird chatter overhead told him it was safe to proceed. Inside, thick dust covered every portion of the dilapidated dwelling, assuring him that no one had used it in a while. Good. It would be his home for now.

Until it was safe to leave.

Rifling through a box holding a few canned goods, he found a can of beans and one of peaches. As the sun went down, he ate the beans cold and savored each bite of succulent, sweet peaches. Then as the darkness grew, he eased out to scout the area.

A man needed to know where his enemies were.

Jack found them about a mile from the cabin. Damn! They were too god-awful determined to get him. He wouldn't be able to stay there after all. He'd have to leave before dawn.

Later, he sat shivering in the night air under the ledge of an overhang of the bluff. Watching. Listening. Thinking.

Someone had once said that it had to get dark enough before a man could see the stars, and damned if that wasn't true.

Now in the midnight of his soul, he saw every detail of Nora's face—from her soft brown eyes to her beautiful smile. The vows he'd spoken had mostly been what she expected him to say. Would they have a forever kind of love that had true staying power and could weather any storm? Or was it the sort that faded over time when a person grew weary of the obligations that came from making a life with another?

There in the darkness, Jack wiped his eyes and puffed out a ragged breath, letting his head sag against the wall of the bluff.

In the quiet, he examined himself and found things he wasn't proud of.

The secret he still kept.

The men he'd killed and the nights when he'd prayed to die.

The irritation toward Nora when she'd only been doing what she thought was right.

He could've shown more patience, more tenderness. An ache rose to hold her, to bury his face in her golden hair, to kiss her soft lips until she begged for mercy.

Nora had shown in many ways how much she cared for him, and she'd even professed her love. Still, in the little time she'd known him, how could she really be sure?

A memory popped into his head of Rachel on their wedding day. The sunlight shone on her reddish-brown hair, and her eyes sparkled like diamonds. He hadn't known her long, but she excited him like no one else he'd ever met.

"I love you, Jack." She'd wound her arms around his neck and played with his hair, her breasts pressed tightly to his chest. "You give my days meaning, and I never want to live without you. If something happens to me, promise you'll find someone else who fills your life with joy and loves you as much as I do."

"Don't talk like that, Rachel. Nothing's going to happen." Yet it had. Oh God, how he'd loved her, even sobbing the words into her cold grave as he dug it.

Now he couldn't say the words to Nora, afraid of being unfaithful to Rachel. Yet here in the dark sky, he saw the truth written in the stars. Rachel had held his heart while she was alive, but he knew she'd be happy he found someone like Nora Kane.

It was okay to love again. It was okay not to shrivel and die while he was still living.

It was okay to love Nora.

And he did.

How quickly she'd stolen past his defenses and wiggled into his heart.

Now, shivering and hungry, he was at rock bottom and

knew the answers he sought. Wanting for the sweet, kind, funny woman shook him to the depths of his soul, and he saw the truth, stripped down and bare, on a pitch-black night when it was dark enough to clearly see.

She was all of his tomorrows, his forever. His always. His life.

Eighteen

Nora rode into the town of Hope's Crossing mid-morning the following day. Like Jack said, the town was a fortress. If he could just make it here, he'd be safe. The smell of new lumber filled the air, and everywhere she looked, buildings were going up. People rushed to meet them, welcoming Tally and shooting curious glances at Nora and Sawyer.

An old man reached for the bridle of Tally's horse. "Glad to have you back, Miss Tally."

"Happy to be back, Tobias." Tally introduced the man as Tobias January, and the sweet woman with silver hair standing at his side as Belle.

"Mama! Mama!" A blind girl with long blond hair came rushing forward, holding a stick out in front of her, feeling her way.

"Violet." Tally dismounted, helped Sawyer down, and rushed toward the girl with arms outstretched. The back of Nora's eyes burned. Such a display of love between mother and daughter. This was what she was willing to do anything for. The baby in her arms wiggled and Nora held her close. Maybe Willow would belong to her and Jack like that one day. Sawyer stayed close beside her horse, staring at the throng of people gathering. Willow's thin cry added to the noise.

A tall man with light-brown hair rushed forward. He wore a dark frock coat and knee-high boots. "Let me help you, ma'am. I'm Jack's friend, Ridge Steele."

"You're the preacher." Nora handed Willow to him and dismounted.

"Depends on the definition. Me and the good Lord don't see eye to eye much anymore." Ridge's amber eyes studied her. "I'm glad Jack found you, Miss Lenora."

"Just Nora, please." She wearily pushed the hair from her

eyes. "Jack and I married each other under the stars two nights ago. We feared the posse would stop us from making it to town, and they did try their best."

"That's just as binding as any. I've given up my calling." Ridge glanced somberly down at Willow, surprise on his face. "Jack didn't tell me you had a child."

Nora put an arm around Sawyer and told Ridge how they'd rescued the boy from outlaws, then found Willow. "Sawyer is old enough to decide where he wants to live, but our door is always open. And Willow…her parents are dead. We have no idea how to find her kin, so for now, she's ours."

"She's a sweet girl." Ridge kissed the baby's cheek before handing her off to Nora. "I'm sure you and the children are tired and hungry. I'll show you to Jack's house, where you can make yourself at home."

"That would be wonderful, Mr. Steele."

"No mister—just Ridge. We're kinda informal here."

Sawyer squinted up at the tall man. "Are you gonna go look for Jack?"

"I am, son. As soon as I can speak with Tally."

"I want to go with you. I have to find Jack."

"Sawyer, that's too dangerous. Stay here with me." Nora couldn't bear to have the kid wandering around the prairie and run the risk of crossing paths with Bittercreek again. But she recognized she had no right to tell him what to do.

"Jack needs me. I hafta go, Nora."

Ridge met Nora's glance. "I tell you what. We'll talk about it and that's a promise."

Dozens of people rushed forward, all clamoring to meet her.

One petite woman, who appeared in her thirties, stood out from the rest, wearing a necklace made of bullets and smoking a pipe. She introduced herself as Dr. Mary. "Let me take the newborn and check her out while you get settled in at Bowdre's. My office is right over there."

Nora followed her pointing finger to a building that was only painted around the bottom, in yellow, as though done by a child. Maybe it had been—a blind one. Violet? She smiled. A large sign over the front said *Doctor*. "She's hungry, and I ran out of milk." Nora passed Willow into the doctor's waiting arms and handed her the empty bottle. "I gave her sugar water this morning. It was all I had."

"Then lucky for us we have a herd of goats. I'll get her fed in no time." Dr. Mary cradled the infant and dropped the blanket back over her tiny face to shield it from the wind.

"I'll milk the goats for you," Sawyer offered. "I'm a good milker."

"I'm sure you are, but we have plenty of milk left from this morning's haul." Dr. Mary must've seen Sawyer's crestfallen face. "I can sure use a hand with some water, though. I'll bet you can fill a pail of water from the windmill lickety-split."

Nora glanced toward the structure. She'd never seen such a tall windmill. Or one that sat in the middle of town.

"Yes, ma'am." Sawyer let a smile curve his mouth for the first time that day.

"You'll find plenty of pails sitting there at the tank," the doctor said. "Bring one to my office as soon as you can."

Sawyer raced off toward the windmill. "Ridge, let's wait for him," Nora suggested. "Everything is so new here and I don't want him to feel lost."

Ridge's sudden smile softened his angular face. He'd looked like he'd been carved from a piece of granite until that moment. "Of course. He looks like a good kid and already has a strong attachment to Jack."

"That he does." She laid a hand on his arm. "I don't want him to go with you. Bittercreek is roaming around out there. I'm terrified for Sawyer's safety."

"I won't lie to him."

"I'm not asking that. Maybe quietly slip out. Please. It's for his own safety."

"I've given him my word to think about it."

"That's fair."

Some women came up and Ridge introduced them, although even a second later, she couldn't recall their names.

Nora liked their friendliness and promised to get acquainted as soon as possible. When Sawyer returned, they walked with Ridge to the house Jack had built.

"He built this for you, Miss Nora." Ridge opened the door of the pretty, wooden two-story dwelling that had rows of windows in front with empty flower boxes underneath. "He didn't know you'd need a bigger place, but there's plenty of room to add on."

"It's lovely." She could picture herself digging in the dirt, planting flowers.

A smile plastered on her face, she stepped into a neat parlor and was struck by the warmth of the frilly curtains, the wallpaper, and the paintings on the walls. The sofa, settee, and rocking chair showed Jack's care. The well-stocked kitchen had everything a new bride would need. They moved up the stairs to a small bedroom that would be Sawyer's if he wanted it. It seemed made with a nine-year-old boy in mind.

"Is this for me?" Sawyer ran his hand longingly over the bed.

Nora's breath hung in her throat, and she blinked hard. "Absolutely. All you have to do is claim it."

He glanced up at her, his face solemn. "I do want it—if you want me."

"Of course, we want you." She pulled him into a hug.

"Will you tuck me in like my mama used to do?" His voice caught. "I really miss that."

Suddenly, Nora couldn't see for the tears blinding her vision. For all his grown-up ways, Sawyer desperately needed to feel loved again.

When she could speak, Nora said, "I will tuck you in for as long as you want."

"Just for a while." The gangly kid looked up through his shaggy hair. "I'll get too big, and I don't think I'll need tucking in then."

"Okay. Just tell me when you want to stop." She followed Ridge into the hallway, and Sawyer went back downstairs to wait.

The house was perfect, but the bedroom she would share with Jack took her breath. The largest wooden, four-poster bed she'd ever seen stood between two large, curtained windows and was covered with a beautiful quilt. A dresser, washstand, wardrobe, and small table with two chairs completed the furnishings.

Tears threatened. If everything had gone according to plan, they'd already have made love and slept in this bed countless times.

Nora's chest tightened. She blinked hard and opened the spacious wardrobe that only held Jack's clothes. "I won't be needing this for a while. I lost all my clothes in the stage wreck."

"Jack will see that you have everything you need as soon as he's able." Ridge stared out the window. "Jack's a very lucky man. We both started writing to mail order brides at the same time, but I'm still looking for one to accept my invitation to come west."

The longing in his voice deeply touched her. From Jack, she knew Ridge was an outlaw too and that Hope's Crossing was once a hideout before they'd decided to stop their lawless ways and get respectable. All appeared to want better. They yearned for wives and children, to be able to walk free.

"Ridge, life is full of surprises." Nora laid a hand on his shoulder. "You never know what's around the next bend. I never expected to find a man like Jack. Lord, I was so scared on my way here, but I'm very happy I took a chance."

"Not sure I'll ever find a woman to settle down with. So far, none seem desperate enough." He colored a deep red. "I didn't mean that you were desperate, ma'am."

"No need to explain."

He shrugged. "Some people were born lucky, I guess. I have too much to atone for."

"Don't we all?"

"I've saved the best for last." Ridge's eyes twinkled as he led her from the room and down the hallway to a closed door at the end. "Are you ready, Miss Nora?"

Anticipation buzzed inside her. "Yes."

Whatever it was must be very special.

Ridge opened the door and stepped back to allow her to enter. She sucked in a breath, astounded at the large porcelain tub and toilet. She hadn't had indoor plumbing since leaving Buffalo and had despaired of anyone west of the Mississippi having anything more than an outhouse, let alone a real bathing room.

"Oh my! This is amazing." She ran her hand over the bathtub. "When I asked Jack if the town had a bathhouse, he just smiled and said no, but we'd manage fine. That man!"

"He wanted to surprise you. He ordered books and studied how to put in a bathing room. Jack has always liked innovations."

She'd married some kind of man. Jack was no ordinary outlaw. "He certainly did surprise me. I assume there's hot water?"

"Absolutely. You have only to turn the knob."

She could have a hot bath! Nora clasped a hand over her mouth, already envisioning the treat. "I can't wait. But I have no clothes to put on except what I'm wearing."

"Tally will fix you up."

"Ridge, surely you jest. I'm two sizes larger than Tally." Why couldn't she have been born petite?

"The mercantile has plenty. We're always prepared for visitors, and Jack has an account."

They returned to the parlor, where Sawyer waited. "Ridge, are all the men in town wanted?" she asked.

"Most are. Clay got amnesty last year. He and Jack both wrote letters to the governor requesting freedom, and Jack had to swallow a bitter pill when he didn't get it." Something shifted in Ridge's amber eyes. Disappointment? Pain? Envy?

"I'm glad Jack tried." She'd help him find the courage to keep fighting for amnesty. "What about you?"

"I'm waiting. All of us here want to be free, Miss Nora. It's a hell of thing to be hunted down like a mad dog. And just because we took justice however we could. We're not murderers. The ones who died by our hand needed to be killed, only the law doesn't see it that way."

Nora was beginning to understand the things that Jack couldn't bring himself to say.

A loud commotion of people hollering and laughing sounded outside the window. Ridge moved the frilly curtain aside. Nora glanced out.

"Luke Legend." Ridge turned to her. "He's the man you and Jack passed letters through. Luke was once an outlaw too but, like Clay, is free now. Want to meet him?"

She stared at the dark-haired man outside. He was somewhere in his thirties and wore black trousers with silver conchas down his leg. Sunlight glinted off the metal disks. She'd never seen anyone quite like this man who sat astride a black gelding. He reminded her of a picture she'd seen in books of Mexican vaqueros. He was the furthest thing from her mind of a mail-order-bride procurer.

"Yes, I've waited a long time to meet him."

Sawyer followed them out. Luke stopped when Ridge called out to him and dismounted.

Ridge and Luke clasped hands in greeting. "Let me introduce you to Miss Lenora Kane. Although she prefers Nora. She just arrived today and has quite a story."

Sawyer glanced up at Luke with curiosity, patting the gelding's neck.

Luke's large, warm hand enveloped hers in a firm shake. "Glad to meet you in person, Miss Nora. Actually, you're why I came. I wanted to make sure you arrived safely. I meant to be here last week but got delayed."

"The stagecoach wrecked, and Jack and I have been walking for many days." The dark eyes beneath the brim of his Stetson were sharp and arresting. She had a feeling there was nothing that escaped his notice. "I apologize for my appearance. Sawyer and I rode in this morning with Tally and haven't had a chance to clean up. Mr. Legend, Jack is still out there. The posse is after him, and we got separated. I'm afraid for his life. One deputy marshal named Belew wants to kill him."

"I want you to tell me everything, but first I'd like to meet this young man. Is he yours?"

"Meet Sawyer Gray." Nora laid a hand on the boy's shoulder. "Jack rescued him from an outlaw named Bittercreek."

At mention of the dirty, yellow-haired barbarian, Luke's face hardened. He quickly shuttered his eyes and turned to Sawyer. "I'm happy to meet you, Sawyer." Luke shook his hand. "Have you met Ely Carver yet? He's about your age."

"Not yet. I have to see to Nora and baby Willow first." Sawyer sniffled and dragged his sleeve across his nose. Nora hoped he wasn't getting sick.

She smoothed his hair. "Honey, Willow and I are fine. Go make friends with Violet and Ely."

Ridge called to some children playing nearby and introduced them to Sawyer. Before long, he ran off with them to be just a little boy instead of a grown man.

Once they were out of earshot, Nora turned to Luke. "Forgive me if I'm mistaken, but you seem to know Bittercreek."

"I do. If the boy was with him, I can only imagine what he went through." Luke lightly slapped the reins of his horse against his leg. "Who is this baby he mentioned?"

"A newborn Jack and I found lying next to her dead mother." She glanced toward Jack's and her little house. "Let's go inside and sit. I have a lot to tell you that you need to know. And I want to thank you for putting me in touch with Jack. We're perfect for each other."

She led the way into the parlor. Luke took a chair and Ridge stood at the window. She told him about the wrecked stage, the posse, Belew, Bittercreek, and the culmination of everything at the soddy.

"And now he's out there alone, running for his life." Her voice broke. "Even now, they might've killed him."

Luke rose and sat next to her on the sofa. He took her hand. "If there's one thing I know, it's that Jack can take care of himself. He's done it for years and has outrun the best."

Ridge turned away from the window. "Clay's already looking for him. Might've found him by now."

"Even better, but I think you and I should head out. Gather

some food for us while I telegraph my wife and eat something. I don't want Josie to worry. She has enough with a sick baby."

"What's wrong with Elena Rose?" Ridge asked.

"Doc says it's measles and she should be fine, but you know how Josie is." Luke turned to Nora. "Josie had to nurse me back to health when I got shot and nearly died two years ago. Ever since then, she goes overboard whenever Elena or I get a sniffle."

Nora smiled. She liked this man, and not only because he'd helped her escape Flynn O'Brien. "I think Josie and I must be sisters. I can't wait to meet her."

She wondered how Luke came to be in the mail order bride business but decided that was a topic for another time. "I can't begin to thank you enough for going to help Jack. Two nights ago, we married each other under the stars. He's as much my husband now as if we'd married in a church in front of a preacher."

"We'll find him. Ridge, we should get busy." At the door, Luke took Nora's hands and kissed her cheek. "Try not to worry. I've never lost a bride or groom yet."

Nora returned to the sofa and sank back, breathing a sigh of relief. With so many looking for Jack, they'd find him and bring him home. A knock sounded, and Nora opened the door to find Tally on her step, her arms full.

"I had to guess at your size, but I think these might fit." Tally came inside and handed her three dresses, then she went back out for a valise. "I brought petticoats and everything else you'll need, except for shoes. We have a good selection over at the mercantile for you to choose from. Clay is a saddler and keeps the store well-stocked with boots."

"I can't believe your generosity." Nora gave her a hug. "I was wanting to use the bathing room upstairs but didn't know what I'd put on." She glanced down at her bedraggled dress. "I'm burning everything I have on. They're beyond repair."

Tally glanced at her feet. "I've been wanting to ask but have held back. Why are you wearing men's boots?"

"I couldn't walk fast enough in my shoes, so Jack first

exchanged them with a dead sheriff's boots, then with a smaller pair he took off a tracker who was looking for me. Jack left Darius Guthrie tied up, unconscious, and stripped of his clothes."

Tally grinned. "If that doesn't sound like Jack, I don't know what does."

Nora recounted that tale, then moved into him using all her petticoats, roping the cow, and the fish down her dress. Before long, they were holding their sides from laughing so hard.

"And Jack has this odd thing where he counts whenever he gets irritated. I tell you I've never heard so much counting in my life. Whoever taught him his numbers should be commended." Both women burst out laughing again.

Finally, Tally left Nora to draw her bath. Dr. Mary sent word not to worry about the baby, that the little darling was warm and fed. Determined not to let anything spoil the moment, Nora sank into the hot bath and couldn't erase the grin from her face.

Sheer heaven. She rested her head against the high back and closed her eyes, letting the warmth seep into her bones. Nothing had ever felt so good, so satisfying in her entire life.

Her thoughts drifted to Jack. Where was he? Was he cold and alone?

Tears trickled down her cheeks. Had she found love only to lose it?

"Please don't die, Jack. I don't want to live without you."

Nineteen

A TWIG SNAPPED. THE SOUND PENETRATED JACK'S DREAM like a rifle shot. He jerked up, bathed in sweat, his heart pounding. His gaze swept left and right, but he could see nothing in the night shadows. Had he merely heard the sound in a dream, or had it been it real? His hand tightened around the butt of the Colt that rested on his stomach.

The enemy was so close he could smell them. He pulled to his feet and moved silently through the brush.

All of a sudden, the figure of a man flew at Jack, knocking his weapon to the ground. Jack swung around and landed a fist in the man's face, sending him backward into a rock wall.

Light from the moon revealed the ugly face and dark, glittering eyes of Bittercreek.

Jack breathed heavily. "You!"

"I came to kill you, Bowdre." Bittercreek wiped blood from his mouth. "You shouldn't have taken the boy. Messed up my plans good. You think you're better 'n me."

"I know I am."

Bittercreek shoved away from the bluff wall and launched himself at Jack. The men rolled over and over on the ground, Jack struggling to get the upper hand. Guttural grunts and groans filled the air.

They got to their feet and Bittercreek delivered a punishing fist to Jack's unprotected jaw. Jack's head whipped back, his spine arching. Sharp pain rushed through him and spread out along his body. Jack gathered his wits and grabbed the man around the middle, slamming him to the ground.

Jack followed, pinning his adversary. "You're crazy. You know that, don't you? Get it through your thick skull—the kid didn't want to be with you. You starved him, for God's sake!"

Bittercreek let out a loud yell and threw Jack off, then scrambled on all fours toward his gun lying several feet away. Jack grabbed his leg and pulled him back, jabbing a fist into the man's kidneys. The air rushed from Bittercreek's mouth. The man bared his teeth like a wild animal and yanked a knife from his boot.

Ice slid down Jack's spine. He held his hands wide, readying for the attack.

Moonlight glinted off the sharp blade. "I'm gonna gut you like a fish, Bowdre."

The first slash missed, but as the outlaw came back across, he caught Jack's upper arm, slicing through his duster and into flesh. Pain seared along his nerve endings, stealing the ability to breathe. Blinking hard, he leaped back, his gaze searching for a piece of wood, anything to defend himself with.

Nothing but small twigs.

His harsh breath fought through his mouth that had become so dry he was unable to draw spit. Nausea rose in waves. For a second, he thought he saw stars and his head swam in a dizzying whirl. Gaining control, he danced out of reach, searching the ground for the gun but could only conclude the weapon must've gotten covered in the scuffle.

Fear rushed through him. To win this fight, he had to stay calm and focused. Slow, measured breaths. In and out. The fear ebbed away and he tamped down his rage. He grabbed a handful of dirt and threw it into his opponent's ugly face.

Blinded, Bittercreek slashed the air wildly before running at him.

A bead of sweat rolled into Jack's eye, stinging. "Is that all you got, you piece of shit?"

Rage burned in Bittercreek's eyes as he lunged again, missing his belly only by a fraction. On the next pass, Jack grabbed the arm holding the blade and twisted it until the outlaw dropped the knife and it landed out of reach.

Jack delivered a hard blow to Bittercreek's belly, doubling the yellow-haired bastard over and putting him on the ground. Bittercreek snarled like some crazed beast, cursing the fact that

Jack had ever been born. The moonlight glinted on a piece of metal on the ground.

The Colt.

Bittercreek saw it too. He got a second wind and rolled over quick as lightning and grabbed the gun.

With only seconds to spare, Jack snatched the knife from the dirt and threw it into Bittercreek's leg. The man let out a loud curse and jerked the gun up. As he fumbled for the trigger, Jack dove onto him and seized the fist holding the firearm.

Wrenching the man's hand down, Jack forced the gun between them, pressing it to the outlaw's chest.

A bullet left the barrel with a loud explosion and Bittercreek went limp.

The air was thick with gunpowder, on Jack's tongue and in his mouth. He rolled off the outlaw and stood, snatching the gun from lifeless fingers, checking for a pulse. The man was dead.

Thanks to the duster, the cut on his arm wasn't serious, although it burned like blue blazes as he approached Bittercreek's horse. Untying the reins from the mesquite, he pulled himself into the saddle.

Ride! The noise would bring the posse.

He didn't bother with being careful. Didn't have time. His breath came harsh and ragged as he raced through the night. The cold air burned his lungs and numbed his fingers.

Each strike of the hooves would either carry him farther away from danger or to it—which, he couldn't say.

❧

Nora woke with a start to the sound of a closing door. She threw a shawl around her gown and hurried across to Sawyer's room. It was empty. He'd left.

The boy had been quiet all evening after speaking with Ridge, been sullen when Ridge had ridden out with Luke. He'd taken a bath, and they'd eaten with Tally and Violet. Afterward, they'd gotten Willow from Dr. Mary.

Tears had bubbled in his eyes when she'd tucked him in, and she knew how much that little gesture had meant.

Now panic burst inside Nora as she hurried downstairs and yanked open the door. But she could see nothing. Even if she had seen him, there was little she could do. Although Sawyer lived with them, he didn't belong to them. He was free to do as he wished.

No one had to tell her what that was—he was going to find Jack.

It was all he'd talked about. She thought she'd gotten through to him about the danger.

Apparently not.

The cool air swirled around her and bit at her toes. She closed the door and raced upstairs. It took no time to dress and slide her feet into the buttery leather boots in her correct size that she'd selected earlier from the mercantile. Bundling Willow in blankets, she hurried to Tally's and knocked on the door.

A few seconds later, Tally peeked out. "Nora, what's wrong?"

"Sawyer's left to find Jack. I have to go after him. He's too young to be out there alone. Can you take care of Willow until I get back?"

"You don't even have to ask. Do you have a gun?"

"No."

"Come in and I'll get one. You have to be able to protect the two of you. Also, take my slicker. You might run into rain. I thought I saw some lightning toward the south."

"Thanks, Tally." Nora hugged Willow close, trying to calm her racing heartbeat. "You'll be just fine here, little one. I'll be back soon," she crooned softly.

She hoped so anyway, but who was to know? The country was foreign to her and she could get lost. Or she could run into Guthrie or Belew again. She put the thought out of her head and focused on Sawyer. He needed her. Jack needed her.

Tally's face was grim. "Be careful. I wish I could go with you, but Dr. Mary laid down the law yesterday after I began spotting."

"I'll—we'll—be fine." If she could figure out how to saddle a horse, find her balance, and remember how to ride. Oh, and please let her remember how to read the compass Tally pressed into her hand. "Go south," she repeated Tally's words.

A short time later, she followed the path on horseback that Tally had pointed to. The gun in her pocket lent her courage to ride through the pitch-black. She could face any monsters that might be hiding in the gloom. By the time the sky had begun to lighten, she spied Sawyer's slight form ahead.

He glanced up. "I ain't going back."

"I know. Do you mind if I come with you? We can rescue Jack together."

"I guess." He rubbed his red eyes. "I think I know where he might be."

"Perfect, because I haven't a clue." She helped him up behind her.

"Bittercreek an' me hid out there some in this rundown shack. He said outlaws used it a lot."

"Just tell me how to get there. I'm glad you bundled up in your coat. This morning's air is chilly. Would you like a biscuit left over from supper?"

"Yes, ma'am."

They rode along in silence. Sometimes when life dumped a bunch of problems on her, it was good to simply be still and listen.

She prayed Jack had hunkered down somewhere and was doing the same.

If he still breathed. Regardless, she meant to find him—whether alive or dead.

⁖

Bloody and sore, Jack limped through some scrub cedar and juniper. Every inch of him stung as though someone had stomped him with a pair of hobnail boots. If he could just find some water.

The horse nickered and nudged Jack with his head. The animal needed water too.

The taste of blood from a split lip sat on his tongue, in his mouth. The fight had loosened a tooth as well. *Hell!*

But he was still alive. More than he could say about Bittercreek.

The sun sneaked over the horizon like a thief, a cloud bank forming where the light hit. Unless he missed his guess, a rainstorm was coming. Maybe it would wash some of the blood and filth off him. He was smelling ripe.

He paused to rest at the foot of a mesa and tend to his cut. As it did very often, his mind wandered to Nora. What he wouldn't give to see her in that bath she'd yearned for, her body slick with sweet-smelling soap, her beautiful hair freshly washed. His thoughts raced, and he imagined what she'd look like stepping from the water, dripping wet and so beautiful.

Ahhhh, his imagination was going to get him in bad trouble.

When would the real thing replace his thoughts? It couldn't come soon enough.

Pushing aside his frustration, Jack forced his thoughts back to survival. If he could avoid the posse, he'd be home in a few hours. But the posse seemed to be fanned out across every path leading to Nora.

He must've dozed off again, because the sound of thunder woke him. Cold raindrops hit his face. Jack rose, determined to make it a few more miles before taking cover. As he reached for the horse, it skittered sideways, then pushed its heavy weight against Jack. He lost the grabbing dive for something solid and stumbled. His boots slipping, he rolled down into the bottom of a muddy ravine.

Jack lay there curled in a ball, shivering.

The raindrops became sheets and soaked him to the bone. His pain-numbed mind told him to find shelter.

It took all his remaining strength to pull himself to the top. He blinked hard at the wet boots standing in his way.

"Now I've got you, you son of a bitch," snarled the owner of the boots.

Jack glanced up through the rain, and his stomach clenched. Seamus Belew stared down, his grin cruel, eyes cold.

Twenty

Deputy marshal Seamus Belew yanked Jack up over the edge of the ravine, giving no heed to his cries of agony. Taking Jack's guns, the lawman tied his hands behind his back. "We've got some settling up to do. My brother demands justice and I've waited a long time to deliver."

Jack gritted his teeth against the searing pain of his bonds and the cuts from the fight.

The gray, overcast sky had lightened a bit, allowing him a good view, although it was nothing to lift a man's spirits. No other members of the posse gathered around. No Guthrie. No one. It seemed odd to see a wagon standing a few yards away. Must belong to Belew. It seemed to be carrying supplies in the bed, and Jack would wager everything he had that the wagon contained a long-handled shovel.

Dread crawled up his spine.

That meant only one thing—Belew meant to kill him and concoct some story. He might even bury him alive and no one would ever know what happened.

"I never figured you as one to get your hands dirty. Always thought you'd order someone else to do the deed. Reckon I was wrong." Jack glanced around for a place to run. He wasn't going to make killing him easy. He estimated the distance back to the ravine he'd crawled from. Maybe he could outrun a bullet.

But not in the rain and on the muddy ground. He'd get no traction.

"On your knees, Bowdre." Seamus jerked him down. "This is as good a spot as any."

Contact with the ground sent waves of liquid fire crashing over Jack. He glanced up at the sad sky, rain pelting his face, and thought of Nora. Thank goodness she wouldn't see him die.

Not like this. Best if she never knew.

He regretted not making love to her just once. Something said that would've been real special. Maybe she'd find another husband to take care of her and give her a good life. She'd raise baby Willow, not looking too hard for kin, and maybe finish Sawyer's upbringing. Nora Kane Bowdre would make a loving mother, guarding her children like a mother lion.

"Say your prayers," Belew growled. He knocked off Jack's hat and pressed the barrel of the gun to the back of his head.

The man was going to execute him on the spot. No judge. No trial. No gallows. One bullet to the back of his skull. Nice and neat.

"Got a cigarette?" Jack forced a casual tone.

"No, besides, you don't smoke."

Jack shrugged "Thought this might be a good time to start."

"Funny." Belew widened his stance. "This is for my brother."

The next second seemed an eternity. Jack closed his eyes and waited for the explosion that would end his life.

Belew pulled the trigger and got nothing but a click.

The gun had misfired. Seamus released a string of curses.

"Go on believing that Max was innocent," Jack snapped. "Won't change the facts, that I was just doing my duty as a lawman."

"Shut up." Another click of the hammer readied Jack to plunge into eternity. He wouldn't get lucky a third time.

He closed his eyes in anticipation of the pain of the searing bullet. He wouldn't beg. "Get it over with, dammit. The rocks are jabbing into my knees."

The sound of horses reached him, but he couldn't turn to see who it was.

"Belew!" a deep voice barked. "Shoot him and you'll be the next to die."

"You don't understand."

"I understand plenty. Lower your weapon."

The gun barrel eased from Jack's head. He swiveled to see

ten of the posse and the old marshal who'd spoken. That one wasn't out for blood—only doing his job and seeing that Jack went to jail.

"Dammit, Hays, he was trying to get away." Belew thrust his gun back into the holster so hard Jack heard the leather complain. He let out the breath trapped in his chest.

He'd lived to fight another day. But he knew Belew well enough to know the man wouldn't give up. They would eventually settle this.

Only which one would walk away when they were finished?

Wearing a rain slicker, Marshal Hays moved to Jack on his bowlegs. "Stand up." He turned to his men. "We'll make camp here tonight. Can't see a blasted thing in this rain. We'll chain Bowdre to the wheel of that wagon. I hope you brought supplies, Belew."

"I did. Figured we should have what we needed."

The men dismounted and roughly took possession of Jack. Two of them were familiar, Gilbert and Red, who'd searched the cave the second day Jack and Nora were on the run. Gilbert removed manacles from his saddlebags. He snapped one end to Jack's wrist and the other to a wagon spoke.

"Mind handing me my hat?" Shivering, Jack motioned to it, lying two feet away.

Gilbert picked it up and handed it to him. "It'll shield your head a little I suppose."

The men stretched a piece of canvas between the mesquites and made a fire. Soon they were drinking coffee and swapping yarns about their days of hunting outlaws.

Unprotected where he was, Jack's teeth rattled. He'd crawled as far under the wagon as the chain allowed, but the hard angle of the rain offered no escape. He pulled his bloody duster together and huddled as deep into the folds as he could.

Even if the storm passed, it was going to be a miserable night. He stared at a large elm tree with outreaching limbs fifty yards away and wished for its shelter overhead.

Just then he saw something move in the brush. An animal?

Hope soared when he heard the familiar duck call.

Clay Colby had found him. This was the first bright spot in the whole God-blessed day.

But, unless he'd brought Ridge and some others, they were severely outnumbered.

❧

Nora and Sawyer crouched, sharing the slicker Tally had insisted she bring. They'd dismounted when the rain started and sought protection under a rocky ledge.

Sawyer shivered. "Do you think the rain will stop soon?"

Lord, she hoped so.

"Oh, sure. I think I see blue sky in the distance. How much farther to that place we're going?"

"We haven't passed the lightning tree yet. Or the big rocks piled up at the turn."

"What's the lightning tree?"

"It's an oak tree that's all black and scarred from being struck by lightning."

That made sense. She tightened her arms around the kid. "How far from the pile of rocks to the turn?"

"Pretty close." Sawyer snuggled against her. "Miss Nora, are you glad you found me?"

"I'm very happy that we took you from Bittercreek. Why?"

"Some people don't like kids much."

"Well, I do. Jack and I want at least half a dozen." She hoped anyway. Strange that they hadn't discussed that over the days they'd spent running.

"And Willow. Do you want her?"

His sad voice brought tears to her eyes. He seemed worried that she and Jack would leave him and Willow on their own. "I'll dare anyone to try to take you or Willow away from us." She meant the bold statement with every fiber of her being. "We love you both, and we want to care for you. You've been through a lot, but try to believe that we'll never leave you to make your own way." She kissed his forehead. "Unless that's what you want."

"No, I never want to be alone."

"Then you have nothing to worry about, sweetheart."

Sawyer sighed. "I like it when you call me that. Makes me think of Mama."

"I'm glad."

"What time it is?"

"I'd say it's early afternoon. We've been here for hours." They'd slept for a good while. It was probably past noon.

The rain slowed and, not long after, stopped completely. The sun tried to come out but never could break through the clouds. They got back on the horse and pretty soon came to the lightning tree.

Sawyer grinned. "The rocks at the turn aren't very far from here."

"Good." Hope rose that she'd be with Jack soon, see his face, his crooked smile, feel his arms close around her. She wasn't cut out to be alone any more than Sawyer was.

Anticipation beating in her heart, they rode to the rocks and made the turn east. They'd almost reached the hideout when riders closed around them. She recognized Ridge, Luke, and Clay.

"Afternoon, Miz Nora." Clay pushed back his hat. "Mind if I ask what you and the boy are doing here?"

"We've come to find Jack. Couldn't bear to wait back in Hope's Crossing. He needs my help."

"Jack needs us." Sawyer jutted out his chin defiantly.

The saddle leather creaked as Luke Legend shifted his weight and leaned his arm on the pommel. "He's in a mess all right, *señora*. The posse has him."

Nora sucked in a quick breath, a vise gripping her chest.

"We're trying to devise a plan now to bust him loose." Clay reached into his pocket and pulled out a sack of Bull Durham and proceeded to roll a cigarette. "They're camped just over that ridge. But it's too dangerous for you and the boy. Go home and wait."

"Respectfully, I can't do that, Mr. Colby. I'm his wife, and we face everything together." They'd be sorely mistaken if they thought she'd leave. She was quiet a second, wrestling with frightening thoughts that lodged in her brain. "How bad a shape is he in?" she asked quietly.

"Not the best, but he'll manage," Ridge answered. "They chained him to a wagon wheel. He's bloody and shivering. Please go home, Miss Nora."

"Sawyer and I will go home when Jack is free." Sawyer's arms slid around Nora from his seat behind her, and she gave him a reassuring pat. The horse danced, apparently anxious to also move on. "That's that. Now, how do we rescue him? How is he chained?"

"With manacles." Clay lit his cigarette and waved out the match. "One handcuff is attached to Jack and the other end to a wagon spoke."

"In other words, you need the key."

"Yes, ma'am. Either that or plan an ambush at some spot along the way, which could get us and Jack killed." Clay blew out a smoke ring. "I overheard the marshals saying they'd head out in the morning for Saint's Roost."

One line of her wedding vows came to mind. *If you get arrested again, I'll search for a key until I find one.*

Did she mean those vows or not? Jack was cold and drenched and hurting. They needed to free him tonight. But how would she get the key?

Sawyer jumped from the horse. "We could pick the lock. Wouldn't need a key. Bittercreek taught me how to pick certain ones."

"No, sweetheart." Nora dismounted and placed a palm against his face. "Not this time. It's too dangerous."

The memory of her and Jack trying to get unhooked flashed into Nora's thoughts. That was it. Maybe.

"Are all manacles alike? Do you think they're using the same kind Jack and I were attached with when we…ah…left the wrecked stagecoach?" Nora felt a flush rising. She hadn't meant to tell anyone about being handcuffed to Jack and how that had come to pass. But she had to convince them to let her try.

Luke's dark eyes sharpened, apparently catching wind that there was more to the tale, and his mouth twitched. "You and Jack were handcuffed together?"

"It's a long story."

"Bet it's a humdinger." Clay drew on the cigarette, making the end glow red.

"I'd like to have seen how that worked." Ridge wiped a grin from his face. "But yes, they could be the same ones. They're all pretty much alike."

"Then I know how to unlock them." One problem though, she didn't have any pins in her hair this time. "If you gentlemen can find me a hairpin."

The trio glanced at each other and laughed.

"I know. A hairpin never works." She watched their laughter fade.

"Jack must've told you," Ridge said.

"Matter of fact, he did." Of all times to wear her hair down. But she'd left in a hurry.

"*Un momento.*" A smile curved Luke's mouth. "I might have one of Josie's in my saddlebag. I seem to recall picking one up that she dropped the other day." He dismounted and began his search, the silver conchas on his trousers flashing. Those glittering orbs would sure be difficult to hide.

Nora waited, planning. After dark, she could sneak under the wagon with Jack and set to work.

Then what a surprise would await the marshals at daybreak. Let them find someone else to arrest. They weren't getting Jack as long as she drew breath.

Luke came up with a hairpin and they all mounted up.

Nora and Sawyer rode with the hard men who'd fought to live free in this harsh land. She felt safe—except from her own thoughts that refused to keep quiet.

What if Jack died at the posse's hands? What would she do? Where would she go?

Flynn O'Brien's wealth and reach was vast. He wouldn't stop until he found her and got his book back. And now that she had Sawyer and Willow to look after, she wouldn't have the freedom to run that she'd had before. The stakes were definitely higher now.

She quaked inside to think about crawling into that camp with a dozen members of the posse on guard, and each an expert shot...she was sure. Still, if Jack was there, that's where Nora wanted—no, *had*—to be.

Besides, she'd vowed to free him if he needed her. The moonlight had been so bright, and Jack's kisses, his arms around her, had made her feel like the most beautiful and the most desired woman in the whole world.

A few miles across the rugged country, they stopped and tied their horses up, going the rest of the way on foot. When they topped the ridge, no campfire burned. Had the marshals extinguished it?

Was this a trap? Needles of worry crawled up her spine and neck. She couldn't breathe.

"Stay here, Miz Nora," Clay Colby whispered. "Let us see what's going on."

She put an arm around Sawyer and watched Jack's friends inch toward the camp, saying a prayer for their safety. The shadows swallowed them.

Time passed very slowly, and the longer it went, the more nervous she became. Had the posse caught them? How many would she have to free? She only had one delicate hairpin.

At last, a voice called out to her, and the trio reappeared, their faces grim.

Nora grabbed Luke Legend's arm. "What's wrong?"

"Jack's gone." Luke huffed out a breath. "Gone."

Twenty-one

How could Jack be gone? What was Luke saying?

Nora bit back a sob. "Gone how? Dead?"

The man rubbed a weary hand over his eyes. "We don't know. The posse packed up camp and there's nothing down there now. They might've taken Jack with them. Or…"

"Or they killed him," Nora choked out. "We didn't hear a gunshot, but they had other ways of taking a man's life." She hated asking the question but she had to know. "Did you look in the trees?"

Sawyer broke free of her. "Did they hang Jack? Did they? We gotta find him."

"We'll have to wait for daylight, son." Clay draped an arm across his shoulder. "Don't think the worst or it'll eat you alive."

Ridge met Nora's searching gaze. "They could've gotten wind of us and decided to head into Saint's Roost early to put Jack behind sturdy bars. They probably didn't want to fight with us. Who knows? Jack's taunted them for too many years. Catching him was a real feather in their cap."

"We have to find him." Nora stalked to her horse. "He may be dead or dying." She untied the reins, put her hand on the pommel, and a foot in the stirrup.

Clay's large hand covered hers. "No. We wait until morning. If Jack's there, we'll find him, and the ground will run red with their blood. I promise you that." The rage coloring his words shocked Nora, yet she knew he meant everything he said. Something told her he'd delivered on those promises in the past with others, and she pitied anyone who stood in his way. "Also, they might've laid a trap for us. We'll find out come daylight."

Anger swept over her. "I have no say in the matter?"

"Not this time. You don't know this country and you could wander out here for months."

That was true. "Darn you for being right." She rested her forehead against the saddle's worn leather, feeling a hundred years old.

Luke laid a hand on her shoulder, then pulled her close. "A storm always leaves the darkest, scariest shadows, but it's only for a little while. We'll get to Jack, and I vow on my mother's grave that I'll not stop until he's back home with you."

His voice trembled with the fervent pledge, and Nora realized just how deep and unshakable this bond between these men and Jack must be. They were truly brothers.

She raised her head and met Clay's gaze. "For the first time since my parents went to glory, I feel like I have family. You and Tally, Ridge, and Luke, are my people." She took his hand. "I belong here."

Luke strode to them. "Yes, you do. We're going to take care of you, Miss Nora."

❧

Dawn found them at the posse's campsite, and it appeared the marshals had left in a hurry. Jack was not hanging in the trees. Nor was there a fresh grave. Nora took her first deep breath since learning of the abandoned campsite.

Sawyer pressed close to her side. "We've gotta find him, Nora."

"We will, sweetheart."

Luke, Clay, and Ridge scoured the area, looking for signs.

Clay straightened. "Tracks lead toward Saint's Roost, Nora. They must've had a premonition that we were close and hurried him behind bars."

Not that bars would hold a man like Jack Bowdre. She strode to her horse. "Let's ride."

It was nearing the noon hour when they galloped into the oddly named town. Nora's gaze swept both sides of the main street. If any saints were roosting there, they must be asleep. In fact, the town appeared deserted except for a few patrons at the mercantile. Strange that there were no saloons, not even one.

Ridge rode beside her and seemed to read her thoughts. "This is a Bible-totin' town. They don't drink, cuss, or allow loose women, and they set the rules for everyone who enters. Even if they have to cram it down our throats."

Clay took a match from his pocket and stuck the stem in his mouth. "Here's the plan. Me and Clay will scout around the town and see if we can find out where the posse went. Ridge, since they're likely to have a wanted poster on you, go to the edge of town to wait and check out who's coming and going."

"Sounds good." Ridge gave his horse a nudge and trotted on.

Nora remembered Ridge saying that Clay and Luke had gotten amnesty for their crimes. She prayed that one day Jack and Ridge would also not have to worry about arrest.

Two women outside the mercantile met Nora's gaze and slid their glances on to the men. They sniffed, jerked open their parasols, and marched down the street, their noses in the air.

Of all things. They'd judged her without knowing one thing about her. Fine. She didn't need them. The way she saw it, they didn't have a whole lot to be proud of. A good many of the buildings were in disrepair; some of the vacant ones stood with broken windows. This was very different from Hope's Crossing, where everyone was working on improvements and the smell of lumber added to the feeling of hope.

"Here, Nora." Luke nudged his horse to the hitching rail in front of the stone sheriff's office and jail.

Her stomach clenched, and she steeled herself for the moment she'd see Jack in such a place. She pulled up next to the men, and Sawyer slid off the back of her horse. She prayed the boy wouldn't throw a fit, demanding to go inside, but he might. She accepted Clay's help in dismounting.

When she swung to the ground, her knees threatened to buckle. "Do we know for a fact that Jack is here?"

"Nope. We figure that you should go in alone and check

things out. Then if he is, we'll have to find a way to get him out." Clay's smile warmed her. "Turn on the tears, demand to see your husband, play on the sheriff's or the deputy's sympathy. If Jack is in there and you see him, tell him we're here and waiting for a chance."

"I want to go in." Sawyer's mouth was set in a line. "I have to see Jack."

Luke slid an arm around the kid's neck, his voice gentle. "I think just Miss Nora should go in first. We'll use you as our ace in the hole. You'll play a big role in freeing Jack tonight because no one notices a boy. All right?"

"I guess. But don't treat me like a kid. I'm nine and a half and my own boss."

"*Sí.*" Luke winked. "We all see that you're a man."

"That's right, Luke." Clay came around the horses. "Sawyer is one of us and he'll have the most important job."

"Really?" A smile curved Sawyer's mouth. Nora ached for him. He tried so hard to fit in and do his part. And, Lord, how he loved Jack.

The kid needed someone to look up to and he couldn't have picked better.

Tears hovered beneath the surface, but she refused to let them fall. They wouldn't do her a bit of good.

What she needed more than anything was a good mirror. She'd frighten Jack half to death with her hair straggling down and mud ruining the hem of her dress. Nerves set in. With luck, Jack was on the other side of the door. Trembling, she finger-combed her hair and shook the wrinkles from her skirt. It was the best she could do.

"You look real fine, Miz Nora." Clay patted her hand. "Now go see that ornery man of yours."

Her gaze swept the men's grim faces, and she knew without a doubt that either would take a bullet for Jack. "Thank you both."

Taking a deep breath and removing a lace handkerchief from her pocket, she strode for the door with confident steps. She turned the knob. One man somewhere in his twenties sat at a desk just inside, reading a newspaper. No one else appeared to be in the sparse office. She assumed the door next to him led to the cells.

He shot to his feet. "Can I help you, ma'am?"

Nora put the scrap of lace to her nose, dredging up a sob. "Are you holding Jack Bowdre?"

"The posse dropped him off this morning and rode on. Sheriff Baxter said I'm not supposed to let anyone see him. Who are you, if you don't mind me asking?"

"His wife." She sobbed harder. "He sent for me from back East and we were married a few days ago. And then the posse arrested him. And they left me all alone. Oh, I don't know what to do." She took a quivery breath. "I'm new to this country and I was so afraid. I heard the most frightening howls, and the animals came very close to my camp last night." She dabbed at her eyes. "Do you know what it's like to be scared to draw a breath, Deputy—?"

"Alan Jones, ma'am." The tall, string-bean man pulled out a chair for her. "I know what it's like to be scared, and I'm sorry you had to go through that."

"I didn't get one wink of sleep, you know." She released fresh sobs and dredged up a few tears, letting one roll down her cheek. "I just have to see my husband. You understand that, I'm sure."

"Sheriff Baxter gave me strict orders not to let anyone back there, ma'am."

She wailed harder, holding the handkerchief over her mouth. "I've just got to. I have to find out what I'm supposed to do. I don't have any family—nowhere to go. Oh, I don't know what to do!" She rocked back and forth, eyeing the large key ring hanging on a nail. If she could distract Deputy Jones long enough to slip the ring into her pocket, she could give the key to Jack. It seemed like a good plan to her.

Deputy Jones fidgeted in his chair. "I wish I could help. Sheriff Baxter will be back in a bit."

"Do you think Jack will—" she swallowed another sob. "Will he hang? My poor Jack."

"I hate to say, but it is something you should prepare yourself for. If you care about him at all, you'd best get him a lawyer. They're itching to hang him and they won't wait long enough for the ink to dry on the execution order."

Nora didn't have to fake the shudder that ran through her. No matter what she had to do, she couldn't let that happen. Real tears streamed down her face. "I've simply got to see him. Maybe he has some money and I can hire one. I didn't know he was an outlaw when he sent for me. I'm a mail order bride, you know." She took a breath and threw out one more thing. "We have children to consider."

"Wasn't that awful fast?" The deputy's large Adam's apple bobbed when he swallowed.

"I was a widow with a son and daughter." She cried harder. "I've been so unlucky in love. Now, I'm going to be a widow again. Who'll take care of me and the children? If I could see him for a moment and find out if he has any money put away, I sure would appreciate it. Money makes every load lighter."

Deputy Jones stood. "All right. Just for a moment. Anything to help your situation."

Nora smiled behind the clenched piece of lace held to her mouth. Only one thing left to accomplish. When the young deputy opened the door to a row of cells, Nora stumbled and fell against the wall. She quickly slipped the brass key ring from the nail and into her pocket, praying Deputy Jones wouldn't miss it until she could put the keys back.

The cells were empty save for one.

At the sight of Jack, lying on a thin mattress in his cell, her knees grew weak. His large form seemed to fill the small space. He slowly pulled to his feet and ambled to the bars. His stormy glare took her aback. What had she done except try to find him? She raised her gaze and put some starch in her spine.

The deputy gave her a smile. "I'll give you a little privacy, but I can't let you stay long, ma'am."

"I understand." She waited until he moved back to his desk before she turned to Jack, wincing. His battered face shocked her, his handsome features hidden beneath the deep bruises.

She didn't miss the anger that turned his gray eyes to bits of stormy ice.

"What are you doing here, Nora?"

The hard words struck her like a stinging blow, but she drew herself up straight and grated low, "I came to get you out."

"You can't. No one can. Go home."

Her anger flared. "And do what? I'm no good at twiddling my thumbs. Just what do you propose I do?"

He pinched the bridge of his nose, his lips moving.

"Are you counting? I cannot believe this." She threw up her hands in disbelief and glared. "I didn't come all this way and ride through a blinding rainstorm, praying not to find you dead, only to hear you count. Listen to me, Jack Bowdre. What you go through is my burden also. We share and share alike—happiness, laughter, trouble. And I'm not leaving until I get darn good and ready." She reached through the bars and jabbed a finger into his chest. "So put that in your pipe and smoke it."

Jack grinned. "Counting is a good way to calm yourself. Ever try it?"

"I have other more effective ways." Her eyes softened and lips parted.

"Do you know how beautiful you are?"

"You must need spectacles. I'm tired, grouchy, hungry, and I could use another bath in your bathing room." Her voice softened. She reached through the bars and cupped his purple jaw. "I love the house you built for me and I want us to go home together, sleep in that big bed of ours."

"I don't deserve you, Nora."

"We don't have much time." She quietly slipped the ring of keys from her deep pocket and through the bars. "Hurry and remove the one to this cell. Clay and Luke are waiting outside, and Ridge is at the edge of town. Sawyer had to come too."

"Sawyer? Nora, this isn't any place for kids."

"I agree, but have you tried to tell him that? He ran off to find you. Jack, he loves you so much."

He removed a key and handed the ring back to her, careful not to make a sound. "Come here, wife." Jack put a hand around her waist and pulled her closer.

Nora's breath hitched. She pressed her face to the bars and he settled his mouth on hers. A small breathless whisper escaped her. "Jack."

Gentle yet persistent, he tugged her bottom lip into his mouth with his teeth, a hand sliding down her throat to the swell of her breasts.

Despite the cold, iron bars, the kiss was raw and left her achy. He ground his mouth against hers as though trying to crawl inside her. She whimpered, weak and hungry for this man she'd married. Her hand bumped the bars when she wound her fingers in his hair.

Her body thrummed, sparks of pleasure running along her limbs and down her spine. The kiss was like how she always felt gulping whiskey would be and feeling the fire travel all the way down to her toes.

"That's much better than counting, Jack. I can't wait to get you home."

The scrape of the chair in the next room alerted her. She broke away. "Sawyer will be in later with more details but be ready tonight."

Jack nodded. "Nora, about earlier—I'm sorry."

"I know. It's already forgotten." She pressed her lips to his for one last kiss.

"Watch out for Guthrie and Belew. They'll hurt you."

"I have a lot of protection outside. I won't stray from them."

Deputy Jones appeared in the doorway. "Time to go, Mrs. Bowdre."

"All right, Deputy. I love you, Jack. Don't ever think I don't. Me and the kids will be fine." Nora followed the deputy out. She didn't know how she'd get the brass ring back on the nail. "Thank you for letting me see my husband. I know what I have to do now."

"That's good." He stood, waiting for her to leave. "Is there anything else?"

"Well, I was wondering…have you ever shot a man? You're so young and all."

"No, I haven't had to face that yet."

He stood between her and the wall and showed no sign of moving. Sweat filled her palms and a bead trickled between the valley of her breasts. She felt ill. Suddenly it came to her. "I feel quite faint. Do you mind if I sit down? I haven't eaten in a while and I'm very dizzy."

"Here, ma'am." He helped her into the chair. "I'll get you some water."

"That would be lovely."

The lawman hurried across the room to a pitcher of water on a stand. As soon as he turned his back, she rose and hung the keys back on the nail. She settled in the chair not a second too soon before he returned with a glass.

"My goodness! This water is so sweet and fresh. Did it come from a nearby spring?"

"No, ma'am. Just a well."

"It's very refreshing and just what I needed. Thank you, Deputy." Nora finished the water and handed back the glass. "You're going to make some lucky woman a good husband one day."

"My mama taught me how to treat a lady."

Nora got to her feet, smiling. "She did an excellent job. Well, I must be going. I have to get back to the children, you know. Thank you so much for letting me see Jack. Now I can go home with a clear conscience."

She moved to the door.

"Wait, ma'am. We have a hotel across the street if you need a room. I've heard they're clean. That is, if you want to stay close by and wait on the circuit judge."

"Thank you, Deputy. You've been most kind." She left the jail with the taste of Jack's lips on hers, his touch branding her.

Soon he would be free, and that thought carried her to the waiting men, the likes of which this town had probably never seen.

Twenty-two

JACK SAT UNMOVING IN HIS CELL FOR HOURS AFTER NORA LEFT, the silence blaring in his head. She filled everything with music, color, and richness. Jack sighed. He'd been such a fool and wasted much of the time they'd had together by being frustrated and put out. Oh, to get those hours and days back.

The piece of metal that would give him freedom warmed in his trouser pocket. She'd put herself at great risk when she stole the brass key ring. Their wedding vows came to mind. She'd promised to find him a key if he got arrested, and damn if she didn't deliver. That was one determined lady.

And she was his.

He could've looked high and low and not found another bride as fine as her.

The sound of voices seeped through the crack the deputy had left in the door, but he couldn't make out the words. One of the people appeared agitated.

Jack smiled. *Sawyer.* The kid was coming to tell him the plans for tonight.

The kid would make a fine man one day—if he got to grow up. It had been Jack's duty to see that he did. Only now, things had changed and there were a lot of ifs and maybes.

The deputy moved closer to the door, and Jack had no trouble hearing the conversation.

"I can't let you go back there. Anyway, kids aren't allowed in the jail," Deputy Jones said.

"But I hafta." Sawyer was persistent to a fault. Jack let a grin curve his mouth.

"Who are you and why do you need to see Bowdre?"

"He's my new papa and I gotta tell him about Mama. She's awful sick. Puking an' everything. And the baby is crying something awful. I don't know what to do."

Jack could picture the frown on Alan Jones's face. The man was caught in the middle. He'd already bent the rules once for Nora. Would he for Sawyer too?

At last the deputy spoke. "I guess I can just this once, kid. But only for five minutes."

Jack hurried back to his cot and pretended he hadn't heard anything. Seconds later, Deputy Jones stood in front. "Got a visitor, Bowdre." Then to Sawyer, he said, "Make it quick."

Sawyer's sorrowful stare told Jack he was hurting bad. He waited until Jones went back into the office. The sniffles were loud in the silence, and Sawyer dragged his sleeve across his nose.

"Hi, Sawyer. It's good to see you." Jack reached through the bars to touch the boy's shoulder. "How are you?"

"I'm scared."

"I know, and I'm sorry for that."

"Everybody I love dies." The pain in Sawyer's whisper cut through Jack like a knife. "My grandpa, my papa, my mama, my sisters." He paused. "Now maybe you."

Sawyer moved closer, and Jack folded his arms around the boy. The admission and the pounding of the kid's heart against him brought a lump to Jack's throat. "I know I'm in a tough spot, but don't count me out yet. We'll get through this." Even if he had to shoot everyone in the way.

"Promise?"

"On my honor."

"I had to come and try to save you. You ain't mad, are you?"

"No, son. Nora said you'd tell me about tonight. Hurry before the deputy comes back."

"We'll wait until the sheriff and deputy leave to make their rounds. Mr. Luke and Mr. Colby think that'll be about eight o'clock. Mr. Colby will give you the owl hoot so you'll know when to come out. You'll unlock your cell and we'll have horses waiting around back, out of sight."

"I'll be ready."

"Jack?"

"What, Sawyer?"

"I'm real worried."

That made two of them. "What about?"

"They might shoot you. Can you get a gun?"

"The sheriff put mine in his desk drawer. I'll get it before I leave the jail." How many things would the kid find to worry about? But then, Jack could understand it, given that everyone he knew and loved had ended up in a grave. "I'll be okay. I promise."

"Will you come home with us?"

"Absolutely."

Sawyer finally relaxed his shoulders. "I like the house and my bed. Nora tucks me in at night like my mama used to do."

"What did you think about that?"

"That Mama must've sent Nora to take her place."

Sudden thickness blocked Jack's ability to swallow. Finally, he managed, "I think so too."

Deputy Jones came to the door. "Time to go, boy."

Sawyer's eyes shone with tears as he whispered. "I love you, Jack. Don't ever leave me."

Before Jack could form the right reply, Sawyer hurried out beside Jones. What the hell had he gotten into? How could he have let such a strong bond form between him and Sawyer?

Hell! Jack could barely take care of himself, and now he had a wife, a boy, and a baby depending on him. The image of his son, Alex, at his mother's feet amid the smoldering, charred ruins of their home, swept across his vision. He'd picked up Alex's little body, limp and lifeless, and held him. Tears had rolled down Jack's face, his heart shattering like fine crystal.

The outlaws he'd been chasing had tied his Rachel to a chair. They broke the oil lamps on the floor. One match had turned his world to ash.

Alex would never marry. Never dream of a bright future. Never fully know the depth of his father's love.

And now, Sawyer had snuck past the defenses he'd erected against that same pain. *Hell and be damned!*

❧

Nora stood on the boardwalk with some time to kill. The name above a small, busy café caught her eye—the Amen Corner. She spoke to the men, and minutes later, all four strolled into the eatery and found a table.

A harried man wearing a long apron rushed by with plates of food in his hands. "Be with you folks in just a moment. The menu is on the blackboard."

When he came over ten minutes later, Nora shouldn't have been surprised to see him wearing a clergy collar, but she was. She ordered a bowl of stew. That was all she thought she could hold after seeing Jack. The men and Sawyer ordered a larger meal. Nora looked around at the full tables, and still people were pouring in. Except maybe a cook in the back, the one minister seemed to be the only person working, and he was drowning in food and tables.

Finally, Nora rose and approached him. "You look like you can use some help, sir."

Relief flooded the man's face. "Thank you. If you'll do that, I'll go to the kitchen and we'll get these people cleared out."

She'd told the men to go ahead and leave and she'd catch up to them later. She worked for an hour before she had a chance to look up.

When the rush ended at last, she sat down with the minister. "I'm Nora Bowdre and just passing through."

He shook her hand. "Brother Paul. I know what you're thinking, but this is only temporary. I'm looking for a congregation, but meanwhile, I have to feed my stomach."

His spectacles made his eyes larger, but they were kind eyes. Other than a smattering of gray at his temples, Nora didn't see any in his brown hair. She put him around forty. Brother Paul had some wear though, as evidenced by the lines in his face. Maybe tending a flock aged a man.

"Have you heard of a new town called Hope's Crossing?"

"I've heard it mentioned. Folks say it's a town of outlaws."

"That's right, but they're good men and they love their families. The town needs a church. Will you come?"

"I can think of no greater need of a ministry. I'll think about it."

She didn't have the heart to leave him with the mountain of dirty dishes, so she went for Sawyer and they set to work. It helped to keep her mind busy and off the impending jailbreak, where anything could go wrong.

⁂

Night fell and Sheriff Baxter came to light the oil lamp. The silver hair and mustache seemed deceptive, and Jack knew by his piercing eyes that it would be a mistake to think him weak. He'd heard how Baxter once stood up against the vicious Vincent gang, sending them all to their graves, and another time single-handedly prevented a jail escape of two murderers.

A man would be a fool to think Baxter easy.

"Supper was good tonight." Jack walked to the iron bars. "You'll have to thank the cook over at the café for me. That apple pie was purely a sin the way it melted in my mouth." Too bad there hadn't been near enough of his only meal of the day. His stomach growled.

"I'll tell him. I doubt he'll be impressed. George has seen a lot of bad men come through here." Baxter stuck a match stem in his mouth. "You won't be here long though, Bowdre. The judge arrives tomorrow."

That was quick. Jack unconsciously loosened his collar.

He sighed. "Guess my luck's about to run out."

"So it seems. Get some sleep." Baxter strode into his office and shut the door.

Jack had no way of knowing what time it was. He could only wait and listen for Clay. He must've dozed off, because at some point, he awoke with a start. The owl hoot came again. He rose, put on his hat, and removed the key from his pocket. In seconds, he unlocked his cell.

Every nerve was taut. A million things could go wrong.

He flattened himself against the wall and crept to the inner door, where he pressed his ear, listening. No sounds in the office. He turned the knob and found the room empty. Quick strides took him to the desk drawer, where he pulled out his gun belt, complete with the Colt in the holster. He checked and found it loaded before strapping it on. The second gun was also in the drawer, and Jack stuck that one in his boot.

Gripping his Colt, he cracked open the door to the street and looked out. Clear.

One more glance and he slid onto the boardwalk. *Damn!* He'd have to pass in front of two businesses before he reached the alley where the horses would be. While he recognized why Nora and his rescue group waited out of sight, he wished they would've left one mount out front. The promise of freedom was worth a struggle though.

His stomach clenched at being exposed a whole lot longer than he'd first thought.

He'd only taken two steps when some kind of large hound bounded from the shadows and came right up to him. It barked and sniffed his leg.

"Go on, dog."

The animal whined and leaped up, barking again.

"Shush now. I can't play with you." For God's sake, of all things! All he needed to make his jailbreak complete was for the dog to hike a leg on him, which Jack wouldn't put past the hound right now. That would add even more sorry luck to his already pissy predicament.

The barking grew insistent. The fool thing would soon draw curious glances.

Lifting the large paws from his leg, Jack ducked low and sprinted to the door of the doctor's office next to the jail. There, he stood in the deep recess, his gaze sweeping up and down the street. The dog followed, panting, apparently happy to have found a new friend.

A soft whistle and slight movement drew attention to the dark figure standing at the alley. Had to be Clay. At least he had help now, but if he didn't get rid of the blasted dog...

Sawyer stepped past the dark figure and called to the animal. "Here, boy. See what I got."

Still the animal stayed glued to Jack. "Go on now."

The dog's long, slobbery tongue snaked out and licked his hand.

"Scat."

"Come on, boy. I got jerky." Sawyer slapped his leg.

Finally, the hound loped toward the boy. But just as it appeared the path was clear, the door to the doctor's office swung open. Ice slid down Jack's spine. He tugged the collar of his jacket up around his neck and tried to act casual.

"What's going on out here?" The man squinted through the darkness. Jack couldn't tell if it was the doctor or someone visiting.

"My dog got loose," Jack mumbled, turning his face deeper into the shadows. "Sorry he bothered you, mister."

"I can help if you need me."

"No thanks. My son caught him. If you'll excuse me, I'll head on."

The door shut behind the Good Samaritan. Jack drew in a lungful of air and limped for the alley as fast as he could.

"Stop!" someone yelled.

Jack ducked around the corner of the row of buildings to join the waiting group.

Just then, another man sounded the alarm that froze Jack's blood. "Jailbreak! Bowdre's getting away!"

"Here." Clay handed him the reins of a horse.

Jack leaped into the saddle and followed behind Nora and Sawyer, who rode double.

Shots rang out and bullets landed around him. He plastered himself to his mount's mane and returned fire, praying that Nora and the boy wouldn't get hit.

A horse and rider gave pursuit. The dog loped along close behind.

Damn! Jack's heart pounded. He spurred his horse and followed close to the others, desperate to find safety, but the rider kept coming.

They raced along the ground, each minute bringing their pursuer closer. Clay, Ridge, and Luke dropped back to protect Jack's flank, laying down a blistering wall of gunfire and forcing the rider to finally turn back.

Jack relaxed and focused on avoiding any holes that could break his horse's leg.

On through the night they galloped like silent ghost riders. A couple of hours later, they stopped at a creek. Sawyer slid off the back of the horse while Jack limped to help Nora dismount. His leg was giving him fits.

She flung her arms around his neck. "You're free. I was so scared."

Clay's voice barely registered, the men moving away to give Jack and Nora some privacy. "Sawyer, let's see to the horses. They need water."

The moonlight shone on Nora's face, illuminating the love shining in her eyes. Jack didn't think he'd ever seen a more welcome sight. He fingered the blond silk of her hair. "God, how I missed holding you. I'm tired, filthy, and hungry enough to eat a horse, but man, how I want you, lady."

Her breasts heaved wildly against his chest. Jack covered her parted mouth with his, the kiss sending that familiar need racing through his body.

Soon, he'd lay her down and make her his wife in every sense of the word. As he drank of her sweet lips, he traced her delicious curves with his hands—touching, kneading, caressing every inch within reach.

Ridge softly called Sawyer's name again, but Jack could barely hear over the roar in his ears. Even if he spent the rest of his life in her arms, he'd never get his fill of Nora Kane. She set his world straight and gave it color. No longer was everything in black, white, and dull gray.

Jack ground his mouth to hers and slipped his tongue through the moist opening of her lips, tasting her need and savoring the fact that she belonged to him.

Nora wound her fingers in his hair and let out a soft whimper. Then, when he released her, she clung to the front of his jacket. Her voice was husky. "You're mine, Jack Bowdre, and I would die inside if anything happened to you."

"So would I if you were taken." He kissed her temple, where her heartbeat throbbed. "But we have miles to go before we reach home, pretty lady."

Though reluctant, they broke apart and Nora kept her gaze lowered and busied herself rifling through her saddlebags. He knew she was too embarrassed to look at the men. Nora had beat a rat to death with her boot, battled a fish down her dress, and faced down Darius Guthrie, but she didn't want to kiss in front of an audience. She didn't have to worry on that score. The men stood talking at the small creek, not paying them any attention.

Hiding a smile, Jack strode to his friends. "I think we should avoid Saint's Roost for a while. Was anyone hit?"

"Nope. How does it feel to be free?" Ridge put a hand on Jack's shoulder.

Jack rubbed his aching leg and grinned. "Pretty damned good."

Sawyer came around the group and hugged him. "I'm glad you're out, Jack." His admission back in the jail that everyone around the boy had died swept into Jack's mind. A thing like that could scar a boy forever.

"Thanks for calling the hound." Jack ruffled Sawyer's hair. "I couldn't get rid of him no matter what. Craziest thing I ever saw."

Clay laughed. "He followed us out of town a pretty good ways before we lost him. The fool dog wanted to go with us. Violet would've loved that. My daughter and animals are inseparable."

Nora buckled the saddlebags and joined them, slipping one arm around Jack's waist and holding a sack with the other. "I got us some food while we waited for darkness. Take your pick." She opened the burlap sack and Sawyer took out a boiled egg.

"Thanks, Miz Nora." Clay reached in for some of everything. "This looks good."

Again, Nora surprised him. She'd thought ahead and made sure to have something to eat.

"I'm starving. Only had one meal in the last two days and it was barely enough to keep a bird alive." Jack took out three eggs, two biscuits, and a portion of jerky. They did little more than take the edge off his hunger, but he enjoyed every bite. "Just curious, Nora, where did you get all this food?"

"While I waited for you, I worked in the Amen Corner café back in the town. Sawyer and I washed dishes and cleaned. In return, the owner let me use the kitchen and paid us in food."

Sawyer grinned. "I helped."

Jack draped an arm around the boy's shoulders. "I'll say you did. I'm flabbergasted. Lady, you beat all I ever saw."

"Well, I needed something to do to pass the time and I knew everyone would be hungry."

"If you don't want to marry her, Jack, I'll sure take her," Ridge teased.

Jack growled low. "Just try it. And for your information, we're already as married as you would've made us."

His gaze met Nora's glistening eyes, and he knew he was one lucky man. If they didn't make it home by noon, Jack was going to cuss a blue streak. He was going to eat, take a bath, and lock himself in the bedroom with his smart and beautiful wife.

A god-awful racket came as something crashed through the brush behind him.

"Get down, Nora!" Jack swung around, his gun drawn. Beside him in a line were Luke, Clay, and Ridge—each with a pistol in his hand.

The hound from Saint's Roost bounded from the thick vegetation, tongue lolling out, and made a beeline for Sawyer.

The hair rose on Jack's arm. He stood rooted to the spot, expecting the lawmen from the town to come bursting through, expecting the order to throw down his weapon and surrender.

Only, no one appeared.

"What the hell!" Jack helped Nora up and turned to his friends. "How on earth did that dog follow us? He couldn't have kept up with the horses."

"Appears he sniffed his way." Clay slid his Colt back into the holster and the others followed suit.

"She's a girl dog." Luke watched the hound leaping up on Sawyer, licking his face with her slobbery tongue. "Bloodhounds have an unbelievable sense of smell."

Ridge snorted. "As ripe as Jack stinks, a blind jackass could follow him."

"Watch it, Ridge. I'd expect better from a friend." Jack grinned and scratched his itchy stubble. "I'm just glad the dog came alone. What are we going to do? Can't take her back to town."

Sawyer glanced up with hopeful eyes. "Can I keep her? Please?"

"Don't see why not." Jack draped an arm around Nora's neck. "What do you think, darlin'?"

"Every boy needs a dog, and she might come in useful. You never know when we might need to find someone." Nora's gaze softened as it always did when she looked at Sawyer. "What will you name her?"

"She's really pretty." The kid glanced up. "Nora, what do you think about Scout?"

Jack didn't have the heart to point out how the name sounded like one for a boy dog.

"That's a fine name. Scout it is." She knelt to rub between Scout's long, floppy ears.

"How about we make tracks for home before something else happens? At the rate we're going, we won't get there by dark." Jack couldn't get rid of the low hum under his skin in anticipation of a bath and making love to Nora.

She reached for his hand, and her smile seemed to say that she meant to hold him to his silent promise.

Twenty-three

HOME HAD NEVER LOOKED SO GOOD TO JACK AS WHEN THEY rode in around noon. For a while he'd doubted he would see it again, especially when Belew had tried to execute him. Jack squinted up at the blue sky and took a cleansing breath before dismounting.

"We made it, darlin'." He swung Nora down, his hands lingering on her waist for a long moment until the din of a gathering crowd broke them apart.

"Been trouble." Tobias January stepped forward. "The bastard took Travis."

Jack stilled. Travis Lassiter had been there since they first started building the town. He was a bit younger by a couple of years, but a man they all counted on.

"Who took him?" Clay barked.

"A damn bounty hunter. He waltzed in here and grabbed Travis. We tried to stop him."

"I fired two good shots, sweetheart." The voice belonged to Tally. She strode to Clay. "One hit him in the shoulder. Not sure where else. He never slowed down."

Rebel Avery ran to them, sobbing. "You have to go get him back. I love him."

"How long ago did this happen?" Jack asked. He was ready to climb back into the saddle and give chase. Hell, this was his fault—Clay, Ridge, and Luke had left the town to come help him. If they'd been there, no bounty hunter would've gotten through the entrance.

"Four or five hours ago. Travis, me, and the children had just finished breakfast." Rebel's green eyes flashed, and the breeze ruffled her black hair. "That bounty hunter didn't even give us a chance. He barged into my soddy and took Travis at gunpoint. Please, go get him."

Luke's eyes narrowed. "Did he give a name?"

Tobias January's face darkened. "Will Spencer's his name. Hung around Cimarron quite a bit, always watching people."

"I know him. There's not much chance of catching him unless Tally hurt him bad." Luke's dark gaze told Jack there was bad blood between him and Spencer.

"I say we ride out and see if Spencer stopped to patch himself up," Jack suggested.

Nora stayed silent but moved closer to him. He knew she was worried. Damn, they'd just gotten home, and he was filthy and tired. Now he had to ride out again in his dirty clothes, on little sleep, and missing his bath as well.

Ridge shifted his weight. "I agree. Even if there's a small chance of getting Travis back."

"It's what we do. Everyone in this town is my responsibility." Clay put his arm around Tally. "I should've been here to stop the bastard."

Dallas Hawk flushed with anger. "Are you saying the rest of us ain't capable? Me and the others raced out, guns drawn, but the bastard kept Travis in front of him the whole time until they got on the horses."

"I'm not laying blame, Dallas." Clay rubbed the back of his neck. "I know you did your level best."

"Stop hem-hawing around or I'll get my horse and go get Travis myself." Rebel's chest was heaving. She turned toward the corral.

"Go back to those kids, Rebel," Clay said softly. "This is my job."

"We should take our new bloodhound," Jack suggested. "We can use her nose."

"Good idea," Clay answered, calling the animal.

Nine-year-old Ely and four-year-old Jenny Carver raced up and latched on to Rebel's waist. Poor kids. If they lost Rebel, they'd have no one. Clay and Tally had rescued the brother and sister when they'd raided the Creedmore Asylum last year, burning the hellhole to the ground. It was nothing but a place of torment, and for a price, the asylum had taken in healthy family members that others wanted to get rid of. They'd kept Tally for a year before she escaped.

He couldn't let these two kids lose a home again.

Jack kissed Nora's cheek. "I'll be back soon."

She clutched his shirt. "Be careful. I don't want this man to get you too."

With a nod, Jack mounted up and galloped away from Hope's Crossing with the other men—Scout loping alongside. Spencer hadn't gone south to Saint's Roost or they'd have crossed paths on the road. Jack's bet was on the wild and wooly town of Mobeetie. Probably had a passel of friends there, ones who'd do whatever Spencer asked.

As he rode, Jack thought of Travis. He was a nice-looking man of about twenty-seven. His dark-blond hair and the deep cleft in his chin made him popular among the ladies, but he had eyes only for Rebel. Folks expected them to tie the knot soon enough.

Only now it might not be possible. Travis had a price on his head, and a judge might be inclined to hang him.

Scout led them to every place Spencer and Travis had stopped and tracked blood the first ten miles. Spencer must've gotten the bleeding stopped somehow.

Luke removed his hat and wiped his forehead. "Appears a wasted effort to go farther."

"Let's ride on a ways," Jack suggested. "We might get lucky." He hated having to go back and tell Rebel. *Damn!* The former saloon girl was tough, but he didn't know how she'd take this. Probably not well. But she had those two kids to think of, and that would help.

Finally, at twenty miles, they stopped again. The saddle leather creaked under Jack as he shifted his weight. "Are we going to ride all the way into Mobeetie?"

"I'm ready for a fight, but that might not help us find Travis." Clay drew his sack of Bull Durham and papers from his pocket. "We'd have to whip the whole damn town."

"It'll be dark before long." Jack sighed. "I'm too beat to whip anyone."

The rest voted to turn back, and Jack was relieved. He was dead tired. Sometimes a man had to know when to fight and when to back away. "Maybe we can send Dallas or Skeet Malloy to ride over and quietly ask around. I'd feel better knowing what happened to Travis. I've been mulling something over in my mind, and with Travis's deal, I have to speak."

The saddle leather creaked when Clay leaned forward, all ears. "Don't be shy now, Jack. Spit it out."

"I think we have a traitor in our midst. Think about it. How else would Marshal Dollard have known where I was and set a trap? And now how damn convenient that a bounty hunter waltzed in and took Travis while most of us were gone."

Luke's face darkened. "If there is, you'd best root him out soon, or no one will be safe here."

Clay pulled out his small sack of tobacco and cigarette papers. "You're not saying anything that I haven't thought, Jack. That whole deal with you stunk to high heaven, and Dr. Mary even said something wasn't right. The woman in childbirth she went to help had a normal delivery, not a risky one as the rider who came to get her said."

"But who?" Ridge asked. "Most have been with us from the beginning, and I will not believe the traitor is a woman."

"Me either," Clay agreed. "But we've had recent single men appear in town and we don't know anything about them."

"We'll have to keep our eyes and ears open." Jack glanced up at the sky. "Let's head for home."

All murmuring agreement, they set their sights on Hope's Crossing. The sun was setting when they arrived.

Nora ran from the house when Jack trotted in. "Did you find Travis?"

"No." Jack wearily stepped from his big dun. "Looks like they reached Mobeetie and we voted to fight another day."

He put his arm around her and stared toward the corral where Clay and Luke were talking to Rebel. Her wails reached them. Damn, she was taking this hard. Dreams died a hard death for people who had little to keep them going.

Tally put a hand on Rebel's waist and aimed her toward the woman's little soddy.

"I feel so sorry for her, Jack. She loves him and now her life seems over." Nora glanced up. "I'd be devastated if anything happened to you. And it could, so easy. You're all wanted men. I don't know how you live your lives."

"One minute at a time and we try not to think about it."

"I have supper ready. You must be starving."

"I'm hungry enough to eat a rabid coyote."

"You are not. No one would be that hungry."

"Pretty darn near." He nuzzled her neck. "There's something else I can't wait to do."

"Any hints?"

"It involves getting you naked and a bed."

Sawyer raced from the house. "You're back, Jack."

"That I am." He noticed the boy's indecision. Apparently, Sawyer wanted to hug him but didn't know if Jack wanted him to. Jack reached for him and put an arm across his thin shoulder. "Did you help Nora?"

"I got to feed Willow and got her to sleep. I think she likes me."

Nora laughed. "She likes anyone with a bottle."

Jack kissed the top of the boy's head and held the door. A warmth dropped over him. The house he'd built for his mail order bride seemed to welcome him with open arms.

He'd lived his life not daring to look beyond tomorrow. But tonight, even as tired as he was, he'd fight like a badger to keep what he had.

Sawyer glanced up and Jack could see he struggled to say something. "Jack?"

"Yeah."

"When I grow up, I want to be just like you." The boy's words were soft but struck Jack like a sledgehammer.

"I'm no one to look up to." He took Sawyer's shoulders and faced the boy. "There are lots better men than me. Why walk in my footsteps?"

"Well, you're not like Bittercreek. You're an outlaw and

I know you did lots of stuff, but you care about people. You didn't have to take me from Bittercreek, but you did. I think you were ready to die for me."

Jack couldn't speak past the lump blocking his throat. He finally cleared his voice, but when the words came out, they were gruff. "Always. For you, Nora and Willow too."

"But not just us. Maybe even a stranger if they need help."

"How you came to this I don't know, but maybe you're right." Jack watched Sawyer blink back tears, trying not to let his emotions get the best of him.

Sawyer dragged his sleeve across his nose. "Jack, thank you for being good to me. You and Nora let me be a kid again."

Again, Jack felt he'd been knocked to his knees. "Because you need that. As far as anything else, be your own man. Don't follow anyone else. You have a good heart and a strong mind and someday you're going to change this land."

"Yes, sir."

"You go on in. Tell Nora I need to see to my horse."

Sawyer's eyes lit up. "I'll do it. Please, Jack, let me."

"Okay." Jack watched the kid take the reins and stride off with his dun. This night called for some serious thinking.

But first, he meant to make love to Nora—even if it harelipped the damn governor.

Twenty-four

THE NIGHT WAS LATE WHEN NORA TUCKED SAWYER IN AND kissed his forehead. Scout was already asleep on a rug beside his bed. Then she fed Willow and rocked her to sleep. Laying the babe in the crib in the corner of their bedroom, Nora put the rosary that belonged to Willow's mother into a drawer. She'd give it to Willow when she got old enough and tell her about her mother.

She undressed and straightened her hair in the mirror. Anticipation leapfrogged inside her as she made her way to the bathing room.

The next hours would belong to her and Jack. Finally, they would cement their marriage.

She opened the door and took in the sight of her husband, lounging in the big tub. Water slickened the parts of his body she could see. Muscles that she'd only felt next to her as she slept on the trail rippled in his chest and arms. Freshly washed hair curled against his neck.

Oh my!

Thank goodness he didn't know what he did to her.

Excited goose bumps rose, her skin prickling, already yearning for his touch.

He'd freshly shaved, all except for a closely trimmed mustache. She found herself missing the stubble that had added a whole other element of danger.

His lazy gaze slid over her, a crooked grin transforming his face. She sucked in a breath. Gone were the grim lines slashing around his mouth that she'd seen on the stagecoach. The sharp angles had softened, and the ice had melted from those hard, gray eyes. He'd been an outlaw fighting to stay alive then. Now, the handsome features and warm smile of the man she'd married underneath the stars replaced the dark, brooding cloud.

A wolfish grin curved his sensual mouth. He crooked a finger. "Come here, Wife."

Nora's knees threatened to give way and her heart raced. She clutched the doorframe for support, intimately aware that she was naked beneath the light wrapper she wore.

"The water's warm and I won't bite."

Her breath caught and hung in her throat at Jack's low teasing. "You promise?"

"As much as I'm able. You sure tempt a man mightily though."

The need to feel him under her proved too much. She slipped off her cotton wrapper, letting it glide to the floor.

A sinful grin reached Jack's eyes, and they glittered like stars under the oil lamp. He wanted her and, oh, how much she wanted him.

A tendril of heat curled along her spine as she slipped into the close confines of the tub, next to all that temptation that she no longer had to resist. He curled an arm around her, and she relaxed her back against his chest as a rush of emotion turned her insides to a quivering, feverish mess.

The heat, the scent of the soap filled the room, and Nora had the sensation of floating. If this was all a dream, she didn't want to wake up. She ran a flattened palm over the muscles of his arm, conscious of the hard planes of his body pressed against hers. She could scarcely contain her nervous jitters, trying not to let Jack see how aroused he made her.

"I've waited forever for this moment, Jack." She caught her bottom lip between her teeth. "And now that it's here, I don't quite know what to do."

"Don't worry about that. There's nothing to do except open your heart and let the feelings take control. You're a beautiful, desirable woman, Mrs. Bowdre." Jack's deep voice, the warmth of his arms, sent shivers tumbling through her. He pushed her hair aside and dropped kisses on the sensitive skin on the nape of her neck.

"I'll bet you say that to all the ladies," she said breathlessly.

"Only this one." He pressed gentle kisses to her temple

and to the delicate skin behind her ear. "I've waited as long as I care to. Tonight, I intend to make love to you if I have to lock the door and hold you hostage." He nibbled his way across her shoulders. "Barred to everyone—with the exception of the children of course—and they'd best stay asleep for the next two hours."

His tender declaration swept past the last of her nerves. Though it wasn't easy, she managed to turn to face him and ran her palms across the hardness of his chest, traced the scars, the hollows along his ribs, the fresh cut on his arm that had come from Bittercreek's knife.

Hot tears burned behind her eyes. But for lucky breaks, he wouldn't be alive. Wouldn't be here with her.

Straddling his lap, she felt Jack's arousal against her bottom, sending delicious heat to her core. A sweet ache she'd never felt before thrummed inside her.

Nora drew in a quivery breath and kissed her way across his collarbone, then nuzzled his muscular neck. "You've been through so much pain, Jack. It's a miracle you survived."

"But I did. You did too, and here we are." He lifted the soap, worked it up into a lather, and moved his slickened hands along her arms and back.

When he moved to her breasts, lifting the heaviness in his big hands, she thought she'd die from sheer pleasure. Never had she been touched like this. And when he captured her swollen nipples between his thumb and forefinger, she hissed in a breath, waves of pleasure crashing over, around, and through her.

"Please, Jack. I want more."

His voice came out hoarse. "We have all the time in the world, darlin'."

"No, I want you now."

"Some things need to be savored." He slid his hand under the water to cup her hot, pulsating core, then massaged the sensitive folds with his fingers until she quivered with a need that was hard to explain. Something teased just beyond reach, a release she craved.

"Oh, Jack, love me."

When she thought she couldn't stand another second more, he eased a finger into her wet entrance. The sensation of pleasure overpowered her, stole her last bit of sanity. She gasped and thrust her hands into the wet strands of his dark hair, pulled his mouth to a breast that seemed to be straining for him.

The real world spun and careened on its axis. She clutched him to her.

"Ride the ecstasy," he murmured, flicking a tongue across the swollen nipple, drawing the protruding bead of flesh into his mouth.

She was alive with searing heat and something strange that demanded fulfillment. Though she was out of her mind with sheer joy, she knew something more waited. Jack Bowdre possessed her, body and soul. And she would never be the same.

The waves became towering peaks that seemed to reach beyond forever, but she didn't care where it took her as long as she was with Jack. The friction of his fingers. The sucking sensation that wrung every morsel of passion from her. Sudden loss of control sent her mind cartwheeling.

Bone turned to liquid. She clung to Jack, gasping for breath, grabbing for every bit of the last uncontrolled, throbbing shudder.

He filled and consumed her so completely she couldn't tell where she left off and he began. She belonged to him.

Love for Jack flowed through her veins like warm, luxurious honey.

She barely knew when he lifted her from the water, dried her with thick, soft cotton, and carried her to the bed.

Heat built in his eyes as he covered her with every inch of his hard body.

A fleeting moment's pain shot through her when he eased into her wet tightness, then blessed spirals of ecstasy replaced it. She began the slow, sensual climb to the stars again—giving pleasure, taking pleasure, knowing immense pleasure each step of the way.

The same kind of raging heat that his fingers had aroused took over her body again, only this time much deeper. With his fullness inside her, she felt each ripple of the delicious shudders and spasms.

Nora clutched Jack to her, tumbling end over end, falling from a tall cliff, exploding in a downpour of fiery sparklers. Jack lowered his lips to hers and the kiss swept her to a place so beautiful and serene, where nothing bad could touch her.

From now until forever, she'd belong to Jack Bowdre.

Twenty-five

JACK SHUDDERED AND FOUND HIMSELF SWEPT ALONG A RAGING current, one of the most powerful climaxes he'd ever felt. Making love to Nora was beyond anything he'd ever experienced.

She was sexy as all get-out, funny, frustrating, and maddening all rolled together into one package. Nora Kane was the only woman for him and would always be.

His breath raspy, he rolled off and onto his side facing her. "Have mercy, woman."

"Jack, I've never felt this way before—so complete, so happy."

He trailed a finger down her sweat-slicked throat. "Me too."

"We waited a long time for this. Maybe the anticipation played a big part in this deep emotion wreaking havoc inside me."

"Several times this past week, I didn't know if I'd ever get to make love to you. So many things tried to keep me from it." Jack brushed a knuckle across her cheek, wishing his hands weren't so rough. "You make me a whole man, and I haven't been that in a long while."

For the first time in years, he wasn't just existing, waiting for his fate. He was living with some kind of purpose. Lord, just don't let it end.

Nora snuggled against him, her breasts pressed to his chest. "What will you do when they come for you? You know they will."

"I'm not sure." He still had the marshal's badge that he'd taken off Dollard after the stagecoach wreck. But what good would it do if the posse recognized him?

"We should leave before they come."

"No. I'm tired of running. Whatever happens, it'll take place here. But just so you know, I'm not going to go easy. When they come, I want you to lock yourself in the house."

"I can't do that. My place is by your side, Jack. I'll not hide. I refuse."

"I don't want to argue. See reason for once. The children need you. If you're with me, a bullet could hit and kill you, and then what would Sawyer and Willow do?"

She was silent for long moment, and her voice held defiance when she spoke. "Then I'll be at the window with a rifle. And don't even think about counting."

Jack chuckled softly. He hadn't resorted to counting since he was in jail in Saint's Roost and she'd waltzed in there big as life, daring anyone to try to keep her out. "You've near broke me from the habit."

"That was just yesterday, sweetheart," she said dryly.

He grinned. "Like I said, you've near broke me from the habit."

"I don't know what I'm going to do with you." Nora touched his short beard. "I like the way you trimmed this up. Makes you look very handsome."

"Glad you approve. I kinda like it too, but what I love more is you naked."

They lay in each other's arms, whispering, talking about the future as though he had one. He told her about Sawyer. "I don't want him looking up to me."

Nora snorted. "If you think you can stop him, go right ahead and try. He idolizes you and has since you rescued him from Bittercreek."

"I want him to be his own man and told him so. He's going to make a difference in this world."

Willow let out a cry from her crib.

"I'll get her, Nora. I've missed holding her." Jack rose and pulled on his trousers. He picked up the baby and went downstairs.

He fed Willow, patted her back until she burped, then rocked her in the rocker. Memories closed in around him. He was back in his other life, before it had vanished. How many nights he had taken care of Alex and let Rachel sleep, Jack didn't know. He'd loved that quiet time—just him and his son. It had seemed that the world outside their door didn't exist. But evil had been hiding in the darkness.

He struggled to swallow. Willow snuggled her small body against his chest.

Jack patted her bottom. "Sleep, baby girl, I'll watch over you."

And that was a promise he meant to keep, come hell or high water. Not only to Willow, but Sawyer and Nora too.

❧

First thing that morning, Nora watched Jack open a dresser drawer and remove an ivory-gripped Colt and slide it into his holster. Now that his gun replaced the ones he'd taken from Dollard and Guthrie, much of the tension in his face appeared to melt away.

"That Colt seems to mean a lot to you." Nora finished buttoning her dress.

Jack turned. "I bought a set of these, but Dollard confiscated my other one before he put me on that stage. Probably never see it again. This Colt is perfectly balanced and shoots true." A smile flicked across his lips. "Something a man in my profession counts on."

Nora wondered how many times his life had depended on the accurate firing of his weapon. Listening to the men talk over coffee the last few days, she knew of some of his near brushes with death.

She moved behind him and laid her face on his back. "Do whatever you must to stay alive. I don't want to be a widow."

"I'll do my best, Mrs. Bowdre." Willow began to fuss, and he went to pick her up. "Ready to feed this little girl and Sawyer?"

She laughed. "Not sure the choice is up to me. I'm sure both have their own ideas."

They met Sawyer at the bottom of the stairs and Nora went to the kitchen to get her day started.

After breakfast, Jack sent a man to guard the opening of the town and warn the others of approaching riders. His preparations for a fight sent fear through Nora. After giving Luke Legend a send-off, Nora was fixing Willow a bottle and listening to Jack teach Sawyer how to tie a decent bowline knot in the parlor when a knock sounded at the door.

"I'll get it, Nora," Jack called. A second later, she heard, "Come in, ladies."

Nora took the bottle out of the hot water and tested the temperature by squirting a little on her wrist. Finding it acceptable, she hurried into the parlor to find Tally and Dr. Mary with three other women. "How lovely to have callers. Make yourselves at home."

Tally held out a pie. "We wanted to give you a big welcome. Hope you like peach."

From his seat on the floor, Sawyer's face lit up. "For us?"

"Yes, it is." Tally laughed. "This dessert seems to have found a good home."

"We're delighted. I haven't had time to bake anything yet." Nora cradled the baby with one arm, clutching the bottle in that hand, and brushing Sawyer's hair with the other. "You seem to know all about little boys, Tally."

"Not as much as I hope to soon." Tally laid a hand on her stomach.

Jack took the pie. "Sawyer, can you take this into the kitchen? You can have one piece now and we'll save the rest for later. Then meet me outside so Nora can visit with these ladies in peace. I think we need to see how Scout is getting along with her new sidekick, Bullet, anyway."

The boy hopped to his feet with a grin, stuffing his knotted string into his pocket. He disappeared into the kitchen with the dessert.

"Stay, Jack." Tally offered a big smile and remained standing. "Our mission pertains to both of you."

"I can't imagine what this is about." Nora didn't think she'd ever seen her husband look so uncomfortable. This group of women were making him as nervous as a rooster in a wolf den. He leaned against the wall, and Nora thought it was to take the pressure off his leg. His limp seemed worse today and that bothered her. She wondered if Dr. Mary could help him and vowed to remember to ask.

"Good. First, let me introduce us to Nora." Tally went around the circle. "You know Dr. Mary. Next to her is Belle January, then Rebel Avery. Susan Worth owns the bakery."

Belle's wrinkled face and gnarled fingers told Nora she'd lived a full life. Nora already loved this old woman, who wore her silver hair up in a little knot on the top of her head. Rebel Avery had a hardness about her as if she was ready to fend off an attack at the drop of a hat. Her hair curled about her shoulders, as black as midnight. Nora got the impression that Rebel had seen some awful hard living. Something in the woman reached out to Nora, though.

Everyone needed a friend. Sometimes in life, that was the best you could hope for to get you through. Here in this outlaw town, they lived on the edge between danger and death, and it took a lot out of a person.

Susan Worth rounded out the three, and Nora found a quiet elegance about her. A few streaks of silver in her brown hair didn't detract from her sparkling eyes and pretty face. She had to be in her late thirties. Nora wondered what her story was.

"This is wonderful. Please sit." Nora settled in the rocker. "I hope you don't mind if I feed Willow."

"No, of course not." Dr. Mary perched on a straight-backed chair.

Tally lowered her swollen girth onto the woven seat of a cane-bottom one. "We came to talk to you about your wedding. We need a date. I think the sooner the better."

"Jack and I really haven't discussed this." Nora tilted the baby bottle and Willow sucked contentedly.

Dr. Mary spoke up. "We want you and Jack to get married with the town in attendance."

Jack pushed away from the wall. "A wedding isn't necessary. Nora and I took care of that ourselves."

"But you didn't let us be a part of it," Rebel said softly. "We—this town—needs a celebration."

"I'll make a wedding cake for the ceremony," said Susan Worth.

Nora met Jack's dark scowl and made the decision for them both. "We'll be happy to oblige. Only I have no good dress."

Tally waved her arm. "A small problem. We'll find you one. Now we need a date."

"Jack, what do you think?" He looked ready to start counting. Nora added quickly, "Please, I want this. And I think a formal ceremony would be much better than our short one, make our marriage even more binding."

"Whatever you want is fine, Nora." His face softened, and she wondered if he was thinking about their night of passion.

For a second, she forgot about their company. It was only her and Jack in the room, and the love they'd found while trying not to die. He moved to her side.

Nora reached for his hand. "We should probably make it soon." Just in case a posse tracked them to the town. She kept expecting trouble to ride in, and Jack had to be too.

He squeezed her hand. "How about day after tomorrow?"

The ladies gasped collectively. But Nora knew they had to hurry.

A clock was ticking in her head and each second brought trouble closer.

Twenty-six

THE NEXT TWO DAYS, NORA FELT LIKE SHE HAD TURNED INTO some kind of whirling dervish. Tally found a dress of robin's egg–blue muslin and Belle altered it to fit. Nora had never seen anything so beautiful. With all the preparations, she didn't see much of Jack, but she could feel his gaze at odd times, or turn around to find him staring at her from across the wide street. The tether between them was strong and held together by mere glances.

At night, after the children slept, she lay in his arms and knew there was no place on earth she'd rather be. Jack excited, aroused her and made her dream. But he still hadn't told her he loved her. Maybe he just couldn't say those words. Maybe he never would.

She knew in her heart he cared for her, and that, in addition to her love for him, might be enough.

Rebel Avery was in the mercantile when Nora went to do a little shopping. "Rebel, how nice to see you. I was hoping we'd have a chance to talk."

The woman swung around, her eyes red and swollen. She forced a smile. "Nora, I've been meaning to pay you a proper visit, but..." Rebel glanced away.

Nora laid a hand on the woman's arm. "I understand. I'm so sorry about Travis. Jack told me what a fine man Travis is and how fond he is of your two children. I'm sure you must all miss him terribly."

"It's this land. People can disappear and you never know what happened to them. You were lucky to find Jack after the posse got him."

The comment jarred Nora but she could see how easily people could vanish out here. That would've been harder back in Buffalo. Although Flynn O'Brien had made it happen with no one the wiser. Looking back, she thought it odd that no one ever came to inquire about this one or that one. But to lose Jack the way Rebel had lost Travis would destroy her. She remembered how she felt when they'd reached the posse's camp and found no sign of Jack. Yes, that had shot fear deep into her like she'd never felt before.

"Try not to worry, Rebel. The men will do whatever they can to find Travis, and from what I've seen so far, they're more than capable."

Rebel glanced down at the boardwalk. "I know. I didn't mean to burden you, Nora."

"You're no burden. Come to visit anytime. I'm an excellent listener and we can get acquainted over tea. I'd love that."

"Me too. But your wedding is coming up. I'm good at fixing hair."

"Oh, Rebel, thank you for the offer. You're hired. I've never been good at that."

They parted, and Nora went about her shopping, but she couldn't get the thought out of her head that Jack might go out to do something one day and disappear, never to be seen again. A shudder swept through the length of her.

❧

Nervous jitters took hold of Nora on her wedding day. Her thoughts turned to the wrecked stagecoach, the wild trek across the rugged land, the rat in the cave, taking Sawyer from Bittercreek, and finding Willow. Nora and Jack had shared a lifetime of experiences in a short span. Despite all the hardships, hunger, and cold nights, she wouldn't trade any of it.

They'd found a purity under the stars that she didn't find in daylight. It was like the heavens sparked a greater truth and inspired the kind of love Nora had waited all her life to find.

She sat in her bedroom and tried not to squirm. Rebel piled Nora's hair on top of her head in a becoming style, and Tally helped her into her dress.

This was the first time she'd had a chance to really talk with Tally. Nora asked if she had everything ready for the baby.

Tally laughed. "As ready as I can be. Clay made a crib for the little thing, and it's a beauty. Belle made a quilt to go in it. Violet is beside herself with happiness at the thought of having a baby brother or sister. I'm glad I don't have long to go. I'm tired of looking like a big fat cow."

"I have a feeling Clay doesn't care what you look like," Rebel said. "He loves you."

"We're three lucky women to be secure in our men's love." Tally wore a dreamy look.

Doubt crept in around Nora's heart. Jack still hadn't spoken of love. Was he avoiding telling her because he was still in love with Rachel? Nora chewed her bottom lip. Maybe he had no love left in his heart for her.

And what about herself?

How prepared was she to take a dead wife's place?

A little past noon, Nora walked out of the house toward a small crowd that had gathered in front of the hotel. It appeared each resident of Hope's Crossing had come. Jack had told her that the population of the town numbered around fifty but that more people drawn to the chance of a new beginning arrived every week. Especially since a stage line had added the town to their route.

Despite the town's growing number, they had no church and she didn't know if Brother Paul would come or not. She guessed standing in front of the newly built hotel for the ceremony would do just fine. After all, it wasn't the where but the who that would give her vows meaning. Maybe they could pretend it was an outdoor tabernacle.

One of these days, she'd ask why Ridge Steele never held services. Jack had hinted at a dark story.

Sawyer was waiting for her. He grinned and handed her a bunch of wildflowers that had a blue ribbon tied around them. He'd slicked back his reddish-brown hair and wore a new shirt that Jack had gotten him.

"Thank you, sweetheart. They're lovely." Nora kissed his cheek.

"Mrs. January has Willow," he reported.

"Excellent. Sawyer, will you walk me to Jack and stand with us?"

"Shoot, yeah. If you want." He slipped his arm around hers. "You look pretty, Miz Nora. Kinda like a princess. I haven't ever seen a princess, but I think they might be real pretty. At least Violet says so."

Tightness formed in Nora's chest. "Those are sweet words, my handsome boy."

Scout ambled up with Bullet, and Sawyer had to tell the dogs he was busy with important stuff. They walked toward Jack, who stood with Ridge in front of the hotel. A crowd had gathered around, but Nora's gaze never left Jack's. He cut quite a dark figure in a suit she'd never seen him wear. The clothing emphasized his wide shoulders and chest, his lean waist. The ivory-handled Colt hanging at his side might've seemed inappropriate, but the sight made her feel safe and cherished.

She stood next to him and slipped her hand in his. "I almost didn't recognize you, Jack."

He put his mouth to her ear, his trimmed mustache tickling. "You're beautiful in that dress with your hair all fancied up. I can't wait to take the hairpins out, strip off your clothes, and run my hands over your body."

"Jack!" She used her head to motion toward Sawyer, who'd taken his place beside her.

Sawyer grinned. Surely he hadn't heard. *Good Lord.* Her face flamed.

Solemn and striking, Ridge stepped forward, still wearing his twin Colts, and opened a tattered Bible. "We're gathered here today to unite Jack and Nora in holy matrimony." He cautioned about entering into marriage lightly and to view it as a binding contract.

There was still no mention of love.

Nora's chest clenched. Ridge pounded home the need to respect each other, listen with their hearts, and be each other's helpmeet. Jack squeezed her hand and looked every bit the hungry wolf he had of late. They said their "I dos" and Ridge asked for the ring. She sucked in a breath. She'd never given any thought to a ring.

Yet Jack seemed calm, not uttering a word.

Sawyer fished something out of his pocket, along with some string, a marble, and a coin, and handed a small item to Jack.

"Thank you, son." Then Jack slipped a silver band on Nora's finger and stared into her eyes. "With this, I thee wed."

Tears filled her eyes. This amazing man she'd married was full of surprises and dreams. He already looked to the future and had spoken of Sawyer's role in making the changing world better. Jack had made her dream, too, of a life where they'd have no fear of being separated by arrest. She prayed they'd see such a day when no one would just disappear like Travis.

Before she knew it, Ridge said they could seal their vows with a kiss. Jack tilted his hat back, put his hands around Nora, and lowered his lips to hers. Mindful of those watching, she'd prayed for a short peck, but she and Jack were like a match and dry tinder. The moment their lips met, flames erupted. She clutched his fancy vest, and for a moment, she forgot they stood in a crowd of onlookers.

Jack filled her senses and put them into overload. She laid a hand on his jaw and gave herself over to the chaos he'd set free inside her.

She heard Ridge's voice as though from a distance. "That's enough, Jack. Save some of that for later."

Heat swept into Nora's cheeks. Finally, he released her, totally unapologetic.

"Oh my stars, Jack!" Nora patted her hair, hoping her cheeks weren't scarlet.

"Toss the bouquet!" someone hollered.

She turned her back and threw the wildflowers over her shoulder. A woman's squeal filled the air, and Nora turned to see Rebel holding the bouquet, and she seemed happy for once. Nora just prayed her new friend would get a chance to marry Travis one day.

"Lucky catch!" Susan called.

Tally stepped forward. "Everyone's invited for cake, and

then my darling husband, Clay, is going to signal for Dallas to get out his fiddle. We've got some dancing to do."

Nora clutched Jack's arm. "I don't dance."

He grinned. "Makes two of us. We'll just stand in one spot and sway to the music. Easy."

"I hope so. Will we have to stay long?"

"Nope. One song and we can go home. We have some celebrating to do tonight." He waggled his eyebrows. "Just you and me. We have a slew of new memories to make."

Nora laughed. Whatever he had planned, she was all for it. Folks gathered around and pushed them toward the cake. Susan had made them a masterpiece. It was designed like the town, complete with the corral and windmill. She'd never seen anything so beautiful. Sawyer planted himself right in front of the table and got the first piece.

There was so much laughter that Nora's sides hurt. Yet despite the jokes and laughter as the afternoon progressed, tears lurked beneath the surface. She and Jack put on brave faces, but trouble lay beneath it all.

Frayed nerves took a toll on her. But when the posse got enough men together to come, then what?

To her mind, Jack's best hope was to disguise his appearance. But how? It would have to be more than getting him out of his customary black clothing. Lots more. Maybe an eye patch and make him walk with a cane.

Nothing more came to mind. She slipped away from the party and went to check on Willow, in Dr. Mary's care.

"You're just in time to feed her," the doctor said when Nora entered the medical office.

"That's good. I need to hold her a bit. I missed her at the festivities. Families need to be together at important times like that."

"I agree." Dr. Mary handed her a warmed bottle.

Nora held Willow to her heart for a long moment, soaking up the feel of the little warm body.

How would she be able to give her up if her family arrived one day?

She kissed Willow's cheek and put the bottle nipple into her bow-like mouth. Dr. Mary bustled around the office, putting things away and straightening.

"Doctor, I've been trying to think of a disguise for Jack so that the lawmen won't recognize him when they come. Have you ever used yellow dye to any success?"

"For fabric, yes." Dr. Mary turned. "Elderberry, sage, or goldenrod make the best yellow dyes, but you need to add alum or tin to give them staying power or else the dye'll wash right out. What are you thinking of dying?"

"Jack's hair."

Twenty-seven

DR. MARY CHUCKLED. "DOES JACK KNOW ABOUT THIS HAIR color change?"

Nora winced. "No, and he's going to dig in his heels at the first word." Frankly, he was liable to do worse than that.

"What are you thinking? Tie him down? Chain him up? Might be best to get some big, strapping men to hold him."

Nora pursed her lips in thought. "I won't force him, even though I wish I could. This has to be his decision, but I think if it comes down to either dying his hair or going to prison, he'll choose wisely. At least I'm hoping he won't kill me for suggesting it."

"Let me get this straight. You want to dye his hair yellow."

Nora glanced at her silver wedding band that shone in the light. "Yes. I think he might look even more handsome with light hair. Don't you?"

"Nora, Jack is a handsome man and will still be no matter what color his hair. What you need is to bleach it. I have a recipe, along with the ingredients of diluted barium, potassium hypochlorite, and lemon juice."

"That would be wonderful."

"Keep it off his skin though." Dr. Mary's eyes twinkled. "Worth a try. Should be interesting."

That wasn't exactly the word Nora would use.

Excitement swept through her now that she knew it could be possible. "We need to do it right away. Today, if there's time. I'll have to talk to Jack first." Nora grimaced. "If you hear a loud explosion, you'll know why."

❧

"You want me to do what!" Jack thundered. Nora had caught him in front of their home, where he'd gone to change clothes. He'd never heard such a harebrained idea. He liked his hair brown. Always had. He was used to looking at that man in the mirror.

"Listen to reason, Jack. Don't you think it makes a lot more sense than trying to shoot your way free?" Nora put her hands on her hips. "I don't know how you can be so hardheaded. Do you want to die? Is that it? Do you have some kind of death wish because you don't think you deserve to live?"

"Of course I don't have a death wish. How can you even ask such?" Jack spun around to Clay and Ridge. "Did you put her up to this?"

"Nope." Clay laid a hand on Jack's shoulder. "Just think about it. Assuming a new identity solves everything with no bloodshed. You have the marshal's badge and won't look anything like yourself. You can be whoever you want."

Ridge spoke up. "In fact, I can't picture you with blond hair. Grow yourself a longer beard, and I probably wouldn't know you myself, and we've ridden together for over six years."

Jack yanked off his hat and shoved a hand through his hair. *Hell!*

Sawyer angrily pushed past Clay and Ridge. Jack had noticed the boy standing silent, listening to the conversation; now he faced Jack. "If you don't at least try, you'll never know. Don't you care enough to live for us? I need you, Jack. Don't you see? Willow and Nora need you too."

Nora put an arm around the boy. "Come, let's leave him to stew in peace."

Guilt skewered Jack's chest as they turned dejectedly to the door of the house. "Wait. All right, but nothing says I have to like it."

"At least you didn't start counting, so that's a good sign. I'm going to get out of my finery. I'll only be a minute." Nora paused. "Jack, I'm glad I married you before you bleached your hair."

"Why's that?"

Nora shrugged. "I wouldn't want to marry a stranger."

He chuckled. "Don't be long."

Clay called, "The dance will start in twenty minutes." Then he and Ridge strode toward the men's gathering spot.

"They're probably going to discuss my yellow hair," Jack murmured sourly to himself.

He had to agree that it would be a pretty good disguise. He couldn't wait to see the look on that sheriff's face. Now, what name did he want? The world was wide open to possibilities. He could take his father's name of Orin. Nope. He'd rather meet the hangman's rope. He thought of all the men he'd known and admired over the years—Johnny Coyote, Joe Moody, Tim Shephard, Joe Long.

Everything stilled inside. He'd stood at Joe Long's side when three bullets felled him in Wichita, Kansas. He and Joe had signed on as drovers, taking cattle up the trail for old man Fancher. They were dirty, bone tired, and thirsty when they finally put that thousand-strong herd into the large corral in Wichita, so he and Joe'd decided to head for the saloon. Joe never made it inside. He died on the boardwalk at the hands of an old enemy. Jack had drawn and fired but it had been too late.

Jack ground his back teeth together. At least he'd killed the bastard. Never knew his name. Didn't matter.

Yes, he'd be Joe Long. Marshal Joe Long. His friend would've found that amusing.

Around three that afternoon, Jack pulled Nora into his arms. Dallas Hawk's song made the melancholy brought by his memories even worse.

"What's wrong?" Nora stared up into his eyes. "You seem so far away."

He breathed in the scent of the fragrant soap she'd used and held her tighter. "Nothing but old ghosts circling. I'll be fine."

Nora glanced up, her doe eyes shimmering. "Is it the thought of having light hair? If so, you don't have to do it. We can think of something else."

"It's not that. Memories of a friend hit me while I was trying to decide on my new name, and I can't seem to shake the sadness, that's all."

"They say that as long as you remember someone, they're not really dead," she said softly. "What was his name?"

"Joe Long."

"And you decided to take his identity?"

"Yep." Jack blew out a long breath. "I think he'd like me being him."

Sawyer copied them and danced in place with Violet, his arm protectively around her. Both kids were grinning, too young to know that love took time. Violet was running a hand across his face, familiarizing herself with Sawyer's features.

Jack ached for both of them and everything they'd lost. He drew Nora closer.

Nora wound a strand of his hair around her finger. "I'll have to get used to calling you Joe. I hope I don't mess up and call you Jack in front of a lawman. And we'll have to be sure and tell everyone here in town."

"No, keep this to yourself for now." Just in case the town did have a traitor. Jack placed his mouth beside her ear. "I'm proud to be your husband, no matter what name I use. You make my life worth living and I don't want to spend one day away from you, Mrs. Long."

Nora laughed. "I'm changing names faster than bullets from a Gatling gun. From Kane to Bowdre to Long, and just when I was getting used to Nora Bowdre. If I go by Nora B. Long, I could *be-long* to you, Jack."

"You do anyway. No matter what name you use, you're mine, lady."

"I do like a man who knows what he wants." She twirled his hair around her finger.

Her mouth drew him like a beacon on a dark sea. He lowered his head. The second their lips met, he couldn't have told anyone what his name was, even if they'd held a loaded gun on him.

She melted against him, one hand gripping his vest while

the other played with his hair. He ran a hand down her curves to her waist, where her hips flared.

The kiss held desire and the kind of heat that soldered metals. She opened her mouth, her tongue softly lashing his. It was almost his undoing. If he didn't get her home and undressed soon, he'd explode.

"You make me crazy, Nora. I have this chaos inside threatening to burn me alive, and then I look at you and everything smooths out."

"Jack, you say the sweetest things. I know I make you frustrated enough to count, so it's good to know I can bring you calm as well."

"And peace. Desire. Passion."

Her cheeks turned a rosy pink. "Jack, thank you for my ring. I hadn't expected that. The band is simple yet beautiful, just what I would've picked."

"I saw it in our little mercantile and thought it looked like you. We could've waited on that, but I wanted to make sure everyone knows you belong to me."

"Foolish man," she said softly. "You don't need a ring for that."

The music stopped and Jack took her hand. "Let's go."

Some of the men blocked their path, asking to dance with Nora.

Jack held up his hand. "Not this time, boys. Tonight, she's all mine."

He swept her into his arms and lengthened his limping gait. At the house, she reached for the doorknob, and he carried her across the threshold and up the stairs to their bedroom.

"Put me down, Jack. I can walk."

"I know." He kicked the door closed and set her down. Turning her around, he began the task of undoing all the tiny buttons. For two cents, he'd rip the dress off her, but since she had so few nice things, he took his time.

Finally, the dress yielded, and soon her undergarments and shoes joined it on the floor. He laid her on the bed, worshipping her with his eyes, thankful for daylight spilling in the window that let him see her clearly. Desire for her made him tremble. He hurried to remove his clothing.

Jack lay next to her, propped on an elbow. He ran a finger lightly across one cheek. "I don't deserve you, Nora Kane. Lord knows you could find a better husband, but you'll never get one who loves you more than me." He brushed his lips across hers. "I love you."

Her eyes widened and her breath came uneven. "You just said—"

"That I love you. I'm sorry I couldn't say it when you did. I had to accept in my head that I could love another woman first. When I sent for you, I wasn't prepared to give my heart. It still belonged to Rachel and I felt I would betray her."

"What changed?"

"The night finally got dark enough to see the stars. I remembered something she once told me, and I knew she wanted me to love again."

"What *did* you expect of our marriage if not to love each other?" she asked softly.

"To fill the god-awful loneliness. Give me a family again, some reason to live." Jack traced the outline of her lips, her jaw. "I found out that it was impossible not to give my heart and that terrified me. Loving someone brings a lot of responsibility with it."

"But now?" Her words came out breathless.

"Now, I'm certain that I never want to try living without you. Whatever problems come our way, we'll face together. And when they put me in the ground, I'll know I loved the best, the smartest, most bighearted woman on God's earth."

"Kiss me, Jack." Love smoldered in her twinkling brown eyes.

His mouth covered hers, the kiss burning with a fiery possession, full of admiration, respect, and passion for the woman who lit up his world.

Nora had his heart—every single piece of it.

The kiss deepened, and he ran his hands down her generous body. He meant to love her as he'd never loved anyone.

When they ran out of air, she pushed him onto his back and left a trail of kisses across his chest, stomach, and below. Every feathery touch of her hands and mouth wound him tight, his patience stretched.

Surprise swept through him when she straddled his hips, her bold gaze raking his body, desire flaming in her eyes. Excitement surged as he reached for her breasts. Every chord, every muscle tightened, straining to fulfill the demanding ache.

He had no desire for teasing this time. This time he wanted it hard and fast, and Nora seemed to want it too. She appeared different, and her newfound confidence fired his blood.

In a swift move, he rolled her over and settled himself on top. One thrust put him inside with her muscles clenching around him. Holding. Drawing him deeper.

Giving.

Taking.

Needing.

Oh God, he couldn't live without Nora.

Her heart raced and her breath hitched. She gave a cry and fell into his frenzied rhythm, her hands clawing at his back, pulling him into her heat.

The climb was swift, and he let the pleasure carry him higher and higher. He shuddered and held on, sparks shattering around him like colorful Chinese fireworks.

Nora gasped and arched her body. Jack held her to him as she took her enjoyment, then rolled off, limp and spent.

"I think you're going to stop my heart, lady."

Her breath ragged, she turned on her side. "Complaints, dear husband?"

"Not even one." He tucked a curl behind her ear. "I'm a very fortunate man. Back in the cave when you were smacking that poor rat with your shoe, I knew you'd have passion. You're all in, one hundred percent with everything you do, and I love that."

He just prayed she'd see reason when the posse came and not get in the thick of things.

"And when you milked that cow and let me have the first

drink, I knew right then that you were a true gentleman—even though you looked anything but." A long, comfortable silence fell over them. She plied him with kisses, his nose filling with the sweet fragrance he'd come to love.

"You keep doing that and you'll see my scoundrel side, lady." He nuzzled her neck and across her collarbone.

"Is that a threat?"

He nibbled her fingertips. "Nope. A promise."

Nora tugged her hand from him. "As much as I hate ending this, are you ready to become Joe Long?"

Jack groaned. *Hell!*

Late afternoon, Nora made her way to Dr. Mary's office, still wondering about the bright-yellow paint around the bottom of the building. So once she got inside, she asked.

Dr. Mary chuckled. "Yes, Violet and the Carver children painted it one day to take their minds off a shooting in the town."

"A shooting?"

"Some drunken blowhard rode in from Mobeetie and Clay had no choice but to shoot him. Then they had to bury the man."

"Does this happen often?"

"No. That only made the second time since I came." Dr. Mary pulled her pipe from her pocket. "But that's the story of the yellow paint. I've been meaning to finish the job but never got around to it."

Nora collected the mixture the doctor had already prepared. "Don't get this in Jack's eyes. Make a thick paste with flour. Leave it on for thirty minutes, no more."

"Doctor, can I ask you something?"

"Sure." Dr. Mary stuck the pipe in her mouth. "Fire away."

"It's about Jack's limp. His leg really pains him sometimes, and he said a bullet is lodged next to the bone. I was wondering if there's a chance you might be able to take it out?"

"How long has it been in there?"

"I think he said about five years. He didn't have a doctor back then. His friends just treated him."

"I'd be glad to examine him and see if it would be possible." Dr. Mary's bullet necklace clinked as she struck a match and lit her cigar. "It's a shame for anyone to be in such pain."

"Jack's a good man and I hate not being able to help him." She paused, thinking about her vow. "Do you mind if I satisfy my curiosity about something else?"

"My necklace?"

"Yes, how did you know?"

"It draws a lot of glances. Everyone wants to know about it." Dr. Mary lifted the shiny brass. "I collect spent bullets from my patients and I wear this to make them stop and consider. Maybe it'll help them make better choices next time."

Nora nodded. "Thank you, Doctor." She hurried back to the house as the sun went down.

So far, the guard at the town entrance hadn't seen any riders. Maybe Jack was right, and the posse was trying to assemble enough men to force their way into Hope's Crossing. Whatever the reason, she was grateful for the time to have a wedding and plan a normal life with this man. Or at least as normal as they could ever have.

Wanted dead or alive. The words washed over her and sent a shudder up her spine.

Not if she could help it. One way or another, she had to keep him safe.

She let herself into the house and went straight to the parlor. Jack sat rocking Willow, Sawyer at his feet. Scout lay next to the boy, her snout on his leg.

Her gaze met Jack's and held it. "I have everything. Are you ready?"

He let out a long-suffering sigh. "As much as I'll ever be. I'll put Willow in her crib. Where are we going to do this?"

"I think the kitchen will be best."

"Can I watch, Nora?" Sawyer asked.

"I guess."

"Why? You thinking of going blond too?" Jack ruffled

the boy's reddish-brown hair. "You and I are going to need haircuts soon, son."

Sawyer brushed a long lock from his eyes. "I just want to see if this works. And I've heard Miss Rebel gives good haircuts."

"That she does. Makes her a good living too." Jack moved up the stairs.

"Don't dawdle," Nora called. "I'd like to be through so I can get used to you before I hop into bed with a perfect stranger. And bring a towel when you come back down."

She went to the kitchen and set down the jar Dr. Mary had given her, trying to remember every instruction. She pulled out a shallow pan, poured the contents of the jar into it and got down the flour. Soon she had a thick paste. The smell was getting to her though.

Sawyer watched from a chair at the table. "Do you think this'll fool those lawmen, Nora?"

"Yes, I do think so."

"What if it don't?"

Good question, and she had no answer. "We'll think of something else. We won't give up until they stop looking for Jack."

"I wish Jack would let me shoot. We might need more guns."

"No!" Jack entered the room, fury tightening the lines of his face. "I never want you to get used to killing! Got that? Remember how it made you feel the first time?"

Sawyer nodded, his head down.

"Jack, don't be so hard. He's just a boy wanting to help you." Nora glared at him.

"I don't want him to be like me. That stain seeps into a man's soul. Sawyer is destined for important things." He touched the top of the kid's head and softened his voice. "Understand?"

"Yes, sir."

Jack glanced at the pan of liquid. "Where do you want me?"

"Sit at the table and turn your chair backward. I think it'll be the right height."

He sat, and she draped the towel around him and began to cover his head with the smelly paste.

"I think it's going to get awfully uncomfortable because you have to stay that way for thirty minutes."

"I'll manage," he growled. "Just don't make my hair green. Anything but that."

Sawyer's eyes widened. "Green?"

"Who knows what's about to happen? I may come out with orange hair."

"I never knew you to be such a whiner, Jack." Nora hid a grin and made sure the mixture covered his entire head. It wouldn't do for him to look like a skunk. He'd never let her live that down. And she put some on his eyebrows, leaving his sexy beard alone.

They waited in nervous anticipation, the clock in the parlor loudly ticking off the minutes. When Sawyer took Scout outside to do her business, Nora took advantage of the quiet to ask Jack about Rebel. "What's her story?"

"Rebel worked in a saloon in Cimarron for a number of years. That's one of the roughest towns I've ever been in. Fights and killings every night. She showed up here one day with Tobias and Belle January and tried to take Clay from Tally. Caused lots of trouble. I don't know exactly what happened, but she changed and her and Tally are best friends now."

"I kind of suspected something similar."

"Why did you want to know?"

"Because she's going through a rough patch and I want to reach out. Everyone needs another friend. I hope she finds out what happened to Travis. I would die if you disappeared like that."

Sawyer returned just in time to watch Nora rinse the mixture out of Jack's hair. He stood and roughly toweled most of the wetness out until his hair stood up on end.

The color was *definitely* different. Scout swung her head around, inched backward, and let out a long howl.

Twenty-eight

HELL! JACK LOOKED AT HIMSELF IN THE MIRROR AND DIDN'T recognize the blond man staring back. The pale-yellow wasn't too bad.

"I've always admired palomino horses. At least my mustache and beard are light enough."

"I like it." Nora touched the light strands. "What do you think, Sawyer?"

"Well, it's gonna take getting used to. Those lawmen won't know him though."

"My own mother won't either. I show up like this at her place and she'll reach for the rifle."

A knock sounded at the door. Nora opened it to find Clay and Ridge. "Come in and see the results."

Jack came from the kitchen, his pale hair glistening in the light. Both of his friends burst out laughing.

Ridge was the first to speak. "I never would've believed it."

"Me either." Clay walked closer. "Are you sure you're Bowdre?"

"Ha-ha! If you only came over to laugh, just keep on walking."

"We're your friends," Ridge said softly. "We're in this thing together—like always."

"I know. It's just that my life as I knew it is over. I liked my hair the color it was for almost thirty years."

Nora put an arm around his waist. "Your life is not over. Your brown hair is over, that's all. And it's only until they stop looking for you."

"I think I'll bleach mine blond too." Clay peered closer. "Tally might find me handsomer. Speaking of Tally—she's feeling puny."

Nora was instantly concerned. "Is the baby coming?"

Jack's thoughts flew to Luke's wife, Josie. She and her baby had almost died in childbirth the previous year, right here in Hope's Crossing.

"I don't know. Doc Mary is over with her." Clay rubbed the back of his neck and went to the door. "Wish this were behind us. I keep thinking of Josie and how she almost didn't make it."

"Tally will be fine," Jack assured him. "Each woman is different, and Tally is healthy."

"I know. Still, a lot can go wrong." Clay put his hand on the doorknob. "I like the hair, Jack."

"Will you stay and visit awhile, Ridge?" Nora asked.

"Better not. I'm on guard duty tonight."

"Next time then. I'll have you over for supper."

Ridge nodded. "Sounds good. Night all."

After the door closed, Willow let out a cry. Nora went up to get her, then to the kitchen for a bottle, returning to the rocker to feed her.

Jack let the warmth of being together and safe wrap around him, afraid to believe fortune had smiled on him. They sat in the parlor discussing everything except the danger that was on all their minds. But he knew they still had some things to discuss.

Finally, Jack rose and let his hand drift down Nora's hair to her shoulders. "When the lawmen come, you and Sawyer will have to stay hidden or they'll recognize you."

"I'd never forgive myself if I gave you away." Nora glanced up with a grin. "A disguise is easy for me. I can put a scarf around my hair and borrow one of Dr. Mary's cigars."

Jack laughed. He could see that now. And she'd do it on a dare, too.

"What about me?" Sawyer got up to stand next to Jack. "I was at the jail."

He draped an arm across the kid's shoulders. "You're too young for cigars. You'll have to wear a low hat. I'll get you one."

"What about your black clothes, Jack?" Nora twisted around in the rocker. "Those will be a sure giveaway. I know you don't want to change, but what about wearing a white shirt and a blue vest at least?"

She had a point and one he'd overlooked. "I'll see what the mercantile has tomorrow."

"I want one of those hats like mule skinners wear and a Mexican serape." Sawyer flopped down on the rug with a grin as though already picturing himself in the role of a desperado.

Scout padded into the room, giving Jack a wide berth, huffed, and lay down next to Sawyer.

If only for one night, they'd pretend they were a normal family in a normal town with a normal life.

Then tomorrow, they'd go back to the way things really were—finding a way to live when others wanted to wipe him from the earth.

⤜⤚

By morning, Tally was in full-fledged childbirth. Everyone seemed quiet and on edge. Nora had no experience with birthing babies, so she gathered the four children—Violet, Sawyer, Jenny, and Ely—and took them to play, away from the pall that had fallen over the town. Many women died giving birth, something Nora had personally known to be true before they found WIllow, for a dear aunt of hers had never woken to see the child she'd created. She prayed Tally would be all right. But Dr. Mary would do all she could, that much Nora was certain of.

Sawyer and Ely carried Willow's crib down and Nora put her in it and tucked blankets around her.

Violet patted her arm, grinning. "I'm going to have a little brother or sister, Miss Nora."

"You certainly are, sweetheart." Nora smoothed the sightless girl's long blond hair. Her heart went out to the nine-year-old who'd never see the baby's face. "Do you have a name picked out?"

"My mama and daddy will choose one."

"Sawyer named Willow. He's good at naming. Do you want a brother or sister?"

"A brother." Violet reached for the long stick that helped her feel her way around. "He won't be blind like me. But if he is, I'll still love him."

A lump formed in Nora's throat. "Of course, you will. We all will."

"I like babies," four-year-old Jenny said, climbing in Nora's lap. "But they cry a lot."

Willow cooed in her crib, the sound spreading joy through Nora.

"Not always, honey." She hugged Jenny to her. Jack had told her about the asylum where the children had been held until the previous year. Jenny and Ely's father had put them in there after their mother died and he didn't want to be bothered with their care.

The rat!

Both were sweet kids, and the anger in Ely's eyes was understandable. Rebel had earned a star in her crown by taking them in and raising them by herself. Maybe they played a role in her giving up the saloon life.

At noon, she was feeding the children when Jack found her. For a second, she didn't recognize him, between his light hair, white shirt, and handsome leather vest. The sunlight winked on the marshal's badge pinned to the vest, and then on the ivory-handled Colt hanging from his hip. Gone was the moody outlaw she'd first met. In his place now stood lawman Joe Long. He handed a wide-brimmed hat and serape to Sawyer, who put them on immediately.

"How do I look?" the kid asked.

"Like a mule skinner who hasn't bathed in a month of Sundays," Jack answered with a wink.

Nora told the children to eat and checked on Willow, who was asleep. With everyone occupied, she slipped an arm around Jack's waist. "You look so different, Joe."

"That's the plan, right?" He grinned, flashing a row of white teeth made even whiter by his tanned face and light hair. "Might as well go whole hog if I'm sticking around."

"Might as well, since you don't have a better offer."

He tucked a lock of hair behind her ear, passion darkening his gray eyes. "They'll have to pry me away from you."

"You say the most romantic things."

Jack released her, and his face turned serious. "Nora, Dallas returned from Tascosa, and he ran into our old friend Darius Guthrie. The tracker was telling another man in the saloon that he knows you hid that book of O'Brien's at the sheepherder's house and he's going back to tear it down one mud brick at a time."

"We can't let him." Panic filled Nora's face. "We have to go get it."

"I agree. We'll go soon. Try not to worry that pretty head of yours. We're going to put O'Brien behind bars."

"It's what I've been dreaming of doing since leaving Buffalo."

Jack's attention swung away from her and his eyes narrowed. Attuned to his every mood, Nora's stomach clenched. She turned toward a group of men gathered in front of the mercantile.

"What is it, Jack?"

"Not sure. There's something about that man over there in the buckskin pants wearing Indian beads around his neck."

"The one wearing tall moccasins with fringe?"

"That's the one."

The man in question was laughing and slapping one of the others on the back. "He looks harmless to me. Very jovial. Do you know him?"

"No. He's new to town. His name's Dutch."

"Jack, what's got you so suspicious?"

"You might as well know. We think we have a traitor in our midst." He laid out reasons for his argument. "Clay, Ridge, and Luke have come to the same conclusion."

"Oh dear." Suddenly, Nora looked at everyone differently. Who was the person who'd led to Jack getting arrested? She'd string him up if she found him. "What do we do?"

"Watch and wait. Go about business as usual."

That would be difficult. She wanted to like everyone

and fit in. "Jack, he might get word to the posse of your whereabouts."

"Maybe—unless we stop him. We have to be on our toes." He kissed her temple. "Try not to worry. We'll root out the traitor."

"What's the latest on Tally?" Nora asked, changing the subject.

"No sign of the baby yet and Clay is biting everyone's head off. He needs someone to shoot. That would make him feel better." Jack stared toward a cluster of silent men.

"What does Dr. Mary say? Is there a problem?"

"She told Clay everything is normal. A first child just takes a while evidently." He put his arms around her. "Fair warning. If one day we should find ourselves in this situation, I will not be waiting outside. Come hell or high water, I'll be with you, holding your hand, wiping your brow, making a real nuisance of myself."

"I'm glad. I wouldn't want to go through that without you." In fact, she didn't want to do anything without Jack.

The one o'clock stage raced through the opening. Jack kissed her cheek. "I need to help Skeet change out the team and take note of the new arrivals. I'll let you know about Tally."

Nora nodded. Putting Sawyer and Ely in charge, she gathered Willow and hurried into the house. After feeding and changing the baby, she went to work looking for a disguise for herself. In a small trunk, she found a heavy black scarf, and from a drawer in the kitchen, she removed a fine gold tablecloth Susan Worth had given them for a wedding gift. After stuffing pillows under her dress to add weight to her, she folded the tablecloth lengthwise and tied it around her larger waist. The long ends of the gold fabric fell past her knees. Putting the scarf around her head, she was suitably disguised.

When trouble came, she'd be at Jack's side like a proper wife. Not hiding.

Nora B. Long.

A smile curved her lips. She *be-longed* to only him. Her thoughts in a tizzy, she gathered Willow and went back out to ride herd on the children, saying another prayer that Tally and the baby would be all right.

The stagecoach made a slow, wide turn in the compound, across the space that would one day be the town square. It headed back out the only entrance. Hope's Crossing was the only town she knew with only one way in and out, but she'd heard the men talk about blowing more of the bluff away and widening the opening—someday, when all was safe.

Jack stood on the opposite side of the square, his gaze on her, probably wondering at her change in appearance. She flashed a big smile and waved.

He limped toward her, and even though she tried not to worry, she wasn't successful.

"Sweetheart, you should get off your leg."

"Soon." He rubbed it, grimacing.

"I spoke with Dr. Mary about the bullet still lodged in there and she wants to examine you." Nora put a hand on his arm and said softly, "It's time. As soon as Tally has her baby, let Dr. Mary take a look. The slug may have shifted or something."

"I know you're right, but I can't stand being poked around on."

"Just think about it." She knew better than to push. Best to introduce the idea and let it simmer. She got better results that way.

"I like the disguise. You've gained thirty pounds. I always liked a woman with meat on her bones. Where did you get the gold fabric, Mrs. Long?"

"It's a tablecloth that Susan Worth gave us as a wedding present. Like it?"

"It's nice. I can think of all sorts of uses for that sash the next time we make love." His positively sinful grin came near to stopping her heart.

Nora slapped at his arm. "Don't be saying that stuff around these children!" But she couldn't keep the smile off her face or settle her racing pulse.

Just then, the guard above the town entrance gave three loud owl hoots.

"Get the children inside, Nora!" The words barely left Jack's mouth before he limped toward Clay and Ridge.

Icy panic gripped Nora as she picked up Willow. This was it. This was what they'd been waiting for. Had she and Jack just run out of time? She caught Sawyer's worried eyes and put an arm around him. "All right, children. Let's get into the house. We're going to play hide-and-seek."

A bloodcurdling scream came from Dr. Mary's office. Tally! But Nora couldn't stop to even consider what that meant. A large group of riders—must've been two dozen—poured into the town. All of them against one man with a limp—it bordered on the ridiculous. But then tears filled her eyes. They were after the man she loved more than all the stars in heaven.

The riders stopped in a cloud of dust in front of Jack and his group of men. Clay's dog, Bullet, circled them, barking and snarling. Scout whipped around from the side of the house, adding her deep, bloodhound howls to the chaos. The townspeople scurried out of sight, slamming their doors.

Clay and Ridge stood in front of Jack, blocking him from view. She knew they'd die before they let the lawmen take him.

Shooing the last child inside, Nora stood in the doorway clutching Willow to her. She recognized several of the riders—the sheriff and deputy of Saint's Roost, Seamus Belew, and Darius Guthrie. She sucked in a breath. She should've known she wasn't rid of the bastard.

"Afternoon, gentlemen." Ridge stepped forward. "Can we offer you food or lodging?"

"Who the hell are you?" Belew snarled.

Ridge drew himself up straight from his seemingly relaxed pose and gave them a bland smile. "I'm the mayor of Hope's Crossing. To what do we owe the pleasure?"

"I'm U.S. Deputy Marshal Seamus Belew, and we've come for Jack Bowdre."

"Who is that?" Ridge asked. "Don't know him."

Nora admired how Ridge restrained his temper, though the strain showed in the clenched fists at his sides.

Sheriff Baxter shifted in the saddle and introduced himself. "Bowdre broke out of my jail a few days ago. We tracked him here."

"Sorry to dispute your word, but he didn't make it to this town."

"Jailbreak is only one of the charges against him," Belew shot back. "I know he's here. Unless you want me to charge you with aiding and abetting, turn him over."

Clay stuck a match stem between his teeth. "We said we don't know him."

Baxter squinted hard. "I heard this used to be an outlaw den. I wonder how many of you have rewards on your heads." He paused to let that sink in. "If I had time, I might just find out."

Ice slid down Nora's spine.

Jack stepped around Clay. Nora sucked in a breath and gripped the door facing. This was the moment she'd dreaded. *Dear God, don't let them recognize him.*

He pushed back his hat a bit where his blond hair showed. "I'm Deputy Marshal Joe Long. Bowdre ain't here. I came myself to arrest him after getting wind that he holed up here sometimes."

Baxter frowned. "What do *you* want him for?"

"Horse thieving and murder."

Seamus Belew swung down from his horse and marched up to Jack, peering into his face. "Never heard of you."

Oh dear Lord! Nora trembled, tightening her hold on Willow, who'd begun to squirm.

"That's because I've only recently been appointed—by Judge Isaac Parker in Fort Smith. If you'd like to wire him, feel free. I heard he has a terrible temper when his word is questioned." Jack released a wad of spit that landed on the edge of Belew's boot. "My assignment is Indian Territory. Came down to Texas for Bowdre, like I said."

Baxter peered at him with an intense stare. "You seem very familiar."

Guthrie also dismounted. "Bowdre travels with a woman

named Nora Kane. She's a disagreeable sort in need of a firm hand."

Nora snorted. He'd think disagreeable if she could get her hands around his scrawny neck.

Belew kicked at the dogs. "Look, their tracks led here. Give them to us."

"Hurt my dogs and I'll put a bullet between your eyes." The hardness of Clay's warning wasn't lost on Nora. She remembered Jack saying that Clay would feel better if he could shoot something.

The old sheriff pointed a finger at Belew. "You're a disgrace to the badge. Hurt those animals and I'll add my bullet to his. Get back to the business we came for. Deputy marshal or not, this is my posse. I put it together, not you."

Nora watched red streaks climb up Seamus Belew's throat.

"Well, first you're looking for Bowdre and now you're looking for this Kane woman." Clay added his spit to Jack's on the ground. "Which is it, Sheriff?"

"Both, I reckon. The woman helped Bowdre break out."

"Can you prove that?" Jack asked.

"She and a kid left town at the same time as Bowdre. To me that says she helped him somehow."

"Hey, ain't that our dog Sadie?" Alan Jones, the kind deputy of Saint's Roost pointed to Scout.

Nora's heart froze. They hadn't given the red bloodhound a thought. She handed the baby to Sawyer, adjusted the pillows under her dress, put the scarf around her hair, and marched out.

"You're crazy, deputy." Clay patted Scout's head. "I've had this dog since she was a pup. Next thing I know you'll be claiming my dog aided in Bowdre's escape."

Jack removed his hat and wiped sweat from his brow. Nora supposed he did that to give them a clear view of his light hair. It was if he was pointing to it. "For your own safety, I think you'd best ride on, Sheriff. Water your horses and be on your way. Good luck in finding Bowdre. He likes to run with wild women—maybe you'll find that Kane woman with him. I'll keep an eye out for your prisoner and telegraph you if I find him."

"You can't tell us when to leave," Darius Guthrie sputtered. "We can go where we want."

Another bloodcurdling scream split the air, coming from Dr. Mary's.

Belew and Guthrie jumped out of their skin and the horses skittered sideways.

"What the hell was that?" Deputy Jones asked.

Her hips swaying, Nora sidled up next to Jack and spoke in a thick accent. "We have sick voman here. Bad, bad disease." She shrugged her shoulders. "Maybe…how you say…cholera."

Belew and Guthrie turned and leaped onto their horses so fast they missed the stirrups.

More screams came from Dr. Mary's. Nora couldn't be sure, but it sounded like more than one voice joining in the chorus.

"I'm getting the hell out of here!" Guthrie yelled and spurred his animal.

Sheriff Baxter directed his words to Jack. "Marshal Long, if you catch Bowdre, let me know."

The riders left the town in a swirl of dust. It was only then that Nora took her first real breath since their arrival. "It worked, Jack." She hugged him. "We're safe."

"For now."

She slapped his arm. "What was that remark about me being a wild woman?"

"Just telling the gospel, darlin'." He slid an arm around her waist and leaned in to whisper, "You are pretty wild with a boot in your hand, declaring war on all wood rats. But most of all, your fiery passion in bed, and that's no joke."

A warm glow filled her. She stared at the entrance to the town and foreboding crept in, squeezing out the happiness. This was only a temporary reprieve. As Belew had said, they'd tracked her and Jack here. They, or others like them, would be back.

Twenty-nine

BY THE TIME THE SUN WENT DOWN, TALLY HAD A LITTLE boy and Clay was beaming. Jack had never seen two people so happy.

Tally was sitting up in bed when Jack and Nora briefly looked in. "I'm real sorry I missed all the excitement. I hear Nora gave quite a performance, and they lit out like the devil was chasing them."

Nora grinned and shrugged. "I just wanted to do my part."

Clay put the baby in Violet's lap and she played the loving big sister, running her fingers across her brother's tiny features, wearing a smile as wide as the Mississippi.

"She's too modest." Jack chuckled. "You should've seen her in that getup and her accent was perfect." He met her brown eyes and drowned in their depths.

"Maybe you gave a performance yourself, Tally." Nora shot her an accusing stare. "I know I heard more than one scream coming from here, and yours seemed unusually loud."

Tally laughed. "Mine wasn't fake, but I did embellish it. And then Dr. Mary and Belle screamed as loud as they could too."

"That gave me the opening I needed to say that we had sick people. We make a good team." Nora stood. "We should be going. There's a whole line of people waiting outside to get a peek at the little one. When you're up and around, we'll have a long talk."

They said their goodbyes and went out into the night. Jack glanced up at the stars and sucked in a deep breath, giving thanks for not being in a cell somewhere. Or dead.

❧

Jack rose before dawn, made himself a pot of coffee, and went outside with a cup. He loved this time of morning, when the air was fresh and crisp. He could get a lot of thinking done in the quiet. With his hat low over his eyes, he walked to the corral and propped a foot on the bottom rail. A couple of the horses moseyed over to nudge him. He rubbed their faces.

He thought about Travis and wondered where he was. Malloy should be getting back anytime now and hopefully had learned something. Jack wasn't above breaking him out.

All of this had to end one day, though. But damn if he knew what he and the others'd do. Except for Clay, who'd gotten a pardon from the governor, and Tobias, they were all wanted men. The lawmen were closing in, and soon they'd clean up this last portion of Texas and kill or arrest every last one of them. With each day, he felt the noose getting a little tighter. How could they escape? Tricks like the day before only worked the once.

Maybe he could wait until the next election and a new governor and try again for a pardon. Maybe he'd have better luck. He just didn't want to be hunted anymore.

To live out his days in peace with Nora and the kids—that was his dream.

Love for her swept over him. She shouldn't have to live this way. Sawyer and Willow either. In them, he had three good reasons to clear the slate.

The sky began to lighten. He took a sip of coffee, and then movement near the town's entrance caught his attention.

A man was staggering toward him. Wet blood created a sheen on his clothes, the red clearly visible even from the distance of thirty feet. He went down on one knee, then struggled to his feet.

On he came, one half-step at a time.

Then the stranger sprawled facedown on the ground.

Jack threw down his cup and ran. He heard no moans, nothing. Jack turned him over. The man's eyes were closed, his face stark white around a light beard. A quick glance revealed bullet wounds to his chest and legs. He'd been shot four times. Something familiar niggled in Jack's brain. He looked closer and tried to imagine him without the beard.

Jack's blood stilled. Pushing up the sleeve on the man's right arm, he found a long scar.

Tait Trinity.

He had a five-thousand-dollar bounty on his head. Every marshal and Pinkerton this side of the Mississippi would give anything to capture this outlaw. Jack had thought his was high at one thousand. Five thousand would make a bounty hunter richer than sin and twice as bloodthirsty.

Trinity would only bring more trouble.

Footsteps sounded as Clay, Ridge, and Dallas Hawk raced up.

"Who is it?" Clay asked.

"Tait Trinity." Jack pushed back his hat. "I almost didn't recognize him. Let's get him to Dr. Mary or he won't make it."

They picked him up and carried him to her office. She took one look and motioned to a vacant bed in her two-bed clinic, then shooed them out.

Outside, Jack met his friends' gazes. "Got a bad feeling about this. Why do you think Trinity sought refuge here?"

"Word probably hadn't gotten to him that this isn't an outlaw haven any longer." Clay struck a match to his freshly rolled cigarette. "Towns are few and far between in this part of Texas, and news travels slow."

Ridge glanced at the doctor's door. "What are we going to do? He's all shot up. We can't turn him away. He saved my life once when he could've turned a blind eye and ridden on."

"Hell, we've all saved each other at one time or another." Clay blew smoke rings. "Didn't you used to ride with him, Jack?"

"Yeah."

Memories of a different time filled Jack's head. He and Tait had a bond nothing would break. Then, they'd gone up against the Reese gang. The gang had taken over a small border town, holding the people hostage, killing at will. Together, Jack and Tait had cleaned it up. Then one morning, Jack had woken to find Trinity gone. That was the last he'd heard of the man until his name popped up in some train and bank robberies.

It seemed Tait was working alone and becoming a force to reckon with.

Which had gotten the Pinkertons on his trail.

Hell! Jack pinched the bridge of his nose and let out a sigh. "We were more like brothers than friends."

"He's going to bring trouble," Ridge said. "Every lawman in the territory will come after him. Can we afford to hide him?"

"He'd do it for us." Jack turned and limped away, wishing to hell he hadn't seen Tait lying on the ground all shot up, barely clinging to life.

⤜∾⤛

To Jack's amazement, Tait Trinity lived through the day. When he looked in on him the next morning, Tait had regained consciousness.

Jack pulled a chair close to the bed. "Glad to see you awake. Been a while since we parted ways."

"Heard you'd built a town here where Devil's Crossing used to be." Tait's gray eyes betrayed his pain, but his voice was strong. "Came to warn you. You have a traitor in your midst."

Surprise to hear it from Tait rippled through Jack. "Hell, figured as much already! Do you have a name?"

"No. I overheard a stranger talking to this bounty hunter named Will Spencer in a saloon in Tascosa. The man bragged about being the eyes and ears for the marshals and others and he's getting rich doing it."

Jack's thoughts raced. "Would you know him if you saw him?"

Tait shook his head. "Had his back to me the whole time and the saloon was dim and smoky. I'd know his voice though. I tried to follow him when he left but lost him in the alley."

"Tait, was he the one who shot you?"

"No. A Pinkerton agent. The bastard picked up my trail after I left Tascosa. Shot my horse out from under me. I hid in a gully until he gave up and rode on."

"He meant to kill you, Tait. You've made the wrong people mad."

"I knew I would when I started robbing trains, but I wanted to hurt them." Tait paused, closing his eyes for a moment. "The railroad company stole my folks' land. They declared eminent domain and booted them off the land that had been in the family for one hundred and twenty-five years. The bastards! Sam Houston gave him that land as payment for fighting for Texas freedom."

"That wasn't right no matter how you look at it, but you can't win this fight."

"Reckon not, but I aim to try. Jack, I'm sorry for leaving with no word the way I did." Tait laid an arm across his forehead. "There were things I didn't want to drag you into. You're a far better man than me. You have possibilities. Me, I'm in too deep to crawl out. I've done a lot of things there'll be no forgiving."

"That's a bunch of malarkey. If you stop now, you have a chance at freedom. Help us settle this town and make it a safe place to raise kids and grow old."

Tait shook his head. "That's crazy, my friend. How can that erase our crimes?"

"Don't know exactly, but if we live right and stop robbing and killing, maybe the law will eventually quit looking for us. I'm still working that part out. In any event, I want you to stay. There's safety in numbers, and the way this place is built in this canyon, we can hold off an army."

Jack left his old friend to rest, his own mind filled with thoughts of a traitor among them. He'd have to alert the others that it was no longer speculation.

Clay met him outside the doctor's office. "How is he?"

"Alive. Tait came to warn us." Jack relayed what Tait had told him. "He never saw the man's face though, so we have nothing more than we did."

"Dammit!" Clay glanced around, scanning the face of each man in the vicinity. He called Ridge and Dallas over and told them their suspicions were fact. "Keep your eyes peeled. I have a feeling the rat will ride out soon."

Dallas rubbed his wild, sandy-colored beard. He looked more like a mountain man than anything else, but he sure could squeeze out the sweetest music from his fiddle. "Except for Dutch, Abel Fargo, and Rex Thompkins, I've known everyone for years."

"I noticed Fargo coming and going a lot," Ridge said. "What do we really know about Dutch? He doesn't appear to have any skill or do any work. Where's he getting his money?"

Jack agreed. "All three are suspect." An ominous silence fell between them as they split up.

"Wait." Rebel hurried to catch up as the group broke apart. "Have you heard anything about Travis? I'm going out of my mind with worry."

"No, Skeet Malloy hasn't made it back." Jack studied her face and red-rimmed eyes. She was a pretty woman but had lost the sparkle in her eyes and seemed to have no interest in her appearance since Travis had been captured. "When did you last eat?"

She pushed her uncombed hair back from her haunted eyes. "How can I eat when Travis could be lying in a cold cell?"

"You have to keep your strength up, Rebel. Are you taking care of the kids? Jenny and Ely need you. They don't have anyone else."

"They're not going without. And me—I'm not important. Without Travis, I'm nothing."

She was dead wrong, but Jack refused to argue. "Come and let my Nora feed you," he said gently.

❧

Nora took one look and put her arms around the woman. "Let's have some hot tea."

Those seemed to be magic words. Rebel stumbled to the table and stared straight ahead while Nora heated water and put tea in to steep.

"I know you're worried, Rebel. Anyone would be, but you can't stop living."

"Travis and me were going to be married. We've been planning on it ever since I took in Jenny and Ely. God, I love those children."

"They need you, Rebel, as much as you need them. You can't worry them like this. You look like death warmed over." One look at Rebel would frighten any child. Nora put an arm around the former saloon girl. "After we drink our tea and have a bite to eat, let's clean you up. You'll feel lots better."

From the looks of Rebel, she hadn't eaten since Travis disappeared with the bounty hunter. Her clothes were hanging on her.

"I don't know." Rebel's chin quivered, and she burst into fresh tears.

"There, have yourself a good cry." Nora gave her a hug.

"I'm sorry, Nora. I'm a wreck."

"I'd be the same way if it were Jack. Do you know how we actually met?" Nora got two teacups from the cabinet. Over the next hour and several cups of tea, she regaled Rebel with her and Jack's adventures. Soon her new friend was laughing and eating lunch.

"That's hilarious. I don't know the last time I felt like laughing." Rebel sobered. "Thank you, Nora. You made me see that I need to be a better mother."

"Glad to help. How about plastering on a big smile and going to play some games with those kids? Let them know how much you love them."

Rebel's mouth tilted up a bit at the corners. "You're right. I have to stop worrying and do something to take my mind off Travis."

"That's the spirit. He's going to be all right and so are you. You can't give up hope. Not ever. The minute you do, you're sunk."

"Did anyone ever tell you that you're a godsend?"

"Not lately." Nora put her arm around Rebel and walked her out the door.

She didn't know a lot about this part of the country, but people were the same everywhere. Trouble and disappointment lay around every corner. For a few days, she'd embrace the calm in Jack's arms. Together, they could face anything.

Jack came in a little past noon with Sawyer, and while she fed them, he told her about Tait Trinity.

"What's going to happen to him once he heals?" Part of her wanted the man to ride on. They had too much trouble already. But she'd noticed the sound in Jack's voice when he spoke of Tait. The connection between the two went deeper than friends.

"He can stay if he wants, but I have a feeling he'll move on. A man like Tait doesn't remain in one place long. Too many demons hiding in the shadows."

Sawyer focused on his plate but kept stealing worried glances at Jack. They should've waited until they were alone to talk about Tait. The boy probably feared Jack would leave with Tait, and that would kill him. Jack was his whole world and like a father.

Nora laid her hand over Jack's. "Tait will do whatever he feels best. I'm glad you offered him a place here."

Every person in the town had demons trailing them. She knew a lot about that subject. When were hers going to jump out and steal her happiness?

Thirty

THAT NIGHT, JACK STOOD AT THE COMMUNITY FIRE WITH THE men. It was the gathering spot for most of the town—the place they shared talk of the day, where they often cooked meals.

Jack tossed a stick into the flames. Tait Trinity was on his mind. And Travis. There were too many problems to solve. All day, he'd watched three men who'd arrived about a month ago—Dutch, Abel Fargo, and Rex Tompkins—and was no closer to arriving at an answer. Dutch was like a loveable bear, helpful and smiling. Fargo kept to himself, a bit too surly for Jack, with never a kind word. And Tompkins seemed committed to the town, caring for the horses while Skeet Malloy was away.

No, it had to be Fargo. That surly smirk and the man's sharp gaze told Jack he wasn't to be trusted.

The darkness had put everyone in a strange mood. Clay seemed lost in thought too. Scout wandered up and lay down next to Bullet.

"The town is having growing pains. We'll soon have to spread out beyond the entrance to find more land," Clay announced out of the blue.

"Yeah, I reckon so. I'm glad to see people coming to settle here."

"A town can't survive without new blood." Clay lapsed into silence while he rolled a cigarette and lit it. Smoke wafted around his head. "We named our son today," he said quietly.

"About damn time. I wondered if the little thing would have to grow up answering to 'boy.'" Jack grinned. "What did you decide on?"

"Dillon. Dillon Colby."

"That's a strong name." Jack crossed his arms. "I've always thought if I have another chance at a boy, I'd name him Charles for my grandfather."

"Dillon was my grandfather's name. He was a strapping man, quick to cuss and just as quick to hug. I learned soldiers burned his house and farm during the war. Shot him and my grandmother. Her name was Amelia." Clay heaved a deep sigh. "Too many memories circling. When was the last time you visited your mother?"

"Been too long. I need to take Nora to meet her and will as soon as I'm able. She's told me that lawmen ride by occasionally, hoping to catch me."

"Best to stay clear."

"You're right. For now, anyway." Jack paused and lowered his voice. "Are we any closer to finding out who the traitor is?"

"Fargo rode out for a while today. I followed him."

"And?"

"He went to where the road branches off to Tascosa. He sat there for about fifteen minutes, then turned around and came back."

"Waiting for someone who didn't show?"

"Your guess is as good as mine." Clay's attention went to Abel Fargo, across the fire from them. Jack followed his gaze to the moody man passing around a bottle.

Fargo claimed to be a surveyor and map maker, but no one ever saw him working. The man's gaze swung to Jack, and his sharp eyes narrowed to slits as though taking Jack's measure. Fargo's pockmarked cheeks and stone-cold face hardened.

He was a man to avoid. But Jack wasn't intimidated. He returned the hard stare, forcing Fargo to look away.

"Do you think maybe Fargo caught wind of you behind him?" Jack asked, although he couldn't imagine that. Clay could trail a catfish through a winding river.

Clay snorted. "Who knows?"

"We'll keep watching. He's bound to tip his hand."

Dutch, the jovial rambler, wandered over from the saloon. The man towered well over six feet five and was built like a bull. But Jack found him easygoing and likeable. Dutch whistled a tune as he joined them, sitting down with Rex Thompkins. Thompkins appeared a little too anxious to please in Jack's opinion. He couldn't put his finger on it, but something about the man seemed off.

Nora stepped from their house with Willow, and Jack's attention automatically riveted on her. She strolled toward him, her hips swaying like a graceful ship upon the waves. Heat stirred in his blood.

Jack shifted. "Clay, do you know how a man can wait and wait for the right woman to come along and share his life, and then one day she just falls in his lap?"

"Yeah, I know. That's how it was with me and Tally."

"It's like me and Nora were made for each other. The heart knows what it knows."

"That it does, my friend."

"Think Ridge will ever find a wife?"

Clay snorted. "Not until he loosens up. That man is wound tighter than an eight-day clock."

When Nora reached them, Jack took the baby and held Willow close, savoring the sweetness. "Clay and Tally named their boy Dillon."

She grinned. "What a cute name. It fits with his red hair."

"Yep. The spitting image of his mother." Clay took a draw on his cigarette.

Never one to miss ribbing his friend, Jack punched his arm. "Thank God!"

"Hey, I'm not that bad looking. At least I don't have hair like mustard."

The back and forth was still going when Ridge joined them, then Jack switched the tone. "Nora and I have to leave soon." He put the baby to his shoulder and told them about the book—about Nora taking it from O'Brien, and the hiding place at the sheepherder's house. "We have to beat Guthrie to it."

"Think that's wise?" Clay squinted and threw a cigarette into the fire.

"No, but we don't have much choice."

Nora slipped her arm through Jack's. "If we're going, we have to do it now."

Ridge met Jack's gaze. "The stakes are awful high with the posse roaming about."

"Seems like I've had high stakes my whole life. No different now."

He felt a shiver run through Nora and suspected the direction of her thoughts. "Making Flynn O'Brien pay for his crimes is all Nora's thought about since escaping Buffalo."

"Then I'm going with you." Ridge's amber eyes glittered in the flickering firelight.

Jack knew of no better man to have near in a fight.

"You'll be welcome, brother." Jack held Willow secure and clasped Ridge's hand. "We'll ride out day after tomorrow. It's only a day's ride, but I don't want to get there after dark, so I suggest we camp out somewhere and arrive at dawn."

"Sounds good," Ridge answered.

"A quick trip there and back, then we start the ball rolling against O'Brien."

"I'd go with you, but I can't leave Tally. She'll need someone to look after Violet." Clay inhaled deep and grinned. "And I have a son to get acquainted with."

"Don't give it another thought." Nora glanced toward their house. "I need to get the children to bed. I'll be over to see Tally again in the morning."

They said their goodbyes and walked quietly toward their house. Jack's attention fixed on the restless horses in the corral. Something had them stirred up. Maybe a cougar on the prowl.

Inside the house, he handed Willow to Nora and got his rifle. "I'll be back soon."

"Be careful, Jack."

He nodded and slipped into the darkness, silently making his way to the horses. The thin fingernail of light in the midnight sky was often referred to as a rustler's moon, a positive thing tonight. Jack stopped in the deep shadows of the livery and blacksmith shop.

Cocking his head, he listened to every sound. To trouble whispering on the wind. To his inner voice that warned of danger.

His eyes were in constant motion, seeking the threat. Clay appeared at his side, and they began a search of the perimeter. Ridge joined them. They were silent ghosts drifting through the night, a thick, foggy mist settling over them and the town.

Watching for any movement, not moving a muscle, Jack stood next to the sheer rock wall of the small canyon that protected the town.

The horses were running around the corral in a frenzy.

Was this threat human? Or animal?

He didn't see his fellow searchers. Maybe they'd caught a scent and moved on to a different area. Jack stayed put.

The thin moon ducked behind a cloud, and that's when a shot sounded. A bullet barely missed his ear. Jack dropped low and raised his rifle, scanning left and right.

Dammit, he couldn't see anyone.

Another shot went wide and told him the shooter was merely guessing at his location. If he could only see a target.

As the moon emerged from behind the cloud, a figure flew at him. Jack barely had time to sidestep the bulk, but something sharp caught his arm. A burning, stinging sensation ripped through him. His rifle landed a short distance away.

He grabbed the assailant by the arm and flipped him over his head. He was a little shorter than Jack, but that was all he had time to see before the bastard came at him again.

His brain was a mass of confusion. Who? Why? How many?

The thin moonlight reflected on the blade of a knife upraised in the man's hand. Jack grabbed his arm and twisted, slinging him around, fighting for leverage. He dropped the arm and delivered two blows to the stomach.

The man grunted, his voice raspy. "I'll kill you, Bowdre. You didn't fool me for a second. The ivory grip of your Colt gave you away."

Just then the thin moonlight shone across the assailant's face.

Seamus Belew.

"You'd better have a damn army with you. That's the only

way you'll kill me." Spinning, Jack reached for his Colt and pulled it from his holster. As he came around, he fired.

Belew dropped to the ground. Jack knelt beside his enemy, listening to the sickening gurgle coming from Belew's throat.

"Why?" Jack asked. "Was Max worth all this?"

"He was my"—blood gushed from Belew's mouth—"my brother. Always looked after…him. Promised."

Seamus worked his tongue, struggling to say something else. Jack put his ear near the man's mouth. "Flynn O'Brien… coming." Seamus smiled, his teeth bloody, and took his final breath.

Clay and Ridge raced up, guns drawn. Behind them stood at least a dozen others in a line, guns drawn, their faces grim.

And off to the side where shadows met the light stood Fargo, his face a chunk of granite.

Jack rose, staring at Fargo, and put his Colt away. "He's dead. It's Belew."

"How did he get past the guard?" Clay asked.

Jack glanced around for Belew's pistol and picked it up from the dirt, examining it. "I'm thinking he scaled down the wall of the canyon. That would be my way. He tried to shoot me first, then attacked with a knife. Now I see why. His gun jammed."

When he swung to where Fargo had been, he found him gone. Had the man been working with Belew and helped him get into the town? Seemed rather likely.

Nora arrived out of breath, her focus immediately on the body. "What happened?"

"Belew." Jack pulled her against him with his good arm. "I killed him."

She must've felt wetness and stepped back, alarm on her face. "Jack, you're bleeding."

"I'm fine." He glanced down at blood dripping from his hand. "Just a scratch."

Nora threw up her hands. "Why do you always say that? Dr. Mary will determine the severity, but if it's too deep, you'll need stitches." She got that mulish set to her mouth.

Good Lord, he didn't need this now. "We should get it seen to right away."

"Not now, Nora!" The danger, the fight, Belew's last words had set Jack's nerves on edge, but he instantly regretted his sharp tone. He pinched the bridge of his nose, trying hard to not count but working to tamp down his anger. After a moment, he softened his voice. "We have the body to deal with. Animals will get to it lying here. We have to figure out how he got in and if anyone came with him. Why would he come alone? Nothing makes sense."

Clay gave him a little push. "Go, Jack. She's right. You're bleeding like a stuck pig." He waved toward the men who'd gathered. "We have plenty of help."

"In that case, I guess…I'll be back later." He aimed his feet toward Dr. Mary, who stood at the edge of the pool of light made by the community fire. Nora walked silently beside him. He knew he'd have to apologize, but he'd need to figure out the right words first.

Dr. Mary took one look at him. "Come into my office. Were you shot or cut?"

"Sliced open a bit. Got into a scuffle." Jack sat in a chair at a small table.

If Nora stood any straighter, her spine would snap. "I'll get back to the children," she managed through stiff lips.

Jack reached for her hand. "Stay. Please. Willow must be asleep, and even so, Sawyer can look after her for a minute."

Tension left her body. "Are you sure?"

"Positive. I want you here."

A smile broke across her face. "No place I'd rather be." She pulled up a chair.

The wound was about three inches long but not too deep. "This cut isn't serious, just nasty. I'll have to stitch you up." Dr. Mary rose and came back with bottles, salves, and gauze. She wet a piece of cotton with liquid from one of the bottles. "This is going to sting like the dickens. Better take a big breath and hold on."

Nora slipped her palm inside his hand.

The second the doctor touched the cotton to the wound, fire raced through him and burned as though she'd stuck a lit match to him. Jack hissed through his teeth and silently cussed a blue streak. But once the initial pain subsided, it became bearable. Nora made the enduring possible. Her soft touch soothed him.

"I'll stitch it and you can go." The doctor reached for a needle and catgut.

Jack gritted his teeth and murmured a few choice cusswords while she sewed him up.

Halfway through, Clay stuck his head in the door. "You were right, Jack. We found the rope Belew used to lower himself down the wall of the canyon. He left his horse tied up top and one of the men is bringing it inside."

"Any sign of anyone with him?"

"Looks like he came alone, but I've no idea why."

"Revenge was too strong, and he wanted me all to himself."

"I guess."

"Clay, I noticed Fargo standing over to the side, glaring at me when you and the men raced up. Made the hair rise on my neck, the way he was looking at me. Then the next time I glanced over, he was gone."

"I should have a little chat with him." Clay turned his attention to Nora. "Take good care of this ol' buzzard."

"Lord knows it's a full-time job."

Clay chuckled and left.

In no time, Jack and Nora made their way home. Sawyer and Scout met them at the door, worry in the kid's eyes. "I'm fine, son. Nothing to fret about. Go back to bed."

"Willow's still asleep." Sawyer yawned and stumbled up the stairs.

Jack dropped to the sofa and pulled Nora into his lap. "I want to apologize for my tone. I wasn't angry at you, just at the situation. My nerves were on edge. Belew finding a way into our town, the fight, and him trying to kill me, then seeing Fargo was all more than a little jarring."

"No, the apology is not yours to make." She sighed and laid her hand on his shoulder. "I should've known to hold my tongue, should've known how that would affect you. I'm still learning how to be a wife and I promise to do better. It embarrassed me that you spoke to me that way in front of your friends though."

"We're both learning. I'm sorry most of all for your embarrassment. If I could take it back, I would." The kiss he gave her stirred sleeping embers, bringing them to life. He yearned to carry her to bed. But first, he had to tell her of Belew's last words.

Nora snuggled against him and rested a palm on his jaw. Her fragrance swirled around him like a mind-numbing drug of some kind. He couldn't get enough of her and had no desire to see what would happen if he tried to live without her. Heaven help him.

He broke the kiss, nibbling along the seam of her lips.

She clutched his new leather vest. "I hate having cross words but, oh, I do love the making up part."

Jack rested his chin on her head. "Darlin', I have something to tell you."

"Belew?"

"Lucky guess. Nora, his last words were a taunt. He said Flynn O'Brien is coming."

She gave a cry, her eyes meeting his. "When?"

"I don't know. That was all he said." He took her hand. "It could've meant nothing more than trying to hit a raw nerve. One last jab."

"Or it could've been that he knew for sure." Her words were quiet.

"We have no way of knowing."

"I've had a feeling for days. I know Flynn, and I know in my heart that he'll come to take care of me himself. That's his way."

Jack didn't hesitate. "We could be back with the book long before he shows. It'll take a while to travel from Buffalo."

"I think so too." She kissed the hollow of his throat. "I'd feel a lot better with it in my possession. And once we get back, I'll take it to someone we can trust."

"Any of the Legend family would do, but I think Sam Legend, Stoker's youngest son, would be the best choice. He's sheriff in Lost Point and a former Texas Ranger."

"If the rest of the family are like Luke, I know they're trustworthy."

"And now that we have that settled, Mrs. Nora B. Long, I have an appointment with you upstairs in the privacy of our bedroom." He stood and swept her up, making long strides to the stairs.

"Watch out for your arm, Jack. You'll bust the stitches and I don't want to have to explain that to Dr. Mary. And be careful of your leg. I'm sure it's killing you."

He silenced her with a long kiss.

Thirty-one

TWO DAYS LATER IN THE PREDAWN HOURS, NORA BENT TO KISS Willow in her crib. The black-haired infant looked straight into her eyes and smiled for the very first time. "Jack, come here. She smiled at me. And I think she knows who I am."

He peered over her shoulder. "Well, would you look at that!"

"I think she's getting prettier every day." Nora picked her up, cuddling the small body. "I'm glad she did it today before we left. We're going to miss so many of these first moments."

"Darlin', she's not going to start walking and talking for a long while." He brushed a finger across Willow's cheek.

"No, but she'll smile more. Maybe laugh."

Jack reached for Willow. "You can't catch every single instance, even if you're right here. She'll do things while we're asleep or at all times during the day. It's not about the first smile; it's all the ones down the road that count."

"Why do you always have to be right?"

"Just lucky, I guess."

A loud noise from the kitchen drew them downstairs. Sawyer was banging pans around like some Salvation Army soldier.

"What are you doing?" Nora asked.

"I gotta figure out how to cook for myself. You said I could stay here in the house."

Nora calmly took a saucepan from him. "Yes, we did, but Mr. Clay and Miss Tally are going to feed you while we're gone."

"What if I want an egg in between meals?"

"Then you need a skillet, not a saucepan. Stand right here and watch me." She pulled an apron over her head. Step by step, she showed him how hot to make the fire, how to judge the heat of the skillet, how to ease eggs into the grease without breaking the yolk, and how to turn them. "Now, you do it."

To her pride, he didn't make too big a mess. Both children were doing first things on the day she and Jack were leaving, and she tried to swallow the lump in her throat, praying for a short trip.

Jack lifted an eyebrow and gave her a smile. "Sawyer, why don't you make me some eggs too while you're at it?"

The boy beamed and shortly carried a plate of eggs to the table.

"You know, you keep this up, and you can go to work in a café when we open one." Jack lifted a forkful to his mouth and chewed. "These are some of the best I've eaten." Most of the yolks were broken but Nora liked how Jack heaped praise on the boy.

Too soon, it was time to leave. Outside, Nora held back a sob and turned Willow over to Rebel's care. The woman had turned a corner and said the baby would help occupy her. Hope now shimmered in Rebel's green eyes, replacing the deep sadness.

Nora gave her what she prayed was a smile. "I know you'll take good care of her, but my heart is breaking."

It was all Nora could do to loosen her hold of the baby and not make a scene.

"Please try not to worry, Nora. I'll treat her as my own." Rebel cooed to the infant and nuzzled her cheek. "I'll keep an eye on Sawyer too. We'll all look out for him."

Jack shook the boy's hand, then pulled him close for a hug. "Nothing's going to happen to us. We're going to be back. Repeat that until you believe it."

"Yes, sir." Sawyer tried to smile but failed. "I won't burn down the house or nothing."

Jack chuckled. "I know."

He could laugh because Nora had overheard him tell Clay and Dallas to look after the kid. She had to admit that Sawyer looked so grown-up standing there, though. He might be only nine, but he was going on thirty-five.

Ridge brought the saddled horses. Nora gave Sawyer a long hug, then Jack helped her onto her mare. Barely holding herself together, she didn't look back as they rode away. The dogs tried to follow, but Clay and Sawyer grabbed them.

"They'll be fine," Nora whispered into the wind. Jack maneuvered his horse closer and took her hand. She held on and squeezed for all she was worth. They said nothing, but his hand in hers seemed to promise that he would always be there when she needed him.

They rode all day, stopping only to let the horses rest, and made camp that night by a pretty little creek. Tomorrow, they'd reach the sheepherder's house. She was glad Ridge had come along. They might need his gun.

Supper was relaxing. Nora enjoyed listening to Jack and Ridge talk about old times and the narrow scrapes they'd had. Although Ridge remained a mystery, little details revealed quite a bit about him. He was loyal to a fault and had once stayed behind with Jack only to be pinned down by some Texas Rangers. They'd badly wounded Jack, but Ridge refused to leave. Time after time, Ridge had huddled by his friend's side instead of riding on and saving his own hide. He never bragged, even though he'd once rescued a group of women and children in the clutches of ruthless outlaws. And through Jack, she learned Ridge regularly sent money to an orphanage, keeping the children in shoes.

The sadness in his voice made Nora want to cry. He'd suffered some great loss in his past that had fueled his need for justice. One thing she knew, Ridge Steele wasn't the turn-your-other-cheek kind of man. He seemed driven to make things right whenever he could.

A quality he shared with Jack, it seemed.

Nora slid her arm through Jack's and laid her head on his arm, admiring how the flickering firelight shone on his light-blond hair. The shock of the change had finally worn off, and she found the new color growing on her.

Later, the sounds of the night drifted around her as she lay facing Jack on his bedroll. She snuggled against his chest, under the blanket covering them. "This is familiar, isn't it?"

"Yep. I wish we'd had this bedroll when we were on the run." His voice vibrated through his clothing.

Ridge's light snores came from his spot on the other side of the fire.

"How is your wound?"

"It's fine."

"Jack Bowdre, I'm going to wipe that word from your vocabulary. I know it is not fine."

"Did you come along just to pick a fight?"

"Of course not, but act human. Admit when something hurts."

"Okay, it hurts. Are you happy?"

"No. I don't want you to hurt."

Jack muttered something under his breath that she didn't catch. She was making him crazy again, and if he wasn't silently counting, he was about to start.

"I'm sorry." She sighed. "I only want to fix whatever is causing you pain."

"You can't. This has to heal on its own. I brought the salve Dr. Mary gave me, and I coated the cut good. Does that settle the question?"

"Yes." She snuggled happily against her husband and inhaled his scent. It seemed nothing and no one could touch them here.

She ran her palm over his chest, feeling the rise and fall of his soft breath under her hand. She loved the little rumble in his throat before he spoke and even his counting—it meant he cared about the other person's feelings and would tamp down his anger before he spoke. He cared about people, the ones in Hope's Crossing and ones who were downtrodden. He especially loved the ones growing up under his roof.

"I snuck in a fishing line and hook this time," she whispered. "Just in case we need to fish, you won't have to freeze your arm off."

"I'm touched." He unbuttoned her dress and slid his warm hand inside against her skin, curving it around her breast. "We got acquainted fast and in a most unusual way. Our fight for survival kind of sped things along. Do you know what I first thought when I saw you sitting across from me on that stage?"

"No." This should be good. She'd always wondered what first impression she'd made on him.

"You spoke with refinement, seemed too perfect. Better than me. A little snooty."

"Snooty? Good heavens, Jack. I was just trying to figure out this strange country, and everyone I met was scary." Nora giggled. When she ran a teasing finger across his lips, he nipped at her. She continued across a jaw and down his throat. "What about now?"

He let out a low chuckle. "You're refined, too perfect, and better than me. Lots better. No contest kind of better."

"I don't think so." She pressed her lips to the hollow of his throat. "Do you know what I saw?"

"A scarred-up outlaw dumb enough to get caught?"

"I wanted to cry. Your face seemed made of carved stone and you had frightening storms in your eyes. I felt your heavy heart, tasted your bitterness. I wanted to wrap my arms around you and hold you."

"All of that while I was trying everything I could think of to get a rise out of you?"

"Yes. You didn't have that hardness about you I was used to seeing in Flynn and his group. I saw deep down where you tried to curl up away from the world. I saw a softness that you tried desperately to hide, and I wasn't scared of you. Not one bit."

"I knew that and thought you must have courage in spades." He moved a hand along her curves. "Do you remember telling me about Flynn giving you that baby boy and ordering you to get rid of it?"

"It took all my strength to tell you that. I was so ashamed for not turning Flynn in."

"I have a secret too, one that's tormented me for years." Jack closed his eyes, tightened his arms around her, and told her about the despicable outlaw Gus Franklin. "I'll go to my grave remembering the blood, the stench of death, knowing that family died because of my mistake."

"You didn't know Franklin would do that."

"I should have. I wasn't green behind the ears. I'd been riding the outlaw trail for years."

"Listen to me, Jack. We do the best we can in each situation. No one expects you to be a mind reader." She took his face between her hands. "We're not perfect and you took care of Franklin. You made him pay and that's important."

"Yeah, too little, too late."

"Stop beating yourself up. You've done plenty of good and don't say you haven't. I've listened to you men sit around the campfire and talk. They like and admire you so much."

"I love you, Nora. Never doubt that for a second."

"Me too." She lay there staring up at the stars after he went to sleep, thinking how glad she was that Flynn was nowhere near. Hopefully, she'd never have to see him again. She never wanted to feel the kind of terror she'd been struck with time and again when he threatened her with his bag of snakes.

She softly kissed Jack and felt his arm tighten around her. Even in his sleep, he was protecting her.

For one moment, one heartbeat, one unforgettable love in an imperfect world, life was pretty close to perfect.

～

The sheepherder's soddy was silent and still in the early morning sun. It appeared even shabbier than before. The breeze ruffled the tall grass and the branches of the trees. Jack dismounted in a stand of cedar and took a pair of binoculars from his saddlebag. Nora and Ridge also climbed from the saddle.

No one spoke as Jack checked the tiny house and the land around it. The goats and sheep he'd freed were gone. He hoped wild animals hadn't gotten them.

The front door slammed back against the house, standing wide open. Jack jumped, and it took him a second to realize the wind had caught it. The door slammed shut again a second later.

"Seems deserted." Jack handed the binoculars to Ridge, then took Nora's hand and found it icy. "I think we need to watch a bit longer. I'll keep you out of danger or die trying."

"I know," she whispered. "I'm going to believe that we beat him."

Jack lightly squeezed her fingers and kissed her forehead. "Even if he's in Texas, he'll have to meet up with Guthrie first."

"True." Some of the tension left her. "But I know Flynn, and he'll retrace every step I've made."

"From what I can tell, it looks clear." Ridge handed the binoculars back to Jack. "I'm going to make a slow turn around the perimeter on foot, look for tracks. But there's a million places a man can hide down there with all the brush and gullies. My gut's warning me."

"I'll go with you and take the opposite direction. We can't do a thorough search, but maybe it'll be enough." He gave Nora a stern glance. "Be as still as possible and don't move from this spot."

She managed a smile and nodded. "Will do."

Jack took the west and kept in the low brush, moving slow, easy, his eyes scanning the ground for any sign of visitors. He saw nothing. He met Ridge back where Nora waited.

Ridge pushed back his worn black Stetson and wiped his forehead. "I don't like this one damn bit. Let's get the book and out of here fast."

"The hair is standing up on my neck. This is not good," Jack agreed. "It's ripe for an ambush."

"Yep," Ridge agreed.

"Then I'll hurry inside and get the ledger. I don't want to stay here any longer than necessary either." Nora shivered. "This place makes my skin crawl. It reeks of death."

"Hold on." Jack took her arm. "Slow down. We're coming with you."

When they reached the house, Ridge broke away into some nearby trees. Jack and Nora went on.

All was well until they stepped inside the door and a large black spider dropped onto Nora's arm. She shrieked and flailed, slinging her arms and stomping, until Jack knocked it off.

"I hate spiders."

"Hurry and let's get out of here." Jack glanced around,

thinking how they'd felt so lucky a few weeks ago to be out of the cold air. And then finding Willow and the fight to save her.

Nora knelt on the floor and Jack pried up the board. "Do you think there are snakes under there?"

It was a clear possibility, but he wouldn't tell her that. "No. Too early."

She reached into the narrow space and patted around. Her face froze. "I can't find it."

"Keep looking. Maybe an animal pushed it farther back."

She leaned into the opening, stretching, concentrating. Finally, she pulled her arm out. Her face was ashen. "It's not here."

"You're sure this is where you hid it?"

"Positive. This was the only loose board, here by the table."

Had they come all this way for nothing?

Jack lifted her up. "Let me look. My arm is longer." He lay down and reached as far as he could until a wooden obstruction stopped him. His fingertips brushed what seemed like paper. "I think I have it."

He stretched farther into the space and got hold of the book. Relief filled him. "I got it."

"Oh, thank you dear Lord!" Nora plopped down beside him. "I feared we were too late."

Jack handed the evidence that would convict O'Brien to her and stood, helping her up. He slid his Colt from the holster. As they stepped from the little house, three men emerged from a stand of scrub oak, guns drawn.

Surprise shot through Jack.

Dutch. Their traitor.

He'd been sure Fargo was the one with a black heart. Not the jovial man everyone loved.

Dammit! Darius Guthrie was holding Jack's and Nora's horses. He must've circled around and got them. This was going to complicate things even more.

The third man in the group, a well-dressed older man somewhere in his early fifties, gave them a cold smile. Had to be O'Brien. He stroked his nicely trimmed reddish mustache and goatee that matched his hair, and when he spoke it was with an Irish brogue. "Drop your weapons."

"Looks like we hold all the cards!" Guthrie yelled. "Do as he says."

"Having you all together will make it easier to kill you." Jack's gaze narrowed on their traitor. "You've finally shown your true color, Dutch—yellow. You'd betray your own mother."

"Dying your hair didn't change anything." Dutch shrugged. "A shame you won't be alive to warn your friends they're next. I'll destroy that town from within and have myself a nice payday in the bargain."

Red-hot anger washed over Jack. "Anything for money, right?"

"I'll be a rich man before I'm through with Hope's Crossing."

If he lived long enough. Jack meant to make sure he didn't.

The horses stamped their feet and their eyes rolled back to show the whites as they strained against the reins.

What else was out there? Who? Had they brought more men?

"He came over to the right side!" Guthrie hollered.

"Enough money can buy anyone, I suppose," Jack answered evenly. "But does it buy loyalty and trust? Will he die for you?"

Where in the hell was Ridge?

Nora pressed closer to Jack while he measured the distance. Too far to lunge. He searched the brush but didn't see help coming.

"Enough." O'Brien stepped out in front, holding a gun. "I'll shoot Nora first. You can watch her die."

"Ahhh, I assume you're Flynn O'Brien. We meet at last." If Jack could get off a single shot, he'd rid the world of the slimy bastard and his brand of terror.

"Throw your pistol over here." The door to the house banged, sounding like a rifle blast. O'Brien jumped.

"Over there or over here?" Jack played dumb and laid his pistol at his feet, within reach.

"Damn you! I told you to throw it over here." A mottled red colored O'Brien's face. "Are you stupid or plain deaf?"

"I can pick it up and bring it to you," Jack offered helpfully. A bullet made a larger hole up close. He'd make sure to get one into the traitorous Dutch.

The wind picked up, swirling around and around, creating a dirt devil between them.

For a moment, Jack couldn't see. He could only feel Nora gripping his arm.

"Leave it and stay where you are," O'Brien barked.

Jack shrugged. "Whatever you say."

O'Brien ignored him, focusing on Nora. "You've caused me a lot of trouble, you little tramp. I demand that book you stole from me."

"No." Nora glared at him. "I don't care about your demands. You don't scare me."

Darius Guthrie edged closer, crowing, "I told you he'd come. Now, you're gonna get what's coming to you."

"It'll take bigger men than you," Jack drawled. Ridge was still absent from the powwow. Jack needed him to tip the odds.

"Shut up!" O'Brien clicked his tongue. "After all I've done for you, Nora. Took you off the street, clothed you, gave you a bed. And this is the way you repay me. For two cents, I'd put a bullet in your head, but give me the book and I'll go on my way instead. I'll forget you bit the hand that fed you."

"How generous." Nora's laugh was forced and Jack could feel her shaking, but she wasn't cowering and he admired her courage. "I'll see you in prison for your crimes, and that's a promise."

A flock of crows swooped down, landing on the brush, raising a loud ruckus. Everyone's eyes were fixated on the squawking birds.

Suddenly, Ridge stole up behind the three men, his gun drawn. He pressed it to the back of O'Brien's head. "Holding all the cards, are you? I'll see your hand and raise you. Toss your weapons. Now!"

The wind died, and nothing moved as clouds drifted over them. The loud flock of crows hushed. The horses became silent and still. Even the tall grass ceased to sway. It seemed as if everything was waiting.

Jack watched. He, too, waited to put a bullet in the three men.

One second passed.

Two.

Finally, O'Brien threw his weapon down, then the other two men at his side followed suit.

Jack picked up his Colt and started toward them, telling Nora to stay put. First, he needed a rope from his horse to hog-tie O'Brien with, then he'd take care of the other two. He'd be damned if they'd ever threaten or hurt Nora again.

But three strides later, he stopped in his tracks, listening.

A rumble of noise grew, rising up from the thick brush. Two dogs sprang from out of nowhere, barking, howling, growling, running for the men Ridge held at gunpoint.

Guthrie's eyes grew wide. He dropped the reins of the horses and began running.

All hell broke loose. The horses reared and bucked, whinnying loudly.

Nora screamed.

Dust swirled around their feet like a cyclone.

The dogs wouldn't stop snarling, running, barking loud enough to make a man deaf.

A flurry of shots went off amidst the rising dirt cloud—from whose gun?

The noise of the chaos made it hard for Jack to think. Gus Franklin exploded into his thoughts. He'd let the man live only to bury his new victims. He couldn't let Dutch walk away or the man would murder the future of Hope's Crossing and the dreams of everyone in it.

Calm swept over him. He barely breathed and placed Dutch in his sights. Saying a prayer, he aimed through the thick haze. He squeezed the trigger, hitting Dutch dead center. The huge man pitched over into a bed of cactus and didn't move.

Jack quickly swung his pistol at Flynn O'Brien, tracking the running target. Just as he fired, the man fell to the ground.

Dammit! He couldn't see anything through the dust or hear over the chaos.

Where had the dastardly mob boss gone?

When the dust settled, O'Brien and Guthrie had vanished—along with the horses and Ridge.

Thirty-two

SHAKING, NORA DUCKED BACK INTO THE SHEEPHERDER'S house, clutching the book to her chest.

Over a thousand miles had separated her from O'Brien. She thought she'd had time. Yet here he was, already in Texas.

She stood trembling in the shadow of the doorway. What now?

Jack ran to her, pulled her close. "You still have the book and we're going to get the bastards."

The two dogs bounded up, tongues lolling out. "Jack, aren't these Bullet and Scout?"

"Hell! Sure seems so. I'd recognize Bullet anywhere." Scout nuzzled Jack's hand with her large nose. He looked for a notch out of one ear and found it. "Yep. This is Scout."

"How on earth did they follow us?"

"Tracked us."

"But why didn't they catch up to us last night when we camped?"

"I'm sure Sawyer kept Scout in the house for a good while. She and Bullet probably started following us once Sawyer let her out to do her business. That's all that can explain it."

Questions swirled in Nora's head until she felt like she was caught in a whirlwind. "What happened to Ridge and our horses?"

"Hopefully, the horses are close and Ridge isn't shot. We'll have to find them."

Nora leaned into Jack, laying her head on his chest. "And then?"

She still shook at coming face-to-face with the man she feared more than death. The desire to run came on strong. Run to her safe little house in Hope's Crossing and hide there. But then everything in her froze. That would not only put

Sawyer and Willow in danger but everyone else who lived there. Flynn O'Brien was capable of destroying the whole town, including the children, and she knew it.

"What are we going to do, Jack?"

"I'll find Ridge and those horses, and we'll ride like the devil is on our tails. Let me have that book. I'll keep it safe."

"Okay."

He put it inside his shirt, then took her hand. "Let's go. We've got to get out of here. Try to keep behind me and don't make a sound."

She saw no sign of anyone when they emerged into the sunlight. The silence was eerie and whispered inside her head like a thousand hissing snakes. She glanced around, half expecting Flynn to leap out any second, kill Jack, and take her.

Colt in hand, Jack moved quickly into the low scrub brush. She kept a palm glued to his back. Scout and Bullet had disappeared again.

Once or twice Jack stopped and raised his hand. After a short pause, he went on. The sun crept higher and still they saw no sign of anyone.

A gunshot sounded ahead of them. Nora jerked but said nothing. The muscles in Jack's back tensed, but he kept moving silently forward.

Was Ridge alive or dead? She feared the verdict.

The brush snapped in front of them. Jack pulled Nora behind the leafy branches of a large cedar.

A second later, the dogs bounded from the brush, followed by Ridge leading his big bay horse.

Relief swept over Nora. "I'm glad you're all right. Who fired the shots?"

"I did." Ridge removed his hat and wiped sweat trickling down his face. "I saw Jack end Dutch's short, traitorous career. I lost the others in a gully. Not sure where they could've gone. The bastards were like ghosts."

"We'll find them. The horses?" Jack kept his sharp gaze moving, still looking for trouble. "We need to beat O'Brien to them and get the hell out of here."

"Your dun headed for the creek behind the house. The others scattered," Ridge answered.

Jack let out a low oath. "With luck they won't be far, but if O'Brien finds them first, he'll leave us afoot."

Nora sucked in a breath. To be on foot with Flynn on the loose awakened full-fledged, terrifying panic in her breast.

"I agree. You check at the creek and I'll ride down the trail." Ridge swung up and trotted off.

Nora stayed at Jack's side, keeping her eyes peeled for her former benefactor, praying he'd fallen into a dark pit with no way out. But slippery as he was, he'd always find some way to escape. Maybe he'd have a harder time with men like Jack and Ridge, who would refuse to roll over like trained dogs.

Neither spoke while retracing their footsteps. There wasn't much of anything to say though. Nora used the quiet time to pray that Jack's horse would be at the creek. Then they could leave, even if Nora had to leave her mare and ride double with Jack. She just had to put some miles between her and Flynn.

Jack's horse was there at the water, although it skittered away at first when he tried to grab the reins. He got the dun horse on the next try and held the animal firm. "I'll help you up, Nora, and we'll try to find your mare."

Ridge, Colt still in hand, trotted up, leading the mare, with Scout loping along beside him. "Found her. Ready to ride?"

"More than ready." Nora shivered. "We have what we came for."

"Wait." Jack handed Nora her precious book. "Put this in your saddlebag. It think it'll be safer there for now."

She nodded and put it inside the large leather pouch, then mounted up, and they trotted away.

Nora turned for one last glance at the sad little house where they'd found Willow. It was already returning to the earth from which it came. If they didn't make it back home and Flynn O'Brien somehow won, at least the baby girl was safe and cared for.

Nerves made her hands shake so much she could barely

hold the reins. Coming face-to-face with Flynn again had awakened her worst nightmares.

∽◦∾

They set a brisk pace for about an hour, then dropped to a walk. At times Scout and Bullet hung back, then caught up. The red hound acted a little odd—skittish and watchful, not the fun-loving dog they knew. Jack kept an eye on her and mentioned his observations to Nora and Ridge.

Nora swiveled in the saddle. "Do you think she senses someone following?"

"Who the hell knows?" Ridge snorted. "Maybe she's looking for more horses to scare."

"Ridge! You'll hurt her feelings," Nora scolded.

Jack lifted a canteen from around his pommel and uncorked it. "I think one of us should drop back and see if someone's behind us. I'll do it, Ridge, if you'll stay with Nora."

"No, let me go," Ridge insisted. Before Jack could answer, he turned around and rode off.

Scout didn't follow. She stayed with him and Nora.

They rode quietly for a bit and Jack listened to the clop of the horse's hooves. Friction crackled in the air like a current, and he kept his Colt ready to fire.

Best to be prepared. Trouble was coming.

"Jack, do you know Ridge's story?"

Jack could barely hear Nora's low voice, apparently mindful of how voices carried.

"Not much of it. Ridge has never liked to speak of the past." Jack met her gaze. "Outlaws have two lives, divided by a before-and-after line. Most hold the before part sacred as a time untouched by violence, before they turned to criminal ways."

She tilted her head and smiled, and his heart flipped over. "I'm glad you told me your story. I understand better now."

"I held it in for too long. It was time to let it out, and a wife needs to know what makes the man she married tick." They were a team, and the better they understood each other, the happier their home would be. Anyway, that was his opinion.

But what the hell did he know? He'd left his Rachel to face a bunch of killers by herself.

The bloodhound suddenly shot up an incline off the trail. What the hell? Jack stared into a deep ravine on the right side of the goat path.

Someone could've ridden along the floor of that ravine and be hiding down there.

The sun was high, midway in the sky. Rays caught on Nora's hair. Jack shook his head to clear it. Sweat covered his palm. He needed to think straight. Just because someone could've ridden down the ravine didn't mean they had.

A second later, a flurry of loud gunshots sounded behind them. Nora moved her mare closer to him. "Ridge is in trouble."

"You can't assume that. Those might have come from his gun." Jack stared up the incline where Scout had gone. Every instinct became raw and heightened. He sniffed the slight breeze and smelled the faint odor of spent gunpowder. The shots were close.

"Get off your horse, Nora. Now!"

She silently obeyed and huddled next to her mare.

Bullets peppered the ground around them. Jack swiveled in the saddle to return fire.

A horse galloped straight for them.

A prairie dog darted under Jack's horse. The dun reared up in panic. Caught mid-dismount, Jack was thrown from the saddle and hurtled down into the steep ravine.

Thirty-three

"JACK!" NORA SCREAMED AND RAN TO THE SIDE OF THE RAVINE. He lay unmoving at the bottom that had to be at least fifteen feet below her.

Was he alive? Her heartbeat roared in her ears as she looked for a way down to him.

The sound of racing hooves alerted her, and she whirled to find Flynn O'Brien astride his horse. There was no sign of Guthrie. Flynn dismounted, a gloating smile on his face, gripping a burlap sack that he untied from his saddle horn. The hisses and rattles coming from the sack turned her to ice. She couldn't take her gaze from it.

Everything she'd tried to forget tumbled back.

The dark room.

The sack of snakes, rattling and hissing only inches away.

Frantic pleas to spare her life. The cold floor where she huddled in fear.

Nora's heart pounded so hard she thought it was coming out of her chest. Her tongue worked in a dry mouth. Heaven help her. Arms held straight out, she backed up until blocked by her mare. The animal's muscles quivered.

Flynn stalked slowly toward her, his tall boots reaching the knees of his black trousers—boots that had stood on a concrete floor slickened with blood.

His voice was as soft as a kitten's meow, yet terror flooded Nora's bones. "For the last time, little mouse, give me my ledger. My patience runs thin."

"Kill me and you'll never get it."

"I have ways of making you talk. Or have you forgotten?"

"I'm going to see you pay for your crimes." What had happened to Ridge? She'd give anything for him to appear. Or the dogs. But she saw nothing. Heard nothing except the wind.

Her heart thudded painfully against her ribs as she glanced over the edge of the ravine at Jack, lying so still and horribly silent.

She was alone and at the mercy of a murdering madman.

Flynn's eyes snapped, his face a dark, gruesome mask. "You know what I do to those who disobey me. I thought I made it clear, but you seem to have forgotten the lesson. Give me my book and I'll let you live."

"You'll kill me no matter what I do." She swallowed hard, needing to buy some time. But she couldn't take her eyes from the wiggling burlap bag and the sickening rattles coming from within.

"I saw your…new benefactor…go into that ravine, my dear. The right choice can save him."

Nora lifted her chin. "He's my husband. We're married."

Disgust crossed Flynn's face. "Does he know how quickly I can make you whimper at my feet?" His voice lowered. "Or your babbling pleas when I took everything from you? You're a filthy, pathetic tramp. The sight of you makes me sick. I knew how to get you to do what I wanted then." His lips parted to reveal his yellow teeth. "And I know how to do it now. Darius proved to be a very able accomplice. He knew where to find what I needed."

Then Flynn did the unthinkable. He opened the sack and carefully removed a twisting, coiling gray-and-brown rattlesnake. It was large in both length and width. Before she could blink, he secured the snake's head between his thumb and forefinger.

He moved to the edge of the ravine, holding the snake outstretched, its tail whipping around.

"No!" Nora rushed forward with her nails poised like claws. "Don't you dare!"

Flynn sidestepped her. "Keep away or you'll force my hand! The book in exchange for your outlaw's life."

Rage and defeat swept over her. The choice was easy. "You win. I'll get it."

"No tricks," he cautioned.

She hurried to her mare and removed the book, holding it for a moment, letting her plan to bring Flynn to justice slip away. But she'd sacrifice that to save Jack. Nothing would be too great to give up for him.

"Hurry, Nora. I might not be able to hold this snake long. It's very powerful. I wonder how quickly your husband will convulse and die. Snakebite is a horrible way to go."

"Here." Clutching the book, she stood several feet away from Flynn. "Get away from the ravine and I'll give you want you want."

"You learn well, little mouse." Admiration briefly filled the reptilian eyes she hated. The burlap bag in his left hand still moved, indicating at least one more snake still waited inside. With his right hand holding the large snake, he couldn't take the ledger. "Lay it at my feet."

Her gaze riveted on the snake in his hand, she obeyed. A growl rumbled in Flynn's throat. She watched in horror as he hurled the snake over the edge of the ravine.

"Jack! Jack!" She scrambled to see, and her heart stopped.

The snake landed next to Jack, slithering onto him, seeking his warmth. She had to get down there. Helplessness shot through her and she couldn't think.

"Wake up, Jack!" She wouldn't let him die. When she looked up, Flynn had collected the ledger and stuck it under his arm. But instead of taking it and leaving, he eased his hand back into the wiggling burlap sack.

His glacial smile chilled her as he pulled out a second reptile, this one even larger. He again secured the head as he had the first.

One slow step, then another, he inched toward her.

He stood so close she could smell his foul breath. She let out a low cry, dreading whatever he had in his twisted mind to do.

"Stand real still, little mouse. Take your medicine." Eyes crazed, his mouth slack, he came closer. Realization that this excited him sent her heartbeat careening. He slowly moved the snake toward her face. "You've been a bad, bad girl."

The reptile's forked tongue flicked out, seeking a target. Ice filled Nora's veins, and her breath hung in her chest. She was afraid to blink, to swallow, to lick her dry lips. The snake's small, obsidian eyes watched her, its rattles shaking. She wanted to close her eyes, but she had to see where Flynn was going.

She had to find a way to escape.

But she couldn't take her gaze from the snake's searching tongue.

"You did wrong taking my ledger and running." His low voice froze her blood and it took everything she had in her to stand still. "You made me chase you all this way. Now you have to pay."

Flynn held the snake's head and placed the cold velvet skin against her cheek. Its tongue flicked out no more than two inches away. A violent quiver raced through her as he let the slender length curl around her neck.

Oh, Dear Lord! Please get it off. Get it off! Get it off!

"No. Please, Flynn."

A sudden calm came over her. Everything she'd endured at Flynn's hand stormed back. In the weeks she'd spent with Jack, she'd become stronger. Wiser.

And Jack's life depended on her.

Quick as a snapping turtle, she kneed him in the groin. He dropped the reptile's head, leaving the body dangling from her throat. Without thinking to consider her actions, she grabbed the snake behind the head and thrust it into Flynn's sorry face. The snake, probably just as terrified, bit down.

Flynn's tortured screams rent the air.

Nora ran to the ravine's edge, not sparing him a second glance. She searched for a way down to the floor. The deadly snake was slithering onto Jack's chest. A roar in her ears was so loud it blocked out all sound. She could barely breathe and shook uncontrollably, rocking back and forth.

The wall of the fifteen-foot ravine was steep but she saw enough brush on the rocky side to give her some handholds. Losing no time, she grabbed whatever brush was growing and scrambled to the bottom, skinning her arms and legs. But she gave herself no thought.

"I can do this," she repeated. "I have to save Jack."

One inch at a time, ignoring the thorns and brambles, she made her way down toward the man she loved, jumping the last two feet.

Her heart pounding in her chest, she closed her eyes for a moment. She had to grab the snake just right, or it would be able to get her too.

Her pulse raced, her breath coming in harsh gasps.

Jack moaned as he came to. "Be still," Nora warned. "Don't move a muscle."

The tail rattled, the snake hissed, warning of danger. It lunged for her, but she jerked back in the nick of time.

Terror raced along her body, paralyzing her and blocking all thought.

Disregarding her plea to lie still, Jack sat up. The snake opened its mouth wide and sank its fangs into his thigh.

He let out a loud yell. Nora kicked the rattler into some brush, then struggled to help him to his feet. "We've got to hurry. It was a rattlesnake—how much time do you have?"

"An hour or two at most."

She had to get him to Dr. Mary, a day's ride away.

But how could she get him up the steep side? Just then, she heard Scout's bark and a horse's answering whinny. "Down here!" she yelled. "Hurry!"

A moment later, Ridge hollered from above. "Hang on, I'll get my rope."

"Watch out for the large snake near Flynn."

"Will do."

Relief made Nora weak. Thank God he'd come.

Tying one end of the rope around the pommel, Ridge dangled the other end over the side of the ravine. "Grab hold and climb up."

Jack motioned to her. "Nora, take the rope."

"You get that rope and climb up or I'll never speak to you again."

He swayed and blinked hard. Sweat popped out on his forehead. Propping him against the rocky wall, Nora snatched the lariat and tied it around his waist. "Raise him up, Ridge, and hurry. A snake bit him."

Once Jack's feet left the ground, Nora grabbed the brush along the side of the ravine and pulled herself to the top. Ridge leaned down to lend a helping hand. When she was on solid ground, she knelt over Jack. His eyelids drooped and sweat was pouring off him.

Ridge pulled out a knife and cut Jack's trouser leg away. Two puncture wounds stood out on his upper thigh and redness surrounded the bite. His leg had started to swell and that couldn't be good.

Scout licked Jack's face with her slobbery tongue. Jack didn't push her away, which said more than anything else about his great pain.

"Can you get my bandana from my saddlebag and bring that small bottle of whiskey?" Ridge asked.

Without a word, Nora raised her skirt and ripped a strip off her petticoat. Jack had used her petticoats to save their lives in the beginning, so it was only right to save him with one. Thrusting the fabric at Ridge, she rushed for the whiskey.

Nora hurried back with it, and Ridge washed the wound with the whiskey then gave Jack a liberal swig. Then he tied the petticoat tight around Jack's thigh, an inch above the angry, red bite. "This is all we can do for now. We've got to get him to a doctor."

She glanced at Flynn. His eyes were closed, mouth hanging open, puncture wounds on his face that had begun to swell. She bent over him and picked up the book. "You deserve a painful death, but even that might not be enough justice after all you've done."

His lips moved. She leaned close enough to hear him say, "Go to hell."

Ridge helped her up. "Leave him. It's no more than his due."

Between her and Ridge, they boosted Jack into the saddle and galloped toward Hope's Crossing.

No one spoke. Nora's thoughts, and she guessed Ridge's too, were entirely focused on getting to Dr. Mary.

Her vision blurred. Jack. She couldn't imagine living without him. That thought refused to take root. She brushed her eyes with an impatient hand, doing her best to hold Jack steady in the saddle. Ridge rode on the other side, keeping him from tumbling off that way.

Although they weren't born as brothers, they loved each other just as much and would give their lives for the other. Their bond brought a lump to her throat.

"Just a little farther, Jack!" she yelled. "Don't quit on us."

They spurred their horses faster and flew over the ground, up hills and down, around bends. She knew they were getting close.

At last, the entrance of the town came into view. Ridge fired his pistol in the air several times and Nora began hollering for help the moment they galloped through the pass and onto the only street.

People ran toward them. Clay reached them first when they stopped. "What's wrong?"

"Get Dr. Mary. A rattlesnake bit Jack." Nora pushed back her hair with trembling fingers and leaped from her mare, watching the men lift Jack's limp form from the saddle.

His eyes were closed, and she could tell he was alive only by the rise and fall of his chest. His shallow breathing frightened her. Which of those bits of air would be his last?

Dr. Mary raced to them. "Hurry. We don't have much time."

Nora followed behind with a prayer on her lips that he'd somehow live to hold her again and keep the monsters at bay.

Thirty-four

NIGHT FOUND NORA BY JACK'S BEDSIDE. SHE WAS BARELY aware of others in the small room. Sawyer came several times to keep vigil with her. The boy held Jack's hand and told him how much he loved him, saying that Jack was his father now and he'd better not die.

"I'm still not used to his new hair." Sawyer glanced up. "Do you think it might change back one day?"

"Eventually. A month or so of washings, and it'll return to brown." She put her arm around the boy. "Go to bed. Tomorrow will bring good news. I believe that."

Sawyer stumbled out and Nora wearily laid her head on the bed, clinging to hope.

Around midnight, Dr. Mary put a hand on Nora's shoulder. "Go get some sleep."

"I can't. I have to be here. He might wake up and not…" Her voice caught, and she swallowed her fear. "Not know where he is." She lifted her beloved's hand and brought it to her cheek. "We've already been through so much together. I can't imagine what else is in store. His leg is swollen twice the size. He has to live, Doctor."

"Try not to worry. He has a good chance. Jack's a healthy man, strong."

Nora let out a heavy breath and gave Dr. Mary a watery smile. "I think I loved him from the first time I saw him on that stagecoach, you know. He was roughed up, his eyes glittering with fury, but I saw a man who would do whatever he could to stay alive. He wears his toughness like a badge. Jack taught me not to be afraid, to dive in and do what had to be done." She kissed his hand and laid it on his stomach. "When I saw that snake and knew no one could save him but me, I put my fear aside and threw it off."

Dr. Mary chuckled. "Someone once said that courage is being stiff with fear but saddling up anyway. I've thought a lot about the subject, and I think fear is there to let you know that something is worth dying for, and if you don't face it, you'll lose something very precious."

"That's exactly it." Jack was her only love, her hope, her destiny, and he was worth dying for.

"After I doctored the bite, I examined that old bullet wound in Jack's leg. I think I can remove it and I want to try."

"That's wonderful, Doctor."

"I can't do it until he starts to heal from the bite. His body is fighting enough right now." Dr. Mary gathered some soiled cloths and went out.

Clay and Ridge entered, their faces grim. Both removed their hats.

"How is he?" Ridge asked.

"Not a lot of change." Nora stood to get the kinks out of her back. "Ridge, what happened after you rode back?"

"I found Guthrie and we had a gunfight." A smile flickered across Ridge's mouth for a brief second. "He lost."

"Good." Darius Guthrie's small crow eyes made Nora shiver. At least she wouldn't have to be afraid of him returning.

Ridge shifted the hat in his hands. "Darius and Flynn had split up. That's why Scout was acting strange. She didn't know which one to follow. They confused her, and Bullet was no help. That dog leads with bared teeth instead of his nose."

"Flynn O'Brien was mean through and through. I'm glad he's dead."

Clay chuckled. "It was pure Texas justice. By the way, Skeet Malloy returned with news of Travis."

"What did he learn?" Nora hoped Rebel could handle this.

"After the bounty hunter got patched up, he took Travis on to Canadian, in Hemphill County. He's in jail there awaiting sentencing."

"Oh no. What do you think will happen?" Her thoughts flew to all possibilities.

The door opened, and Dr. Mary came in with an armload of clean cloths.

Ridge watched her putting them in a cabinet. "I know the judge up there to be a fair man. I don't think Travis will hang."

"But you're not sure, are you?"

"As Clay will tell you, anything can happen." Ridge put on his hat. "I'll go let Rebel know."

"Tell Jack he'd better not get too used to that bed." Although Clay's voice was gruff, she knew it came from deep caring.

After the two friends left, Nora's attention caught on movement in the room across the hall. She walked to Tait Trinity's door.

The unshaven outlaw glanced up in surprise to see her. "Come in. How's Bowdre?"

"The doc thinks he'll make it but he's still unconscious. Is there anything I can get you?"

"A cup of coffee if it's no trouble."

"None at all. Anything else?" Nora liked Jack's friend. Tait had kind eyes, the intelligent type that seemed to notice every detail.

"Any news drifting into town?"

"Travis Lassiter is in jail in Canadian awaiting trial. We're hoping the judge will go lightly."

"I know Lassiter. Good man. Hope he finds a way out that doesn't involve a rope." Tait rubbed a hand across his bristly jaw. "Have you heard anything from Dodge City?"

"A fellow came in on the stage a few days ago and said the Santa Fe Railroad got held up at gunpoint. He said the robber was shot and killed."

Tait sagged against the pillow. "I'll take that coffee now."

Nora hurried to get it, wondering why Tait had asked about Dodge City so specifically. Maybe he'd known the holdup would take place, and the man involved was a friend. When she returned with the coffee, Tait thanked her without saying anything else.

An hour later, Jack's moan alerted Nora. She leaned over him. "I'm here, Jack. Can you hear me?"

His eyes fluttered for several moments before they finally stayed open. A loud groan filled the room.

"Who's sitting on my head?" He opened his eyes and put a hand in his wheat-colored hair.

"That's good news." She grinned and brushed her lips across his mouth.

"Not good news from my side of things." He frowned. "What happened? Am I shot?"

Evidently, he remembered nothing. That could be a blessing.

"A snake bit you." She tenderly smoothed back his hair. "I'm very happy you're back. You had me worried there for a bit, sweetheart."

"Sorry." He winced and touched his bandaged thigh. "How did I get snakebit?"

Dr. Mary leaned over him and looked in his eyes. "Glad to see you back with us, Bowdre. Gave us a quite a scare. Get some rest and quit nagging your poor wife. She's barely left your side since she and Ridge brought you in."

His eyes searched Nora's face. "I got me a keeper, Doc."

After the doctor left the room, he pulled her next to him on the small bed. Nora smiled and laid her head on his chest and told him all about her encounter with Flynn and the snakes.

"Glad you found the courage when you needed it. I'm sorry I wasn't able to kill the bastard with my bare hands."

"It took all the strength I could muster and then some, but I wasn't going to cower in front of him ever again." She drew circles along Jack's ribs with a finger. "Snakes don't scare me anymore. I guess seeing you lying there so helpless toughened me up. I might go hunt them and skin each one I find."

His chuckle was a bit raspy. "That's a tall order, lady. I think you'll turn out to be one hell of an outlaw's wife."

"Skeet Malloy got back with news. Travis is in jail in Canadian and awaiting sentencing."

A stillness came over him along with a frown. "I don't

think we can get him out. The walls of that jail are a foot thick and have no windows."

"Ridge knows that judge and thinks Travis will get a fair trial."

"It's the best we can hope for. But I damn sure hate it."

Nora slipped her hand inside the nightshirt Dr. Mary had put on Jack, loving the feel of his broad chest.

"Jack, Dr. Mary wants to operate and remove that bullet in your thigh."

"Hell!" Jack glanced down at her and tightened his hold. "Maybe it'll be good to get rid of that damn pain though. As long as you'll be my nurse."

"That's a deal."

O'Brien's last words kept rolling around her in her head like marbles. Filthy, pathetic tramp, was she? Her eyes locked with Jack's and the love she saw there made her feel like the most beautiful, desirable woman on earth.

Thirty-five

"I'M GOING TO OPERATE ON YOUR LEG, JACK," DR. MARY announced cheerfully a week later.

A growl rumbled in his throat. He glanced down at Willow, lying asleep in the crook of his arm. Other than the babe, he saw little to be cheerful about. Although a lot of the swelling in his thigh had gone down, the snakebite still hurt like hell. He'd like to empty his gun in O'Brien. "What's the hurry? I've lived with it this way for five years."

Her bullet necklace tinkled as she leaned over to adjust his covers, reminding him of the misery a lot of other men had endured so she could make that damn piece of jewelry.

"Why drag it out, Jack? The snake bite is going to pain you awhile longer, so you might as well get everything over at once while you're laid up."

Jack didn't know her age, but he'd guess somewhere in her thirties. The rich brown hair that she kept in a knot at the nape of her neck had a few silver streaks in it but not many. He liked her gumption and the fact that she didn't take any crap from anyone. Not a bad-looking woman either. Slender, standing not more than five feet. But God almighty tough. Good Lord!

Nora stepped through the door, looking like the ray of sunshine she was. The way the light caught on her hair put him in mind of an angel.

"I'm back," she announced. "Is he giving you trouble, Doctor?"

"No, I'm not giving her trouble." Jack's sour mood was amplified by the sugary sweetness surrounding him. "Just asking questions, as is only my right, seeing that she wants to cut me open."

"Well?" Nora bent to give him a kiss.

Her fresh fragrance calmed him, a reminder that he'd been

unable to hold her or make love in ages, and he was getting an itch he couldn't scratch.

"The jury's still out. Dammit, I want to be up and around. Before I know it, I'll have bedsores oozing pus. A man needs some fresh air, to feel the breeze on his face and blow the stink off him."

"You will soon, Mr. Grumpy."

"How's Tait?"

"He's out of here and staying at the hotel now." Dr. Mary stuck an unlit cigar stub in her mouth. Waiting like a vulture. She shifted her cigar. Still silent.

"Oh all right," Jack spewed. "If you're going to do it, get it over with."

"Wise choice." Dr. Mary turned to Nora. "Will you assist me?"

"Sure, but I don't know anything about surgery."

"I'll tell you what to hand or fetch me." Dr. Mary scurried around, assembling everything she'd need.

Jack watched with the knots in his stomach getting tighter. Why had he agreed to this? But Nora sat with him, telling him about the children. Willow had gurgled at her. Imagine that? And Sawyer had taken charge of the kitchen, either helping her or making things by himself.

"He's really diving into cooking, Jack. It's not just something he was curious about. And as you saw before, he's pretty darn good."

"If we had money, I'd open up a café."

"I know. Maybe someone will put in one soon and he can work for them."

Jack took her hand. "Darlin', when I'm healed up from this, I want to take you to meet my mother. I think you'll hit it off."

"I'm sure we will. I'd love to get acquainted. But isn't it dangerous to leave Hope's Crossing? You could run into Sheriff Baxter again."

"He won't know me with my new hair. Hell, I don't even recognize myself anymore."

Dr. Mary came in with a tray of bottles and silver instruments. "Ready?"

Jack swallowed hard and gazed into Nora's beautiful eyes. "Go easy on me, Doc. I have a lot of reasons to live."

❦

Nora stilled her trembling hand and held a cloth soaked with ether over Jack's mouth and nose, praying for a good outcome. It would be wonderful if Jack could live pain free.

She almost gagged when Dr. Mary made the incision on Jack's hip, but she held herself together by sheer will. She handed the lady doctor everything she asked for.

"I'm having trouble seeing the bullet." Dr. Mary probed inside Jack with a silver instrument. "It's been in there so long the muscle has grown around it."

The clock in the room ticked off the minutes one by one.

Tension squeezed Nora's chest and doubts crept in. What if this didn't work? Would the surgery leave Jack worse off than he'd been before?

Finally, Dr. Mary exclaimed, "Found it."

"Thank God." Nora let out the breath she'd been holding. "How's Jack doing?"

"He's still asleep. His eyes aren't fluttering at all."

"Perfect. I'll clean away the blood and sew him up now."

"You're an amazing doctor. Some would call you a healer. This town is very grateful you gave up your practice in Indian Territory and came to Texas."

"I like it here. Always wanted to live in Texas."

They finished, and in no time, Jack woke up. "Is it over?"

Nora took his hand and smiled. "All done. It's out and hopefully you should be able to walk without pain."

"Imagine that. Come here, woman." He pulled her down for a kiss.

She braced herself with a palm on his chest and found pleasure in the love winding through her.

"Now, that's the sorriest sight I've ever seen," Clay said from the doorway. "Here Ridge and I have ridden all over

Texas, dodging bullets with no sleep and little food. And here you are laying up in bed with pretty women waiting at your every beck and call."

"I think you're a sight for sore eyes." Jack pulled himself to a sitting position with Nora's help. "Maybe you'll help me get shed of here."

Tall and lean, coated with trail dust, Clay looked every bit the outlaw. He took off his hat. "Too busy."

Jack narrowed his eyes. "Doing what, for God's sake?"

"Making sure O'Brien is dead for one thing. Which he is. Not much left after the wild animals got through with him."

"Good." Nora found that immensely satisfying and probably so would his victims.

Clay propped himself against the door facing. "But this place is crawling with lawmen led by the sheriff of Saint's Roost. They're still looking high and low for you, Jack."

Ridge moved to the foot of the bed. He lifted his hat and poked a finger through a bullet hole in the side. "They chased us awhile, shooting. Came near to parting my hair."

Nora let out a cry. Baxter wasn't going to let this go. "Will they mount a raid here?"

"No. They don't have enough men. It would be suicide on their part." Clay pushed away from the door facing. "I'm going to take a long bath, kiss my wife, and play with my kids."

"Clay?" Jack called.

"Yeah."

"Dr. Mary took that bullet from my hip. You always regretted not being able to get it out. Now you don't have to anymore."

Clay's dark eyes seemed to smile. "Best news I've heard in a month of Sundays."

"I'm glad, Jack." Ridge straightened. "I need to go too. Rest up and get out of that bed soon, brother."

The door closed behind the two friends, leaving the room quiet. Nora thought about Flynn O'Brien and the ledger she still had. It wasn't of use now, with Flynn dead.

Or was it? An idea came to mind, but she wasn't ready to share it with anyone yet.

"Why so serious, darlin'?" Jack made little circles on the inside of her wrist. "The monsters are gone. You don't have to be afraid of the shadows."

"I'm just wondering what to do with the ledger now. I hate to just throw it away after the trouble I had getting it here."

A commotion outside drew Nora to the window. The dogs were barking at two men in a covered wagon pulled by oxen with bells around their necks. One arrival stood on the wagon seat. He was tall and lanky, wearing eyeglasses and a dark suit. When he turned, she noticed a white clerical collar around his neck.

Brother Paul. He came.

He was clean-shaven, whereas the other traveler had a nicely trimmed reddish-brown beard and mustache and sported a jaunty bow tie. He wasn't as tall as Brother Paul.

"What the devil is all that racket about?" Jack leaned, trying to see out.

"Stop that, Jack Bowdre. You'll tear your stitches out. It's the minister I told you about from Saint's Roost, the one I helped out that day while waiting for night to fall. He's in a covered wagon with a stranger." She pushed him back onto the pillow. "I can see you're determined to be a horrible patient."

"Let me put you in this bed and see how you like it." He brought her hand to his mouth and kissed the back. "I need to see what's happening, to see trouble coming. I might as well be locked in a prison, bedfast like this."

Nora chuckled at the longing in his voice. He sounded like Sawyer. "You're not in any prison. My stars! This is only for a few days and you'll be up and around. But if you don't behave yourself, you'll only prolong everything. If you'll lie here and be good, I'll go welcome Brother Paul and his friend."

"When you come back, bring my gun and holster."

"Why, so you can shoot them?"

"So I can defend myself if I need to. You forget I'm a wanted man."

"So are half of the men in town."

"My point exactly. Lawmen could ride in at any moment." His eyes darkened. "I'm a wanted man with a price on my head, and there is no escaping that fact."

She didn't need the reminder. She was terrified enough. "I'll bring your gun."

She hurried out and pushed through the crowd that had gathered around the covered wagon.

The eyeglass-wearing preacher stood in the wagon box, where everyone could see him. "Hello, I'm Brother Paul and I heard you had no church here. If you'll have me, I'd like to build one and preach the word of God." He turned to his partner. "This is Todd Denver. He's a schoolmaster. Perhaps you're in need of someone to teach your kids."

Ridge climbed up into the wagon box with them and shook hands, introducing himself as the mayor. "We welcome you both to Hope's Crossing. We'll help you build a church and school. The town is new, so we don't have much to commend it except a bunch of hardworking people with big hearts."

After the clapping died down, a young voice hollered, "I don't want to go to school!"

Nora swiveled to find Ely Carver with his fists on his hips.

"Tough," Rebel Avery answered. "I'm not going to let you grow up to be a heathen, young man. Do you understand?"

Ely wilted. "Yes, ma'am."

Nora's gaze went to Sawyer, leaning against one of the oxen. He stared up at the schoolmaster, a big grin on his face. "I only got to go to second grade before my ma and pa died. Can you teach me to read and sign my name?"

Todd Denver jumped down from the wagon. "I'll have you doing both in no time, son. We'll start with classes under a tree until we've got a roof over our heads."

Everyone pressed forward to welcome the two, obviously excited they would soon have a church to attend, where they could have weddings, and a school for the children. Happiness bubbled over inside Nora as well. They would be a real town now.

Nora hung back until the crowd dispersed, then went to welcome the kindly minister. "I'm glad you came, Brother Paul. I was afraid you'd changed your mind."

Brother Paul grinned. "I had a few things to wrap up first. I'm impressed with Hope's Crossing. It's a friendly place with a nice feel. Let me introduce Todd Denver."

"Welcome, Mr. Denver." She liked the young, red-haired schoolmaster's handshake. "You're a godsend—you both are. You're very much needed."

"I'm happy to be here and in on the ground floor of building a town," Denver said.

"I talked him into coming." The minister chuckled, his eyes twinkling behind his spectacles. "A week ago, I didn't know Todd. He was passing through Saint's Roost, dejected that they already had a schoolmaster. When he said he needed a new direction in his life, I asked him to come along."

"I'm glad you did."

Ridge returned to get the travelers settled, and Nora hurried to retrieve Jack's gun from the house and tell him about the interesting developments. Life seemed to be looking up.

Soon, she'd meet his mother and possibly his sisters. Maybe they'd make her part of their family. Yearning filled her heart to have a family again—even if it was borrowed.

Thirty-six

DESPITE NORA'S BEST EFFORTS TO STOP HIM, JACK THREW back the covers and got out of bed the next morning. He met her shocked glare with one of his own. "I've had all of this I want. Any more coddling and hovering and I'll turn into a worthless derelict. I'm going home. I need to hold my daughter and see Sawyer."

Anyone thinking to stop him had best get out of the way. He didn't care what anyone thought. He was going home. He'd been missing out on far too much. He needed his wife.

"Fine." She pitched him his clothes. "Go right ahead and pull out your stitches."

"I will." Glaring, he pulled on his trousers and shirt. But when he put his full weight on his leg, he gave a cry and almost went down. He gave her a sheepish glance. "Do you think maybe you can find me a cane?"

Her smile seemed to gloat. She reached around the outside of the door and held out a roughly hewn cane. "I knew you were going to try this, so I was prepared. Sawyer made it."

"He did a great job for a nine-year-old. I'll be sure to thank him." When he finished admiring it, Jack pulled himself to his feet. His first tentative steps were shaky, but he draped an arm around Nora's shoulders and they headed for home.

Sawyer spied him and broke into a sprint, a wide grin on his face. "You're getting well, Jack."

"I certainly hope so. Thank you for making this handy cane." Jack released his hold on Nora and pulled Sawyer close. He could feel the kid's wild heartbeat. He'd hadn't been the center of a child's world in a long while, and the realization brought a lump to his throat.

The boy glanced up, tears in his eyes. "I missed you."

"Missed you and Willow too." Jack swallowed and steadied his voice. "I hear you're a pretty good cook."

"Nora's teaching me lots. She doesn't even yell when I burn stuff."

Jack met Nora's gaze and winked. "Maybe that's because she's too busy yelling at me."

She gasped. "I do not, Jack Bowdre!"

Sawyer paid them no mind and went on, "We got a schoolmaster named Mr. Denver. We haven't started yet, but he's gonna teach me to read books. Shoot, by the time Willow gets big enough, I'll be reading newspapers."

"An education is important. Don't forget that when the fishing hole is calling you."

"I won't." Sawyer paused. "Jack, I'm glad you didn't die."

"Makes two of us, son."

Ely Carver came from Rebel's sod house. "Wanna play marbles, Sawyer?"

"Yeah." The boy hurried to his friend.

Nora lifted Jack's arm and put it across her shoulder. "Now, I guess you feel properly appreciated. He worries about you."

"The boy's going to get white hair before his time." Jack lowered his head and dropped a kiss on her tilted mouth.

Fresh air that didn't smell like medicine, the sunshine, and his family was all he needed to make a full recovery.

❧

That night, he crawled into his own bed with Nora snuggling at his side. Although he wasn't up to making love just yet, he ran his hands down the soft lines of her back and kissed every inch of her naked body. When he placed his lips on hers, he tasted desire on her tongue, felt yearning in each touch.

In turn, his passionate wife stroked and kneaded his body into a heated mass of desire. He was as hard as a brick and aching.

She flicked, nibbled, and kissed her way down him. In short order, he found himself aroused—too aroused. Afraid-to-breathe aroused. The tiniest motion of her warm breath feathering across his skin threatened to send him over the edge.

Jack hissed between his teeth. "Stop."

"Am I doing something wrong?"

"You're doing everything—" He fought to steady his breath. "Doing it too right. I won't last more than two seconds the way we're going."

"I see. I don't want to spoil anything." Nora scooted herself up.

He ran a finger down her throat to the swell of her breast. "Thank you for having patience, darlin'. I know you get frustrated with me, but I hope you never quit loving me."

"Slim chance, cowboy." She raised up and pulled his mouth to hers.

Heat swirled inside him and settled in his core. He used his hands to pleasure her and soon brought her close to rapture.

"*Jack*! More!" She arched her back and flung herself against his hand.

Judging by the strength of her clenching muscles and thundering heartbeat a few seconds later, her climax was immensely satisfying.

She panted, stiffening, clutching him tight.

"That's it. Ride it out all the way." Jack held her to him and let the shudders carry him with her.

Nora gradually relaxed as her last quiver died away.

"Jack." She lay back, gasping. "You haven't lost your touch, sweetheart."

He caressed the curve of her cheek and jaw. "Good to know." It wasn't like he was going to forget how to make her breath hitch, how to cry out in the clutches of passion.

After her breathing slowed, she positioned herself between his legs and, though unsure of herself and her movements at first, Jack helped her.

As randy as he was, it didn't take long under Nora's willing hand until he found paradise, and that shook him to his core.

They lay in each other's arms until dawn. Jack gave thanks for all he'd found. It had taken a long while, but his life was worth living again.

Nora surprised the hell out of him. There was nothing

much she wouldn't try, and she adapted to each situation like a trooper. He thought of Darcy Howard, and how different his life would've been if she hadn't gone to the nunnery. His fervent hope was that she'd found peace and was healing.

Jack kissed Nora, holding her close. She was his lifeblood. His every breath.

⌘

Nora saw Tait Trinity almost every day, sitting in front of the hotel in the sun. He'd turned out to be quite a handsome man once he'd cleaned up and shaved. His question about the railroad up at Dodge continued to puzzle her, but Jack had told her it was best to drop it. She agreed. It would break her heart to see the man arrested or go to jail like Travis.

Although Jack never said much about his relationship with Trinity, the men sat visiting often. She knew they'd been close and that Trinity had meant a great deal to him.

Maybe he'd open up soon and tell her some more about the man he worried over. Although there were things Jack wouldn't speak of and times when his face darkened. She was already aware of the men he'd killed who haunted him, and she also knew when to keep silent. This was Jack's penance to work through.

Although he continued to improve, he'd stumbled over the cane twice and fallen, and he kept laying it down and losing it, which meant stopping everything and searching until they found it again. Nora watched, knowing his breaking point was coming. And soon.

The moment arrived the next Sunday. He and Sawyer had put the finishing touches on a chicken coop and Sawyer had run off to play with Ely. Jack picked up his cane and hobbled toward the stage that had just rolled in.

"Slow down, Jack. You're not supposed to run a race on that cane." She shifted the baby and readied to try to catch him if he fell again.

"I *am* going slow."

Instead of pointing out the obvious, she clamped her mouth shut and saved her breath.

His foot caught the cane and he went down to one knee. Immense pain colored his face white, and he muttered cusswords that singed her hair.

"Are you all right?"

"Fine." He stood with considerable effort and glared at the offending piece of wood.

His eyes locked firmly on hers, he picked the cane up, placed it over his knee, and snapped it in half.

Nora gasped. "Jack Bowdre! I can't believe you did that."

"I'm done." He threw the two pieces aside and limped toward the stage, where a passenger was alighting.

She hurried to catch up, and they went to meet the woman stepping down from the coach.

"Mother, how nice to see you." Jack kissed her cheek.

His mother? Shock ran through Nora.

"I never would've known you with that blond hair." The woman laughed. "I sense a story."

Silver streaked the attractive woman's brown hair, at least the tresses not pinned up under her pretty hat. Doing some quick math, Nora put her in her early fifties. She instantly loved the twinkle in Mrs. Bowdre's blue eyes and the way her slender fingers lay easily on her son's arm.

Jack drew Nora close, introducing them. "I'm glad you came. I wanted you to meet my wife and family. Nora and I had talked about going to visit, only I've been laid up."

"I figured something like that." Maggie Bowdre slipped her arm through Nora's. "I want you to tell me what my son won't. He always says he's fine."

Nora laughed. "Yes, he does."

"Gang up on me, will you?" Jack huffed.

∽

Supper that night was a happy affair. Jack loved having his mother there, and she seemed to dote on the kids. He didn't think he'd ever seen her more at peace and wondered what had put that new glow on her face.

Maybe one of his sisters was in the family way again.

Maggie reached for a slice of homemade bread. "Sawyer, you remind me so much of my Jack when he was a boy. I think your hair is darker, but you have the same way of looking at a person as if you're trying to figure out what makes them tick."

"Yes, ma'am. But mainly I'm trying not to mess up." Sawyer stared at his plate. "I like it here and I don't wanna leave."

"My dear boy, I don't think that will ever happen. Tell me about school."

"We just got a schoolmaster and he's going to teach me to read. We ain't started yet though."

"Haven't started yet," Nora gently corrected.

Jack passed the beans and potatoes. "Sawyer helps Clay milk the goats every morning, and he loves to cook. Mother, maybe you can show him how to make your chicken and dumplings."

"I'd be delighted to."

A cry came from upstairs.

"Please let me get her." Maggie pushed back her chair. "I'll only be here for a few days."

Nora smiled and curled her fingers around Jack's. "I love your mother. Thank you for saving her. She seems really happy now."

"More than I've ever seen her," Jack admitted. But he knew her, and there was something she wasn't telling him.

After the women cleaned the kitchen, they sat in the parlor with the children.

"Mother, what's going on?"

Maggie sat rocking Willow. She stopped the chair's motion. "I'm free. A Texas Ranger brought word a few days ago that your father met his end in a shoot-out."

Anger washed over Jack. "I hope he suffered. He was a bastard if I ever knew one."

"I know, son. He made our lives a living hell, and I've had to live every day with guilt that I couldn't protect you and your sisters."

Nora patted her knee and said softly, "We've all had our share of situations we couldn't control. Don't let it eat at you."

"I know." His mother gave her a sad smile. "It's better than it was."

Jack rose and stood looking out the window. "You did the best you could. None of us fault you for it."

Nine-year-old Sawyer lay on the rug at Maggie's feet, petting Scout. "Bittercreek forced me to become an outlaw. I'm glad he's dead. I'm glad Jack killed him."

"Oh, honey, I'm so sorry."

"It's okay. I have a home here now with Jack and Nora and I'm gonna be a cook, and as soon as I learn to read and write, I'm gonna be smart."

"Yes, you will. Keep those dreams, honey."

Before long, the dark mood lifted, and they were entertaining Jack's mother with the story about dying his hair. It was great to see her laugh and forget all those times when her tears could've floated a child's boat.

He just wished he could dig up Orin Bowdre and kill him all over again.

That night in bed, Nora told him of her plan for Flynn O'Brien's ledger. "I want to force a judge into dropping the charges against you. I think it can happen."

"Darlin', I've tried for amnesty and it didn't work. I don't know if I have it in me to try again." He let out a long sigh and kissed her.

The bed creaked when Nora moved closer. "If you think I'm going to let you give up, you don't know me well. We'll try as many times as it takes. I have a feeling this ledger will be worth a lot to the right person."

Ever the optimist, but that's why Jack loved her.

Maybe this time *would* be different. A tendril of something resembling hope unfurled deep in a small corner of his heart.

Thirty-seven

A WEEK LATER FOUND NORA AND JACK IN THE TOWN OF LOST Point in Sam Legend's office. Apart from their height, Nora didn't see a lot of physical resemblance between him and his brother Luke. Sam had brown hair to Luke's black. But Nora loved the warmth in his eyes and ready smile and knew she could trust this lawman.

Sam shook their hands. "I don't exactly know why you're here, but it's good to meet you. Luke speaks highly of you both."

A white scar around his throat drew her gaze. Jack had told her that a mean bunch of rustlers had tried to hang Sam during his tenure as a Texas Ranger and, but for Luke's arrival, had nearly succeeded. She didn't know what being hanged would feel like but suspected it caused a great deal of pain. Sam was the right man for the job.

Nora removed the ledger that had almost cost her and Jack their lives. "I want to bargain. This belonged to a very bad man and in it he recorded every murder he committed, every bit of money he collected, and every name of the men he was in cahoots with. Some are governors, mayors, rich businessmen."

"May I see it?" Sam asked and took it when she handed it over.

Silence filled the sheriff's office while he glanced through it. Jack squeezed her hand and gave her a smile. Yet beneath his calm exterior, fear lurked. He'd suffered extreme disappointment in obtaining his freedom thus far and was afraid to even hope.

She leaned to brush her lips across his. "Relax."

Nora recognized that this might well be a fool's errand. But she would try.

Finally, Sam looked up. "What do you want?"

"A clean slate," Jack answered firmly. "All my crimes erased."

"When that happens, I'll turn the ledger over to you," Nora added. "Not one second before."

"This is gold. I think I can arrange that." Sam handed the ledger back. "Put that in a safe place. I'll notify the governor right away, then I'll telegraph his answer the moment I receive it."

"Thank you, oh thank you." Nora flung her arms around Sam's neck. "You don't know what this means to us."

"I think I do."

Nora's face burned to have been so forward with him. "I'm sorry for attacking you."

"No apology needed. Stay with Sierra and me. She'll be hurt if you don't. I want to hear all about Hope's Crossing. I've been eaten up with envy every time Luke and Houston talk about it. Clay Colby and I go back a long way. How's he doing?"

For the next two hours, they talked of home and the people they loved. Nora kept stealing glances at Jack, trying to imagine what a difference his freedom would make. She'd do anything to give him a future free of bleached hair, dark shadows, and a heap of worry.

∽

A month later, Sam Legend rode into town and dismounted at Nora and Jack's. She took one look at the grin and knew before he even spoke. Excitement washed over her.

"Jack's crimes have been expunged—that is, if you still have the ledger."

"Come in and I'll get it. Jack's in the parlor."

Jack stood when they entered. "Sam, how nice to see you."

Nora put an arm around him and met his gray eyes. "You're free, Jack."

He blinked hard and cleared his throat. "Are you sure? This isn't a joke?"

Sam clapped him on the back. "No joke. The governor wiped your record clean and thanks you and Nora for helping clean up a criminal ring in New York. The lawmen there have been trying to get them for years."

Tears sprang into Nora's eyes. Everything that she'd suffered hadn't been in vain. Flynn O'Brien was dead, and Jack was a free man. There was justice in the world after all.

As night began to cast shadows and the breeze cooled, Nora threw her shawl on and invited Sam to come with them. With Jack holding Willow, they went to join the others at the community fire. A good many of the town sat around, talking about their days.

Nora loved these times when a warmth drifted around her shoulders and she knew she belonged here.

It didn't matter about a person's past. Here, their futures blended and pieced together like an old colorful quilt.

She and Rebel had gotten close. Good thing, because the woman needed someone to help prop her up occasionally. She still pined for Travis but didn't dwell too much on the fact that he was gone. They'd received word that the judge had sentenced him to five years in prison.

That seemed an eternity when you loved someone, but it was better than being hanged.

Tally brought Violet and the new baby out to join the others. She gave Nora a bright smile. "You've worked wonders with Rebel. She needs all the friends she can get."

"I like her. She's just trying to find her way like the rest of us. It's hard for her, though, with those children and Travis not here to help. That's when friends really count."

Tally leaned back with a wide smile. "I'm so glad you came here. I would've missed never knowing you."

"And I you."

"Did Jack lighten his hair again?"

"This morning, but he won't have to ever do it after this. He's not wanted anymore."

"Nora, how wonderful!"

"I know. We're celebrating tonight." Nora gave her a hug and kissed baby Dillon, then went to stand with Jack near the fire.

He slid an arm around her. "You've made a difference here, Nora, and I love you for caring about these people."

"Why does that surprise you? How could I not?"

"Some wouldn't. Some would see criminals, killers. Not men wanting to straighten out." He gazed at the new buildings and the increased number of men and woman at the fire. "You should've seen this place before we started making it a town. It was god-awful dreary, the men's eyes dull and hopeless."

She could imagine. "You were all at the end of your roads. Change had to happen."

"Clay saw what Devil's Crossing could be, and he got us thinking that we didn't have to live like we were." Jack chuckled. "We'd follow that man anywhere."

"Everyone needs a good leader." Nora smiled up at him. Jack didn't know that he was every bit the leader Clay was, but one day she'd tell him.

There was nothing like the smell of new lumber to signal progress. The frame of the new church and school sat in a prominent place next to the windmill. It wouldn't take long to finish the buildings and Sawyer couldn't wait. He was like a sponge, soaking up everything that had been denied him.

A new couple—the Trumans—had arrived with their ten kids—all boys—so Sawyer had plenty of playmates.

Jack's hold on Nora's waist tightened. After she completed her ceremony, they'd go back to their house and make love. Her pulse raced. She would never tire of loving Jack Bowdre, no matter what color hair he had or how many canes he broke. Or how stubborn he got at times.

He put his mouth next to her ear and tingles swept over her. "Are you ready?"

"Yes, I am."

Jack whistled sharply to get everyone's attention. "If we can have a moment, my wife and I have something to say."

"Evening, all." Nora flashed a smile around the group. "We have something to celebrate and I want to do it with you. The ledger that came near to costing me and Jack our lives has bought and paid for Jack's freedom. In it, I recorded every crime Flynn O'Brien committed. The names of the dead are in here and I hope, with Jack's help, that I bought them some justice. Most were simple folk like you, just wanting to make an honest living. That's all any of us want. Just to have families and raise kids. O'Brien tortured and killed with a zest I've not seen in anyone else. I lived as a prisoner in his house over ten years and feared for my life every single day."

She took a breath. "But that's not the only thing I'm celebrating. It's you and the sacrifice, the pain you've had to bear. We are strong and we are mighty! Let's embrace our power! Let's take back what was stolen."

After the cheering stopped, Jack stepped forward. "I'm glad I can celebrate this here with you. It's been a long time coming and there were days when I thought I was foolish for hoping. But my wife, the most positive person I've ever known, changed all that and she changed me. She never let me stop dreaming." He put his arm around her, and she melted against his warmth. "Once I wished for a wife with rough edges that I could control, that I could shape as I wanted."

A voice yelled, "Shame on you, Jack Bowdre!"

He chuckled. "I am truly ashamed. I like Nora's rough edges just the way they are, and I wouldn't change one thing about her. I'll stand by her side through every storm, every happy day, and most importantly, through every dark night. Men, if you're single, keep looking."

A loud whistle sounded amid the clapping. Nora beamed at Sam Legend, watching it all in amazement.

He moved closer. "Now I know why Luke and Houston love this place. I want to help more men like Jack."

Brother Paul moved beside her and spoke to the gathering. "From what I hear, this is one brave woman. She had guts to stand up against a killer. You're all brave people and I'm privileged to be in your midst. Lumber to finish our church will soon arrive, and I look forward to putting my shoulder to the wheel beside you. Together, we can accomplish everything we want."

Ridge rose and raised a hand. "We've barely begun with this town. We have a lot more work ahead in order to make it safe for all of you, and it's going to take every hand. We have a lot to be proud of."

"I'd like to say something." The mysterious Abel Fargo removed his hat and held it to his chest. "I came here looking for freedom from persecution. My name used to be Gabe Vargas and I changed it to hide my nationality. You see, my wife and children were dragged from their beds and murdered in the street. I was afraid to let anyone get close, and I hate that it cast suspicion on me. I have nothing to fear here, and for that, I thank you."

A chorus of "Welcome, Abel!" went up.

Nora stood with Jack, her heart near to bursting.

This was her town.

Her people.

Her life.

Jack's lips were moving but no sound came out. She poked him. "I swear, Jack! Are you counting again?"

"Yep." A sinful grin revealed white teeth in his tanned face. "Just tallying up all the ways I love you."

He lowered his head and pressed his warm, sensual mouth to hers. The kiss sent sizzling sparks through her and she had to clutch his leather vest to hold herself steady. This husband of hers sure knew how to stake a claim.

A tortured bounty hunter must protect a gentle
Englishwoman in an epic new love story from
USA Today bestselling author Rosanne Bittner.

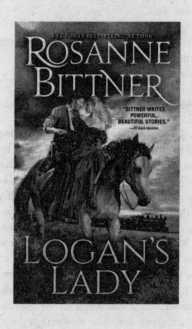

ONE

London, England, April, 1870

"You have disgraced the family name beyond recovery!"

William Baylor looked away from his brother's dark, accusing stare, never sure how to deal with the man's fits of judgmental rage. He licked at his cut, swollen lower lip as he struggled for the right words to explain himself.

"This is the end of your foolishness," Lord Jonathan Baylor roared. He towered over William with a face as red as an overheated stove plate. William couldn't think straight.

He'd lived his whole life under his brother's stern rule and intimidating temper. Now the man leaned over him with fists clenched. "I…I cared about her," William finally answered.

"*Cared* about her? I asked one of my friends to go to that theater and ask about her. The woman's reputation with men is even worse than her profession! An *actress*! I'm not sure which is worse."

"She's just a woman, young and pretty and alone."

"She's a *slut*! No man who cares about his family and his reputation hangs out with actresses, let alone one who is talked about in smoking parlors. What am I going to tell my business acquaintances? It's bad enough you failed in your education—"

"I *told* you! I can't see letters in the right order!"

"Some people think you're slow in the head. And please, get up and face me like a *man*."

William slowly rose, glancing at the doorway to the parlor. His dear sister and best friend, Elizabeth, stood watching with tears in her eyes. "Jonathan, you know William has a soft heart for those less fortunate than we are," she tried to argue.

"I don't want to hear it," Jonathan snapped in reply, his gaze still on William.

Jonathan's wife, Caroline, also witnessed the argument, but her eyes showed the same cold disappointment as Jonathan's. Her husband suddenly whipped around to glare at Elizabeth.

"I am tired of you constantly defending your brother," he told her. "He needs to grow up and be a man."

"He *is* a man," Elizabeth answered boldly. "A kindhearted man who is brave enough to go into the poorer neighborhoods and—"

"And disgrace this family!" Jonathan interrupted. His eyes grew even darker. "Stay out of this, Elizabeth. With our parents dead, it's been my job to look out for *both* of you for six years. *I* will decide what is best for you and this family." He turned back to William. "I managed to get you a fake diploma to prove you have normal intelligence, William, and I've supported you since you finished school because your job at the family accounting business is a *farce*. We both know it. I've done all I can to save the family name and your reputation, even after that mess last year when you got drunk at your sister's cotillion and fell into the food table. But this..." Jonathan threw his hands into the air. "This is about as bad as it gets!" He glanced at his wife. "I'm sorry about this, Caroline. I can't begin to advise what you should tell your society friends. And here you have an embroidery tea tomorrow afternoon. By then, this story will be in all the newspapers."

Caroline heaved a deep sigh, glaring at William. "You have left me in a disgraceful position, William, having to defend you getting arrested for beating a man nearly to death, and over an actress and a *harlot*—"

"He was *hurting* her," William argued. "And she's not what

you say. She's a sweet young woman who was left on her own at ten years old and—"

"Stop!" Jonathan demanded. "The fact remains that you were caught in the dressing room of a disreputable actress and in a fistfight with a drunken, low-class chimney cleaner who'd probably been sleeping with her. Have *you* slept with her, too? For God's sake, you probably already have a venereal disease."

Elizabeth again interjected. "Jonathan, he was just defending her."

Jonathan glared at her, the scolding look in his dark eyes as fierce as a slap. "Need I remind you that you are only nineteen years old and know nothing of that seedy side of life? Your brother has shamed and embarrassed the Baylor name since he was old enough to go out in public. It's time he stood on his own and learned true responsibility. I am kicking him out of this house."

Elizabeth's eyes widened in disbelief. "You wouldn't!"

"*Wouldn't* I?" Jonathan stepped closer to Elizabeth, flaunting not just his size but the power and influence that came with it. "I've had all I can take, Elizabeth. You should be upset, too, after what happened last year. I cannot go on like this. The man, if he can call himself that, has to leave this estate and this family and learn to survive on his own."

Elizabeth's eyes teared. "He's your *brother*," she reminded him. "His only problem is that he has a big heart, and that *you* have *no* heart."

"And you have no right talking to me this way after all I've done for *both* of you," Jonathan answered. "Your brother's big heart, as you put it, doesn't excuse the fact that he disgraced the family name yet again by hanging around disreputable people. I have babied him long enough. He's done too much damage this time." He stepped closer and grasped Elizabeth's arms. "And I might remind you that you are beautiful and have your own reputation to think about. You are a woman of honor and intelligence and talent, and as long as William is part of this estate and continues to bring shame to our name, the harder it will be for you to find a decent man to marry.

Until you *do* marry, I will always care for you, but the best way to ensure a proposal comes sooner than later is to send William away."

Elizabeth jerked her arms from her brother's grip and faced the man squarely. "If William goes, *I* go!"

"Don't be ridiculous!" Jonathan shook his head and sneered. "You'd never survive away from the shelter of this estate."

"I am old enough to do anything I want. And I can claim my share of the money that is rightfully mine, and so can William. And mother left her jewels to me. All of that should be enough to survive just fine, out from under your rule and away from this depressing, boring life."

William spoke up. "Elizabeth, it's okay. I'll be fine."

"It's a matter of what is right and what is wrong," Elizabeth answered, still holding Jonathan's gaze, determination in her eyes.

"Don't be a fool," Jonathan told her. "I'll *never* allow you to leave this estate."

"I am free to leave any time I want."

"And your air of independence has always been as much of a burden to me as your brother's *stupidity*. You are Lady Elizabeth Baylor. A woman of your station should leave home only because she has a husband, and I might remind you that Lord Henry Mason is very interested in marrying you."

"And I'm *not* interested in that old lecher!"

"You are close to becoming an old maid, Elizabeth. Women whisper, and men wonder. I have had requests from others besides Lord Henry, men younger than he. I held that cotillion last year so you could meet other men. Why on earth are you not interested in such things? It's natural for a woman to want—"

"*I'll* choose whom I marry, and I will have to *love* him. I'm sure that is something a man like you would never understand, Jonathan. I'll not marry just for a man's title and money. Thanks to Father's connection to the monarchy and the approval of the Queen, you don't own me. And you are obligated to give me my share of this estate whenever I ask for it. I will not have what is mine used as a dowry for some old man who is already wealthy. I'll choose my *own* path."

Jonathan pressed his lips together in disgust. "You have no idea what it would be like out there on your own. I'll not allow it! You are my *sister!*"

"And William is your *brother!* You should be just as concerned about *him.* And don't talk about not giving him his fair share. If you insist he leaves, you are obligated to give him money to survive."

Jonathan stiffened. "How and when did you become so independently minded? That, too, is a disgrace! Women are not meant to make demands of those who keep them."

"*Keep* them? I'm not a zoo animal, Jonathan."

"Nor are you getting any younger. Think about what you are saying. Men swoon over you. And if you married Lord Henry, you would live like a queen, what with his money and your own. I have suffered enough disgrace because of William. How would I explain allowing my beautiful young sister to go off on her own when she knows nothing of the world outside this estate?"

"I'd have my brother for an escort. There is no shame in that."

Jonathan closed his eyes. "You're a *fool.* William can't care for you like I can, and you know it. To leave this estate would be to throw your life away."

"Staying here and marrying a man I don't love would be throwing my life away."

A new coldness moved into Jonathan's eyes. "You'll never have the courage."

Elizabeth put her hands on her hips and raised her chin. "*Watch* me."

William couldn't help a small grin. Elizabeth had a brave way of handling Jonathan that he himself had never possessed. More than once she had actually backed the man down.

Jonathan drew a deep breath, as though someone had socked him. He took hold of Caroline's arm and pulled her with him as he suddenly swept past Elizabeth with an arrogant air. "William, you have two weeks to decide what you will do and where you will go," Jonathan called as he walked out of the room. "And if you take your sister with you, what happens will be on *your* head, not mine. You think about that!"

Elizabeth watched him leave, then turned to William, arms folded. "There," she announced. "I've done it. William, we are leaving the Baylor estate. It's time to live our lives the way we choose."

William wiped at unexpected tears in his blue eyes. His thick, light-brown hair hung over one eye, and he quickly swept it off his forehead, revealing another bruise. "I'm sorry about all this, Liz. I'll be fine. You don't need to leave with me. Really. Jonathan's right about it being dangerous for you."

Elizabeth walked closer. "It's been six years since our parents died, but I remember Mother always seemed to understand your good heart. She had one, too, and she also was an independent woman. I remember her having a gentle way of bossing Father around." She smiled, and William broke down, covering his eyes as he wept.

"I miss them so much, Liz. I still feel them with us. If they hadn't decided to take that trip to France—"

"No one thought such a violent storm would hit the Channel in the middle of a lovely, calm summer." Elizabeth put her arms around him. "The fact remains we were left in Jonathan's charge, and I hate it as much as you do. I think he always resented the responsibility. He probably hopes both of us *do* leave. He was always the mean-spirited, spoiled firstborn, and since he inherited the estate, we have both felt like prisoners."

William sniffed and pulled away as he wiped at his eyes. "I don't mind leaving, Liz, but you shouldn't go with me."

Elizabeth shook her head. "You always say I'm the strong one, William. And I *hate* the fact that my future is mapped out for me as long as I stay here. I *am* strong, and I've already been thinking about leaving, *alone*, if I have to. Now we both have an excuse for going, and you can be my escort, so I won't shame Jonathan." She took a deep breath, summoning her determination and warding off any doubts. "And you and I aren't just brother and sister. We're good friends. We understand and trust each other. We've grown so close since Mother and Father died, and we both want to get out from under Jonathan. This is our chance."

William shook his head. "Where on earth would we go? By tomorrow, everyone in London will know about me. I'll be a disgrace, and you'll be looked down upon for leaving with me. I don't want that for you." He watched Elizabeth's brilliant blue eyes light up with excitement. A beautiful young woman with an alabaster complexion and thick, golden hair, she would catch any man's eye. "It makes me nervous to think of being responsible for you, Elizabeth. And people in London—"

"We won't stay in London. We'll go to *America*!"

William's eyes widened in surprise. "*America!* Are you crazy? I thought all your talk about gold and cattle and mountains and outlaws was just from those penny dreadfuls you read. Those are just silly, made-up stories, Elizabeth. I'm sure they make America sound more romantic and adventurous than it really is."

"They're called dime novels in America, and they're wonderful," Elizabeth answered, grasping her brother's hands. "Just think of it, William. With an ocean between us and Jonathan, we'd be completely out from under his control, and we'd have a lot of money. We could make investments in gold mines and maybe buy lots of land and—"

"Elizabeth, that's foolish."

"*Is* it? We'd be free to go where we please and make our own decisions. We will have enough money to go anyplace we want and live well. We can pay the best guides to take us to the gold mines in Denver once we reach America. I've been studying about all of it longer than you know. And I've been wanting to get away from here since our parents died and Jonathan took over." She squeezed William's hands. "If I stay in London, even living separately from Jonathan, I fear that somehow he will be able to force me into marrying some boorish man I don't love, and into a life of nothing but teas and cotillions and embroidery clubs and constant gossip. I have a need for adventure and independence, William, and everything I read about America tells me that a woman can have independence there that she could never have here. I'm nineteen and you're twenty-two. We have our whole lives ahead of us. Why not go to America and see what's there for us? If we don't like it, we'll come back to Europe, maybe France." She let go of his hands and smiled excitedly. "Once we're away from here, our futures are in our own hands. *Think* of it, William."

William smiled. "It does sound exciting."

"You can be your own man there. And you *are* a man, William. Don't listen to Jonathan when he insults you the way he does. This is our chance to be free from him."

William sighed deeply. "Are you sure?"

"Of course I am! We just need to buy passage on a ship to America, but first we'll need to set an appointment with the family solicitor to claim our inheritance."

William breathed deeply with a mixture of excitement and doubt. "You're so brave, Liz."

"I just want out from under Jonathan's thumb." Elizabeth leaned in and kissed her brother's cheek. "I'm going to my room to make plans and think about what I should pack. Tomorrow morning, I want you to take care of the solicitor and get some schedules for passage to America." She took his hands again. "Promise me, William. Don't change your mind."

"I won't. I promise."

Elizabeth squeezed his hands again before hurrying off to run up the grand staircase to her room. William watched her go, his heart heavy with the knowledge that his name would be notorious by morning. He wanted to be strong for Elizabeth. He couldn't let her know he was scared to death to leave and go to America, but then he'd face just about anything to get out from under his brother's constant badgering and insults. Jonathan was right in saying he needed to stand up for himself, and he had to admit that going to a place like

America sounded exciting. He'd read about the place, too, and he supposed there couldn't be a better chance at making a good investment than in a place that was growing like wildfire, where a man could do anything he wanted.

He sighed and sat down on the fainting couch, putting his head in his hands. "God, help me," he whispered.

Two

THUMP!

Sheriff Jack Teller awoke with a start when cold air rushed over him from an open door and something heavy hit the floor of his office. His first reaction was to reach for his gun.

"Leave it!" a deep voice told him. "It's just me." The intruder slammed the door shut. "Jesus, Teller, somebody could have come in here and helped a prisoner escape and you would have slept right through it."

Teller looked up at the tall man with long, sandy-colored hair that stuck out from under a wide-brimmed hat. His sheepskin jacket made his six-foot frame and broad shoulders appear even larger. And he was in bad need of a shave. It took a minute for Teller to realize who it was. "*Logan?*"

"I brought Sol Weber to you."

Teller turned to look beyond the end of his desk to see a man lying on the floor, still wearing a wool jacket, his frozen eyes staring up at the ceiling. An ugly hole in his forehead made Teller shake his head as he looked at Logan Best. "Is it possible that someday you'll bring one of these men back *alive*?"

Logan shrugged. "If the poster says dead or alive, I might as well keep things safe and kill him. Then I don't have to worry about feeding him and staying awake half the night watching him so he doesn't try to put a bullet in me and escape." He glanced at the dead body of Sol Weber. "Besides, when he robbed that bank in Sheridan, he killed two kids as he was trying to get away. He doesn't *deserve* to live."

"Says a judge and jury, in most cases," Sheriff Teller answered. He hoisted his too-heavy body out of his chair with a grunt. "Need I remind you yet again that your only job is to get wanted men back here? Let the right people decide if they should live or die."

Logan took a thin cigar from his pocket, then struck a match and lit it. "Why bother, with a man like that?"

Teller snickered, his belly jiggling when he did so. "You have the strangest set of values I've ever known in a man." He ran a hand through his thin, graying hair. "You kill a man at the drop of a hat with absolutely no regrets, but you worry about the right and wrong of what he did and get upset because a couple of kids died. Obviously, most men agree that's a terrible thing, but most men don't turn around and put a bullet in a man's forehead with no feelings at all."

Logan puffed on the cigar for a moment. "The weather helped. This sudden spring snowstorm froze his body pretty quick, so I didn't have to worry about burying him because of the smell. Besides, burying the men I go after isn't in a bounty hunter's job description."

"I didn't know there was such a thing as a job description for men like you," Teller grumbled.

Logan sniffed and ran his coat sleeve across his nose. "When do I get my money?"

Teller rubbed at tired eyes. "I'll wire the authorities in Cheyenne. It usually takes a few days, so stick around. In the meantime, get that damn dead body out of here. Frozen or not, it will stink damn quick." He studied Logan's sorry condition. "Or is that *you* I smell?"

Logan grinned. "Both, I reckon. I'm fixing to head over to Martha's place and let one of her girls give me a bath. I'm in need of a woman, or more than one. Maybe I can get two or three of them to scrub me down, all at the same time."

Teller walked around the desk and took his hat from a hook near the door. "I expect you won't have a problem there. The ladies at Martha's love you. I don't doubt you're well known at every whorehouse in Wyoming, and probably in Colorado and Kansas, too."

"A man's gotta do what a man's gotta do."

Teller put on his hat and looked up at the much taller Logan Best. "I've always wondered where you come from, Logan. What led you to do what you do?"

Logan kept the cigar between his teeth. "Lotta things. I come from everywhere and nowhere, and there isn't a person alive who gives a shit about me. Not since—" He hesitated, deciding not to finish the sentence.

Teller took down a wool jacket and pulled it on. "Since what?"

Logan frowned. "Never mind."

"You ever think about marrying and settling?" Teller asked.

"None of your business."

"Suit yourself, Logan, but some day you'll get tired of this life and want to settle. I don't doubt there are any number of women who would gladly oblige you."

"I'm not losing any sleep over it. I'm still trying to get over the fact that this territory allows women to vote."

Teller grinned. "Gotta agree with you on that one. In the meantime, I need you to drag that body out of here and have someone carry him to the undertaker. He'll dress him out and put the bastard on display for the newspaper. I'm going to the telegraph office to see about collecting your money."

The sheriff turned and opened the door for him. Logan kept the cigar between his teeth and reached down, taking hold of Sol Weber's ankles and dragging the man's stiff body out the door.

Teller left, and Logan closed the jail door, leaving Weber on the boardwalk. He nodded at two women walking past the jail. Both gasped at the sight of the dead body lying there with a hole in its forehead.

"Dear God!" one of them exclaimed. She looked up at

Logan Best. "*You* again! You're a merciless killer, Logan Best! You're no better than the men you murder in the name of justice and only for money."

Logan nodded to her, taking the cigar from his mouth. "Believe what you want, ma'am. That man killed two little kids in a shoot-out after robbing a bank in Sheridan. Could have been one of your own."

The woman sniffed. "The man still deserved a trial."

"Maybe so, but he would have been hanged. I just saved the Territory a lot of money by taking care of things myself."

The woman shook her head in disgust and pulled her long, black wool coat tighter around her neck before stepping over Sol Weber and walking past Logan. Her friend stared at Logan a moment longer, then turned and followed.

Logan watched after them with a sigh, thinking about Teller's remark that he should settle. He doubted that a woman existed who'd put up with the kind of man he'd become. He'd settled once, and it had destroyed everything good in him. Whores pleased a man in all the ways he needed pleasing, and he didn't need to love a whore, so there was no danger of hurting anyone's feelings.

He turned to leave, and three men approached him with scowls on their faces. "Another dead one, huh, Logan?" one of them commented.

"Yup."

"Sheriff Teller told us to come and take him to the undertaker," the second man said.

"Be my guest," Logan answered. He shivered into his jacket and headed for Martha's Female Boutique for a hot bath and the best whiskey in town.

THREE

"I AM HAVING TROUBLE AGREEING TO THIS." IAN TYLER frowned at Elizabeth and William Baylor. "I have been the solicitor for your family for many years, long before your parents died."

"The Writ of Title to the estate includes me," Elizabeth told him. "That means I have a right to my share whenever I want it, whether you like it or not. I am over eighteen. Neither you nor Jonathan can keep me from what is mine, nor William from his."

Tyler leaned back in his large, leather chair. A streak of sunlight highlighted the many wrinkles in his very white skin. Elizabeth thought him so pale that he could easily be mistaken for a ghost. His shoulder-length white hair was thin and spindly, his pink scalp the only color on him. Even his eyes, which showed only a bit of blue, were pale.

"Lady Elizabeth, it would be one thing if you were marrying, or if you wanted to start your own separate account but remain living with Lord Baylor," the old man told her. "But to take this kind of money to a place like America is outrageously dangerous and foolish." He glanced at William. "And you, William, are nothing but a troublemaker, with no common sense whatsoever. Men belonging to a family like yours don't hang around on the wrong side of the tracks with lower-class people who have no standing among the elite of London."

"I refuse to look down on them. Some of them are good people who need help."

"They would rob you of every last shilling you own if they could!" Tyler, obviously angry, straightened in his chair. He turned his attention to Elizabeth. "It goes against every grain of good judgment in me to allow this."

Elizabeth caught the way the old solicitor looked her over. She'd often seen the same disturbingly hungry look in Lord Henry Mason's eyes when he talked of marrying her. She kept her hands folded properly on her lap. She'd worn a handsome silver-and-burgundy-striped day dress, with ruffled pagoda sleeves trimmed in burgundy lace, and a crinoline skirt with six rows of ruffles at the hem that matched the ruffles of the sleeves. Her tall, crowned hat in burgundy velvet sported one white feather, the color, she thought, looking splendid against her light hair. Her white gloves were decorated at the wrist with tiny burgundy buttons. She wanted to look mature and womanly, older than her real age. She kept an authoritative look on her face as she raised her chin, determined to have her way.

"And I could take you to court over this if you refuse to give me what is mine," she reminded the man. "That would make all the newspapers, and Jonathan hates publicity. I have the necessary paperwork to prove my inheritance, and I want it. *Now!* William and I have already booked tickets on a ship to New York City."

"And then what?" Tyler asked with a hint of sarcasm.

"Then we will take a train to a town called St. Louis, where we will take one of those wonderful paddle steamboats on the Missouri River to Kansas and then a train to Denver, where there are gold mines in the Rocky Mountains and any number of other possible investments. Do not forget, sir, that I am well schooled. Not all women care about nothing but embroidery and proper dress and marriage. Some of us have loftier ideas, and under Jonathan's heel I will never be able to enjoy the kind of freedom I dream of. With the money we have coming, William and I can build our own home in Denver. We will have maids and cooks and all the other things we enjoy here. And they say that in western America everything is clean and beautiful, not like the smog and filth we have here in London."

Tyler glanced at William. "Is this what *you* want? You are not nearly as ambitious as your sister, William."

William glanced at Elizabeth and smiled. "Elizabeth has always been good to me." He turned his gaze to Tyler. "I want whatever *she* wants. I will be her escort and protect her along the way. And I think that once I am out from under Jonathan's control, I'll be stronger for it."

Tyler shook his head and leaned back in his chair, glancing at Elizabeth again. "And where did you hear all these stories about America?"

Elizabeth straightened her shoulders and held her chin proudly. "I *can* read, you know. The newspapers are full of stories about America, and some of my friends' fathers and husbands have already made investments there. I would not be surprised to learn you've looked into it yourself."

Tyler nodded. "I have considered it, but I am a man of wealth and experience. You, on the other hand—" He stopped and sighed when Elizabeth glared at him for trying to embarrass her and insult her intelligence. "Tell me," Tyler continued in a change of subject, "when you say you have read a lot about America, are you referring to those penny dreadfuls? Dreadful is the right word for those things. I hope you know those stories are a bunch of lies and exaggerations."

"They are exciting and adventurous," Elizabeth answered with a sure tone to her voice, "but I know better than to believe all of it. I must say, though, that it will be exciting to find out what is true and what isn't. Either way, I have studied about America, in books far more dependable than the penny dreadfuls. America has succeeded in supporting a democracy that promotes independence and entrepreneurship. We have little of that in England. Our lives are too controlled by the Queen's rule. And America just recently completed a railroad that goes all the way from New York City on the Atlantic coast to San Francisco on the Pacific coast. William and I just might take the whole trip. Who knows? San Francisco is another city that offers opportunities for investments, especially in shipping. They trade with China and—"

Tyler put up his hand to silence her. "Enough! Have you considered the fact that America just got over a civil war? There is great unrest there now. And if you go anywhere beyond the Mississippi River, you will find life is very hard and very dangerous. There is little law of any kind in western America, or so I am told. Raiders and killers and robbers abound. Men get hanged for stealing a horse. Someone as young and beautiful as you would be in terrible danger. The only women in the West are cooks, laundresses, and whores. Is that what you want to become?"

"Of course not! I assure you, sir, that I have been secretly studying America longer and more thoroughly than you know. I have wanted to get out from under Jonathan for a long time, and to be free to do what *I* want to do. This is my chance."

"And what about Lord Henry Mason? Your brother promised you to him."

"He had no right to do so! I will not be a bride to that lecherous old man. I'd rather die."

"And die you might, if you go to America," Tyler answered. "Americans are nothing like the elite of England. They are barbaric, uneducated, far too independent, rough, and unruly. They have no proper manners. A young lady like you would be repulsed by most of them. At least let me find out if there is a proper family in New York who might be able to take you in for a while until you know what you want to do, where you want to go. You can't just land there with no plans for what you will do next."

"That is what makes it more exciting," Elizabeth answered. "We will stay at the finest hotel in New York City and find someone to help us get to Denver—a guide of some kind."

Tyler turned his attention to William again. "I can see that your sister will be more in charge of this trip than *you* will be. Be that as it may, are you sure you can properly protect her in a new land?"

"I know how to use a gun and my fists," William answered. He straightened, with a proud look in his eyes. "I would do anything to protect her, in every way possible. In fact, we have decided that while we travel we will pose as husband and wife. That will keep away men who might have wrong thoughts about Elizabeth. We have it all worked out and have even decided what to pack in our trunks."

"And you just might need to use that gun and your fists more often than you realize," Tyler said, looking William over scathingly. "If any culprit finds out how much money you two have on you and that you have expensive jewelry in your possession, there will be a target on your backs. I am telling you that America is a dangerous place."

"We will be fine," Elizabeth declared. "And speaking of money, just how much exactly will each of us receive?"

Tyler closed his eyes and sighed in resignation, reaching for a heavy ledger and pulling it over in front of him. "I already did the figuring once Jonathan told me what you two were up to." He opened a drawer and took out something that looked like a receipt book. "I will give each of you a withdrawal slip from the Bank of England. Each of you will receive ten thousand pounds. In America, that comes to roughly twenty-four thousand dollars—*each*. That is a very large amount of money, especially in America, and it is enough to invest in a gold mine or whatever you choose to do with it. I hope you understand the enormous danger of traveling with that kind of money. I suggest once you get to New York you put most of it in a bank for safe keeping, along with any jewels you take along. Please tell me you will do at least that much."

"We will speak with a banker or investor when we arrive in New York," Elizabeth answered. "We will decide then how to handle the money."

Tyler handed Elizabeth and William withdrawal slips. "Whatever bank you choose to deal with in New York will know how to convert your money to American dollars." He rose. "I still think this is a dangerous and foolish idea, but you are of age and free to choose your own life, so all I can say is, God bless and protect you both."

Elizabeth looked at William, seeing the same excitement in his eyes as she felt. "We'll be fine. Thank you for your blessings and cooperation." She put the withdrawal slips in her handbag and rose, reaching out and shaking Tyler's hand. William did the same before walking out with Elizabeth and closing the door.

As soon as they were out in the hallway, Elizabeth turned and flung her arms around William. "We're free, William! Jonathan can't run your life anymore, and I can make my own decisions now!"

William hugged her gently, then grasped her arms. "Thank you, Liz. I have to admit, I wasn't sure we could really do this."

"Of course we can! We're free and rich and we're going to America!"

William sighed deeply. "Kind of scary, isn't it?"

Elizabeth shook her head. "I'm not scared at all, and neither should you be." She patted William's chest. "Come on. I can't wait to see the look on Jonathan's face when he realizes we are really doing this. And we have packing to do and plans to make. Once we get to America, maybe we'll see buffalo, maybe real cowboys and Indians. And I can't wait to see the mountains, and Denver." She took hold of William's wrist and pulled him along with her, heading down the hallway and outside, where their driver waited for them. They climbed inside, and Elizabeth turned to her brother. "Our lives are going to change completely, William."

He smiled a bit nervously. "Indeed they will."

"An adventure awaits us." Elizabeth looked out a small window at the crowded street. The sun was shining, but its brightness was blurred by smog, and the air smelled foul today. She couldn't wait to see the beautiful, clean American West and breathe deeply of that air, and to wake up in a new land where Jonathan could no longer control her life, where the threat of being forced to marry a man she didn't love no longer existed.

About the Author

Linda Broday resides in the Texas Panhandle on land the early cowboys and Comanche once roamed. Their voices often float in the stillness and tell stories of the days when the land was raw and unsettled. She grew up loving museums, libraries, and old trading posts and credits those and TV westerns for fueling a love of the Old West. There's something about Stetsons, boots, and tall, rugged cowboys that fan a burning flame. A *New York Times* and *USA Today* bestselling author, Linda has won many awards, including the prestigious National Readers' Choice. Visit her at lindabroday.com.